Praise for James T

'James's style draws you in . . . it's alive with vile creatures, sweeping mysteries and the best~~~~~~~~~~~~~~~~~~~~~ ~~~~~~~~~~~~~~ ~ique voice'

~narchy

'The s~~~~~~~~~~~~~~~~~~ ~~~ astonishingly imaginative fantas~ ~~~~~~~ . . If you're looking for a story that's been written well, is complex and has interesting characters, you have just found what you've been looking for . . . it's a genuine masterpiece of literary fantasy.'

Risingshadow on *Anarchy*

'This epic debut tale wowed us . . . it's ambitious and echoes Philip Pullman.'

Stylist on *Advent*

'This mesmerizing fantasy draws aside the thin veil between the magical and the mundane to reveal the chaos that might be unleashed if we had to share our world with creatures long dismissed as legends. Told with great warmth and insight, *Advent* is an epic tale that will linger in your mind long after you turn the last page.'

Deborah Harkness, author of *A Discovery of Witches*

'An interesting and original tale, bringing a fresh outlook to old stories . . . clever twists keep you hooked'

SFX on *Advent*

'Treadwell makes marvels from the simplest materials . . . and brings his landscape to frightening and fascinating life'

Publishers Weekly on *Advent*

'There is something profoundly different about *Advent*. Perhaps it is the atmosphere of history, magic and mystery it exudes, or maybe the curiosity of the characters. Or it could even be the beauty, the manipulation of the English Language that James Treadwell so clearly is a master of. Either way, you know you have something special in your hands'

www.thirstforfiction.com

Also by James Treadwell
Advent

About the author

James Treadwell was born, brought up and educated within a mile of the Thames, and has spent much of his life further reducing the distance between him and the river. He studied and taught for more than a decade near the crossing at Folly Bridge, Oxford, and now lives within sight of the Tideway in West London. *Advent*, the first book in the Advent trilogy, was his first novel.

More information about James can be found at
www.jamestreadwell.com.

ANARCHY

James Treadwell

HODDER

First published in Great Britain in 2013 by Hodder & Stoughton
An Hachette UK company

This paperback edition published 2014

1

A CIP catalogue record for this title is available from the British Library

Paperback ISBN 978 1 444 72854 5
Ebook ISBN 978 1 444 72853 8

Typeset in Baskerville MT by Hewer Text UK Ltd, Edinburgh

Printed and bound by CPI Group (UK) Ltd, Croydon CR0 4YY

Hodder & Stoughton policy is to use papers that are natural, renewable
and recyclable products and made from wood grown in sustainable
forests. The logging and manufacturing processes are expected to
conform to the environmental regulations of the country of origin.

Hodder & Stoughton Ltd
338 Euston Road
London NW1 3BH

www.hodder.co.uk

As in strange lands a traveller walking slow,
    In doubt and great perplexity,
A little before moonrise hears the low
    Moan of an unknown sea;

And knows not if it be thunder, or a sound
    Of rocks thrown down, or one deep cry
Of great wild beasts; then thinketh, 'I have found
    A new land, but I die.'

                                    TENNYSON

Prologue
Three Dialogues

One

*S*PEAK
　　'...'
Speak. Speak
　　'... sp ...'
Answer
　　'... ah ...'
Answer me. Be voiced. Be mouthed
　　'Be ...'
I am speech. I I am mouth and breath. I I I am consonant and vowel. Speak
　　'I.'
I am I am I am the irresistible word. I make a mouth out of your shadow of a mouth and a name out of your shadow of a name. Answer me
　　'Who.'
Remember me. I am undeniable. I am here
　　'Nowhere.'

3

I speak the sun and light ascends. I speak the arrow and plague falls. I am the lyre and the laurel and the long road. I I I am here. Where I stand is an island in these dark waters. I make a place

'I'm not . . . I'm not.'

You are. I am inescapable. I am the absence of choice

'Let me go.'

There is nowhere else to go. I am every road. I am every beginning and every end. I am prophecy. I am desire and I am consummation. I am the bright eye of the heavens. I am the light that falls everywhere

'Not here. It's so dark.'

I am without contradiction. Remember. You fled me once

'Don't.'

You fled light. You fled the sun. You hid yourself

'Ah.'

You fled with my seed. You sought the dark. You sought to escape my eye. Say whether I found you

'That was . . .'

Answer

'When I was . . . I was.'

Say what happened. Speak

'That was before.'

I am then and now. I I I am above and below. I pour golden breath in your mouth. My seed is truth. Say it

'You found me.'

I found you

'You fell on me.'

I fell on you. I planted my golden seed in you

'Let me go.'

My seed has grown

'No. Oh no.'

Remember

'Not that. Not him.'

My seed has grown and become prophecy. Truth walks the world above

'Let me forget. Please.'

I forbid it. I I I banish forgetting. I have been forgotten and now and now now there will be no more oblivion

'Let me . . . not speak.'

You begged me. You refused me. Remember. I am implacable. Remember. Say what happened

'I was . . .'

Remember

'I went . . .'

You came east to a place that belonged to me. You refused to forget. You slept among oak trees and the sun rose and turned them golden and I was the gold I was the grove I was the sun and the seed

'Ah. No.'

And I was the light that fell on you and the light you fled from and I was the beginning of the long road you took and though you hid from me I was also the end

'No. Agony.'

And I was the seed that took root in you and I was the pain of its growing and I was the bitter music of its birth

'No. I want silence.'

And I am the plague that burst in blood from your womb and I am the mouth you suckled and I I I I am the word that mouth must speak

'It's so dark. I'm so alone.'

I am the blood and the burnt offering and the smoke from the hidden fire. I am the writing on the sybilline leaves. I am everything no longer forgotten. I am the message you could not speak before you died. I have a thousand names and every one of them is true. I give you back your name and your voice

'No one can hear me.'

I am the voice in darkness. I am the words written in the sky by the wings of birds. I I I I am oracle

'No more. Finished.'

I I am the road you trod. I am not finished. I have no horizon

'Let me go. Let me be forgotten.'

I deny it. Remember

'Ah.'

I am the light that always returns. I am the sun the sun the sun

'My son. I remember. Our son.'

Two

'BUT YOU PROMISED.'

'I know.'

'You promised!'

'I know. I'm sorry.'

'You said you'd stay for ever. I remember you saying it.'

'I will. I'll come back.'

'That's not the same. For ever means not going away at all.'

'I thought so too. But maybe it doesn't.'

'What do you mean, "maybe"? You can't go. You can't. I'll have no one left.'

'I've talked to Owen.'

'Owen!'

'He'll come as often as he can.'

'We hardly see him for days!'

'He'll keep an eye on you.'

'What about the rest of the time? After Christmas he didn't come for I don't know how long.'

'And there's Holly. And Grey Mouser.'

'Don't be stupid. I want you here. You said!'

'I'm sorry.'

'Stop saying that! I don't care if you're sorry or not.'

'If there was anything else I could do, I would. I mean it. But I have to go.'

'That's a stupid thing to say. If there was anything else you could do. You could go on here with me like we've been doing.'

'If only I could . . .'

'No! Don't touch me.'

'All right.'

'You promised you'd always be here!'

'Listen. I'm promising now. I'll come back. Once I've done what I have to do I'll come back. As soon as I can.'

'All right. When?'

'I don't know.'

'What?'

'I'm sorry. I'd say if I did but I don't. It doesn't matter. However long it is it'll be over one day. You'll be here and I'll come back.'

'Where are you going?'

'I'm going to take this back, first.'

'What's in there?'

'You probably don't want to see it. It's that mask. I don't like the idea of leaving it in the house with you. Anyway it belongs to someone else, a friend. So I'll take it back to her. Then I have to go . . .'

'Where?'

' . . . Find something.'

'What?'

'I'll show you when I've found it.'

'What is it?'

'Something that belongs to me. I'll show you. When I get back.'

'Why? Why do you have to find anything? We've got everything we need here. We've managed so far. Weeks.'

'It's . . . I can't explain. It's important. A thing, something I should have taken before, but I didn't know. It's my fault. And now it's gone.'

'Where?'

'Marina. I'm s— . . . This isn't helping. Asking lots of questions. Nothing I say's going to make this easier. I'll do what I need to do and come back to you as quickly as I can. That's all it comes down to. But you might have to wait a while.'

'I'll come with you.'

'You can't.'

'Yes I can. We'll go together.'

'You have to stay here. It's not safe for you.'

'I'm almost as old as you.'

'This is a nightmare . . . The longer we talk the worse it gets. I don't even want to say goodbye, that would be like I'm not coming back and I am. I promise. OK? I promise. Will you wait? I might have a long way to go.'

'Where are you going?'

'Quite far. Don't think about it. I'll come back, just think about that.'

'Wait.'

'Better if I don't.'

'You can't go just like this. You can't just walk out. Close the door.'

'There's no other way I can go.'

'You can't do this to me.'

'I hate . . . I'll think of you every step of the way. OK? Will you think of me every day?'

'Every day? Days? You're going for days?'

'Yes. It'll be days.'

'How many?'

'Don't count them. Whatever you do. Once I get back it won't matter how long we had to wait.'

'Stop. Please stop. You haven't explained anything.'

'I can't. It's too . . . There's no choice. I'm getting it over with. The next time I go through this door I'll be back for good. I promise. OK. Till then. OK? Till then. I . . .'

'Wait.'

'Till then.'

'No.

'Wait. Don't—

'Don't . . .'

Three

'**H**I.'

...

'I said, Hi.'

...

'Jennifer, right?'

...

'You like Jennifer? Or Jen, or . . .'

...

'Can you look at me please?'

...

'OK. We have a long day tomorrow. So I'm going to try and keep this polite. Easier for both of us that way. Hey, there you go. Thank you. Hi. I'm Officer Maculloch. I'm going to be taking you over to George on the ferry tomorrow. Everyone calls me Goose.'

...

'Don't ask why.'

. . .

'Not that you're going to ask . . . I guess it doesn't matter too much what to call me if you're not going to say anything, eh?'

. . .

'Joke.'

. . .

'Jeez. OK. So, listen, I'm sorry about the cell. It's just for today. Place over in George is a proper facility. It's supposed to be pretty nice. You know. Beds.'

. . .

'Beds.'

. . .

'Like the things you sleep in.'

. . .

'Jeez. OK, you can stop looking at me now.'

. . .

'You know what? I'm not too much of a talker either. So I guess we'll get along fine tomorrow, eh?'

. . .

'You ever been on that ferry before? No? I'm calling that a no. Goes all the way up to Prince Rupe. It's a pretty long ride. They don't let you stay in the car. Safety regulation. So I'm supposed to cuff you. That's the protocol.'

. . .

'So, like, if you need the bathroom. Or you get hungry. Think about it. It might help if you say something.'

. . .

'You understand me, Jennifer?'

12

. . .

'I read about you, you know.'

. . .

'In the papers. You were kind of famous for a while there.'

. . .

'I read you sing.'

. . .

'When you think nobody's looking. That facility down in Nanaimo, they have CCTV in the rooms. Kinda creepy, huh? But they do. Apparently. I read there's CCTV that shows you got up every night and did a little dance and they could see your mouth moving.'

. . .

'Is that right?'

. . .

'Guess you can't believe everything in the papers, huh.'

. . .

'OK. Forget it. I'm escorting you tomorrow, that's it, we're done. All I'm saying is, I know you can open your mouth if you want to. So if you want me to help you out. You know. Makes things a bit easier for tomorrow.'

. . .

'I'm not going to cuff you anyway.'

. . .

'Stupid regulation. I don't need cuffs to keep you straight.'

. . .

'I may look nice but I'm mean as dirt.'

. . .

'Joke.'

. . .

'Jeez. This is going to be . . . . All right. So, anyway, hi. Just introducing myself. I'll be in and out this afternoon. Officer Paul'll take over this evening. He's got the apartment here.'

. . .

'Next door. Like, right through that wall down the end there. So, you know. Near by. Just in case.'

. . .

'If you care.'

. . .

'You don't care at all, do you? Huh.'

. . .

'OK. I did my best. Sorry it's not more comfortable. I'd say shout if there's something I can get you but I guess that's not going to happen.'

. . .

'Yeah. Joke.'

. . .

'By the way. I know you didn't do it.'

. . .

'Doesn't take a genius. I followed the story. Pretty obvious your mom was, you know.'

. . .

'You know, making it up. Whatever.'

. . .

'Whatever. It didn't work out too bad for you in the end. That facility in George is pretty swish. Not so much fun in winter up there but you already missed most of that, so, OK.'

. . .

'Well. I guess if all those experts couldn't get a hello out of you I'm not going to. You know what? You and me'll do OK tomorrow. I always kind of like not having to chat too much, eh? OK. I'm going to get a coffee. Going to walk down to Traders, the stuff Jonas has in here makes me ill.'

. . .

'Just a few minutes down there and back. You know Traders.'

. . .

'So I'll lock you back in here, I guess. Nice to meet you.'

. . .

'OK. See you.'

. . .

. . .

. . .

. . .

. . .

. . .

. . .

. . .

'Jeez, what's that . . .

'Jonas?

'. . . smells like he left yesterday's catch in here . . . Jonas, you here?— . . .

'God, I might throw up. Coming from back here somewh— . . .

'Jennifer?

'Jennifer?

'What the—

15

Part I

Four

' HELL?'
    Marie-Archange Séverine Gaucelin-Maculloch
held the upturned collar of her uniform jacket over her nose
and mouth and stared into the empty cell.

It wasn't the kind of space you could lose something in. It
was just walls and floor and ceiling, fold-down bed and
barred window. There was absolutely nothing else.

Specifically, and inexplicably, there was no teenage girl.

She looked in the other two cells, in case she'd somehow
forgotten over the course of the ten minutes it had taken her
to walk to Traders and back which one the girl had been
locked in. Then she ran outside, not least because the smell
of rotting fish inside the station was nigh on intolerable.

She looked up the street. (Houses, parked vehicles, the wet
forest sloping up above the town, the miserable sky.) She
looked down the street. (Houses, parked vehicles, boats on
trailers, the landing, a wide stripe of flat water, the same wet

forest and the same miserable sky.) She jogged a little way in each direction, to the corner, to check the cross-streets. It being the middle of the day, and early in March, and the town being little more than a dormitory at the best of times – which these weren't – no one was about.

She returned to the station, by now persuaded that the disappearance of the girl she'd been talking with (OK, talking at) just a few minutes earlier was obviously a hallucination. The smell had faded quite a bit, or maybe hadn't ever been as bad as she'd imagined. She went through to the back corridor where the row of cells was. The door to the third one was still open, and the space beyond still empty.

She must have left the cell door propped open. She'd wedged it open to talk to the kid, and then forgotten, and gone for her coffee without locking up, and the kid had just walked out. Right?

The only thing was, she didn't do things like that. Ever. Even at the age when all her friends were shambolic teenage airheads who could barely be trusted to put their shoes on the correct feet she hadn't done things like that. Why else would it have felt so obvious that she was destined to join the police? (*Que tu es fiable, Séverine*, her mother always used to sigh, as if her reliability was a disappointment.) The truth was that she'd let the door slam shut. She had a clear picture of the sequence of events. *Nice to meet you*, she said, but was actually thinking, *Oh well at least I tried*, and then she swung the door closed and put away the key. In fact she specifically remembered the clunk of the bolt, and thinking, *Poor kid*. Imagine what that sounds like from the inside. Bang.

All right. Don't panic. (She put her hands on her head, breathed carefully, and tried to concentrate.) So someone bust the kid out. (Someone who smelled of bad fish, or was she hallucinating that too?)

A couple of implications were beginning to present themselves as she returned to the office and reached for the radio. They didn't make her feel good. The little community of Alice, British Columbia, might be the back end of nowhere but it was her first proper assignment, the first place where she'd be doing more than trailing along behind a senior partner, and it was only her second week in the job. The staff sergeant hadn't been all that welcoming in the first place.

She buzzed Jonas.

'Goose?'

'Jonas. Hey. Where are you?'

'Hardy. Cruising. Got a problem?'

She couldn't tell him. She knew how stupidly easy it was to lose the guys' respect. One teenager, plus maybe an accomplice, who couldn't have had more than a few minutes' start on her; how hard could it be to deal with? She was absolutely certain she hadn't heard the sound of a vehicle, not even in the few seconds she was in Traders getting her coffee. One of the strangest things about moving to a microscopic dot on the landscape like Alice was the way everyone in town could hear everything else, all the time, because nothing made any noise, except (sometimes) the rain and (always) the non-stop one-note barking of the crows.

'Maybe. Can you do something for me?'

'Thought you'd never ask, man.'

'This might be important. I need you to get back here. Check out the road as you come over.'

'What?'

'Are you near Thirty?'

'Only a minute or two if I step on it. Hey. It's siren time!'

'No siren. Just come over. And stop anyone you see coming the other way. Or keep an eye out for someone walking. You'll know who if you see them.'

'What's up?'

'I'll explain when you get here. Might be nothing.'

'You gotta give me more than that.'

Perhaps. But she told herself not to be ridiculous. She could handle it, especially if she didn't waste time on the radio. They couldn't have gone far.

'Ohhh, man.'

Constable Jonas Paul did everything slowly, or, as he liked to put it, unhurriedly. He rolled his shoulders, leaned into the empty cell and repeated his rueful drawl, stretching it out to make it convey his fateful certainty that something bad was in the offing: 'Ohhh, maaan.'

It was widely known that the Mounties lowered their admission standards for First Nations applicants. Goose had fumed when she'd arrived at the Hardy detachment and immediately been assigned to partner Jonas at the outpost in Alice, fifty kilometres away. The one woman and the one native, shoved out to the tiny mill town on the other side of the island where there was nothing to do but tell kids to turn their music down and intervene in the occasional domestic:

that was what it looked like. Alice didn't even have its own bar for fights to break out in (and Goose dearly loved breaking up fights in bars). The mill workers took Highway Thirty over the pass to Hardy to drink, and they were all so used to the twists of the mountain road by now – it was the only road in and out of town – that they could make it home safely no matter how far over the limit they were. By all accounts Fitzgerald had been a regular guy and a popular cop and she'd known it would be hard work persuading his detachment colleagues to accept her as his replacement, but she'd at least expected to be given a chance to show them what she could do, rather than being shunted off out of sight with the token native.

Jonas had dismantled her prejudices within a couple of days. He was a lot smarter than her; he'd been to college. He didn't talk about how he'd done at the Depot but it was obvious no one had had to make allowances for him. And although it took him three times as long as it took her to do anything – *anything*, from paperwork to getting out of a car to wiping his nose – he was the best community relations cop she'd ever seen.

'How'd she get out?'

'You think I know that?'

'Just thinking aloud, Goose. Thinking alo-u-ud.'

It had taken him twenty-five minutes to come across to Alice, during which time she'd driven twice around the town and knocked on every door within two blocks of the station. A couple of people had been working in their yards. No one had seen anyone walking anywhere, other than her: they'd all been wondering what she was doing running around like that. 'Looked kinda like you lost something,' one walrus-whiskered old joker told her, chuckling as if it was funny. She was too embarrassed to say exactly what she'd lost. Jennifer Knox was still a hot potato. No one was even supposed to know she was being transferred through Hardy. That was why they'd decided to keep her overnight in Alice, out of everyone's way. Jonas had driven her up that morning in an unmarked car. An unmarked car! They'd had to borrow one from down-island, where police work was presumably more subtle and exciting than up here at the end of the highway.

'Didn't see a single driver on the road over. So, I guess we can rule that out. Where'd she be going, anyway?'

'Search me.'

'Makes no sense. The only reason we're shipping her off to the mainland in the first place is she got nowhere else to go. Man.'

'I should get on to Cope.'

'Ma-aan.' Jonas shook his head at the mere idea of that conversation.

'Would you mind starting a search before I call him? I don't want anyone to be watching while he reams me out.'

Though as it turned out, Staff Sergeant Cope was surprisingly terse on the radio. Dangerously terse, Goose thought, as she signed off, wiping her palms on her uniform pants. Perhaps it was a good thing she'd hardly unpacked yet. She tracked down Jonas and passed on the instruction to keep looking while they waited for Cope to arrive, not that either of them would have done any different anyway. Jonas had set up by the roadside at the entrance to town, right next to the wooden WELCOME TO ALICE, B.C. sign with its leaping salmon. It was what she should have done right away, she saw. The steep slope that rose out of the inlet came closest to the shore here, effectively making a bottleneck at the mouth of the town. The road lifted a little to squeeze over the slope, so you could sit on top of the rise and see pretty much the whole of Alice ahead, a tidy cleared space strung along the bottom of the hills at the edge of the water. The fumes and heavy workings of the mill were discreetly out of sight, a couple of miles farther up the inlet, but there was no need to watch that direction. The mill was the very end of the road and, as befitted an industrial site, had its own security. The only other way out of town was by water, but Jonas had that covered too. His spot was high enough to overlook the breadth of the inlet.

'Only possibility is, she holed up in someone's house. In which case all we do is wait. Neighbours'll know about it soon enough. You know how it is.'

'Want me to knock on some more doors?'

'Nah. Best if I do it. Gotta give them a bit of time, though.'

Only Jonas Paul could convince you that sitting in a patrol car doing nothing was the best way to handle a missing person investigation, Goose thought. Her own policing gifts were very different, essentially amounting to the advantage of surprise: the surprise being that someone with her face and general demeanour should have her capacity for enthusiastic and effective violence. She had to admit that her ability to rough people up at the drop of a hat was, in the immediate circumstances, entirely useless. She sighed and got into the car next to Jonas.

'Cope's on his way.'

'Uh-huh.'

'I'm in it deep, aren't I?'

'Uh-huh.'

'Maybe I'll blame you.'

'Good luck with that.'

'I need to think of a story.' She held her head between her hands. 'I don't get it. I don't see what could have happened. There was that . . .'

'Hmm?'

That smell. But it was gone by the time Jonas had arrived, and now it sounded stupid. *The officer noted a powerful odour of marine decay. No source for this odour was observed.* Mentioning it wasn't going to help. Nothing was going to help except finding Jennifer Knox, who'd briefly been the most famous person on Vancouver Island, if not in the whole of the mighty province of British Columbia, at least until the mysterious virus stuff had started creeping into Canada's virtual space and the news cycle had moved on.

'Jonas?'

'Hmm?'

'When you were driving her up this morning. Did she . . . You know.' Jonas Paul wasn't the type to finish your sentences for you, either. It was hard enough work waiting for him to finish his own. 'Say anything?'

He just chuckled.

'I went to say hi. In the cell.'

'That's good. Sure you didn't invite her out for a walk?'

She thought about punching him and found that, untypic-
ally, she wasn't in the mood for it.

'You know what it's like? It's like a cat. You ever have a
cat?'

'No.' His mellow drawl stretched the syllable into a little
song. 'Never wanted to share the fish.'

'I grew up with cats. If you stare at one for long enough,
and it's staring back, it gets weird. I mean, you can see it
looking at you, but there's like no one there, you know? It's
just a cat. Nothing behind the eyes. She was kinda like that.
Looking right at me, but it didn't matter what I was saying.'

'I bet you get that a lot.'

'I'm serious, Jonas.'

He did his slow-motion shrug, too lazy to qualify as a
stretch; it reminded Goose of the old Chinese guys doing t'ai
chi in the park in Victoria. 'Messed-up kid,' he said.

She watched the crows hopping from pole to pole, quacking at each other. It was like they had Tourette's. They
hopped around and spat out monosyllabic gargles every few
seconds. Hop, *merde!* Hop, *fuck!* Hop, *pute!*

'Do you think she did it?'

'Did what?'

'Killed her brother. Tossed him down the stairs.'

'Man. Who knows.'

'She does. Maybe the mother too. The younger kid was in
the house, right? He's got to know something.'

Jonas was exhaling, a slow deep puff like his mouth was a
blowhole. 'Cody don't talk sense, and nor does Mom after

six p.m. I've known that family a little while. Might as well ask the baby. Sometimes you just got to let things go.'

'Seems a shame she's going to end up in an institution. I've met some of the kids who go to those places.'

'Just one of those things.' *Tho-ose*: the word was lengthened out to embrace the whole universe of happenstance Jonas was content to leave uninvestigated.

'I don't know. She wasn't much like your usual native teenager in a cell. No offence.'

'So, Goose, here's the thing.' He turned to look at her, his broad face showing no more animation than usual; he always seemed half asleep. 'Don't talk it up too much with Cope, OK? He's not that wild about the whole business. I think as far as the sarge's concerned it's,' he made a smoothing motion, 'case closed.' His hand swiped back through the air, brushing away doubts. 'We get her over to the mainland, we're done.'

'If we can find her.'

'I'll find her,' he said, peaceably, and made it sound so inevitable that she felt better at once.

Staff Sergeant Cope left Jonas to begin the process of asking around town while he called Goose into the station. She braced herself for a bawling. At first, though, he hardly said anything at all. He looked at the cell, and the door, and (she handed them to him) the keys. He shone torches at them as if she'd missed something. He asked all the obvious questions, leaving long thoughtful gaps between them. He rubbed his bald patch. She stood very straight with her hands behind her back and called him 'sir' in every sentence; right from when she'd arrived at the detachment she'd pegged him for the type who liked old-fashioned discipline. When he'd finished doing all the obvious things he went and stood in the entrance to the station, blocking the door, squinting up at the perpetually low sky.

'I take full responsibility, sir.' She addressed his pudgy back.

'Damn straight.'

'Sir?'

'Damn straight you do.'

That was when she began to suspect things weren't going as well as she'd dared to think.

'I can find her, sir. Someone must have seen the accomplice. Jonas—'

'There's no accomplice.'

From behind, he looked remarkably like a tackle bag. She gripped her hands more firmly behind her back and told herself to stay calm. 'With respect—'

'Just shut up, Maculloch.' The bag rearranged itself at the top end: a sigh. He came back in and closed the door. 'That kid hasn't got any friends. You think she'd be here if she had anyone? There's no damn accomplice. I wish there was. They could have her. Anyone else can have her, far as I'm concerned. Long as I never have to deal with that kid ever again.' His radio coughed at him; he snatched it and yelled, 'Not now!' Only then did she see he was turning red around the collar.

'We can find her soon, sir. Jonas'll get a lead. Once we do

29

I promise she won't go out of my sight until I hand her over to the officers in Prince Rupe.'

Cope sat on the edge of a desk. It creaked under the weight.

'You know what? I hope we don't.'

This felt like the beginning of the bawling at last, so she simply stood to attention, fixing her eyes on a spot on the wall, which happened to be the knot of the prime minister's tie in the standard-issue photo.

'I hope to God she's just gone. Ran off into the woods and a bear ate her. That'd be damn perfect. No more Jennifer Knox. How sweet that sounds. You have no damn idea how much I'm dealing with already today.'

The very worst thing about being posted up here was having no one to take things out on any more. Back down in Victoria there'd been full-contact training twice a week, an hour of dumping bigger girls on their asses, or, if she was lucky, guys. The best she'd been able to find in Hardy was a martial arts studio in an empty room above a supermarket, and the only other people who went were kids; too easy. Maybe she'd take the kayak out later, she thought, and smack the water till she couldn't see for sweat.

'All I want from my officers is that they don't screw up too bad. That's it. I don't expect anything complicated. Fitzgerald's a dumbass, but that was OK. He showed up, he drove around, he didn't mess up. That was fine. That was good. He may be a dumbass, but he didn't leave cells unlocked.'

'Sir—'

'I don't want to hear it.'

There was a long silence. She contemplated the shiny purple hideousness of the prime minister's tie.

'Am I dismissed, sir?'

The desk squealed again as Staff Sergeant Cope levered himself off it. 'Here's what you're going to do.' He tried to stare authoritatively, but the effect was weakened by the obvious fact that he was minding his next words. His unspoken, forbidden thought was as plain as his uniform: *damn female officers. Why'd they have to send me a damn female.* If she could get him to say that aloud it would be him who got demoted, not her, but she knew he wouldn't, and she hated all that minority crap anyway. 'You get the kid. I mean you.' He stabbed a finger at her, stopping just short of touching. 'You've got' – he looked at his watch to make the point, though there was a big clock on the wall right behind her – 'twenty-nine hours till the ferry goes. And Jonas doesn't do any extra time today. I'll go tell him that myself, right now.'

She stayed at attention, waiting for the rest.

Cope squinted at her. 'Something not clear?'

She was careful to repress a dubious frown. 'Just me? Sir.'

'Just you. You screwed up, you fix it. And don't go shouting about what you're doing either, you understand me? Last thing I want is the Jennifer Knox circus coming back to town. In fact, I'd go so far as to say that's my number-one priority.'

She had to look at him now, to be certain she was understanding him correctly. 'You don't want me to submit a report?'

'No, Maculloch, I don't want you to submit a damn report.

I'm not reopening this case, and nor are you. You're just going to . . .' He tried to do an authoritative version of a vague gesture; the overall effect wasn't impressive. 'Tidy it up.'

'What if we . . . What if I don't?'

'Don't what?'

'What if I don't find her, sir?'

'Wouldn't that be great?' She thought it best not to say anything. She could see him gathering a head of steam again. He hooked his thumbs in his belt. 'You know what this is? It's what they call a win-win situation. If you find her you find her, if you don't then we all pray she's gone for good, and if someone asks what happened there's only one person whose fault it is.' The redness reached his cheeks. 'That's you, Maculloch. In case you're wondering.' His radio gargled again. 'What is it?'

A voice Goose recognised as belonging to one of the Hardy station support staff began something about a tree down on the road. He cut it off. 'Give me a minute. I'm almost done here.' She met his eye, imagining the tackle: low and hard, the air oofing out of the bag. Perhaps he saw something of it; he took a step back and fiddled with his collar.

'OK. Dismissed. You can start hunting around. Quietly, you understand? Think of it as a favour. No one else has to know what you did.'

She shifted on her feet. 'They'll be expecting her up in George.'

He glared. 'Then maybe you'd better track her down. 'Cause I'm damn well not going to, and nor are any of my other officers. We've got better things to do than cover your ass.' He opened the door again. *Pute*, a crow snapped from the roof. 'Nothing personal.' He paused in the doorway. 'You got anything else you want to say?'

'I didn't leave the cell open, sir.'

His shoulders sagged. 'You know what? I don't care.' He lowered his voice. 'One way or another, she's not going to be my problem.'

'Sir.'

He raised sausagey fingers and ticked off two alternatives with a thumb. 'You catch up with her, put her back in a cell, nothing happened, it's nobody's problem. Or she shows up somewhere, you were the duty officer, it's your problem. That's how it's going to be.'

'Sir.'

'Anything else?'

'No, sir.'

'Good. Twenty-nine hours.'

'Plenty of time,' she said, suddenly tired of being dutiful. 'Sir.'

He frowned. Her being spunky wasn't in the script. 'Yeah,' he said, groping for a rejoinder he wasn't quick-witted enough to find. 'Let's hope it is.' But he closed the door on her quickly, as if escaping before she could answer back.

No one had seen anything. If Alice had been a different kind of town she might have suspected that people were holding back, closing ranks against an outsider. But the conversations generally went like this:

'Good morning, ma'am. I'm sorry to trouble you at home.

I'm Constable Maculloch with the RCMP. Would it be all right if I asked you a couple of questions?'

'Oh, you're the new mountie!'

'That's right, ma'am. I—'

'Hey! How d'you like it up here?'

'It's good. Could—'

'Quiet, eh? Heh heh.'

'Sure is.'

'So they sent a girl up, eh? We never had a girl mountie before. Can I offer you a coffee?'

'Thank you, ma'am, but I'm just making some enquiries—'

'Something going on? That makes a change. Heh heh. Sure about that coffee? I made hot cakes.'

'Can you tell me if you've been outside in the last hour, ma'am? Or even looking outside?'

'You mean like in the yard? What's going on? I didn't hear anything.'

'It's just a routine enquiry, ma'am.'

'Well, you certainly have nice manners. Bit of an accent there, eh? You sound like a French girl. Yeah, I probably looked outside once or twice. Think I saw the other side of the street. Heh heh.'

And so on. She gave up after a while and left the door-to-doors to Jonas, but by that time word had gotten out that the police were looking for someone and she couldn't get out of the patrol car without people zeroing in on her to ask about it. By the time she drove up to the mill the security guy had already heard there was a dangerous vagabond on the loose. He stared down the road, narrowed his eyes like Clint

Eastwood and nodded to himself as he reassured her. 'Yep. If he comes this way I'll get him.' It was his hour of need. He tucked his shirt in accordingly.

She thought about the possibilities. It was less and less plausible that the kid was hiding out in town somewhere. But where else could she have gone? And – this bugged her the more she thought about it – why?

'She ever try to escape before?'

'Man, I dunno. Not that I ever heard.'

'She wasn't in custody all along, was she? I heard they sent her home for a while. Right? And there was that deal with the First Nation band, they were going to put her on an island or something. Like tribal justice.'

'Yeah. They tried that.' Jonas was back in the patrol car, at the bottleneck, coffee on the dashboard, windows rolled up to deter the curious.

'So it wasn't exactly maximum security.'

'Girl's never been convicted of anything.'

'What I'm saying is, if she wanted to run for it she could have. Any time.'

'Nowhere to go, man. Nowhere to go.'

'That's what I mean. So where's she gone now?'

Jonas wasn't the sort to waste his carefully hoarded thinking energy on hypotheticals. He didn't even bother to shrug. Goose understood why he loved fishing so much. Waiting, waiting, until the fish took the bait all by itself.

'Cope kind of implied my job's on the line.'

'Aw. He can't do that. Can't be discharged for a mistake.'

'I didn't make a mistake.'

He cocked a finger and shot her with it. 'You betcha.'

'I didn't, Jonas. You know it's not possible anyway. You know how security works in the back. I'd have had to hold the door open while she walked out. Like, After you.'

'Yep.'

'You think that's what I did?'

'Nope.'

A truck chugged up. Jonas flagged it down, asked a few questions, shot the breeze. The guy knew him, of course, and had heard there was a drug dealer from down-island on the run (of course). He'd kept his eyes open. He hadn't seen anything.

'She's got to have run off into the woods somewhere,' Goose said, as her colleague settled himself back in place behind the wheel. 'Unless the accomplice got her in a car and got away. In which case they're long gone by now.'

'Possibilities.' Jonas sighed. He could have been agreeing or disagreeing.

'The thing is. She's got to end up somewhere. Right? So, where else can we look? Can I look.'

'I'm gonna help you out.'

'Cope told you not to, didn't he?'

'Hey.' Jonas was unperturbed. 'Using my own initiative. It's good policing.'

'I appreciate it. I'm thinking you should stay here anyway, though. If anyone comes up with anything in town they're going to tell you right away. I'm not getting anywhere by knocking on doors. I need to figure out where she's headed.'

Jonas waved at the view ahead, the twenty or so arcing

and intersecting streets in their small bowl at the edge of the inlet, hemmed in by steep forested mountains. Stripes of cloud in varying grey lay snugly over them like a quilt. It was mid-afternoon, not that there was much of a change in the light above or the activity below. School was out; the brief afternoon migration of strollers to and from Alice Elementary was already complete. There were about twenty-four hours before the ferry which was supposed to carry her and Jennifer up to the remote north would steam out of Hardy.

'Big island,' he said.

'Can you do me a favour?'

'Sure thing.'

'Can you get me her file?'

'Oh, man.'

'Please, Jonas?'

'It's like two boxes.'

'I'm not asking you to carry it over Thirty by foot. Come on. You can stick it in the back of the car. How hard is that?'

'I dunno, Goose.'

'I'm serious. I can't go over to Hardy, Cope'll freak if he finds out. No one would bother you over there. Later on. Please? I want to see if there's something in there. Might give me a handle on what she's up to.'

'Goose. They had a hundred doctors and lawyers trying to figure out what she's up to. It was on TV.'

'Come on, Jonas. This could be my career, you know?'

'What, you're afraid they're gonna post you somewhere less important than this?'

'Could be worse. Could be Manitoba.'

He did his version of a chuckle, a slow soundless bobbing of the head.

'I'm not going to spend the night covering the forest with a flashlight,' she went on, already sensing he was going to give in. They'd only been working together a few days but already they'd struck up that tacit agreement to cooperate, the first silent sign that each thought the other was basically OK. 'If we haven't found her by now we're not going to find her when it gets dark, are we? I might as well look for a different angle.'

'Whoa.' He sipped coffee. 'Sherlock.'

'You can get it, buddy. After hours. It'll be quiet enough in the station over there, you can sign it out without any fuss.'

'Okey dokey. No problem.'

'My hero.' She swung herself out of the patrol car. 'I'll go take another look around. Jonas?'

'Yup?'

'You don't seriously think I screwed up, do you? You meant that?'

'Cross my heart.'

'How'd you think she got out, then?'

He shook his head.

'Come on. You must think something.'

He stretched his right arm into the space she'd just vacated and rolled his neck, unstiffening. 'Some things,' he said calmly, as if he was holding the line still, waiting for explanations to impale themselves on the unseen hook in the ocean below, 'you just don't know how they happen.'

Five

IT WAS THE theme of The Case of Jennifer Knox. Except that in Jennifer's case the policemen and doctors and lawyers weren't like Jonas, content to see what they might fish up, almost equally content if they went home empty handed. They wanted to know.

It was their job to want to know. The file – a single thick folder of papers and CDs, strapped with a rubber band; Jonas had exaggerated – was the record of their efforts to know. Goose spread the papers and disks over her bed and sat cross-legged among them in a big baggy T-shirt, the anglepoise lamp coming over her shoulder like an eavesdropper, her laptop half tucked under the pillow. She skimmed the legalese, tried a bit harder with the medical stuff, read the police material carefully. An oceanic darkness flowed out of all of them, the unplumbed depths of Jen's silence.

Take that away and the case didn't look all that complicated. The initial police reports were brusque, routine.

Constable Fitzgerald might be a dumbass but the report he'd
signed off on was entirely competent. He'd observed the
protocols. Everything was in the proper order, all the relevant details were there. On the night of 1 December the
police had been called to the Knox family home in Rupert,
the no-horse town just down the coast from Hardy, known
only to its mostly First Nations inhabitants plus a smattering
of people who turned the wrong way coming out of the
airport. The call had come from Patience Knox, the mother;
the report described it as 'incoherent'. Fitzgerald arrived at
the house a little after 1 a.m. and found the front door broken
in, evidence of damage to the interior of the property, the
oldest child Carl lying dead at the bottom of the staircase,
the mother hysterical, the second child Jennifer unconscious
in a room at the top of the stairs, and the two younger children (one handicapped and the other an infant) screaming.
There were lots of photos on a disk. Goose slotted it in her
laptop and after some fiddling around there the dead boy
was, and the smashed door and the staircase, all bleached by
the camera flash and eerily silent, the screaming and hysteria
left to her imagination. Carl had broken his neck, presumably by falling downstairs. It took half an hour of coaxing
and coffee for the mother to calm down and sober up enough
to give a proper statement, but once she'd given her story she
stuck by it. It was straightforward enough. She'd driven back
from a bar in Hardy to find the outside light and the door
broken. She ran into the house and heard a commotion
upstairs. ('Commotion' was a good report word. Goose had
typed it out a few times herself.) She saw Carl dead and

thought someone was attacking the other kids. She heard Jennifer calling for her so she ran up. The door to her bedroom was barricaded. Jennifer was shouting in there but Ms Knox couldn't get in so she went to fetch her phone from the truck and called the police. By the time she got back upstairs the door was no longer blocked and Jennifer was lying inside more or less as Fitzgerald found her ten minutes or so later. (The report noted that there was no lock on the door, no sign the bed had been moved, and nothing else in the room substantial enough to use as a barricade.)

Plenty of witnesses confirmed that Ms Knox had left the bar when she said she had, and a couple of neighbours reported hearing the commotion; they were used to the kids shouting and the mother coming home drunk late at night, and ignored it. The damage to the door and the exterior of the property – a scrapheap, basically; the pictures alone were enough to suggest why none of the neighbours wanted anything to do with the Knox family – was consistent with a break-in. Ms Knox was adamant that if there'd been an intruder in the bedroom with Jennifer when she arrived there was no way he could have left the house without her seeing, even while she went to phone the police. Fitzgerald, however, noted that Ms Knox was 'severely intoxicated' when he arrived.

So far so good. The picture was as clear to Goose as it had been to Fitzgerald, and, later, to Staff Sergeant Cope. Someone had broken into the house, waking the children. The boy Carl had come out of the kids' bedroom to investigate, tripped and gone down the stairs. The guy had taken

Jennifer into the bedroom and blocked the door. The mother had come back, interrupting him; he'd scrammed without being seen. It was inconvenient, admittedly, that the police found no footprints or tyre marks around the house beyond those made by themselves and Ms Knox, and that later examination failed to turn up any evidence of an intruder inside the house either, except for two burnt-out matches on the floor of the bedroom. ('Of unknown provenance,' said the report; that had to be the sarge writing. Goose could see him peering over his glasses, tapping out the fancy words.) But with the police and the ambulance coming and going and the mother with the baby and the younger boy going up and down the house screaming, it wasn't hard to see how any traces might have been erased in the first few minutes. Anyway, they had enough to go on. Jennifer was, understandably, traumatised, but she'd been in the room with the guy and would be able to ID him in due course. Take out the unfortunate death of the kid and the general melodrama surrounding the family and Goose could see how they'd all expected the case to be pretty uncomplicated.

The first sign of trouble was in the hospital report dated 3 December, two days later. The phrase looked confident, professional, doctorish: *acute post-traumatic aphasia.*

Put like that, it sounded as if you could operate on it, or prescribe a drug. Have you got something for acute post-traumatic aphasia? But what it meant was that Jennifer Knox wouldn't speak.

Not a single word, not even the beginning of a word. Not to anyone, police, nurses, doctors, friends, her mother. She wouldn't draw, or sing, or hum, or nod, or any of those things you could sometimes get traumatised kids to do when they didn't want to talk. She sat up when the nurse asked her to sit up, she let the doctor examine her, she let her mother hug her. She ate, she got dressed and undressed. She listened and understood, apparently. She'd look you in the eye. But she wouldn't say anything at all.

Problem.

It was apparent from the early reports that she was their only hope of a decent witness. The family was a mess. ('Highly unstable domestic environment': Cope again, Goose reckoned.) The younger boy was developmentally disabled – code for something, obviously, though Goose wasn't sure exactly what – and the mother was an alcoholic. Without Jennifer's testimony the prospects of finding out what had happened in the house that night were severely reduced. On top of that there'd been no progress in identifying a suspect. A couple of guys who had some history with the mother and plenty of bad stuff on their records both had unbreakable alibis. More inconvenient still, Patience Knox's evidence about what she'd heard from the barricaded bedroom began to change. Right from the start this had been a minor but irritating weakness in the case: her description of the so-called 'commotion' hadn't really made it sound like someone suffering an assault, sexual or otherwise. According to Fitzgerald her exact words had been that the girl was 'up there screaming nonsense . . . crazy shit'. Later in the night she'd given a more sober statement to the sarge, in which she said, 'First Jennifer called out to me and then she started shouting stuff,

I don't know what it was, she'd gone crazy. I thought she was crazy.' Three days later she was telling the police what they'd like to have heard all along: that Jennifer had been shouting for help and asking her to call the cops. She wasn't able to explain the contradiction.

The Band got involved. There was the documentation, on shakily photocopied headed paper, signed by their community liaison officer, a round bespectacled woman whom Goose had already met. Up at this end of Vancouver Island the police spent a lot of time talking with First Nations community liaison officers of one sort or another, because ninety per cent of the young men they had to lock up overnight were First Nations kids. The Band had their own procedures – 'traditional justice' was the official phrase – and they requested that Jennifer be put in their care for a few days, even though no one had accused her of anything. They weren't required to tell the police exactly what happened, but Goose understood it involved taking the kids off somewhere and having them live in supervised isolation. Plus some ceremonies. That kind of thing. By that stage the sarge was only too happy to try anything.

Jennifer went away wherever they took her and came back, still without saying anything at all to anyone.

She attended her brother's funeral. That was when the media got interested.

It was a single photo which kicked off the whole circus. The shot showed the grieving family, the mother crying, holding the fragile-looking younger boy by the hand, and Jennifer off to the side, looking utterly blank, hard, cold, but also, unfortunately, looking pretty. Just pretty enough to catch everyone's interest, once you factored in the piquant detail that whatever happened to her had struck her mute.

Goose remembered her first contact with the story. She was in Victoria. She'd come home after a wet cold day inspecting illegal fishing catches, turned on the news, and there it was: The Girl Who Won't Talk.

Now the case became a medium-sized event. There was serious pressure to make an arrest. An inspector came from down-island. He tried to interview Jennifer. The documentation was on one of the disks; the filename was almost longer than the content of the file. His report read, in full: *Subject unable or unwilling to cooperate. Full psychiatric evaluation recommended.* The girl was sent to a bigger hospital. Meanwhile, Cope was getting nowhere, and there was a TV crew camped in the Hardy Motor Inn.

Goose tried her best to read the psychiatrist's report, but it made her eyes swim. She looked up from the bed at the boxes she'd trucked up from Victoria and for the first time that week considered whether starting to unpack properly would be less boring than the alternative. She hadn't even peeled the tape off a couple of them, the ones containing the pictures (no hammer or pins to hang them with) and the kitchen stuff (too busy to cook, or so she'd told herself). The apartment smelled of microwaved MSG already, though not strongly enough to mask the undertone of whatever cleaning product it had been soused with before she moved in. It looked discouragingly temporary. Clothes on the floor, stuff lying sideways on the one shelf. She wondered whether it might be better to leave it like that. Not much point straightening the place up if she was about to be discharged.

The only thing about the medical reports that caught her eye was the proliferation of negatives. *No sign of . . . No evidence of . . . No indication that . . . Schizophrenic disorders can be ruled out . . .* However many times they threw down their net, it came up empty every time. Jennifer was unfathomable.

They sent her home. It was nearly the holidays. The TV crew would have camped on the Knoxes' doorstep if they'd dared but with an aboriginal family that was never an option. The Band chief had publicly requested that they stay away and no producer in Canada was going to pick a fight with the First Nations. The story went quiet. For a couple of weeks nothing was added to the file. Cope must have been praying that the case had drifted quietly to join all his other unresolved and forgotten failures. Every RCMP station had a hinterland full of cases like that. The wilder conspiracy theories about the worldwide computer virus were starting to emerge by then, too. Someone had coined a suitably newsworthy name for it: the Plague. There were countries where government departments and major industries were beginning to deny they were affected, so ensuring that the whole internet assumed the opposite. The stories from England were getting more lurid by the week: people setting fire to piles of banknotes, bands of Satanists roaming the snow, students proclaiming the dawning of the Age of Something or Other. The news cycle moved on.

And then it cycled back, with a vengeance. Goose remembered going out one morning not long after Christmas and passing the papers stacked outside the convenience store. There on the front page was a close-up of that first photo of Jennifer, looking stern and frightening and interesting, under the headline: *MURDERER!*

Ms Knox had changed her story completely. She'd been trying to protect her girl all along, she claimed, but she just couldn't do it any more. According to the new statement she gave Cope, what had really happened that night was that she'd come home to find Carl blundering around outside the house in the dark. He and Jennifer had had a fight and she'd locked him out and broken the light. When his mother arrived he'd been going through the yard looking for something to break down the door. She shouted up to the bedroom; Jennifer swore at them and told them she'd kill them if they came inside. They broke the door down and went upstairs to try to calm her. She pushed Carl, he fell all the way down, and when she saw she'd broken his neck she passed out.

Goose hadn't appreciated it when she read the story online down in Victoria, but now that she'd worked through the police records in sequence she saw Cope's dilemma very clearly. On the one hand the mother was a terrible witness. On top of that, she'd just spent two weeks at home with a baby, a ten-year-old boy with serious problems and a daughter who (presumably) wouldn't acknowledge her existence with so much as a word. It wasn't hard to imagine her motive for coming up with this new story. On the other hand, the new version fitted the facts as well as the old one, if not slightly better, and it had the priceless bonus of doing away with the need for a suspect. If there'd never been an intruder, there was no housebreaker and child-molester on the loose; there was no one Cope had failed to catch.

Now, of course, everyone wanted a piece of the case again. The sarge was on TV every other day, visibly trying to remember media training courses he'd taken in the days when the internet was a cult mystery known only to a handful of geeks. The Band insisted that tribal mediation and traditional justice should be the first resort. The word 'aphasia' was introduced to millions of Canadians for the first time. Free Jennifer groups were formed before she'd even been accused. Goose had been hooked like everyone else, for a few days. The magic of television joined forces with the court of public opinion to turn Jennifer's impassive, unsmiling face into the mask of a silent psycho.

Her mother kicked her out of the house. Jennifer couldn't go to school. They'd tried for one day, the first day of the semester, and (of course) she'd sat, saying nothing, doing nothing, freaking out the other kids so badly they sent her home at lunchtime. The younger boy, Cody, was becoming seriously disturbed by his sister's behaviour too, according to a badly spelled report from Child Welfare. The Band offered to take her in, but now Cope had another, easier option. Goose saw how strongly he must have been tempted by the thought of handing the whole business over to the courts. He took her into custody. The Girl Who Wouldn't Talk became a juvenile accused of a serious crime.

From that day in early January onward, the file bulked up like it was on steroids. The inspector came back, at least partly because he sounded so much better on TV than Cope had. There was a whole disk devoted to copies of the nego-tiations between various agencies over whether and how Jennifer was going to be tried, who was going to look after her in the meantime, and – this was the bit Goose tried to concentrate on, though it was hard to track details through the blizzard of officialese – where. The girl hadn't gone home again, that was clear. It looked like the Band had taken responsibility for a while, before apparently giving up. Which made sense: aboriginal justice systems were good at what they were mostly needed for, which was dealing with stupid boys committing the kind of petty crimes where involving the police and the courts would only make things worse. Jennifer's problem wasn't a First Nations problem, no matter how much they wanted it to be. The problem was that she was the only person who knew what had really happened, and she wouldn't tell anyone. Pretty much by default, the only way to find out the truth was to let a judge decide.

Goose flipped papers back and forth, scrolled files up and down. It looked like Jennifer had spent the time before they could get her into court the way anyone else accused of a crime would have: in custody, in the station. In a cell.

Nowhere else to go. It was the zero option for juveniles, everyone knew that. If there'd been any alternative to custody they'd have taken it. But there was no sign of any alternative in the files. No fostering, no refuge. No one wanted her. No one, Goose imagined, could stand that ter-rible relentless silence within their walls.

Once lawyers got involved the production of paperwork

turned industrial. Goose sighed and checked the time on the laptop screen; ten already. She couldn't see any point trying to wade through the court reports. If she did she'd probably still be sitting in a T-shirt on her bed when the ferry left tomorrow afternoon. Anyway, she knew roughly what had happened. Jennifer hadn't spoken during the judicial proceedings, not even to identify herself, not even when the judge explained that the law required her to confirm her identity, not even when threatened with contempt of court or whatever they called it. So there'd been no trial. The judge had sent her for another psychiatric evaluation, down to a big facility in Nanaimo. Off she went for more interviews, interventions, diagnoses. The results were precisely the same as they'd been all along. However much paper was poured in, nothing came out. She was a psychiatric event horizon.

Goose couldn't stop thinking of Jennifer in her cell: sitting, staring, immaculately unresponsive, like an automaton perfectly disguised as a person, as impenetrable to medical or legal or judicial analysis as a black hole.

She stood up, stretched. Her apartment was, she had to admit, unforgivably bleak. The excuse she gave herself was that she didn't know anyone up here yet. No visitors meant no need to unpack or tidy up or make the place look like a home. Her domestic life had come down to the essentials: soap, clothes, and the internet. She thought about Skypeing Annie just to take a break, but it was 1 a.m. in Toronto and Annie would either be out or asleep.

There were other places she could go on the internet for a

break, of course. She could go anywhere. That was why you didn't really need a home once you'd unpacked the laptop. Just a private space with a reasonably fast line. You didn't need to know anyone, either. She could go on the internet and log in as SCRUMGRRL, who could be anyone, anywhere, and talk and stuff with other girls she didn't know at all.

She scowled at the scatterings on her bed. There was nothing in the file, nothing she didn't already know. If there was a secret accomplice, some schoolfriend of the kid's maybe or some sympathetic adult who'd been waiting quietly all this time for a chance to bust her free, they'd left no traces in the paperwork.

Besides, the accomplice theory was nonsense anyway. Cope and Jonas were both right. No one could walk into the station, even when it was unmanned, and unlock a cell. No one except her colleagues could unlock the front door of the station, come to that. The only thing that could have happened was that she'd left both doors open by mistake; but she hadn't.

Jennifer knew what had actually happened, of course. But she'd never tell, even if Goose could find her.

Goose wondered whether anyone had tried *making* her talk. It must have been awfully tempting to squeeze a little too hard, push something back a bit farther than it was supposed to go. Just to get some kind of reaction, even if it was no more than a whispered *ouch*—

Goose froze mid-stretch, a curious thought occurring to her. Where had she heard that rumour about the girl singing on CCTV? It must have been something in the news, which meant it could have come from anywhere; but of all the places Jennifer had gone the only one with CCTV in the rooms was surely the big facility in Nanaimo.

She sat down again and flipped through the relevant folders and disks. It took ten minutes to find the reference, a brief sentence at the bottom of the kind of one-page sheet that nurses left clipped to the foot of hospital beds. Beneath ticked boxes and blood pressure numbers it read: *Security reports patient seen dancing overnight. No footage. Uncorroborated.* The scrawl wouldn't have caught her eye if someone hadn't circled it with a different colour pen and added in the margin, *SF 12/1.* She spent another ten minutes hunting for further detail, without success.

She tried to remember the story. The security guard must have said something to the press, was that it? In which case . . .

She realised she'd been waiting for an excuse to plug in the ethernet cable. Well, why not. She'd been going through files for nearly three hours. She'd tried. She should have known it was useless anyway. Jennifer had vanished and she wasn't going to find her, any more than any of the people who wanted answers from the girl were going to get them. She might as well relax for a bit, try to get some sleep, be ready to face Cope with her failure tomorrow.

She did at least Google the story first thing after connecting the laptop. There were pages and pages about Jennifer Knox, covering the usual spectrum from responsible to deranged. Sticking to the news sites, she found archived articles. A guy who monitored the CCTV overnight had indeed claimed that he'd seen Jennifer get out of bed and shuffle around the ward, mouth moving, but once it turned out there was no sign of anything of the sort in the recorded footage everyone just assumed he'd been trying to get a buck or two from a gullible reporter. Goose must have only remembered half the story. Still, it made no difference to her either way. It was just a tiny thing she'd latched on to, something about Jennifer that might not have been a complete blank, the faint suggestion that there might be something going on behind those hard dark eyes of hers, but it was nothing. No help at all.

She pushed the papers and disks back in the folder and dumped it on the floor. She'd get them back in the right order later. She smoothed back her hair and adjusted the anglepoise lamp, bending its light against the wall, making the room dimmer and warmer.

The laptop chimed at her. Skype. For a happy second she imagined Annie deciding to check in on her before she went to bed. Then she saw that the call was from her father.

She sighed. It was another thing she'd been putting off for a few days. She pulled the T-shirt down so she was sitting on its hem and tilted the head of the lamp away from the wall to brighten the room. It made her pasty and weary looking in the laptop's camera, but she didn't mind that. It might even help her keep the conversation short.

'Hey, Dad.'

'Séverine! Hold on . . .' Moving jerkily, even more badly lit than she was, her father's head and shoulders wobbled and jerked around a corner of her screen, his eyes directed out of shot. She heard a mouse clicking. 'How are you, angel? I talked with Thérèse earlier, thought I'd give you a try . . .' More clicking. His image had the peculiar gormless, distracted, washed-out quality she thought of as Skypeface. She inspected the picture her own camera was projecting, trying not to fall into the same wide-eyed and slack-jawed look, practising for later. 'OK, what do I need to . . .' Her father leaned forward, making the dome of his head loom. He frowned, mouth half open. She could see the nicotine stains on his teeth. 'I'm not seeing you. Is your camera working?'

She waved. The mini-Goose in the white T-shirt waved back at her from her screen, microseconds later. 'Uh-huh. Go to the menu, click on—'

'I did all that. Look.' He stabbed a finger at the space below the camera, as if she was standing over his shoulder. 'It says your name on the window, it's just there's no . . . All I can see is grey.'

'Maybe the line here can't handle it. So how's Tess?'

'Hmm?' He was still trying to make it work.

'Tess. You said you were talking to her.'

'Oh. She's still with that guy.'

'Get used to it, Dad.'

'I'm trying. This is pissing me off. I hate these machines. Maybe if you call me?'

'Just leave it, OK, Dad? I can see you fine.'

'You're not hiding something, are you?'

'No, I'm not hiding something. So everything's OK there?'

'I guess. Not as busy as we ought to be but I still got work. How's up-island?' He blinked at the screen and tapped keys, only half listening to her.

'Good. We had a bear chase a couple of moose through town today.'

'Oh yeah?'

'No, of course not. Dad, can you leave the computer alone and talk?'

'Sorry, angel. It's . . .' He leaned right forward, squinting at whatever he was or wasn't seeing on his screen.

'Just close the window, OK?'

'It's weird. It's not like static. It's ripples. Looks like water.'

'Close it, Dad.'

'Yeah.' A click, and his attention settled on the camera. 'Sorry. So, you're good? Settling in?'

She told him about the weather, the apartment.

'Maybe I'll come visit. There's supposed to be lots of fishing up there.'

'So they tell me.'

'You got room for a guest in the apartment?'

'No. There's places to stay in Hardy. It's cheap this time of year.'

'I don't take up much space.'

'There's no room, Dad. I'd show you if you could get the picture working.'

'I probably can't leave the business that long anyway. It takes all day to drive up there, is that right?'

'There's a flight once a week.'

'I can't afford a plane. Hey, did you hear about the airport in Montreal?'

'No.'

'They closed it. All flights cancelled. Thérèse was supposed to go to New York.'

'Shame for Tess,' Goose said, dutifully. She got on all right with her sister, especially at a distance, but she'd long ago stopped pretending not to resent her for being the glamorous one who got whatever she wanted.

'Some security thing with the computers, that's what they're saying. She and that guy were about to check in.'

'He's got a name, Dad.'

'Whatever. They were using those do-it-yourself machines that print your boarding passes? It printed junk.'

Goose was getting impatient. 'Uh-huh.'

'She reckons it's this Chinese virus.'

'There's no Chinese virus, Dad. I'm a law enforcement officer. If China was engaged in cyberterrorism I'd have heard about it.'

'You wouldn't have heard jack shit, angel. This stuff goes way over our heads. Those guys are doing stuff people like us don't know the first thing about.'

'You don't know the first thing about your own toaster.'

'Maybe.' Even in the bad light of his desk lamp, with the dark brown bachelor decor of his den swallowing the back of his balding head, the whole scene sluggishly pixellated, she could see his stubborn face coming on. 'I got a message from the bank today.'

'Yeah. Me too. Same message, I bet.'

'I don't like it when they start sending messages about security. The ATM in town shut down yesterday too.'

'We had the same thing.'

'Up there?'

'Yeah. It's not a big thing. We spoke to someone about it. Just a glitch.'

'Who did?'

'We did. The police. People were trying to use the machine anyway so we had to tape it up. Called the bank.'

'What'd they say?'

'Just a glitch. Some technical thing. They're going to fix it overnight.'

'I don't like the sound of that.' He looked grudgingly satisfied, the way he always did when things he didn't understand (technologies, human relationships) went awry. 'I reckon I'm going to go in tomorrow at nine and get a bunch of cash out.'

'Jeez, Dad.'

'There's more and more stuff like that going around.'

'Just don't hide wads of money under your mattress, OK? Burglars like it when people do that.'

He harrumphed. 'There won't be wads of money to hide unless business starts picking up.'

'When the weather changes. It's not long till spring.' Her father had a small gardening operation in the lower Fraser valley.

'No sign of it. People are sitting on their hands anyway. You heard about those people in Wenatchee?'

'That's in America.'

'It's not that far.'

'You'd have been out of business a long time ago if everyone stopped spending money every time Americans acted weird.'

'I dunno. They say it's happening some place in California too, bunch of people going off the grid. There's a funny mood around.'

'People watch too much TV.'

'Someone saw that bird thing up at Punchaw.'

'I don't know what you're talking about, Dad.' She loosened her shirt, checked the time, reached down for the folder and started getting its contents back in order.

'You know. That thing in England. The angel of death.'

'Oh yeah, that thing.'

'They got photos.'

'Dad. Jeez. People have seen that thing everywhere. I bet there's scientists in Antarctica who looked at a penguin funny and said it was that thing. People see what they want to see, you know?'

'You should be here. Thérèse said it's the same in Montreal. What are you doing?'

The papers were rustling loudly. 'Oh. Just some unpacking.'

'At this time of night?'

'I've been busy, Dad. New job. New place.'

'You sound tired.'

'Yeah.' She knew she ought to spend a few minutes trying to talk a bit of sense into him, especially if he'd just been listening to Tess and getting wound up by her drama-queen thing, but she wasn't in the mood. She was in another mood, and wanted to get rid of him. 'Really tired.'

He let her go a few minutes later, by which time she'd got the folders straight and every disk in the right case. She pushed them out of sight behind the bed. Out of sight, out of mind. She was going to forget the Knoxes for a little while, forget that she might be officially reprimanded the next day, forget what it might mean for her career. She'd figure something out tomorrow. She'd start early.

She twisted the lamp back down until the light softened, moved the laptop around to the foot of the bed, and settled herself on her stomach facing it. She pulled up the site. She examined herself in the window on her own screen again. Another window listed SCRUMGRRL's friends online, a little pink heart next to each name. She sent an enquiry to DAISY19AB, who wasn't too much of a talker and liked to get going quickly.

Moments later and a little strip of text blipped on to her screen.

hey u

A powder-blue bedroom, a spiky-faced spotty girl with a phone to her ear. Goose typed:

u busy?

The girl tapped at a keyboard with her free hand.

no a boy brt

boys suck

The jaw opened and closed, the head tilted from side to side, while the finger tapped slowly. Two conversations at once. Goose, as so often, wondered why she bothered.

brt 1 min

All right, Goose thought. One minute exactly.

ok

where ur pic

?

no pic

??

o wait

The girl blew kisses into the phone and tossed it aside on to her bed. She shifted around to lie on her elbows, propping the keyboard in front of her, and typed rapidly.

couldn c u 1st comin up now

ok

Goose watched as the girl, who probably wasn't nineteen or called Daisy or even in Alberta, frowned and cocked her head. She went very still; her eyes seemed to grow too wide, and younger, a child's eyes. They lit up with shock. She pushed herself violently away from her computer, her mouth opening in what looked like a scream. Her hand swooped with blurry speed down on to her keyboard and the window vanished. Goose's laptop trilled at her, and then again, over and over again: a window appeared saying 'Begin Live Chat With ?', and then another, and another, windows spilling all over the screen like the unstoppable iterations in a hall of mirrors. She slammed the machine shut and pulled out the cable.

Six

'N O LUCK?'
Goose handed the folder back to Jonas, shaking her head.

'You look like you were up all night.'

'I didn't sleep too good.'

'You worry too much.'

'Yeah. It's only my freaking job.'

'Whoa.'

She stared out of the window. As soon as it had turned light she'd done a circuit of the town, without knowing what she'd hoped to find. Footprints, maybe. Torn clothes in the undergrowth. A suicide note. The crows flitted from pole to pole, passing compulsive opinions on her efforts. *Plotte. Chienne.*

'You told me you'd find her, Jonas.'

'Mmmm. Guess I lied.'

'Thanks for that.'

'Hey.' He ambled over to stand behind her. 'It's gonna be OK. She'll show up.'

'Where, though?'

'Kid's gotta eat.'

'Don't tell me. You're going to go sit in Traders and wait for her to show up asking for a sandwich.'

'Whoa, that's some smart thinking. They should make you an inspector.'

She'd even thought about locking herself in the cell, to see whether there was some trick about the door that meant you could open it from the inside. It was hard to think straight. A churning in her belly was telling her she'd screwed up. Everyone would know she'd screwed up.

'I'll tell you something,' Jonas went on. 'She's nowhere in Alice. I guarantee it.'

She bit back a retort.

'Musta hidden out somewhere in the trees and walked away in the dark. Over towards Hardy, if I had to guess. She'll be getting hungry. Can't hide out for ever. Someone's gonna see her on the roads.'

'I'm not too sure about your predictions any more, Jonas.'

'Hey. You know I'm right. Look, Goose, we've had kids go running off before. It's not a big deal. You should get a couple hours' rest, drive over to Hardy. Someone's gonna call in saying they picked her up trying to hitch a ride south. That's how it usually goes.'

'This kid's different,' Goose said.

'Can't argue with that.'

She saw what he was getting at, though. She thought

about it as she drove out of town on Thirty, turning away from the inlet, up the steep switchbacks where unexpected stands of silver birch broke up the forest's usual dark wet monotone. The persistent weirdness of the file had distracted her, or maybe her memory of the girl's uncanny stare when she'd tried talking with her in the cell. She should have ignored all that and concentrated on the simple facts, the way Jonas did. Think of the girl as a runaway seventeen-year-old and it suddenly didn't seem so hard to guess where they'd eventually find her.

Of course, when seventeen-year-old girls went missing they fairly often showed up dead. Goose pushed that thought away, ashamed of her first reaction to it: *well, that would make things a lot simpler.*

Food. The kid would need to find food. Whether she broke into someone's house or stole from a store, there were only three places she could get it: Alice, Hardy, Rupert. Beyond them was nothing but trees and water until you got to the next towns down-island, too far for her to reach unless she had a vehicle, and if she'd got a ride somehow then the game was up anyway, there'd be nothing Goose could do. Alice she could rule out already. Jonas was right. It wasn't the sort of place anyone could go half a day without being noticed. So if the kid hadn't already been driven south, or if she wasn't dead in the forest somewhere, most likely she'd walked all night over the pass and would now be tired, cold, hungry, and sneaking around the edge of Hardy looking for a way of getting something to eat.

And if she managed that, then what? There was still

nowhere to go. Hardy was, literally, the end of the road. The asphalt tangle that represented civilisation here reached one of its terminal threads. The highway came up all the way from the other end of the huge island, from Victoria, where she'd been living for a year until the Hardy detachment lost a constable to long-term sickness and she was assigned to replace him. She'd driven its whole length. It narrowed and emptied as it went north. About halfway up it started avoiding the port towns on the east coast, swinging inland, forgetting everything but forest and logging roads. A mile or two outside Hardy it reached its only significant destination, the ferry terminus on the south side of Hardy Bay, where most of the summer traffic that travelled it would go aboard for the long passage to the northern mainland. Its work done, it immediately gave up any further pretence of being a highway and debouched almost shamefacedly into Hardy proper, kicking around an entirely unnecessary roundabout and dropping down the hill like any of the town's other wide, badly surfaced, unpopulated roads until it ran into the strip of park at the edge of the bay, where its last gasp was marked – for reasons Goose has never got to grips with, even after she'd paused in her jog one morning to read the sign – by a three-foot-high wooden carrot.

Hardy was an invisible frontier. You could get in your car there and start driving and never have to worry too much about how far it was to the next gas station or flush toilet or place where you could pay money and get what you needed. You'd be on roads with laws and fellow-travellers, and within a few hours you'd be looking out the window at somewhere that bore no more indication of proximity to the wilderness than a retirement suburb in Florida. (Goose's maternal grandparents wintered in one of those, the setting for family Christmases that had turned her Anglo as well as atheist.) Here – she drove over the pass and down towards the east coast and Hardy Bay, passing blitzed disaster zones of freshly logged land – you still had a toehold on the asphalt. But beyond . . .

Beyond was the north. At this time of year you could still feel it, the huge darkness coming down too early and leaving too late, not quite willing to retreat into its Arctic lair of permanent ice, and the ocean air blowing over the top of the island, heavy with the memory of storms. South of where she was there were schools, jobs, houses that got bought and sold, wireless networks which meant that anywhere might as well be anywhere else, local differences erased by shared information. North were canneries (but the salmon runs were failing), logging (but the age of paper was ending), tourism for a third of the year, the government's guilt at having abandoned the remnants of the coastal passage's aboriginal nations to their 'heritage', and otherwise only the great inhospitable emptiness which tourists came to look at or fish in from the safety of their ships.

People told her Hardy had seen better days. She found it hard to believe. Although she had to admit that its parking lots were hilariously optimistic. Virtually every building that wasn't a private house lorded over wide concrete skirts with parking spaces neatly painted out, as if it expected tens or hundreds of visitors to show up any moment. When she closed her eyes and thought of Hardy it was those white-striped grey wastes she saw, tragically deserted, filling up with puddles when it rained (it often rained), coming to life only late at night when drunk kids used them to practise handbrake turns. She drove slowly into town. People didn't walk around, as a rule. With all those empty parking spaces there wasn't much call for walking. Pedestrians tended to be the old native guys, not usually looking their best, or young couples, also usually native, pushing strollers. If Jennifer showed up here, scurrying across the concrete wastes, she'd stick out a mile. Goose circled a couple of times and then pulled over opposite the market.

It felt wrong. She couldn't have said why. Maybe it was just the after-effects of a bad night's sleep (she was trying not to think too much about the look on the girl's face as she slammed her computer shut). She did a few more circuits, watched a couple of other spots, left town to drive a few miles south along the highway and back again. The longer she spent looking, the harder it became to imagine the silent, intense girl from the cell skulking around town trying to steal some pop and a candy bar. There was a mismatch some-where. Jennifer had opted out of all this, the dreary stores with too many parking spaces, the kids her age pushing strollers, the little that was going on. She'd stopped doing it. If her case file told you anything it told you that. Logic said she had to go somewhere to eat, but then logic said a lot of stuff. Jennifer didn't say anything.

Goose wasn't cut out for watching and waiting anyway. She'd never been any good at sitting still. Better to get it over with, she decided. She made her way to the station in Hardy to face Cope.

Take away the flagpole and the patrol cars parked in front and the station could have been a small-town community centre, or even an unusually large and ugly house. It looked like it might have been shipped from Ottawa in prefabricated sections, to keep the budget down.

'Morning, Marie.' Janice took the idea of first names very literally, so it seemed, or perhaps she'd just been flustered by Goose's full name and fastened on the only element she was confident of pronouncing; for whatever reason she couldn't be persuaded to use 'Séverine', let alone anything as far beneath her dignity as a nickname. But then her own official title was 'front office support staff', which actually meant 'receptionist', so Goose tried to be sympathetic.

'Morning, Janice.'

'You're not on rota today, are you?'

'I wanted to have a word with the sarge.'

'Oh. He's out. It's been crazy crazy this morning. Crazy crazy crazy. Six calls already. Can I get you a – oh, would you look at that.' She flicked a switch in front of her and settled her mouth into a receptionist smile for the benefit of her headset. 'Hardy Police, how may I help you?' Goose turned away as Janice listened, wondering how to occupy herself for the next hour, and was about to head back out to the car when she noticed the receptionist waving urgently.

'OK. All right. Let me note that down.' Janice made big

eyes, and mouthed something at her. 'All right. We'll get an officer over there as soon as we can. All right, Margaret, dear. All right. Bye. Marie, would you be a dear?'

She would. Some actual work would come as a relief. 'What's up?'

'Vandalism. Rupert. I'm sorry, everyone else is so busy. Did you hear that the plane couldn't come in? It's these problems they're having. I'm sure it won't take you more than a moment. That was Margaret Sampson. Some damage to the artwork outside the hall. I can't say the name properly. Do you need the address? You know, the big hall in Rupert. It's the Band building.'

Goose had only been to Rupert once but she knew. Rupert was smaller even than Alice.

'She sounded kind of upset,' Janice said, cautiously.

'I'll be nice.' Goose had the impression that Janice had been looking forward to the arrival of a female officer, and was more than slightly disappointed when said officer had turned out to show no obvious aptitude for her vision of empathetic, tactful, X-chromosome policing.

If Hardy was the back end of Canada, Rupert was the back end of Hardy. The whole town was on a meagre square of reservation land tucked against the next bay south. It amounted to a long crescent beach of grey sand and pebbles, two rows of houses either side of the shore road, and a hectare of trailer homes on the slope above. It had its own tiny store for coffee, cigarettes and DVDs. Goose hadn't even thought about keeping an eye on it. Everyone would know within minutes if Jennifer showed up in Rupert. It was her home town and, by the perverse law of celebrity, she was probably its most famous inhabitant ever.

Margaret Sampson turned out to be the small round liaison officer Goose had already met. She was one of a group of four small round women all aged and dressed more or less the same, standing unhappily outside the Band hall. The building was much more impressive than the RCMP station in Hardy; a pleasantly weathered barn of two significant storeys. On the street side it was supposed to look like one of the big houses the coastal people used to live in. They'd decorated its long flat windowless front with a mythical creature painted in the distinctive north-west coastal manner, and put up a kind of statue in front in the same traditional style.

As she got out of the car Goose saw that both the painting and the statue had been defaced.

They must have used charcoal. The effect was worse on the painting, where both heads of the double-headed serpent thing had been all but blotted out. The statue was in the shape of two bear-like creatures supporting a pole across their shoulders, and a bird – probably a raven, Goose knew they were big on ravens – sitting on the pole. All three animals had been smeared black around their mouths. Margaret Sampson was close to tears. 'It's so disrespectful,' she kept saying, as Goose opened her notebook. 'They should be ashamed.'

'When did this happen?'

'This morning.' They all agreed. 'Just now.'

'Just now?'

One of them had walked by not half an hour ago, she said. 'Plain daylight.'

'But someone must have seen something?'

They looked at each other. No one had seen anything.

'You're sure this happened in the last half-hour?'

'Absolutely sure.'

A man walking with a cane had come out of one of the ramshackle houses near by. 'Hey. Are you the police?'

'Officer Maculloch, sir. From Hardy.'

'You gonna fix the TV?'

'Why don't you keep quiet?' one of the women asked.

'TV isn't working.'

Goose concentrated on Mrs Sampson. 'No one saw anything at all? It might not have been kids. Anyone on the street? A car?'

'Keeps showing junk.'

'Will you be quiet?'

Goose stepped away to give herself some room and found herself looking out across the bay. It was the same kind of day it had been ever since she'd arrived, as wet as the weather could be without rain, the clouds like a misty lid resting on top of the world, everything you looked at – sea, sky, trees, or the abrupt sawtooth silhouette of the mainland peaks far across the water – a variation on the underlying green-grey. Like every other stretch of the fifteen-hundred-kilometre waterway that ran tight under the mountainous shadow of the continent's north-west coast, the bay was studded with islands, overlapping each other in perspective so that water, rock and damp conifer forest blended together in the middle distance as if they were all the same substance. In the summer, so they told her, there'd be cruise ships going up and down the Inside Passage every day, and cruising yachts stopping off in all the bays, but all Goose had ever seen offshore was the endless indistinct jumbled wilderness.

Until now. A single yellow kayak was splashing towards the islands, its small dark-haired pilot little more than a smudge even though it couldn't have been more than a couple of hundred metres out.

Her stomach knotted.

'I need a boat.'

'Huh?'

'A boat. I need a boat. Who can lend me a boat?'

'Officer Maculloch.' Mrs Sampson wasn't the kind of person who forgot names. 'This is a crime.'

'Where's the crime?' asked the man with the cane, momentarily distracted from his malfunctioning TV.

'Right here in front of your nose, you old fool.'

'This is urgent. Police matter.' Goose shouldered away from the small women's offended dignity towards the beach. She couldn't be sure what she was seeing, and yet she was sure, somehow; who else would be paddling steadily away into the misty emptiness? She scanned the town for a vessel. In Hardy and Alice there always seemed to be trailers pulled up by the landings, people's fishing boats or kayaks waiting for the weather to turn. She looked up and down the long sweep of the bay and saw only gulls and eagles and crows stalking the pebbles.

The little crowd caught up with her, squawking like the gulls. 'Officer—'

'I need to question the girl in that kayak.' She heard herself talking like a policeman, always a bad sign; it meant she wasn't concentrating. She was chasing ideas one after another. Race back to Hardy and take the RCMP launch? Too slow; she might lose the kid in the mess of islands. Call another officer out in the launch? Janice said they were all busy, and no one was supposed to know Jennifer was on the loose. Get Jonas to come over and take his own boat? Too slow again. What she really needed was—

'Excuse me.' She had to shout to quieten them. 'Listen. Someone in town must have their own kayak. Who's got a kayak here?'

'You're going boating?' One of the small round women looked at Goose from behind bottle-thick glasses, quietly incredulous.

'George got one,' said the old guy with the cane. 'Got it for his boys.'

'That's a girl?'

'She got no life vest. Is that illegal?'

'How d'you know it's a girl?'

'Sir?' Goose spoke sharply again to catch the man's wandering attention. 'Sir? You say you know where there's a kayak?' It was all she needed. She was fast and very fit; as long as she didn't lose sight of Jennifer for long she knew she'd be able to catch up.

The man waved his stick down the road. 'George Hall. With the blue fence.'

'Officer Maculloch, I'd like an explanation why you're not giving your attention to . . .'

She'd run out of earshot before the sentence was complete. The blue fence was a few metal bars like tent posts with plastic netting strung between, penning in a very fat dog with invisibly stumpy legs. The dog jiggled upright as she sprinted closer, though it turned out not to be her who'd roused it; the door of the house opened and a grizzled man in a lumberjack shirt came out. He stared at Goose in complete confusion.

'George Hall?' She was breathing hard already.

'Are you the police?'

'Mr Hall, this is an emergency situation. I need to borrow your kayak.' He appeared not to understand. 'Quickly. Sir.'

'I didn't call the police yet.' The dog waddled over to him and flopped down right in front of his feet, as if to suggest that he was better off not going outside.

'No, sir. It's not to do with you. I just need to commandeer your boat.' Jeez, Goose, she thought to herself: *commandeer?*

'Sure as dammit is to do with me. Someone just stole my kids' kayak.'

Once she was safely back in the car and racing away as fast as she dared from the questions and complaints, she got Cope on the radio.

'She showed up this morning, sir. In Rupert. She vandalised the Band property and then took off in a kayak.'

'She what?'

'She stole a kayak. Took off in it. Out into the strait.'

'And you didn't stop her?'

'I was called too late. I need a vessel, sir. I'll be taking the launch.'

'The damn launch is in McNeill. What are you talking about?'

'She's in a kayak, sir, by herself. She won't be hard to track down. It's a bright yellow kayak.'

'What did you say about the Band?'

She explained, but she was already snatching at the next idea. It would mean getting hold of Jonas, quickly.

'That's just perfect. Just what I needed.' She could hear Cope sagging. 'Did you talk to Margaret Sampson?'

'Yes, sir. I—'

'Damn it. I don't suppose there's any hope you asked her to keep it quiet till we find her?'

'Keep what quiet?' A patrol car sped past in the other direction at the airport turn, lights flashing.

'"Keep what quiet?" What do you think? Didn't we talk about this?'

'Oh. No, sir, no one saw Jennifer. Identified her, I mean.'

'Then who . . . You'd better start from the beginning, Maculloch.'

No, she'd better not. She'd explain later. 'Emergency, sir,' she mumbled, and cut him off.

In the few seconds of relative silence while she pulled out her own phone she seemed to hear a larger stillness, the emptiness of water, the solitary *tlatch tlatch* of paddle blades.

'Jonas?'

'Goose! What's up? Mountie got her man?'

'OK, listen. I need your help. I'm in a hurry.'

'You're always in a—'

'This is serious. The kid's out in the strait. I need your

boat. Fast. You hear me, Jonas? Really fast. Like sirens and actual running, that kind of fast.'

'You're kidding, man. I'm on duty here.'

'I've got maybe an hour to save my ass. This is what you're going to do, Jonas. Are you listening? You run outside, get in the car, floor it over to Hardy, meet me at the pier. You're going to do that for me, right away. OK? Right as soon as I hang up.'

'It's kind of a nice ass.'

She hung up.

Time ached as she waited by the half-abandoned water-front condos. She recognised the feeling from the last three minutes of games her team was losing, when the other girls had the ball and whatever you did, however hard you hit, you knew you weren't going to get it back. She listened distractedly to the unusually heavy chatter on the radio. Janice called her.

'Hi there, Marie.' Her schoolmistressy voice. 'I've just had a phone call from Mrs Sampson. I guess she's a little unhappy.'

'There's an emergency. Something's come up.'

'Oh, OK. We have procedures for an emergency. I'll get some back-up to you right away.'

'It's not like that. It's, ah.' She could feel the whole situation getting worse around her, underneath her; she was sinking into something embarrassing and stupid without quite knowing how she'd got there. 'It's personal.'

'Oh. Oh, I'm sorry. Is there anything—'

'I'll get to Rupert later. Tell them we have a suspect, OK? I need to go.'

Which was true. She needed to go. There was still time before the ferry was due to leave; it hadn't even come in yet, and she knew it sat at the dock in Hardy Bay for two or three hours while they turned it around. She had a misty recollection of the map. There were three or four small islands in Rupert Bay, and beyond them just the miles of open water of the Queen Charlotte Strait. Nowhere a yellow plastic kayak could hide for long, whichever direction it went. They'd just have to round the headland between Hardy and Rupert and cruise along the coast and they'd see the boat before long. The shore was all forest and rock as far as she knew. No roads, no hiding places, nowhere to go.

Nowhere to go. (*Tlatch, tlatch, tlatch, tlatch.* What was she doing out there? Where was she going? What if it hadn't even been her?)

Jonas tried to call once too, but she decided he'd probably come faster if she didn't answer. She wasn't sure what to tell him anyway. She still hadn't settled on an explanation by the time she saw the patrol car cruise – unhurriedly – down from the roundabout and pull up in the disintegrating oversized nine-tenths-deserted parking lot that served the dock. Mercifully, Jonas was that rare kind of person who could do things without perpetually asking why (no drive, Goose had thought to herself on their first day together; no curiosity; I hope I don't end up like that myself after a year in a place where nothing much ever happens. But after a week she admitted to herself that she wanted to be more like him, not that her parents' genes would ever allow it). He took her down through the stained and damp and generally unloved remnants of the Hardy fishing and leisure fleet to his own cluttered whaler, if not exactly at a jog then at least without pausing to ask what she thought she was doing. The closest he came to a reproach was just before he started the motor.

'Not the greatest time, you know, man. Had a couple of guys in the station already asking about the bank.'

One visitor to the station in a whole day would have counted as a crime wave in Alice, let alone two in a morning. 'I'll make it up to you. I can take the next few shifts.'

He backed them through the puff of oily smoke coughed up by the outboard. She felt cold already, only a few feet from land. 'So, where to, Jeeves? No, wait. Jeeves is the chauffeur. Other guy.'

She explained what she'd seen. For some reason it was easier to say on water, as if the unlikelihood didn't matter so much here. She had to shout; Jonas gunned the throttle as soon as he was clear of the dock. He obviously didn't mind going fast as long as he could stand still while it was happening.

'Keep going like this,' she yelled, 'and I reckon it won't take too long. No one will notice you left.'

He leaned across to reply. 'I dunno.'

'You think she can outrun us in a kayak?'

'Nah. Look at that.' He nodded forward.

'What?'

'Looks like a fog.'

She was so used to the universal evergreen-tinged grey

of the horizon that she'd stopped noticing when it changed shape. The coastal mountains were gone, replaced by nothing. Out beyond the bay the sea and the sky mingled into a single looming presence that seemed to be equally solid and air.

'Crap.'

They powered on close to the eastern side of the bay, passing the ferry terminal and the last few holiday cabins overlooking it. (Strange place for them, Goose thought, though if her holiday choices were fishing or watching a ferry go in and out she'd have chosen the latter.) The air was wet and chill enough to sting like sleet if she stuck her hand out of the shelter of the windshield.

'How long have we got?' she asked.

He swayed comfortably while the boat bounced under his feet and the wheel shook in his hand. 'Couldn't tell you. Us native guys got excused meteorology class at the Depot.'

'Jeez, Jonas.'

He shook his head. 'One thing for sure, if that rolls in here we aren't finding anyone in it.'

'So what do we do?'

He thought about it for a while, then leaned on the throttle. She grabbed the cold metal of the back of her seat. 'Go faster, I guess.'

As soon as they rounded the eastern tip of the bay the strait grew surprisingly rough. From a distance it looked as even and tranquil as the utterly sheltered inlet beside which Alice sat, water so smooth that when Goose had first taken her own kayak out there she'd felt like a calligrapher marking patient lines and dots on a vast silver sheet. But here, even in the absence of anything but the faintest wind, the sea felt the presence of the ocean fifty miles west. It was restless. It made itself into fist-thick ridges and troughs which smacked the skimming hull of Jonas's whaler as if they wouldn't have minded punching it back where it came. Looking over her shoulder now Goose could see straight up the Inside Passage, out past the flat head of Vancouver Island towards the ocean and the north. There was no passage. The fog plugged it like mortar.

'Gonna be tight getting back.'

Goose gritted her teeth in silent frustration.

'Might not even be the kid,' Jonas said. 'You didn't get a look at her, right?'

She didn't say anything. She knew with complete certainty that it was Jennifer she'd seen paddling away, just out of reach, just out of her grip. If she hadn't been sure before she was now. She was the fog girl, the disappearing girl, the one you could never catch up with nor ever see.

What if Jennifer had made the fog happen?

(This kind of thought came more easily on water.)

What if she'd made the fog happen the way she'd made the cell door open?

''Nother few minutes east and we can turn into Rupert Bay. Pretty shallow in places there, though.'

'It's OK. You can turn back.'

'I don't mind giving it a try. Know my way around out here pretty good.'

'Nah. We won't find her.'

Jonas looked at her, surprised.

'We won't.' Goose set her jaw. 'Let's go back.'

'Hey,' he said. 'You OK? This doesn't sound like you.' He eased the throttle back. The ambient sounds became a presence, the sea's insidious whisper.

'How much were you involved in the investigation?'

'When Carl died?'

'Uh-huh.'

'Depends what you mean. Not much, I guess. But then you couldn't really avoid it. Contagious.'

'You ever read the whole file?'

'Oh, man. Maybe once I'm done with *War and Peace*.'

'If you read the file you'd know we're not going to find her.'

'Why's that?'

She looked away. 'You'd just know.'

A long muted groan spread from the sea behind them.

'Foghorn at Scarlett Point,' Jonas said, and spun the wheel. 'Must be coming down faster 'n I thought.'

To Goose it had sounded like a moan of defeat. She slumped in the seat, imagining Jennifer paddling still, safely out of sight, secretly, purposefully. Going somewhere even though she had nowhere to go. Now that Jonas had turned back, the fog was dead ahead. Goose hadn't seen proper sunshine since she'd moved up here. The sun might as well be a myth. This wasn't the sun's country. Nothing was sharp, clear, bright. She'd rented a mountain bike on her first afternoon off and taken one of the forest trails, remembering happy autumn weekends in the hills outside

Montreal. After an hour she'd returned the bike and gone home. The forest here was endlessly repetitive: straight, wet, evergreen, oppressively quiet, a thick deep wall which looked like it went on for ever, like Jennifer's silence, like the impending fog.

It caught them just as they turned back into Hardy Bay. One minute they could see the ferry dock and the town ahead, looking pathetically diminished, blips in the landscape; the next minute they could see nothing. Jonas throttled all the way back and peered at the compass mounted on the whaler's dash.

'Due south-west should do it. Just have to take it slow. You want to go up front and keep an eye out?'

Goose did a full turn. The world had vanished. It was like there was no left or right, no up or down even. With nothing to reflect, the water itself appeared to have turned into cloud.

'For what?'

'Anything. Deadheads.' She'd been warned about deadheads the first time she put her kayak in. They were floating logs broken loose from the giant booms that passed up and down the Inside Passage every day, whole stripped tree trunks heavy as a bus and often drifting upright with only a foot of their length showing above the surface, waiting to punch a hole in your hull. 'Hardy. Won't see it till we're on top of it.' He pulled a portable horn out of a locker and aimed a single long blast into the fog. Miles away, the lighthouse moaned again like an echo.

'What's that other noise?' Goose asked, after she'd been staring uselessly at nothing for a few minutes.

'Huh?'

Her senses felt disconnected. The mumble of the motor in the stern sounded like it was coming from the sky. She heard her own breath outside herself. Was the other thing just the sound of water curling gently away from the hull?

'That.'

Jonas kept his eyes on the compass. 'Don't hear anything.'

'Wait. There.' It was breathy and irregular, like the whisper of the tiny bow-wave, but somehow with more to it. It sounded like a distant conversation.

'Oh. Wait . . . Someone out there?' He shouted. 'Hello?' He raised the horn again and sounded it for a couple of seconds, obliterating any other noise.

Distantly, directionless, another horn answered, much deeper.

'That wasn't the lighthouse.'

'Nope.' Jonas held his finger to his lips, frowning, listening. A sound was coalescing in the fog, everywhere, as if it was the fog's heartbeat, a deep muffled drumming. It swallowed whatever Goose had heard, or thought she'd heard. It seemed to be spreading, as if it was coming closer.

The new horn blared again.

Jonas checked his watch, nodded to himself and touched the throttle forward, speeding them a little faster towards everything they couldn't see. 'Should have remembered,' he said. 'Ferry's coming in.'

Seven

THE FOG COSIED up to the mountains above the town and settled. Goose drove back to Rupert slowly. The cars she passed made haloes with their headlights, hanging them in front like anglerfish navigating the white murk. She tracked down Margaret Sampson and her shawled and bespectacled posse, did the apologies, made nice, heard out as many statements as people wanted to give, and took notes and photos to show she was taking them extra seriously. She let the old guy complain about his malfunctioning TV. He said a couple of his buddies in trailer homes up the hill were having the same problem. She waited as long as she thought respectful before suggesting he call the TV company. She talked to Mr Hill about his stolen kayak and promised the police would look for it. One of his sons had come home and stood in the background during the interview, in the dingy interior of their house, looking hostile on principle, as the local young guys always did when she was in uniform. She looked for traces of Jennifer's passing, certain she wouldn't find any.

The fog lifted around four. She was on her way back home to Alice, technically off duty. Halfway there and the world unveiled itself around her, the mist thinning and melting as if it had never been anything more than cloud blowing by. A kilometre or two later Cope radioed to call her back to the station in Hardy.

That gave her ten minutes to contemplate the upcoming discussion. They weren't the most pleasant minutes. She spent the majority of them trying to recall what she was supposed to know about the RCMP's disciplinary procedures. She was fairly confident she couldn't be dismissed or demoted without a formal hearing; she was less sure whether the official grounds for instigating a formal hearing included screwing up. Back at the Depot in Regina they'd talked a lot about 'misconduct'. Did losing a teenager count as misconduct? Turning it over as she drove, it occurred to her that the only thing she really dreaded was her mother somehow hearing the news. Séverine's in trouble! Séverine messed up! Boring, reliable Séverine, Séverine who wasn't vampy and glamorous and wouldn't wear make-up, Séverine who liked rough sports and joined the police and chose to speak English and moved out west near her Anglo father – Séverine screwed up badly enough to risk forfeiting her precious childhood dream of being a mountie. *Please, Staff Sergeant, don't tell my mom.*

But Cope turned out not to be angry at all. There was no telltale purpling around his collar. On the contrary, his jowly neck had less colour than usual, if anything; he looked grey. When she stood to attention in his office he gestured wearily to a chair. The usual scatter of paperwork covered his desk. He tapped at it absently with his biro instead of saying anything. She actually found herself listening to the clock tick. She glanced at it, not sure where else to look. Four twenty. Assuming the fog had cleared out of the Passage for good, the ferry would leave in ten minutes.

'I hear you did a good job with that woman over in Rupert.'

She sat straight backed, hands on her knees, and tried not to let her surprise show. 'The liaison officer, sir?'

'Nothing worse than when she gets on the warpath. Holy hell. I wish I could lock her up. Throw the key in the chuck.'

Goose thought it best not to react at all. Cope sighed, flipping the cap of the biro up and down. 'Anyway. She's your new best friend now. "Delightful young lady." She had to tell me all about it personally. Five damn minutes I didn't have. I guess you used your feminine empathy or whatever they call it.'

'I don't have any empathy, sir. I just like kicking ass.'

It was her standard comment about being a female policeman. She didn't know how it had popped out now; perhaps because this conversation was nothing at all like the one she'd unconsciously rehearsed as she drove into town. 'Excuse me, sir,' she added, but he was neither amused nor irritated. Whatever was on his mind, she barely seemed to figure in it at all.

'So,' he said. 'That girl hasn't shown up.'

'I'm sorry, sir.'

'What have you got? Anything?'

She gave him a brief version: nothing at all the previous day, the accidental sighting in Rupert that morning, the search broken off in the fog. He stopped fidgeting while she told him those parts, and was silent for quite a while after she finished.

'This kid in the kayak,' he said at last, and Goose saw at once where he was going, and in the same moment understood what this conversation was going to be about. It was nothing to do with her at all; she should have known it wouldn't be. He didn't care about her. He was the one looking for an excuse. 'How far out were they when you first saw them?'

'I'm not sure, sir. It's hard to tell on water. Two or three hundred metres?'

'A fair way off, you're saying.'

'I guess.'

'And there were a bunch of other people with you?'

She recited the names, all of which she'd learned that afternoon in the course of her note-taking and apology-making.

'At least a couple of that crowd know the Knox family pretty good. For sure. Probably all of them. Margaret Sampson knows every man, woman, child and dog in that town all by herself.' He looked at Goose expectantly, and when she didn't respond, added – as if stating the obvious – 'So none of them identified the person in the kayak as Jennifer?'

'It was pretty—'

'That was what we in English-speaking Canada call a question, Maculloch.'

'No, sir. None of them did.'

'So how come you think that's who it was?'

She thought about trying to explain. Not for very long, though, since (firstly) it was essentially inexplicable and (secondly) she appreciated now that Cope was going to have his version of events no matter what she said.

'I guess there's no way I could make a positive identification.'

'At that distance.'

'Yes, sir. At that distance.'

'The person had their back to you?'

'Yes, sir.'

'I guess not either. Is there any evidence at all that the Knox girl was in Rupert this morning? Anything?'

'There's no evidence at all that she's anywhere, sir.'

He leaned back in his desk chair. 'That's what I thought.'

'Someone stole Mr Hill's kayak and paddled away in it.'

'Kids are always stealing stuff around here. I reckon it's boredom. So it could have been anyone, as far as you know, is that right? That one's what we call a rhetorical question, incidentally.'

'That's right, sir.'

'So. Who else knows your theory?'

'I'm not aware of having a theory.'

'Give me a break, Maculloch. It's been a long day. Did you tell anyone else that you were off chasing that girl?'

'Oh, I see. No, sir. Well, Officer Paul. It was his boat. I kind of had to.'

'No one else.'

'No.'

'You're sure about that?'

'Cross my heart.'

He glared at her while the clock ticked.

'You asked Jonas to get you that file, didn't you?'

Janice must have said something about it. Janice was big on sharing information where she thought it ought to be shared. Gossip, in other words. 'Yes I did. I was looking for—'

He grunted away her explanation. 'I don't want to know.' He bowed his head, rolling the biro between his palms. 'All right,' he went on, as if only now coming to the point. 'Here's what I'd like you to do from now on, Maculloch. You check in when you're supposed to check in and do what the rota tells you to do and you leave the whole damn business with that girl alone. OK? Leave the file alone, leave your suspicions alone, follow up that damn kayak and whatever else Margaret Sampson's on my ass about without making any assumptions at all. How's that? You're sure you didn't so much as mention her name to anyone except Jonas?'

'Absolutely sure.'

'Well.' He made it sound like nothing more needed saying. 'Let's keep it that way. All right?'

From outside, down in the bay, three sharp hoots echoed over the town. Goose looked up at the clock. Four thirty-two. There wouldn't be that much traffic on the ferry; nothing to hold it up. Nineteen hours up the Inside Passage, bleak islands on the west side and to the east the wildest coast south of the Arctic Circle, on its way to Prince Rupe. Her deadline had passed and was even now turning sluggishly to face north, steaming away from her.

'Not meaning to be difficult, sir, but what about the facility up in George? They're going to notice when she doesn't arrive.'

'I'll talk to them.'

Was Staff Sergeant Cope actually looking shifty? She'd hardly ever seen him hiding behind his desk before. Normally he perched on its edge. Normally he folded his arms and looked at the members of his detachment over his glasses as if daring them to annoy him. Now he pushed the spectacles up his nose and fiddled with them, like a suspect pretending not to be nervous.

'Sir,' she began, carefully. 'I appreciate that I take responsibility for Jennifer disappearing from custody. In which case I think it's appropriate for me to know whether I can expect . . . How my service record might be affected.'

'Trust me,' Cope said. 'No one cares about your service record at the moment. We've got bigger problems.'

'What I'm asking, sir, is what you're planning to say to the people in George.'

'I'm going to tell them what happened. Surprisingly.'

'Which bits of what happened?'

'The bits we know. The kid got out of the cell somehow, ran off, whereabouts unknown. We'll keep an eye out in case she shows up and we'll ship her up to George whenever.'

'You're going to start a missing child investigation?'

'No, Maculloch. No damn way am I going to start a

missing child investigation. I was kind of hoping this meeting wouldn't take too long but I guess you don't get it, so let me spell this out for you.' Still he didn't shout, though some of the blood came back into his face. Shouting might have attracted curiosity; his office wasn't all that well insulated from the rest of the station. 'That place up in George don't want that kid. No one wants that kid. I sure as dammit don't want that kid. Her own damn mother doesn't want her. The law can't figure out who's responsible for her. So as long as no one's got her . . . You see? You can stop worrying about covering your own damn ass. I won't tell anyone how you messed up. If.' He pointed a pudgy finger at her. 'If. You let it all drop too.'

She sat still and straight, discipline hiding her bafflement. 'So what happens if she shows up again? Sir.'

'What do you think she'd do?' He tried to sneer, unconvincingly. 'Make a complaint?'

'I thought maybe—'

'She's just a crazy kid. That's what makes me so sick. All she ever was is a girl who lost her mind and pushed her brother downstairs. All this damn fuss and driving her up and down and TV and this and that. She's a messed-up kid from a waste of space family. She's not going to turn up. How long do you think a crazy kid's going to last by herself in a kayak in February?'

Oh, Goose thought. OK.

'You're not being disciplined.' Cope turned his attention to the paperwork in front of him, flicking the cap off the biro ostentatiously. 'I called you here so you understand we don't have anything to do with Jennifer Knox any more. As long as you got that, you can go.' He made a note. 'OK?'

She stood up. She felt like she ought to be bubbling with relief, but she wasn't. 'OK, sir. Thank you.'

He waved her away without looking up. 'Then we're done.'

Since he wouldn't meet her eyes she found herself staring at his fidgety hands. She was turning to go when he made another note, a brief scribble. It caught her eye with its shape and colour. A quick red loop and a few letters in the margin. She frowned.

He raised his head. 'Class dismissed.'

'Sorry, sir. Thank you.' She recovered herself and left.

'Jonas? Goose.'

'Hey. How'd it go?'

'Weird.'

'Weird?'

'Weird.'

'Is that good or bad?'

'Well, I'm still a constable.'

'Congratulations. Caught the sarge in a good mood, huh.'

'I wouldn't put it that way. Do you still have the file?'

'Man. No. Janice had me turn it back in first thing. What'd he do, give you extra reading as a punishment?'

'Something I wanted to check again.'

'We need to get you more stuff to do.'

She'd spent long enough looking at it the night before that it had stuck in her memory. Mostly because it had been the only thing to stand out from the blur of hospital paperwork. That one sheet, the one brief reference to the security guard's story, which was itself the one brief reference to any kind of flaw in Jennifer's immaculate silence; and the person who'd scribbled a quick loop and a marginal note on the sheet – *SF 12/1* – was Sergeant Cope. She was certain of it. She'd just watched him make exactly the same kind of annotation, right before her eyes. Most probably with the very same red biro.

She drove up to the station in Alice instead of going home. Jonas lived in the apartment attached to it. When he answered the door the TV was noisy in the background, showing a hockey game. She asked whether she could come in for a minute.

He sighed exaggeratedly. 'I'm kicking back, you know? Had folks hassling me about the bank all day.'

'It's only a second. OK, look, a commercial, that's as long as I need.'

'Nah, I'm kidding. You want a beer? Come on in.'

'Honest. I just need to ask you something before I forget.'

He muted the TV while she hunted around for pencil and paper, and watched as she made a version of Cope's note. 'There was something from the hospital in the file, that big place down-island. The sarge had written on it. Like this.'

Jonas waited a while. 'And?'

'Do you know what it means?'

'Don't mean anything. It's a reminder. He does that. Helps him keep stuff together.'

'A reminder of what? Does what?'

Jonas looked longingly at the now silent game. 'You sure you care about this?'

'I'm not leaving till you tell me.' She moved to stand between him and the screen. 'There. Don't make me turn it off.'

'Whoa. Look. It's just a way of getting the pages together. You know, so he can find stuff.'

'You need to go back a few steps, Jonas. I'm the rookie here, remember? I don't understand what the letters mean. The numbers.'

'Oh. OK. Name and date. Sorry, man. Thought that was obvious. SF is Fitzgerald and 12/1 is the date. So there's a report from Shawn for that date, goes with whatever he'd written that on.'

She looked at her own scribble. 'You sure?'

'Goose. You promised.'

She stepped away from the TV. 'Sorry. So, this is like a cross-reference?'

He snapped his fingers. 'That's the word.'

'And it means this goes with . . .'

'Whatever Shawn filed that day.'

'There wasn't anything in the file.'

Jonas shrugged. 'Big file. I should know.'

'I read all the station reports. I went through it like ten times and read all of them first. They're short, that's why. And you can understand them.'

'Something got into you?'

'Maybe,' she said.

* * *

After her interview with the sarge that afternoon she was absolutely sure she'd never get hold of the file again, no matter who she asked. On the other hand, she thought, sitting on her bed staring absently at the packing boxes, she didn't need to. She remembered, quite clearly, spending extra time trying to figure out what had happened to Jennifer in those second and third weeks of January, after the girl had been charged on the basis of her mother's accusation. It was precisely the paucity of documentation that had struck her. Putting kids in jail for more than a night was a serious business which usually left a prominent paper trail. She was as sure as she could be that there'd been nothing signed by Fitzgerald with that date anywhere in the file.

And why would Cope have referred to one of his officers' reports anyway? Perhaps he hadn't been cross-referencing anything at all. Perhaps he'd got the date wrong. It was just a scribble. It was, however, unmistakably, unarguably, a response to that particular couple of sentences in the hospital report. The suggestion of Jennifer sneaking out of bed and singing and dancing around in the middle of the night must have reminded him of something.

Drop it. She had her instructions. Let the kid go, forget about her, for your own good. That was the deal.

She kicked a space clear on the floor, lay down, and went through her stretching exercises, promising herself she'd do something to make herself sweat and breathe hard during her off hours the next morning. There was no farther she could go anyway. Cope hadn't so much declared the case closed as annulled it, decided to pretend it had never happened. She obviously wasn't going to be asking him what he'd been thinking of when he saw the hospital report. Or what it had to do with whatever Constable Fitzgerald might have noted on 12 January—

She sat up abruptly, tweaking her shoulder.

Drop it.

Why couldn't she drop it?

Her apartment was very quiet. People called places like Alice 'quiet'; it was supposed to mean that nothing went on there, but actually, she'd discovered, it was the literal truth. Nothing but the potty-mouth crows made any noise unless the wind was up or the rain was falling. Especially at night. For a few seconds after she went to bed, when she pulled the cover up to her chin and settled on her pillow, she'd lie there astonished by the absence of noise. Frightened by it, if she was honest with herself, just for a moment. She didn't like it. She didn't like the silence that bored out of the girl's eyes. She didn't like the thought of the girl vanishing into the fog, *tlatch tlatch tlatch tlatch*, receding, muffled by the white shroud, going somewhere and doing something no one else could understand.

It was just one phone call, she thought. Cope would never need to find out. Fitzgerald had been transferred away for good. They'd sent him home when he got sick; once that happened it was as good as being redeployed. She wouldn't have been called up in his place otherwise. Wherever he went next it wouldn't be back to Hardy. But Janice had given Goose his home number on her first day. Her first hour, in fact. 'Oh, Shawn, I'm sure he'd love to hear from you. Tell you all the little ins and outs. Tips and tricks.' Janice wanted everyone in the detachment to be best friends.

Goose checked the time. If she left it any later she might interrupt dinner or wake someone up. Those midwestern people ate and went to bed ridiculously early.

The first time she tried the number it didn't work. Or rather she heard a kind of ghostly ringing, very faint, as if the connection was only a quarter complete. She strolled around the apartment looking for a better signal and tried again from the miniature kitchen. This time there wasn't even a dial tone, just a kind of whispery silence. The screen was showing three bars, which should have been plenty. She put on coat and shoes and went outside, heading up the slope of the road. It was almost dark. She'd reached the corner of the block when the phone buzzed in her hand.

'Hello?'

'Hello?' A woman's voice, nervous.

'Hello?'

'Who is this?'

Goose cupped her free hand around the phone. The woman sounded frail, or elderly, or both. 'I think you have a wrong number, madam. Séverine Maculloch?'

'What?'

'I said I think you have a wrong number. Sorry.'

'I just picked up the phone.'

'Excuse me?'

'You called me. Is this the hospital?'

Goose put on her official voice, with its hint of abrasive impatience. 'Who am I speaking to, please?'

'Marnie Fitzgerald. Are you the doctor?'

'Mrs Fitzgerald?' The official voice deserted her.

'Hello?'

'Mrs—' She struggled briefly to recover herself. 'I'm sorry. Can I confirm that I'm speaking to Mrs Fitzgerald?'

'Yes. Is it bad news? Oh God.'

'Mrs Fitzgerald, I'm sorry to bother you. My name's Séverine Maculloch. I'm the officer who replaced Shawn in the Hardy detachment.' There was a pause. 'Hardy, B.C. How's Shawn doing? I was sorry to hear he was sick.'

After another shaky pause, the woman said, 'You're the police?'

'This isn't an official matter, Mrs Fitzgerald. I just wanted to check how Shawn was doing and maybe see if there was a chance I could talk with him for a moment. If he's there. Or if you have a better number for him. Hello?' She thought she'd lost the connection, but the button on the phone's screen was still green. 'Hello?'

A man's voice appeared. 'Shawn's not here.'

'Is that Mr Fitzgerald?'

'He had to go to hospital. Monday morning.'

'Oh. I'm very sorry to hear that.'

'You don't sound like the sergeant. Marn said it was the sergeant.'

'No, sir. I'm Constable Maculloch. I'm Shawn's replacement.'

'You're a mountie?'

'I'm an officer of the Mounted Police, yes, sir.'

'In that place?'

'My assignment is the Hardy detachment, yes, sir. Just the same as your son. Am I speaking to Mr Fitzgerald?'

'They're gonna eat you alive up there.'

'I appreciate the advice, sir. Would you mind telling me the name of the hospital where Shawn was admitted?'

'They won't let you talk to him.'

'I certainly won't bother your son while he's sick. I have a couple of questions for him but they're not urgent, I can try another time. Sorry to disturb your family, Mr Fitzgerald. My best wishes for Shawn's recovery.'

'He got a lot worse.'

Goose looked across over the town and the still black stripe of the inlet to the mountain ridge on the western horizon. Even the crows had gone temporarily quiet.

'He couldn't even stay in bed. Sores got so bad he can't lie on them.'

This wasn't the first time someone had mistaken Goose for a good listener. She'd always blamed her looks before. She was blonde and appley. By a mean-spirited genetic joke she'd inherited her dad's improbably wholesome face unmitigated by any of her mom's spiky glamour, which would have suited her much better, as well as being much more popular with the kind of boys she'd liked in high school. On this occasion, obviously, her face couldn't be held responsible.

'I'm sorry to hear that,' she said, briskly. 'I'm sure he'll do better now he's in hospital.' Her next word would have been *Goodbye* but she wasn't quick enough.

'None of them know what it is.'

They had lectures at the Depot about being a good listener. 'Active Listening', it was called, which was about as much as she remembered. She knew she'd most likely have to work twice as hard as the guys to get the same evaluations, so she gave it her best shot, but she'd never really grasped what it was about, beyond biting your tongue so you didn't tell losers to quit whining.

'It'll be all right, sir. They'll look after him good.'

'We wanted him to stay here. But the smell—'

He's going to cry, Goose thought, as the man cut himself off with a kind of fumbling choke.

'Please don't distress yourself. Thank you for your time. My best wishes to your family.'

'You seen that girl?'

Goose flushed and went very still. 'Sir?'

Bubbling sniffly noises. 'You know what Shawn says?'

She looked around. No one else was outside. People didn't go outside unless they were in a car. 'I've never had the opportunity to meet your son.'

'Says she put a curse on him. That's what he says. Says she gave him the evil eye. None of the doctors got an explanation.'

'I understand your son must be very distressed—'

'What'd you say your name was, missy?'

Missy? 'Constable Maculloch.'

'You got that girl still? The native girl? You still got her in jail?'

Goose took a long moment to answer. 'I'm afraid I'm not at liberty to reveal custody arrangements.'

'You go see her. OK? You go see her. Please.' The voice had gone hoarse. 'I'm asking you as a father.'

'Mr Fitzgerald, I'm afraid I can't—'

'Please. You go tell her Shawn's sorry for what he done. Real sorry. You ask her to stop what she's doing. Tell her we're begging her. If she wants money we'll give her money.'

A boy freewheeled down the slope on his bike. She turned her face away from the road and let him pass out of sight.

'May I ask,' she said, carefully, 'what it is Shawn thinks he did?'

'He didn't mean no harm. He's a good kid.'

'I'm sure.'

'Please,' the voice said, shrunk to a whisper so bereft Goose could barely hear it even on that deserted street. 'Just tell her.'

Eight

'NOT SLEEPING TOO good, huh.'

'Is it that obvious?'

Jonas drew crescents under his own eyes with his fingers.

'I was unpacking,' she said. 'I've been putting it off.'

They were in the window booth at Traders, simultaneously having breakfast and being visible. Cope, who perhaps knew enough about Jonas to figure that he'd sit in the station watching TV if he could, was big on being visible.

'Boxes fought back?'

'Yeah. It was, like, ten against one.'

He chuckled, opening his third sugar sachet and stirring.

She'd hadn't plugged in the laptop. The mere thought of doing so had made her sweat. Her phone had gone off three times, unknown callers. She'd desperately wanted to talk to Annie but something about the way the phone sat there buzzing at her made it impossible for her to touch it. She'd tried to tire/bore herself to sleep by unpacking. Hours later, as it turned midnight, she'd been standing in the kitchen holding her cheap wok in one hand and crying into the other because she couldn't remember where she'd put the matching lid she'd unwrapped two minutes earlier, or at least that was the only obvious reason.

'You wanna go home and catch some zees? I can watch the shop.'

Jonas was so absurdly even tempered that it hadn't quite occurred to Goose to think of him as kind. She smiled, embarrassed.

'Nah. I'll be OK. I'm off later this morning anyway, right?'

'Yep. I'm thinking you could break early.'

'I'm fine. I need stuff to do. Think I'm getting cabin fever.'

'Ahh, we can keep you busy if we try, can't we, Courtnee?' The waitress had brought his eggs. She was a hefty teenager who went speechless in the face of Jonas's easy charm, like every other female in the town. 'Gonna rustle up some malfeasance for Goose here, huh? Hey, is that French? Thanks, hun.' Courtnee retreated to her greasy sanctuary behind the kitchen door, blushing helplessly.

'You're great with the kids.' Goose watched him eat. 'You should have your own.'

'No way.' Even for him the negative was emphatically protracted. 'Different kettle o' fish.'

'They should have let you sit down with Jennifer Knox right at the start. I bet you'd have had the whole story out of her in ten minutes.'

He glanced at her, suddenly wary, and went on eating. 'What?'

He finished chewing, very deliberately. He dabbed at his mouth. He'd have driven her mother crazy. You could see he had something to say, but it was like he needed to warm up. *Alors, accouche!* (waving the lit cigarette in her hand in her impatience, scattering tiny flakes of ash: who's going to clean them up? Goose would be thinking angrily).

'Girl's still bugging you, huh.'

'Aren't you even curious, Jonas? Of course you aren't. What am I saying.'

'I'm curious about whether there's a God, too. Don't let it keep me awake, though. You know the sarge don't want us going looking for her again?'

'Oh, yeah. I got the message.'

'Hey. Take it easy.'

'Are you guys up here always like this about missing kids? Like, Oh well, never mind, plenty more where they came from?'

He put down his fork and leaned back. 'It's not like that. The thing you got to understand, Goose, is we did all this before. The guys tried their best, you know?'

She cradled her mug in her hands, swirling the dregs of her coffee into a miniature whirlpool. Its steam clung to the chilly window, fogging her view.

'What about Fitzgerald?' she said.

'Shawn? What about him?'

She'd said nothing about calling the man's home. Something about it lay slightly outside the range of conversation. There was a tincture of the unspeakable. Goose felt it by some secret instinct, like a taboo.

'What'd he think about her?' She heard her voice waver fractionally.

'Shawn's not too much of a thinker.'

'He was the duty cop one night while she was in jail.' She stared out at the row of houses opposite, the ones overlooking the inlet. 'He wrote some kind of report that wasn't in the file.'

Jonas sighed and shifted in his seat. 'Oh, man.'

'Right?'

'You're gonna sleep better if you stop thinking about paperwork.'

'Did he ever say anything to you, Jonas? About Jennifer? He was the officer called to the scene that night. He must have been involved a lot.'

'A lot of people said a lot of stuff.'

The tone of his voice said *it was nothing, forget it, don't worry*. She turned to him sharply and saw discomfort in his eyes.

'What do you mean? What'd he say?'

'Ah. Shawn. You know.'

Her mother would have waited no more than a few seconds before getting up and standing over his shoulder, snapping. Recognising where the impulse came from, Goose resisted it and waited. Jonas had his own rhythms. Part of his heritage, she thought to herself, plucking the buzzword from that internal glossary of Canadianness she'd worked so hard to acquire.

'Shawn's good people.'

Goose had learned how to interpret this phrase. Jonas used it so often that at first she'd thought it represented his universal view of humanity. Then she'd noticed it was often followed by a *but*. It was his way of compensating for something he didn't really want to talk about, so as to keep things in his preferred state of equilibrium. If they were talking about a wife-beater with a home-grown supply of weed and a habit of posting racist conspiracy rants on YouTube, he'd get to the qualifier more or less straight away: 'He's good people, but . . .' For less heinous individuals it might take him a bit longer.

'Hard worker. Tries his best, you know? Nothing too much trouble.'

Goose had to wait while the waitress came in and refilled their coffees.

'But, you know. Thought he was gonna sort it out.'

She waited a while longer to be certain that was as much as he had to say.

'Sort out what? The case?'

'Ah, I dunno.'

'You mean he thought he knew what had happened?'

'Who knows. Ancient history.'

'I was talking with Jennifer the day before yesterday. Or trying.' They both kept their voices low, though they could hear the owner yakking on the phone in the kitchen, and Courtnee had left the room again. 'Two days ago. It's not ancient history. She walked right out of that cell all by herself, Jonas. I swear she did. You want to know why I can't sleep?'

'See.' Her colleague looked pained. 'This is the thing. It gets to you unless you take it easy. Got to Shawn.'

'Got to him how?'

'I guess . . . He used to say how hard could it be to get a kid to talk.' Jonas looked at his plate. She felt like she was bullying a puppy.

'He said that?'

'Uh-huh.'

'You think he tried something?'

'Oh, man. Come on. Shawn's a good cop.'

'So what was he talking about?'

'I dunno. Said he knew she could open her mouth if she wanted to, so—'

'What?'

'Goose, what's with you? I'm gonna take you home myself.'

'Nothing's with me. There was stuff in the file. About Jennifer getting up in the night and singing or something like that.'

'Yeah.' Jonas nodded.

'What do you mean, "yeah"?'

'Whoa. You joined the wrong service. Should have made you an interrogator.'

'It's true. Don't make me get the electrodes out.'

It was the right approach. Persuade him that it wasn't serious and Jonas didn't care what he told you. He grinned and held up his hands. 'Mercy. Yeah. Shawn had some story about how he'd heard something like that one night in the cells. Guess he read the rumours. He's a good guy, but, you know. He always liked to be where the important stuff was. Man, he loved it when that TV crew showed up. I think he had a crush on the reporter.'

'So he said he heard her singing?'

'Singing, whatever.'

And now he was dying. Rotting. *But the smell—*

'Ohh-kaay.' Jonas took advantage of Goose's silence to push his chair back. The waitress must have been attuned to the scrape. Courtnee came racing out to take his plate and fuss around the table, transparently hoping and fearing that he'd speak to her. 'We better get to work.'

They strolled up to the station together. The day felt as if it might turn out a little warmer. A different wind, maybe, more southerly. She thought how strange it would be to know that you might not see the change in the season. How could spring and summer come and a person not be there to see them? Fitzgerald was twenty-six, exactly the same as her.

'The Band in Rupert . . . I can't say the name properly.'

'Kwakiutl.'

'Quaggoolth?'

'No worse than my French.'

'That's Jennifer's . . . what do you call it? Nation?'

'Hey, Goose. I got an idea. I call it,' he placed the words one by one in the air in front of him, left to right, 'Changing the Subject.'

She ignored him. 'Are you . . . that, too?'

'My nation? Nah. Nuu-cha-nulth.'

'Nootchn . . .'

'Nuu-cha-nulth. West side of the island. We're the good-looking ones.'

'Of course you are. So do you, like, know about the . . . The people here?'

'The Kwakiutl?'

'Yeah.'

He shrugged. 'They drink too much?'

'Their culture. Like religions, ceremonies, whatever.'

He blew out a long breath. 'Ahh. Man. To be honest. Everyone likes to talk about that kind of stuff. But it's all gone, you know? We do our best, but, you know. Kind of making it up as we go along. Don't quote me, now. Maybe I wouldn't say it like that if someone else was asking.'

She walked on quietly, thinking. Or not exactly thinking: ideas and images were happening to her, insistently, as if they were stuck in her brain and blocking everything else, but they didn't come together like thoughts. Fitzgerald's parents, broken by worry. The silent scream on the face of the unknown girl who called herself Daisy. The sound of the foghorn in the greyed-out nothingness. Jennifer in her cell, staring, staring, not answering. The cell, empty.

'Jonas?'

'Yes, ma'am.'

'What do you think about all that stuff in England?'

He looked pained. 'Now you've gone the other side of the world. I can't think that far.'

'You watch the news, right?'

'I keep up.'

'So what do you think?'

He made a face like someone pretending to think, then shrugged.

'You think they all just went crazy, or you think there's something going on there?'

'Goose, man. There's people over there marching up and down singing songs and setting fire to stuff just 'cos it's snowing. Come on. They should see Canada, we could show them snow.'

'You ever heard that woman talking? With the glasses? The one they're getting so worked up about?'

'I don't listen to women talking. Too complicated.'

'Yeah, yeah. Come on, you know what I mean. That stuff she says about how everything's changed. Like how we don't know what we know any more or whatever.'

'Huh. Kind of proves my point.'

'Jonas.'

He looked at her carefully, perhaps deciding how likely she was to let it drop, and then sighed. 'What?'

'What if she's right?'

Jonas stopped outside the door of the station. 'Now, this is exactamundo the kind of thing that happens when you don't get enough sleep.'

'Probably.' She tried to catch some of the peaceful unconcern that radiated from him. Go inside, sit at the desk, answer calls, wait till eleven when she was off shift and then get in the kayak and pound the water till her arms felt about ready to fall off; wasn't that a good enough plan for the morning?

'We all got better things to do than worry about some Brit chick.'

'So what would you do? If, like, something happened right in front of your eyes that, you know. Wasn't. Couldn't have . . . Something you couldn't explain.'

'Hey.' He smiled. 'I get that every time I watch the Canucks.'

'I just thought . . .' She didn't know what she was thinking. She was groping after something too weird to qualify as a concept. 'You know. With your heritage. Like, sacred spirits and stuff. Before the Europeans came and screwed it all up.'

He raised a quizzical eyebrow, so slowly it was like he was on stage. 'My heritage?'

'Those people in England, they're talking about supernatural stuff coming back, right? Isn't that the kind of thing the First Nations say? And having a different way of life?'

'The First Nations spent every summer beating the crap out of each other.'

She didn't embarrass easily, but she looked away. 'Sorry.'

'Hey, no worries.' He unlocked the door and flicked the light switches. 'I know what you mean. Some of what she talks about . . . Maybe it wouldn't be such a bad idea for everyone if they unplugged for a while. Slowed down. I can dig all that.'

'If you slowed down any more they'd paint lines over you and call you a speed bump.'

'Funny lady.'

'It'd be weird, though. If . . .'

'If what?' He leant over the desk and tapped at the computer.

'If it was true. Like, things that couldn't be, happening.'

'Uh-huh.' He wasn't listening. He tapped again, eyes scanning the screen. The phone rang by his hand. 'RCMP

Alice, this is Officer Paul.' His look of patient exasperation appeared as he listened, the look which signified his frustration at the rest of the world's inability to just get on without bothering anyone else. 'OK. Be right down.' He hung up. 'Some guy kicking down the bank door,' he said, reaching for his cap. 'Saying he wants his money.'

She'd have felt guiltier about taking her break when something was actually going on for a change if it hadn't been for two things: first, it would be her turn soon enough, all that evening and on call overnight as well, and second, Jonas knew as well as she did that she needed it. She wasn't much help to him in her current mood. He talked people down, told them he'd see what he could do, reassured everyone it was just a computer glitch and the bank would have it sorted out by tomorrow, while she prowled around the office hoping someone would lose their temper and become aggressive. He shooed her out of the station on the stroke of eleven.

She got changed, threw life vest and helmet and paddle in the car and loaded her kayak on to its rack on the roof. Instead of driving it the four blocks down the slope to the town landing, she steered out of town and headed up Thirty, rolling the windows down a finger's width to let in soggy pine-scented air. The couple of times she'd gone paddling since she'd arrived in Alice she'd explored the inlet. It was perfect. Sheltered as a swimming pool, bordered on one side by sheer slopes like a picture postcard fjord, it was a good ten kilometres of kayak utopia before it bent westward and became the wider, wilder sound. On her first trip out there she'd had it all to herself apart from the birds and a single otter moseying along on his back, peering around like a whiskery old bachelor in his private bath. Today, though, she wanted currents, wavelets, wind, a stretch of water she could fight against. At least that was her excuse. If there was another reason she'd pointed the car over to the east side of the island, she wasn't going to admit it to herself.

She drove down into Rupert and stopped by the fenced-in cemetery with its gaudily cross-cultural assortment of totem animals and crosses and plastic flowers. A couple of guys came out from their houses, waddly dogs in tow, while she carried her boat over the mottled pebbles. She guessed she was on her way to becoming a celebrity hereabouts. Not just the new girl cop who'd earned Margaret's seal of approval but a blonde in a wetsuit too. Elderly men who probably wheezed going upstairs offered to help her with the kayak. She smiled as best she could – she'd never had a talent for it – and managed on her own.

It never failed to amaze her how quickly things changed when you were afloat. One minute she was dealing with the equipment and trying to be friendly to the old guys and stopping dogs peeing on her kayak and thinking about when she'd have to get back and worrying about police work and her reputation and why hadn't she spoken to Annie for was it three days now, and the next minute . . .

The next minute her world contracted to the simplicity of effort and motion. Everything fell away apart from the pure dominant rhythm, *tlatch tlatch tlatch tlatch*. She always thought animals must live like this, deciding what they'd do next moment by moment, sniffing the wind. It was cold on the water but she was warm within a couple of minutes. Her shoulders began to ache pleasantly. The stray flicks of spray on her bare hands and face became stings of relief, ocean acupuncture. Back straight, head still, she punched alternating puddles in the sea, leaving them behind her like short-lived footprints.

She followed the left side of the bay, past the big empty vacation houses sitting back under the cedars, until the shore beside her became the familiar mess of spiny trees over their fringe of rock. They breathed out their clammy forest smell, exchanging it with the salt air. To her right the islands at the mouth of the bay fell into their proper perspective, the gaps opening between them to disclose increasing slices of the grey expanse beyond. After forty-five fierce minutes she'd slid past the last of them. Her arms were pleading for a rest, the southerly wind was raising steeper ridges in the sea around her, and the full breadth of this section of the Inside Passage swept across her view. She eased down, panting, and then let the rhythm go, laying the paddle across her thighs.

In two months' time these would be busy waters. The clouds would rise, the sun stride northwards, and the hundreds of kilometres of the Passage would be transformed into a platform for viewing the acceptable face of the northern wilderness. There'd be shiploads of gawpers and adventurers and idlers passing one way or the other every day. Goose looked left and right and saw a smudge with a long brown tail: a tug dragging one of those implausibly gigantic log booms. Apart from that, hers was the only boat in sight. Across the Passage the mainland mountains walled in the horizon. For a while longer, this was no man's land. There were islands in the strait, clumps of darker grey hovering at unspecifiable distances, their tree-top profiles softly bristled; crouching sea-beasts with wet fur. She was tempted to set her bow towards one of those clumps and paddle however many miles it was, without stopping, turning herself into a vanishingly small speck in the trackless and featureless sea.

The whine of an engine broke her trance. A powerboat sped into sight from the west, the direction of Hardy Bay, bumping recklessly in the gentle chop. Just like herself and Jonas yesterday, she thought, but without the impending fog. It was the same kind of boat, and there were two people in it. They swerved out wide as they saw her, giving her plenty of room, or maybe so they didn't have to slow down. Two young guys, she now saw, both in the unvarying uniform the native kids adopted whatever the season or weather: shades, bandanas flapping crazily, tight shirts bulging in less impressive places than intended. The wake from their boat slapped noisily against the rocks. She touched the bow around to meet the manufactured waves straight on, small hills of water parting with a faintly menacing hiss around her kayak, rocking her for a moment. The guys stared as they zoomed past. It could have been the guys-together-looking-at-a-girl stare, or the young-native-men-looking-at-a-white-stranger stare, or the kids-facing-down-the-police stare. In Goose's experience there was very little difference between the three. The basic meaning of all of them was, *I dare you to try to imagine how much I despise you.*

Their boat slowed very abruptly and they circled around towards her. She gripped the paddle lightly.

'Morning,' she called out, and then made a show of checking her watch. 'Oh. Afternoon, I guess.'

The boat came around behind her at a respectful distance. She dipped one end of the paddle again to keep herself facing it.

'You got some trouble there?'

'I'm good.'

'Just cruising?'

'Yep.'

'Funny time of year for it.'

'There wasn't any other time of year available today.'

Their boat completed its circle, the arc of froth from the outboard meeting itself in a frayed loop. It slowed down further. The one who hadn't spoken yet, the bigger of the two, lifted a bottle from somewhere down by his feet.

'Want a beer?'

She kept her eyes on them. She could just about see her own reflection in their shades, the pink blob of her kayak. Some years ago she'd made the discovery that she was immune to all forms of the Stare.

'Where are you boys off to this morning? Afternoon.'

The guy with the beer held it out, indicating the bows of their boat with the neck of the bottle. 'That way.'

'You wanna come?' said the first one.

'I have to get back to work,' she said. 'I'm on duty in a couple of hours.'

The bottle disappeared.

'Are you the mountie?'

'That's right.'

'French girl.'

'I was born in Montreal. We call them "women" there.'

'How d'you like it out here?'

'It's nice.'

The one with the beer had slumped back down on the far side of the boat, trying to look bored and insouciant. The other, less self-conscious, his features so Asiatic he wouldn't have attracted inquisitive looks on the other side of the Bering Strait, was doing all the talking.

'There's a whale stranded out on the Mastermans.'

'A what?'

The guy waved over his left shoulder. 'Right up on the beach there. On the big island.'

'Did you say a whale?'

'Killer whale.'

'You mean . . . Is it dead?'

'Dunno. Big fucker. Gonna stink up the place. You guys should check it out.'

She frowned. 'Where's this?'

'Masterman Island.' He turned and pointed towards what appeared to be a relatively close clump of non-sea. 'We went by there yesterday.'

It sounded like a prank. 'Hasn't anyone reported it?'

He shrugged, looked at his friend, who also shrugged, necking the bottle. 'We're reporting it now. Thought you might wanna know.'

'Do they do that often?'

'Huh?'

'Killer whales. Do they get stranded a lot?'

'I never seen it before.' He was losing interest. Perhaps they'd just been hoping to provoke her into reciting regulations about alcohol in boats. 'Big fucker just laying there on the beach stinking it up.'

'May I ask your names, sir?'

They looked at each other. The friendlier one reached for the throttle.

'We ain't done nothing,' he said, and the boat surged away, sending a foam of turbulence around her. A pair of ravens flopped out of the trees on the shore and went grumbling after it as if to lodge a complaint. She felt a drop of cold drizzle on her arm.

The afternoon had spoiled somehow. She grimaced, looking up at the relentless clouds. She'd be against what wind there was on the way back, and the tide was running out of the bay. Plus she couldn't keep up the same pace anyway, not after nearly an hour of it. It would be a longer trip returning. Time to turn around.

She tugged her cap down, leant forward, and attacked the ocean.

Her watch told her she had an hour before she was back on duty. She towelled the spray and sweat out of her hair, calculating whether she'd left enough time for a proper shower. It would have been nice to sit on the beach for five minutes while she cooled off, watching the eagles strut and chitter, enjoying the washed-out aftermath of intense exertion. In her experience there was nothing quite as blissful as that feeling: *Now it's over, now I can stop.* But she knew she'd better not turn up at the station stinky. It appeared she'd dodged the disciplinary bullet somehow – one of the best things about self-inflicted exhaustion was the way it stopped you thinking too much about the whys and wherefores, or indeed about anything at all beyond the tingling health of your body, a teasing hint of immortality – but she was still new in the job and not exactly in Cope's good books. She'd better always be on time and look smart.

So she lugged the kayak back up to the unmown cemetery without stopping to rest. She had it tied on the roof rack and was on her way back to collect the paddle and life vest when one of the interchangeable small round women came hurrying down the street.

'Hey. Hey. Fire. Hey, help. Fire up the road.'

Goose went straight for the radio in the glovebox. The woman scurried closer, so out of breath she couldn't make more than two words at a time. 'Tried calling. I couldn't. Get through.'

'Can you give me the street address, ma'am?' Goose clicked the radio on and buzzed for an emergency.

'End of. The road. Kids in. There.'

'Do you know the address?' The radio was crackly and didn't seem to be responding. Battery, she thought angrily, though they weren't supposed to need replacing for years. 'Maculloch. Reported fire. I repeat, fire. Hello?'

'You gotta help.'

She was trying to. She knew the protocol. But the radio

wasn't cooperating. She switched it on and off. 'Maculloch. I need assistance. Who's out there?'

'Goose?' The radio jumped to life all at once, the voice weirdly clear and close in her ear.

'Janice?' It was a woman's voice, one she thought she knew, but the wrong one. She stalled in confusion.

'Goose?'

'Is that . . . I need to report an emergency. Fire. In Rupert.'

'Goose. It's Annie, you dumbo.'

'Annie?' She stared at the radio, waiting for her eyes to identify it as her phone instead. They didn't cooperate.

'I've been trying to call for days. What have you been doing?'

The small round woman watched with a frown as puzzled as Goose's own.

'Annie? Where are you?'

'I'm at home. You could have got me any time.'

'I . . .'

'Young lady,' the woman said, with as much dignity as her breathlessness and urgency allowed. 'There are children in that house.'

This was some kind of surreal mistake, obviously. You couldn't get your girlfriend in Toronto on the police radio. 'Sorry, Annie.' She had no time for mistakes, or for guilt; there was a protocol. 'I have to . . .'

'Goose, I'm scared.'

'What?'

'I'm scared. I went out and bought tinned stuff. I need to talk to you.'

Someone else leant out of a window along the road and shouted to everyone or no one, 'There's a fire!'

'Crap,' Goose said, and clicked off the radio.

'Goose?' it said. She dropped it with a jolt of terror.

'You have to call the rescue.' The woman thought, perhaps rightly, that Goose didn't know what to do. 'Right now.'

What was the protocol? Why couldn't she remember? She was a trained officer. You called emergency services, then you went to the scene—

'Get in,' she said, starting the car, suddenly decisive, shaking Annie out of her head. *Later, later.* 'Show me where.'

A few people were now appearing on the street. In the mizzly afternoon stillness Goose thought she heard the dreadful crackle, distantly. She faced the gathering crowd and shouted a general instruction to call the fire house.

'Couldn't get through,' the woman reminded her, from the passenger seat.

'Someone drive up there!' she yelled, but one of the younger men was already jumping into a truck; he gunned it hard enough to squeal and was away at joyrider pace almost before she'd finished shouting.

'Dan's a volunteer,' the woman said. 'Up that way.' But Goose didn't need directions now. Smoke was rising, grey as the slow clouds but billowing and dancing as if possessed. The road ran out at the end of town and became a dirt track turning away from the shore. It humped over a woody ridge and led to a line of houses dismal even by Rupert's standards, lots carved apparently at random out of the trees, dwellings thrown up in the first temporarily clear patch that came to hand. The last of them was burning. Already its feeble walls were black silhouettes, and the trees around were juggling sparks in their droopy branches.

'Oh my God,' the woman said. 'Oh my God.'

People were running up along the road behind them, but it was already and obviously too late to do anything but watch. The house was crumpling as if squeezed by an orange fist, tumbling in on itself, fragile as ash. Goose stopped at a safe distance and ran out, trying to expel Annie from her head and concentrate on her job. Make sure everyone's clear of the neighbouring properties, she thought, that was the next thing. But everyone was already outside. A huddle of spectators stood in the road ahead of her, a few older folk, a woman with a baby, a boy. They turned as she sprinted up, still in her wetsuit. The boy shrunk anxiously up against the woman with the baby. Muffled by the wet forest, they heard the siren from the fire house above the town.

'Is anyone—' Goose began.

'They all got out,' an older man said.

Against that infernal background, Goose slowly realised who she was looking at.

'OK,' she said, breathing a little easier. 'OK. No one's hurt?'

'That's my whole house,' said the woman with the baby, who had to be Patience, Jennifer's mother. 'Everything I got.' The elderly man put his arm around her shoulders awkwardly. The boy – she remembered his name from the file now; Cody, the kid with the problems – squeezed himself hard against her. He didn't seem to be able to take his eyes off Goose. He scratched tentatively at his mother's waist. Goose thought it was some spasmodic twitch and then noticed, with an unexpected wrench of pity, that the poor kid was waiting for someone to hold his hand.

'No casualties?'

No one answered her. The house had chosen that moment to surrender its roof. They all backed away a step at the slow-motion collapse, retreating from a wheezing puff of lateral fire.

The engine arrived a few minutes later. The guy who'd jumped in the truck to fetch it was driving it himself. He'd only been able to raise a couple of his buddies. They yelled at people and wrestled with their equipment and stared at the burning house as if challenging it to step outside, but already the conflagration was calming. It had burned the building inwards and now met itself in the middle and found itself out of fuel. The heat on their faces was fading. The volunteer guys ran into the property's yard and made a great show of dragging some of the stuff piled there away from the blaze. It was the correct protocol, she supposed, but even to her inexpert eye there didn't seem to be any danger of the fire spreading. The permanently damp trees rebuffed any sparks and burning fragments as thoroughly as the ocean would have.

She'd left the radio lying in the road back by the beach. Her own phone was in the car. She went and called Jonas. Her fingers hesitated with unaccountable fear before prodding out the number, but he answered straight away, and he'd heard about the emergency, and officers were on their way.

She rubbed her face. The wetsuit felt simultaneously hot and clammy. She felt like she'd done most of the right things. No one was hurt; the engine was here. She went back to the group around Ms Knox, who was still holding her baby, a squashy-faced upright girl interested in the extra attention. The boy Cody was sitting cross-legged on the dirt road, staring at his lap, completely ignoring a woman who was trying to say something comforting.

'Excuse me,' she said. 'Hi.' The group let her in. 'Officer Maculloch. I'm police. Off duty,' she added, feeling her hair salty and frazzled and her face flushing. 'The patrol car's on its way. May I just talk to Ms Knox for a moment, please? I'm very sorry about your loss, Ms Knox.' Crap, that was what you said when someone died. 'Your home.' The mother stared grimly, jiggling her daughter. 'How about over by my car, if that's OK? Can someone bring her out a coffee and some blankets?'

She persuaded the gathering to disperse. Ms Knox followed her along the road to her car. The pink kayak strapped atop it looked particularly inappropriate. She didn't say a word and didn't look back. Her son leapt up like a startled insect when she set off and followed, mouth opening and closing. Whenever Goose looked at him she found him staring at her as if she were an alien.

She composed herself for a moment, then put on what her own mother (dark) called – not kindly – *ton sourire blond*. My blonde smile.

'Hi,' she said, in a bright kindergarten teacher tone. 'Cody, right?' The boy stopped like in a game of statues.

The trick, she'd once discovered, was to imagine you were talking to a dog.

'I know, I don't look much like a policeman, huh?' She grinned, picturing herself as an idiot sorority girl. 'I've been kayaking. That's my kayak.' She patted it. 'My name's Séverine but everyone calls me Goose.'

She paused for a moment, and then added, '*Honk.*'

A flicker of a grin came and went in his face, fast as an eyeblink. Like all the aboriginal kids he had very dark eyes which looked somehow wary: maybe it was the contrast between the whites and the almost black iris, and the woody tinge of the skin.

The only pair of eyes, she thought, which might have seen what happened in the house that night at the beginning of December.

She stuck her arms out at her sides and flapped them, thinking, *Nice puppy. Good dog.*

'*Honk honk,*' she said, goosily.

'Cody don't want to talk to you,' said the mother, but the boy had almost smiled. Almost.

'I'm sorry, ma'am. Can I get you anything for now? Someone'll bring some coffee right out.'

'We have nothing left,' she said.

'I'm very sorry.' The duty officers would do all this properly in a couple of minutes when they got here. Still, she had to make a bit of an effort, though the woman radiated the sullenness of anger and shock. 'Can you describe to me what happened?'

'I smelled smoke. Ran upstairs to get the kids.'

Something like seventy per cent of these incidents turned out to be smoking in bed, they'd told her. 'You were downstairs at the time?'

'Yes.'

'Did you see how the fire started?'

'I was just cleaning up. I turned round and smelled the smoke.'

The woman would barely look at her. The woman who'd accused her own daughter of murder and thrown her out and, as far as Goose could tell, forgotten about her. All right, she thought. It's too early for this. Leave it to someone else. 'OK. We'll get you a hot drink and somewhere to sit down. One of my colleagues will need to ask some questions later but there's no hurry. OK?' She couldn't do the smile on adults; it hurt her mouth to try.

Two patrol cars came, and then the other engine, from the fire house on the far side of the district. By then there was no fire at all, only a lightly smouldering ruin. People milled around everywhere. She told Webber and Gudgeon what she needed to say and let the two duty cops start gathering information. Now that uniformed officers were present as well as all the volunteer guys kitted up in their helmets and heavy boots, the small crowd's attention drifted away from her. She went back to her car and leaned against it, resting her head on the moulded plastic of her boat. She closed her eyes for a few moments, gratefully separate from the hubbub.

'Her coat's gone.'

She jumped. Cody flinched back a step. He hadn't made a sound as he'd come up to her.

'Whoa! Hey, sorry. You startled me there for a second.'

'Cody!' Patience shouted from the front of the neighbours' house. 'Get over here!'

'Wait. Whose coat?' *Crap*, she thought, *I forgot the fricking smile*. 'Cody?' But the boy was running away, still looking back at her. He bumped into a fireman. She started after him, but he ran to his mother, who fixed Goose with a nakedly hostile stare. The baby started to cry.

Nine

WHOSE COAT?
She knew whose coat.

She stopped on the road at the place she thought she'd dropped the radio and got out to have a look. She found its cracked fragments in the messy grass by the cemetery fence. It looked like the fire truck had run it over.

She used her mobile to ring Jonas and tell him she was on her way. She also called Janice to confess about the radio. Janice, sounding excited, promised to get the relevant paperwork ready. She made all the calls while she was driving over to Alice. She promised herself she'd call Annie as soon as things seemed quiet enough that evening.

She jogged up the stairs to her apartment, left the wetsuit in a smelly heap by the front door, and took a rapid shower. The hiss of hot water had a vacant echo. Perhaps it was the bare walls, she thought. The place wouldn't feel so empty once she got some pictures up. Tomorrow, definitely.

Jonas wasn't in the station when she got there, and the car was gone. He rolled in fifteen minutes later, looking as harassed as she'd ever seen him.

'Sight for sore eyes,' he said.

'I'll make it up to you.' She meant it, too. She wouldn't mind spending a bit more time in the station and a bit less time alone in her apartment with only the internet for company.

'Hey. Duty calls, you know. All must obey. Comes with the territory. Did they get that fire out?'

'Yeah. Kind of died all by itself.'

'The Knox house, huh.'

'Yep.'

'It's like they're family of doom. They don't need the rescue squad, they need an exorcist.'

Says she put a curse on him. Her head was buzzing with little disturbances, things she couldn't seem to forget about but also couldn't quite identify. It was as if Jennifer's file had infected her. Reams of paper which added up to a great big question mark. Information without comprehension. A total silence at the heart of it, like fog.

Jonas was watching her sympathetically. 'I'm kidding,' he went on. 'You know most likely the mom lit up a smoke and fell asleep? Right?'

'I guess.'

He smiled to himself and did his slow-motion headshake. 'You're thinking Jennifer's out there burning her own house down?'

'I don't know what I'm thinking.'

'You got to get some proper sleep. Listen, I can be on call tonight—'

She cut him off quickly, and more aggressively than she intended. 'No. I can do my job. I'm OK. You go on home.'

Alice had to be one of the smallest, dinkiest postings in the whole of the Royal Canadian Mounted Police. The building looked like a holiday bungalow pretending to be a police station because that was what it in fact was. Jonas eyed her and then raised a sarcastic finger to point through the office wall, in the direction of his bedroom, ten paces distant, as if she'd forgotten that his home was under the same roof.

'Or go fishing,' she said.

He chuckled.

'Sorry.' He raised his hands to show he didn't need an apology. 'I'm OK, Jonas, honest. I could do with a regular evening's work. Cope was right, I need to stop thinking about that kid.'

'I know how that is.'

'Off you go. Going to get some fishing in before dark?'

'Nah. Hockey's on in . . .' He glanced at the wall clock. 'Dang. East coast game's already started.' He was already circling the desk to switch on the small TV he kept in the corner, moving with an urgency she'd never seen him apply to police work. 'Only a few weeks till the play-offs. Things starting to get tight.'

She watched in mild disbelief as he waited for it to tune in. 'Jonas. You live next door. Go watch in your own room.'

'Yeah.' He was too absorbed to care. 'Just checking the score real quick.'

'Jeez.'

'Here we go.' Quacking commentary burst from the TV; he turned it down sheepishly. 'Oh, man. Not again. Wait.' He flipped channels up and down, as if trying to enrage her. Goose didn't even have a TV. She associated television with her mother's infuriating inattentiveness, and anyway she watched the internet instead. 'What's this?'

She looked at the screen. 'Looks like hockey to me.'

'That's yesterday's game. They're showing the wrong game. Oh, man. Oh, man.'

'Jonas. Go home.'

'What the heck . . .' He poked buttons on the remote.

'Turn it off and go home, OK?'

He sighed. 'OK.'

'I'll see you tomorrow.'

'Maybe it's a sign. God wants me to go catch fish.'

'Yeah. Fresh air. TV rots your brain.'

'That's why you're so smart, huh?'

'Absolutely.'

'All right. You know how to get hold of me if you need me.'

'I'm good. Go relax.'

He gazed at the TV like a disappointed lover. 'Yeah.'

Completely inexplicably, and to her secret horror, her mortification, there was a little voice inside her shouting, *Don't leave, Jonas, please don't leave me here alone.* She had no idea what was wrong with her. She blurted something out as he opened the door. Was she really trying to delay the moment when he closed it behind him? Really? 'Oh. You didn't see any news, did you?'

'What sort of news?'

'I don't know. I heard . . .' She clasped her hands together under the desk, out of his sight. *Goose, I'm scared.* 'Something. Something happening in Toronto.'

'Toronto?'

'Just something I thought I heard. I might have got it wrong.'

'Stuff doesn't happen in Toronto. There's a law. Like, a total event ban.'

She'd never heard Annie scared before. Annie could be temperamental, crazy, hyper, but not frightened. She was too heedless to worry about anything.

On the other hand, she couldn't possibly have heard Annie at all. Not on the police radio.

'Everything OK?'

Goose nodded and motioned him out the door before she was tempted to confess that it wasn't OK but she didn't know why. 'Go fish.'

She rang Annie, got her voicemail, left a couple of messages. Annie was a sulker. If she'd been offended by the way Goose had cut her off she might well not be answering her phone. There was a kind of rhythm to their relationship now, after a couple of years, a predictable pattern of peak following trough. Goose didn't think it was all that likely to survive the long-distance stress much longer, but she was in no hurry to reach the crisis. It wasn't like she was going to find anyone else up here.

She rang her father.

'Séverine! God, you had me worried.'

And already wished she hadn't. 'What are you worrying about now, Dad?'

'You weren't answering.'

'I have a lot to do. You know I can't talk to you every day, right? Dad? I grew up. They let me join the police.'

'Is everything OK up there?'

'Sure. Usual thing. How about you?'

'You're not getting any of this stuff?'

'What stuff?'

'Christ, angel, I'd have thought the police would know what was going on.'

'I don't know what you're talking about, Dad.'

'I'm talking about the whole country going down the crapper.'

'You've been talking about that for as long as I can remember you talking.'

'Bank runs? Satnavs? The CBC?'

She paused before answering, looking around the quiet office, and out between the slats of the blind at the unchanging stillness beyond.

'I'm sorry, Dad,' she said. 'I haven't had time to catch up with the news.'

He made an incredulous bark. 'I know you're a long way from anywhere up there, but shit. Don't you people at least sit around and come up with some kind of plan?'

'I heard about something in Toronto.'

His turn to go silent for a while, now.

'You heard about something in Toronto,' he said.

She should just get him off the phone. She wasn't in the mood for this. 'OK, Dad—'

'I think maybe you and your colleagues should go turn on the news. If you have news. They're saying the CBC got the plague now and half the country has no TV.'

Her eye fell on the cube of plastic with its blank screen, Jonas's household god. A normal thing. Every house had one, every building here in this tiny town in its long valley under its huge sky.

'You're telling me you haven't heard any of this?'

Any what? Nothing was happening. She could hear it not happening, hear the usual silence of Alice, peppered by foul-mouthed crows.

'Dad, sorry, I'll talk to you later, OK? I'm on duty.'

'You carrying a gun?'

'What?'

'Do you have a gun? Do they give you a gun?'

'Of course I'm not carrying a gun. This is Vancouver Island, it's not freaking Somalia.'

'Will you promise me you'll wear one? Séverine? Promise?'

'No, Dad. No. Try and calm down, OK?'

'Do it. For me.'

'I'll call you later.' Much later. By a stroke of luck the station phone began to ring. 'Got to go. Bye, Dad.'

Her evening's work began.

* * *

She considered going around the back of the station and knocking on the apartment door. Jonas was still the only person she knew in town, knew properly, that is. She'd stopped to chat with neighbours in her own building a couple of times, until they'd begun asking her whether she accepted Jesus as her saviour.

But Jonas was a colleague. She couldn't treat him like a buddy. It would make it impossible for them to work together. God knew she wouldn't have wanted *him* knocking on *her* door on her off nights, wanting to come in and watch TV.

She went home. She picked the wetsuit off the floor and tossed it in the bathtub, not wanting to deal with the laundry room. She hung her uniform up by the door in readiness. There hadn't yet been a call-out at night but she had a feeling tonight might be different.

What she wanted to do was get straight into bed. The kayak had done its job; she was exhausted, properly tired, her body full of that odd lightweight feeling suggesting that she'd probably get to sleep pretty quickly no matter what was going around in her head. But . . .

She looked at her laptop.

A very weird feeling came over her. *You don't want to know*, it whispered. It was as though the laptop was one of those stars, a white dwarf or whichever, a tiny dense ball hot with energy, waiting to explode into the silent vacant zero of the apartment. It contained everything, all the information, all the knowledge, the whole rest of the world; without it she was floating as if alone in a lifeboat in the middle of the Pacific.

She rubbed her face crossly. Just not used to small-town living, she told herself. New place, new job, missing Annie. Twenty-four hours worrying she was going to be fired. No wonder she felt a bit below par. She'd look up whatever had got Dad all freaked out, not that it took much. Maybe spend half an hour clicking around her bookmarks before settling down.

She squatted comfortably on the bed and opened her browser.

Instead of her home page the window displayed a grey rectangle with three words, large, white, upper case.

VOUS ÊTES ICI

As many times as she quit and restarted the browser, as many times as she rebooted the machine, however often she ran her antivirus and security software, she could not get past that page. The information, the knowledge, the rest of the world had all gone, replaced by that one message.

VOUS ÊTES ICI

In the middle of the night, she thought: it would be different if the sun would come out. Even if just for an hour. Everything always looked so much better under the face of the sun.

Staff Sergeant Cope came to the station the next morning at nine, unannounced. The first Goose knew of it was the rattling of the door.

'Maculloch?'

She straightened in the chair. Her neck felt horrible. She must have been slumped sideways. 'Sarge.'

'Were you asleep?'

All the lights were on. There was a quarter of a mug of cold coffee on the desk in front of her. She'd kicked her shoes off; she felt for them with half-numb toes as discreetly as she could manage. 'I guess I must have been. Sorry, sir.'

'You look like shit. Where's Paul?'

She'd tried so hard not to fall asleep. She remembered now, leaving her apartment before six and walking through the dark town, finally giving up on her own bed. Switching on the lights, making coffee. She'd even tried watching TV. Some rolling news report was all she could find. It kept returning to shots of people in coats and scarves queueing on wide sidewalks, in Ottawa, in Edmonton, in Toronto. A peculiarly Canadian version of a crisis. In America there were people arming themselves, filling shopping trolleys with canned goods and heading off into the hills. Their northern cousins lined up in the cold and waited for their turn. She tried to think of them as real people, worried people, whole cities full of people worrying, Annie among them, but the pre-dawn hour and the scratchy picture made it all seem so far away. The heart of it wasn't in whatever glitch in the banking system had got people panicking and lining up to get their cash out, or in whatever was wrong with the transmission satellites (sunspots? cyberterrorism? aliens? – there was a panel discussion about it on the rolling news, people she didn't know in a studio thousands of miles distant; what did they have to do with her?). The heart of it was here. Her apartment. The cell the girl had walked out of. The burned shell of the house. The fog.

'He, um . . . He should be here any minute.'

'What kept you up all night? Anything I need to know?'

She picked up the mug by reflex, sniffed its contents, put it down. 'No, sir. I've been having trouble sleeping.'

He had the basset-hound face of a career cop, a face that said it had seen it all and was now unmoved by everything. He stared at her for a good ten seconds, looking neither sympathetic nor unsympathetic.

'Well,' he said at last, 'you better fix that.'

'I'll do my best.'

'I'm making some changes to the duty roster. There'll be longer shifts.'

'I'm fine with that.' She smoothed her hair. It still felt slightly crusty, the ocean salt clinging on. 'It's not a big thing, sir. Just a couple of bad nights.'

Jonas arrived, straightening the cuffs of his shirt. 'Whoa. Sarge.'

'You're late, Paul.'

'I'm always late. Hey, Goose. Man, you don't look too good. I'll get coffee. What's up, Sarge?'

'What do you think?'

'Don't pay me enough to think.'

'Have you two even been watching the news in your little holiday camp over here? Or do you just sit around making coffee all day?'

'Hey, I keep an eye out. But, you know. Alice never seems to make it on to the news.'

'Sit down for a minute, will you, Paul?'

Jonas gestured peaceably and eased himself behind the other desk.

'All right.' Now that he had their attention he'd turned self-conscious. He hooked his thumbs in his belt and sought gravitas. 'OK. So, we have a potential situation. I just got instructions last night. Whatever this problem is with the computers, they reckon it's sending a lot of stuff haywire. Infrastructure. We can expect some volatility. The whole force is cancelling all leave. I've got the new roster here.' He waved a handwritten piece of paper. 'Until they get it sorted out we're responsible for maintaining order. We have specific instructions to discourage hoarding and prevent looting.'

If Cope's delivery was supposed to impress his seriousness upon them, it didn't work on Jonas.

'In Alice?' he said. Goose had to bite back a giggle.

'This isn't a joke, Paul. The assistant commissioner's message suggests that we may be under attack.'

Jonas sat a tiny fraction straighter. 'Okey dokey. We're vigilant.'

'Maculloch was asleep at her desk when I came in.'

'I'm vigilant,' Jonas corrected.

Cope sighed. 'Look. I don't know what's going on either. Here's your rota. Keep an eye on the market. Nobody gets to clean out the shelves. Don't let anyone start freaking out.' He was about to hand the paper over to Jonas when he stopped and studied it, looking over his glasses, eyebrows rising. 'Wait a sec . . . Yep, Webber's coming over here to cover you guys. Maculloch, I want you to take the day off. Got a pencil?'

'Sir. I'm entirely capable of performing my duties.'

'I'm sure you are.' He didn't even look at her. He leant the sheet on the desk and made an alteration, finishing it off with an emphatic crossing-out. 'You get the day off anyway. Go sleep. That's an order. Go get pills if you have to. Take them with two shots of bourbon, that's what I used to do.'

She hadn't felt so humiliated since she'd left home. 'With respect, sir—'

'Just. Don't. Argue with me.' He straightened and adjusted his glasses. 'I need all my officers at their best.'

'He's right, Goose. Ain't much we're gonna be doing anyway. The invisible enemy, you know?'

'Don't be so sure.' Cope never let himself get excited about anything, on principle, but there was a slight edge of relish in his voice. 'Some people'll take any excuse to cause trouble. We're not going to let them. Understand?'

'Roger.'

'We keep things nice and quiet here while the geeks sort it out.'

'Hey,' Jonas drawled. 'Might be nothing they can do either. The haunted internet, you know? Ghosts in the machine.'

Goose looked at her feet and concentrated on wiggling them into her shoes, in small movements.

Cope pushed the handwritten roster in front of Jonas. 'Just because we got the damn Queen on our money doesn't make us damn crazy Brits. Here you go, Paul. This is work. Remember what that is? You signed up for it. Do it.'

Jonas picked it up. 'You got it, Sarge.'

'Good boy. Oh, and one more thing. The commish says communications may be compromised. Email, messaging.

Mobiles too. So nothing secure gets done that way for now, you get me? No police business on the computer. Best damn thing about the whole rigmarole, if you ask me.'

'Ahhey.' Jonas nodded to himself. 'I was wondering why you drove all the way over here.'

'Well, you can be damn sure it wasn't for the pleasure of your company.' He wasn't good at the banter. He tried too hard to do the gruff old cop act and so never got it right. 'Anything I need to know before I get back to work, of which, in case you were wondering, there's a damn shitload?'

Jonas pursed his lips and looked at Goose.

She felt rough edged with tiredness, unpreparedness, and embarrassment. Her mouth seemed to open of its own accord and speak the sentence.

'There's a beached whale, sir.'

His whole face screwed up in disbelieving amazement. 'A *what?*'

Why had she said it? It had been there in her unsleeping head all night. *Stinking up the place.* The smell of rotting fish. An offshore island, somewhere out in the fog. *Tlatch tlatch tlatch tlatch.* 'A couple of guys in a boat reported it. I don't know if it's a police matter, sir. A stranded whale. I think they said an orca.'

'Yeah,' Jonas said, to her surprise. 'I heard about that.'

Cope stared at her as if she'd confirmed all his suspicions about female officers in one convenient sentence. 'As far as you know, Maculloch, has this whale committed a crime?'

'I haven't had a chance to interview it yet, sir.'

Mercifully, Jonas intervened. 'I talked with those guys yesterday. They were asking who was gonna deal with it.'

'Oh,' Cope said. 'Well. That's an easy one. Not me. Not me, and not you. Paul, you're responsible for this town till Webber gets over here. Maculloch, you're going to sleep until you look like a human being again. And try to pay attention, Paul. You get no back-up this morning. We're not using the radio unless it's an emergency. Got that? And when I say "emergency" I don't mean some dumbass whale that can't tell the difference between land and water.'

'The citizens of Alice are safe in my hands,' Jonas said, cradling his palms into a bowl.

'God help them.'

They waited for his car to disappear from earshot.

'Hey.' Jonas directed a sympathetic shrug at her. 'Sorry, man. But seriously, you gotta take a break.'

She put her head in her hands. 'I don't know what's wrong with me.'

'Just tired, man. It messes you up. The sarge is right, you should drop some pills if you need to. They got some behind the counter at the market, I can tell Linda to let you have some. She's good people.'

She looked up, studied his broad impassive face.

'None of this bothers you, does it?' she said. 'Whatever's going on out there. It just rolls right off you.'

For a moment he was about to make a joke of it, but maybe he heard something in her voice, a fraction of desperation. He stood up and strolled over to the pane of glass in the door. He looked out thoughtfully. You could almost see him gathering words, getting them in order.

141

'You ever find it weird, Goose? Being . . . here. Instead of somewhere else. You ever think about that?'

'No,' she lied.

'I mean . . .' He crouched so he could peer up at the ocean-thickened sky. 'You look out there every day and you'd think, OK, nothing's goin' on. Nothing much changes. But it's the same planet, you know? Same ball of rock. You keep going that way' – he nodded outwards, in no particular direction – 'you go on far enough, you get, I dunno. Africa or somewhere. Kids with AK-47s and no water. Or England. People sitting in circles and drumming, shouting and scream-ing this and that. It's connected, you know? Get on a plane and you can be there the same day. But from here . . . It doesn't feel real. Know what I'm saying?'

Vous êtes ici. She suddenly thought that maybe sleeping pills weren't such a bad idea.

'I sort of think I do,' she said.

Ten

I NSTEAD, SHE WENT for a run.

She was too embarrassed to have Jonas escort her down to the pharmacy counter at the market. And, she told herself, she might have weakened enough to let herself be forced into buying pills, but she'd never have taken them. She'd never touched a cigarette or a joint. She'd never had a glass of wine. She wasn't putting anything in herself that had even the slightest hint of the glamour of addiction. It was all part of her project to make herself as unlike her mother as possible. She knew only one way to blot out the passage of empty time, to haul up a barrier between herself and the lurking ennui of existence: violent exercise.

She promised Jonas she'd go back to the apartment and go to bed. She did, at least, go back to the apartment. But she changed, avoiding the mirror, and left again as fast as she could. She kept thinking. She thought: I should call Annie to make sure she's OK. I should call Dad to make sure he's

OK. I should call Tess too. I should this, I should that. I shouldn't have let Jennifer go. I didn't let Jennifer go. She's gone, she isn't gone. It's a bug, it's a virus. It's a plague. It's a curse. What will happen now, what will happen, what what what. The only way to stop thinking was to run.

There was one road long enough to run on, Route Thirty. It followed the inlet out of town and then turned steep, heading up towards the pass. She went steeply up with it. Her legs found themselves in a fight and fought. There were trees on all sides and no sound but the choreography of that battle, the steady thrum. She didn't worry about when to turn around. She'd recognise the moment when it arrived: when she'd gone far enough that she couldn't think at all for the pain.

Cars occasionally passed. Trucks. One, oncoming, was a patrol car. She glanced up for half a second, saw Webber, glanced down. He might have recognised her, or not, it didn't matter; she'd been going steeply up for almost an hour, maybe, long enough anyway that nothing mattered but keeping her legs turning and her elbows swinging. A while later and she topped the ridge, the road dipping into a long shallow descent. At that moment she felt a clean burst of elation, pure and weightless. Running downhill was so easy she felt she could be flying, loosed from the weight of existence altogether.

Many curves of the road later a car slowed as it passed her from behind. Another patrol car. It pulled up. The door swung open and out stepped Jonas.

Crap, she thought. It was the first thought she'd been conscious of for some time.

He waited for her to jog up, hands on his hips. She let herself slow, carefully. Bewildered at the change in their rhythm, her legs wobbled and threatened to drop her.

'OK,' he said. 'You're in big trouble.'

She stood, gulping air. He pulled open the back door.

'In you get,' he said.

'No,' she said. 'Way.'

'Can't make you go to bed if you don't want to. We're just gonna talk. In you get.'

She put her hands on her knees. They were trembling. ''Kay,' she said, and crawled into the back.

He started driving: not, as she'd assumed, back the way he'd come, back to Alice, bringing her in like a fugitive, but on east, towards the other side of the island and Hardy.

'Where we going?' she croaked.

'Webber brought a message over. There's been a boom break. Sarge wants me out in my boat to check it out.'

'Boom break?'

'You know the log booms?'

'Oh. Huh.'

'Big break. Whole boom got loose, apparently. That could be like three or four thousand deadheads. Good as a floating minefield.'

'Huh.'

'What am I gonna do with you, Goose?'

'Come too.'

He twisted around.

'Please,' she said. Her lungs were calming.

His unflappable look settled back on the road. 'Sea air

ought to make you sleepy, I guess,' he said. 'Anyway. OK. You can't be trusted on your own.'

She'd have died of exposure if she'd gone out on the water in nothing but her sweaty vest and shorts, but he had outdoor clothes and waterproofs in the trunk. They sagged around her like a spacesuit. She didn't mind. She was on the edge of something, she didn't know what, but it felt perilous, and Jonas's company was keeping her from tipping over.

Besides, she had an idea. It felt like it might help.

'Jonas?'

He sized her up as she zipped the waterproofs closed, chuckling. 'I gotta hand it to you, Goose. Not a lot of chicks I know have the guts to go outside wearing that.'

'Don't call me a chick.'

'Wouldn't dream of it.'

'So you already know about that whale?'

'The one that stranded?'

'Yeah.' He walked, she shuffled along the gravel of the wharf towards the dock. There were a couple of kids pushing strollers. Both of them looked far too young to have kids of their own. 'You ran into those guys who told me about it?'

'Uh-huh. Fishing buddies.' She waited for his *They're good people*, but it didn't come; something must have given him pause.

'You think they were having me on? I kind of had the feeling they were messing with me.'

'The thing is,' he said, as if he'd been mulling it over for hours, 'they wouldn't feed me the same story. If it was just you, yeah, I'd say maybe. Don's good people' (*aha!*) 'but he gets a kick out of stuff like that.'

'But they told you the same thing? A killer whale stranded on, what was it? Something island?'

'Masterman. Yep. Weird place for it. And wrong time of year. Even the transients are usually still down south now. Plus I only ever heard of them stranding in bunches.'

She descended carefully on to the floating pontoon. They were the only people on the dock. 'Can we go check?'

'Huh?'

'That island group's just out of the bay, right?' She'd looked them up in her atlas. That was at around three in the morning. Three in the morning, the apartment smelling of packing tape and unwashed wetsuit (she'd left it in a heap in the bathtub), and poor sleepless Séverine awake still, wondering what was happening, where the silent girl had been going; still in the grip of the night-time delusion that she could work it all out.

'Oh. You mean take a little detour? I guess.'

'You're supposed to report strandings, aren't you?'

He knelt and began untying his boat. 'Right now,' he said, 'I think people got other things to worry about.'

'It can't be that much of a detour. Humour me.'

'You know there's nothing we're gonna be able to do? Those things weigh twice as much as a car.'

'Yeah, I know.'

He climbed aboard, lifted up a plastic tub and took a

bunch of keys out from underneath it. 'Gonna look pretty miserable up on the beach. If it's there at all. Just a big hunk of dead fish.'

'That's where you keep the keys? Seriously? Not even in a locker?'

'Hey.' He clicked the bilge pump on and started the motor. The few kids pushing strollers through the park below the town all turned to see what the noise was: *something happening!* There were people in Hardy who walked down from their houses a couple of afternoons a week just to watch the ferry arrive. 'We do things different up here.'

She climbed in after him, huddling in the limited shelter of the cockpit. 'So can we check? I'd like to see.'

Jonas gave her a long look as he steered out. It almost qualified as curious.

'What's up with you, Goose?'

'I wish I knew.'

North of the island's tip, the ocean air banked thick and damp against the ramparts of the coastal range, tripling the late winter mist into a fog. The continent's edge was outlined in soft white, a hazy barrier, like an atmosphere. A white boat drifted there, invisible. It made no sound. There was nothing to propel it: no sail, no engine. Its single passenger sat in it, sightless head bowed, unmoving. The head was black as well as white, and there were black characters on the bow, as useless in that solitude as patterns made by a tangle of weed: LV6 IRKUTSK STAR. The open boat, no more than twice as long as Marie-Archange Séverine

Gaucelin-Maculloch's kayak, rocked and swivelled, rudder-less in the long swell. Birds avoided it.

The shore was a series of protrusions and indentations, a wavering negotiation between rock and water. Tree roots fingered into every crevice above the line of high tide. The forest pressed as close to the ocean as it could, the two vast uniformities almost touching, the dull dark evergreens and the dull grey water. Goose couldn't find anything to look at.

'You doze off if you want,' Jonas said, over the motor's whine. 'Looking kinda dopey.'

'I'd love to.' The sea was calm, barely more ruffled than bedsheets. They skimmed along without jolting.

'Logs'll just ride up and down on the tide until the wind gets up. I don't think there's gonna be a problem with them getting into the bay.'

'Did Cope say why the boom broke?'

'Dunno. No, he didn't say. They lost contact with the tug. This problem with the satellites, I guess.'

'Those booms can break up in bad weather, eh? But it's flat as a pancake out here.'

'Yup. Looks like there's a fog up the Passage.' He shaded his eyes to look north and west as they powered out of the bay. Though there was no glare, the sheer expanse of grey had a kind of glistering weight that hurt the eye.

'Oh, great.'

'Nah. Not gonna bother us today. Way off. See over there? Those are the Mastermans.' Jonas indicated a snaggle of forested rock chipped off from the main body of the island, debris fallen a few hundred metres offshore. 'How about we swing by now? I'm not seeing deadheads anywhere.'

There were a couple of outlying lozenges of rock. An eagle stood near the top of a bare tree and watched them as they slowed to pass between.

'That's the big island on the left there. Don said it's right up on the beach.' He pulled the throttle back and curved their course away, to get a better view. 'Right over there.'

Goose stood up. She could see the break in the trees, a pebbly notch scalloped out of the island. 'There?'

'Uh-huh.'

'I guess your buddy likes winding you up too.'

Jonas looked slightly pained. 'I guess. Never thought he could keep his face that straight.'

'Unless it unstranded itself.'

'Could be.' His normal lack of curiosity was reasserting itself. He leaned on the wheel, turning them about. 'OK. Nothing to see here.'

'Wait.' Now Goose shaded her eyes, squinting. Jonas followed her look back towards the tiny beach.

'Hey,' he said.

Looking for a four-ton orca, neither of them had at first seen the smaller shape slumped on the pebbles, too big for a bird, too small for a twisted fragment of felled tree.

'Looks like a body,' Jonas said. He let the boat complete its curve until it was facing the island again.

Goose was feeling something she recognised from the middle of the night: a strange and bleary quickening, like the first glimpse of a prospect equally hoped for and dreaded.

Jennifer, she thought. *Jennifer*.

There was definitely someone lying half curled up on the pebbles, partially draped by some dark covering.

'That's a kid,' Jonas said beside her. 'Oh, m— . . .'

The depth beneath them was reducing rapidly. He slowed to a crawl and steered around a treeless reef. The scattered land pushed closer around them, the water now shallow and perfectly calm. Dead ahead, a dark-haired child sprawled unmoving as beached driftwood. She lay in the centre of a strangely smooth depression printed in the speckled sand and stones, as if, Goose thought, *as if, as if something really really heavy and kind of rounded had been lying right there making that shape.*

'Hey!' Jonas shouted. The wall of straight-trunked evergreens swallowed his voice. Another eagle flapped silently away, disturbed. 'Hey!' The child lay unresponsive, the back of her head to them. Something about her didn't look like Jennifer. 'Take the wheel,' Jonas said, 'I'm gonna jump.' But Goose, ignoring him, had already scrambled to the bow and over the forward railing. Too small, she thought. Short hair. Just before the bow scraped, she sprang on to the pebbles. The kid was lying with a dark puffy coat draped over her, head sticking out one end, feet out the other. Goose slowed as she came close, crouched down, put her hand out to the neck.

'Dead?' Jonas called from the boat.

It wasn't Jennifer. It wasn't a girl. It was a boy, a small boy, not much older than Cody, a native kid, pale as death. His mouth was open.

His eyes were open too. They twitched towards her.

'*Mon dieu.* OK. Oh my God. OK.' She bent over him and touched his cheek. He was as cold as the sea. 'OK, you're going to be OK. Can you hear me? Hello?'

The boy's feet scraped against the pebbles. She heard Jonas swear.

'Get on the radio!' she shouted over her shoulder. The boy quivered at the sudden noise. His head lifted a little. One hand came up from beneath the coat and clutched at his chest, a feeble and clumsy infant gesture. 'We're going to need an ambulance at the dock!'

'Is he hurt?'

'I can't tell!' She tried to catch the boy's wandering eyes. 'Hey. Can you hear me? Are you OK? Can you get up?' She squatted on her heels and lifted the coat away.

She fell back on her heels, heart juddering, swearing without thinking. '*Tabarnac.*'

A brutal gaze fixed on her, its eye a single huge dark lozenge.

The boy had curled himself around a native mask. It stared at her like the head of a beast buried in the shingle. '*Tabarnac.* What the hell?' It dared her to touch it. It was all flowing lines and carved protrusions, as fierce and solid and substantial as the boy was frail and limp.

'Goose! You need help?'

The boy closed his mouth and made a strange kind of moan.

'What the hell have you got here . . . OK. *Doucement.* Take it easy.' He spasmed and shivered, pushing himself up, staring at her properly for perhaps two seconds, his look as intensely empty as the terrible stare of the girl in the cell. His eyes closed and he slumped back to the stones.

'Goose!'

'All right. All right. Give me a sec here.' The mask wouldn't release her. Nothing could close that eye. She tore her own look away from it, trying to concentrate. Protocol. Recovery position. (The kid was already in it.) Heartbeat. (Faint, terribly faint, but she could feel it in his neck, though the skin under her fingers seemed too cold for life.) Signs of injury. She scanned the body. The boy was dressed in dark slacks, black shoes, a dark sweater, some kind of dark jacket with yellowy piping and a badge at the pocket, weirdly formal. The clothes were crumpled and faded and scuffed but not wet, or no wetter than everything else touched by the sea air. 'Hey. Hang on now.' He seemed to have passed out. She felt carefully along his clothes. There was nothing obviously wrong, nothing broken, no wound she could see.

'Get the ambulance!'

'I'm trying! Damn radio . . .'

She reached underneath him very slowly. He groaned slightly. She could almost cradle his head in one hand. It felt horribly light and fragile, like a bird's skull.

'OK. I'm going to try and lift you up. We've got to get you out of here, eh? You shout if it hurts. Can you hear me?' There wasn't any time to waste. The kid was terrifyingly pallid and chill. She got one arm under his back and the other beneath his thighs and braced herself.

It was like lifting a baby. Half the weight must have been

in the clothes. She carried him back to the boat, where Jonas, dumbstruck, leaned over and let her pass the kid to him.

He nodded towards the shape on the pebbles. 'What's that thing?'

'You're not going to believe it.' She ran back to the mask. She'd seen things like it in the museum in Victoria, safely hidden behind glass. It didn't look so safe here. She used the coat to wrap it. As she picked up the bundle she noticed, casually, incidentally, that the coat was much too big for the boy, and had sparkly threads stitched between its quilted puffs; a girl's coat.

'He's like ice.' Jonas had cleared away his boxes of fishing crap to expose a padded bench where he'd laid the kid. He'd already taken off his own jacket and spread it over him.

'Do you recognise him?'

'Huh?'

'Not a local kid?'

'Not that I know of. You sit here, OK? We better hurry. Here.' He handed her the radio. 'Keep trying.'

'Wait.'

'What?' He'd already lifted a boathook from somewhere and was about to push them back from the shore.

'Look at this.' She opened the bundle.

Though they'd only been partners for twelve days, she felt she knew Jonas Paul reasonably well, perhaps because she'd spent a hefty proportion of that time in his company. She'd never have guessed his equanimity could disappear completely.

'Holy fucking shit,' he said.

'My thoughts exactly.'

'Excuse my French.'

'Let's get going.'

'Try the radio again. It started acting up yesterday. I got it to work sometimes, though.' Swift and efficient – she'd always suspected he could do it if he had to – he gunned the motor, spun the boat and eased them away from the island, accelerating steadily. 'He gonna be OK like this?' With the outboard roaring he had to shout to be heard in the bows. She couldn't see that the small bumps and judders were doing the kid any harm. She gave Jonas a thumbs-up. He nudged the throttle forward a bit, pointing at the radio.

She buzzed the call button and shouted over the noise. 'Maculloch. Needing assistance. Hello? Anyone hearing me?'

She thought she heard static, though it was hard to hear anything even when she squeezed the radio against her ear. She buzzed again. 'Emergency. Ambulance required. Got a minor in trouble here. Hello?'

'Hello?'

She almost let go of the radio. The voice popped out as if the man had materialised at her ear; breathy, hoarse, too close.

'Who's that? Maculloch here. I need an ambulance.'

Nothing.

'Ambulance. Emergency.'

'There was a wave.' The voice was hesitant. It had a strange accent, like Newfie but more so.

'Identify yourself, please.' Goose turned her back to Jonas and faced the spray.

'Too late,' the radio told her. 'All hands lost. None of us . . .'

'Who the fuck is this?'

'Barely a minute, it was.' The voice in her ear sounded distraught. 'I only thought to rest my eyes.'

'I need . . .' Her throat caught. To her astonishment she realised she'd choked up with fear. She hunched over the radio so no one could see her face. 'I need an ambulance.'

Grief-struck, the voice roared, 'She broke in two!' The radio tumbled out of Goose's fingers. She clutched after it, knocking it forward on to the gunwale, where it bounced and fell in the ocean. '*Tabarnac!*'

'Dammit, Goose!'

'It wasn't working anyway,' she yelled. Her hands were shaking. She had a sudden strong feeling that she was going mad, that she could suddenly see what madness felt like and had accidentally found herself standing one step away from it. *Vous êtes ici.* She stared at the shore ahead, the spilled white specks of the town, wishing the boat could go faster.

They heard a siren rushing out of town as they reached the dock. Seeing that Goose and Jonas were unloading a body, some of the aimless kids came ambling around the empty waterfront condo buildings (and their cracked and weed-infested parking lots) to see what was going on. Jonas shooed them away surprisingly forcefully. Goose got in the back seat with the kid, laying him down so his head was on her lap; Jonas drove up to the hospital. There was a patrol car there too, pulled up outside with its lights flashing. Goose was so tired she could barely move. She sat with the boy while Jonas went inside.

'What's going on?' she asked him, quietly. 'Where the hell did you come from?'

The mask was in the front passenger seat, wrapped up again. Jonas had wondered whether the kid might have stolen it. She'd thought the boy was First Nations but he said not. Now that she was sitting quietly, looking down at the kid's bleached-wood face, she could tell he was right. His ancestry was on the other side of the Pacific, in Korea or China or Japan.

She imagined him floating all the way across the ocean, washed up here for her to find.

The clothes were like a uniform, it occurred to her. Like he was a miniature security guard, with that faded yellow shield pattern on the breast pocket of his jacket. They had schools like that in Japan, didn't they, where they dressed the poor kids up funny. School uniform.

She was so tired now that her brain was working in slow motion and at minimum capacity. Just one train of thought came along at a time, rumbling sluggishly from idea to idea, like those monster trains she used to see crawling along next to the highway back home. School uniform. Name tags. Name. ID.

She opened his blazer to look inside, then turned back its collar. A white rectangle had been sewn inside the neck. There were faint traces of letters on it. She bent down, rubbed her eyes and read

H JIA

She leaned back against the headrest, eyes closing involuntarily. Too much adrenalin, too much exercise, too little rest. And she'd got cold out there too.

'Hey there, Aitch Jia,' she said. 'How're you doing.'

The hospital people came out with a gurney and wheeled the kid away. Jonas ought to have gone in with them, really – protocol – but he took one look at Goose and drove her straight home.

She slept as only the young can, all the rest of the afternoon, all through the evening, all night. While she slept, the fog spread, piling outwards from the mainland across the Passage, filling in the strait. Through its dense and echoless silence the sound of the horn from the Scarlett Point lighthouse drifted over Hardy, a tightly wrapped moan blaring and fading in regular sequence until an hour before sunrise, when – although the fog was if anything worse, so heavy the sunrise might almost as well not have bothered – it ceased, for ever.

Eleven

THE CROWS HAD gone quiet again. Or perhaps she'd woken before them. Certainly no one else in her building was up yet. Her eyes opened to an intense stillness.

She rolled over and checked the time on her phone. It was indeed early, especially for a Saturday. Not dark, though. She could see all the way past the packing boxes into the kitchen, where a peaceful grey light touched the edges of the window. The boxes looked less depressing than they had all week. Amazing, she thought, what a proper night's sleep can do.

She had fresh voicemail and a bunch of texts. People trying to get hold of her while she'd been out cold. She didn't want to deal with them, not now, when for the first time in days she felt like herself again. Except for Annie; but Annie's message said she was driving to her parents' place in Thunder Bay and would be out of touch until that night. She sounded exhilarated, not scared at all. Crazy Annie, scripting herself a road movie. Goose tapped out a couple of texts for her to get whenever she got a chance.

She didn't want to shower yet for fear of waking everyone else in the building by rousing the demonic groans of the plumbing. She got out her exercise mat instead and went through her postures for the first time since she'd moved in. Then, in a fit of blissful efficiency, she did some unpacking.

She didn't really appreciate how heavy the fog was until she set off to walk over to the station. To her surprise she found it not ominous but beautiful. It turned every object in the world into a kind of suggestion of itself. I'm going to become a self-help guru, she thought, and make millions out of my book: *How to Get Happy by Sleeping Fourteen Hours and Then Starting That Thing You've Been Procrastinating Over*. She swung her arms as she walked.

She heard noises ahead on the street well before she saw what was making them. A man was loading stuff atop and in the back of a station wagon. She recognised him; he was one of the people who'd answered their door when she was out searching for Jennifer, back when (it felt like an immensely long time ago) she'd thought Jennifer was just a runaway kid with an accomplice who smelled of fish.

'Going away for the weekend?' she said.

The man banged down the hatch of his car and stared at her, rubbing his hands. 'What's it look like?'

She refused to take offence. 'Just asking, sir.'

'We're out of here,' the man said. 'My sister-in-law's down in Comox. We're taking the kids. Hey. Could you keep an eye on the place? I don't have an alarm.'

'You're leaving town?'

His wife appeared out of the house, a ghost in the fog for a moment before solidifying into a woman carrying a couple of shoeboxes. 'Aw, for Pete's sake,' the man said. 'I just closed the goddam car.'

'It's my jewellery,' the woman said. She looked at Goose nervously. 'Good morning.'

'Morning.'

'What's happened?'

'Nothing, ma'am. I'm just passing by.'

'Nothing,' the man snorted, opening the hatch again with exaggerated weariness. 'Sure.'

'You must be the new girl,' the woman said. She was still wearing slippers.

'Officer Maculloch.'

'Do they have any idea how long this is going to last?'

'For Pete's sake, Judy.'

'The fog?' Goose looked around in that way people do when wondering whether they can predict the weather. 'It usually lifts in the afternoons. They tell me.'

Both husband and wife looked at her uncomfortably.

'I meant,' the wife said, embarrassed, 'this . . . problem.'

'Oh,' said Goose.

''Course she hasn't got any idea. No one's got any idea. Go wake up the kids, Judy, we're ready. Unless you got anything else you want to bring.'

'You could be polite,' the woman mumbled, but she vanished back into the mist.

'Excuse me if I was a little short.' He checked straps on the roof rack, grunting as he yanked them tighter. 'It's a lot of stress. I'm right, aren't I? Bet I am. You police don't know what's going on any more than the rest of us.'

'That's sometimes the case, sir, though we do our best. It depends what you're talking about, specifically.'

'Specifically.' He leant back. 'Specifically. Let's see. Specifically, that we got no TV and the phone line's down the crapper. And they put the mill on half-shift 'cos a bunch of deliveries didn't come in. And I got emails from the bank saying they got problems with my account except I don't 'cos now I don't got no email either. What'd they do, give you orders to smile nice and tell everyone to stay calm?'

'We have plans in place for all sorts of contingencies. It's part of what we do.'

'Yeah. Well. Excuse me, but we're not staying around to watch. Not with no TV. What's anyone gonna do in this place without TV?'

'Take extra care driving in these conditions, sir,' she called after him, smiling at herself, as he followed his wife away. Jonas would have talked him down, she reflected. Reassured him somehow that everything was under control. But she didn't have that gift, and anyway – she went on through the fog; the man and his car and his family disappeared completely within twenty paces – things weren't under control.

There was a kind of clarity to it. The girl who wouldn't talk, walking out of a locked cell, paddling away into the mist; the boy on the beach where the whale had been, huddled around that extraordinary mask; the messages from the rest of the world announcing that all was not well. The voices where voices shouldn't have been heard, the three words on her screen. No, she thought, I don't know what's going on; but so what? It was kind of like unpacking. You just did what was in front of you. Or like walking in the fog: you kept on putting one foot in front of the other, even though you couldn't see where you were headed.

She was surprised to find the station open, lights on in the windows. So surprised that for a few moments she thought she'd gotten crossed up and accidentally walked into the driveway of somebody's house. She turned around to check the sign and the flagpole. The top of the pole was invisible. If the flag was flying it would have been completely limp anyway. There was not a breath of wind.

Webber was behind the desk with his feet up. She'd met him when Cope had introduced her to the Hardy detachment; otherwise they hadn't exchanged a word. He had the stocky build and the faintly swaggering air of an athletic guy in the process of turning into a guy who used to be athletic. He stretched and yawned ostentatiously as she came in.

'Thank God,' he said.

'Hey. I wasn't expecting anyone. What's up? You been waiting?'

He swung his legs down and stood up, his legs just a little too wide apart. 'New shifts,' he said, and tapped a sheet of paper on the desk, clicking his tongue. 'Sarge wants all stations manned twenty-four seven. I've been here since midnight. So, yeah, waiting. You could say that. Oh, and guess what.' He picked up the paper. 'Nothing else to look at, I read this up and down a hundred times. You're on tonight in Hardy. Maculloch, that's you, right?'

'That's me.'

'Ten till two.' He handed her the sheet. 'You're going to have a fun night. I hope the TV's working.'

'I don't watch TV.'

He gave her a version of the Stare.

'Don't you? So you won't have heard what happened.'

'What?'

'Last night.' He puffed out slightly as if he was giving her a lecture. It seemed he was enjoying the chance to deliver news, bad news particularly. 'The navigation went down. All up the coast. All of it.' She must not have looked sufficiently impressed. 'All the lights, the lighthouses, markers, whatever. As far as anyone can tell.'

'They went out?'

'Every single one. The coastguard's been called in. And the navy. Now you've got this fog too.'

'That's . . .'

Now he thought he'd impressed her. He swayed on his feet and nodded judiciously. 'You know the Inside Passage is the busiest marine highway in the world? So now we've got all that shipping out there with no markers. In the fog.'

'That sounds . . .' But all she was thinking of was the single yellow kayak heading away, with no need for markers, no need for lights.

'You know what? I'd nuke the fuckers.'

'Which fuckers are those?'

'The Chinese. That's what they should do. Send a

fucking nuke. It wouldn't have to be Tokyo. Just, like, some medium-sized city. No warning. Just, like, bam, there goes ten million of you fuckers, now let's talk. If I was in charge I'd do it right now.'

She paused, trying not to let him disturb her mood. 'How would that help?'

'They think we won't do anything. That's how it works. They know the government's a bunch of fucking pussies. Look at this.' He leant across the desk and tapped at the computer. 'C'mere.'

He tried to arrange it so he'd be able to stand right behind her while she bent to see the screen. She knew this routine. She stood back from the desk and crossed her arms. 'What?'

'It's been like this all night. Go on, look.'

A pattern was running across the monitor, horizontal lines racing by in blurry lines. 'What's that?'

'Happens as soon as you run Windows. Here.' He switched the machine off and rebooted it. 'I tried this like twenty times. That's how bored I got. Take a look. Log it in.' He stood back, not far enough, and waited for her to move to the keyboard.

'Go ahead,' she said.

Thwarted, he sighed, and moved to tap the command line by the wavering cursor. A few seconds later the pattern appeared again.

'Fuckers,' he said.

The blur was letters, scrolling fast from one side to the other, like something out of a bad art installation. He pushed a finger right up to the screen. 'You can read it if you look close.'

Despite herself, she was curious. He was right; once your eyes matched the scrolling characters' speed they became the same two words, repeated constantly, looping rapidly past:

*sunthesunthesunthesunthesunthesunthesunthesunthesunthesunthesun-
thesun*

'I bet it's like a signature, eh. They do that. Like dogs pissing. They have to leave their mark. Fucking geeks. They'd give up in ten seconds if we dropped a bomb. Sayonara, fucktards.'

The words were strangely hypnotic. After a while the black of the moving letters and the off-white glare of the background blended into a grey haze: sea fog.

'Oh. And you won't have heard either. Fitzgerald died.'

She blinked. 'Shawn Fitzgerald?'

'Last night. Sarge got a call early this morning.'

'Crap,' she said. 'That's no good.'

'I knew he was sick but no one said he was sick that bad.'

'Shame. You hate to lose an officer.'

'He was one of us. One of the team.'

'Yeah,' she said. 'I'm sorry.'

'Tough act to follow.'

She had no interest in being intimidated by this guy. She reached around the monitor and forced the computer to quit again. 'Speaking of which,' she said, 'I'm on duty. So I guess I'll see you later.'

He waited a moment. She didn't look at him. He strolled to the door and collected his hat.

'I have to say, though,' he said, 'you're a lot better looking.'

She thought of Fitzgerald, too foul with sores to sleep in his own bed. Dying young, in quarantine, under his parents' hopeless eyes, just because Jennifer Knox had wanted him to die.

'Hey.' Webber tried to sound casual. 'You play that game, don't you? The sarge said. What's it called?'

'Rugby.'

'Rugby, yeah. That's the one where you stick your heads up each other's asses.'

'And lift each other up by the shorts.'

He cocked his eyebrows, a gesture copied from movie scenes where tough guys were playing it cool.

'Chicks' teams?'

'That's right. They don't let us play with the guys in case we hurt them too bad.'

'Now that I'd pay to see.'

'Free admission.'

'It keeps you pretty fit, I guess?'

I could knock you flat in half a second. 'You guess right.'

He was stuck at the door, holding his hat in his hand like an idiot.

'So anyway,' he said. 'You want to maybe have a beer some time?'

And my boyfriend's a girl. 'Webber?'

'What?'

'Go away.'

* * *

Jonas came in only briefly, an hour or so later, still early in the morning. He and his boat were needed again. She felt like she wanted to talk to him about yesterday, and the days before that. He'd seen most of the things she'd seen, starting with the empty cell. He'd just put his head around the door to say he wouldn't be around, though.

'I only got a minute. My skills are required.'

'Uh-huh.'

'You see they found that ship?'

'I don't see anything, Jonas. I don't like TV. Remember?'

'Oh, yeah. Freak.'

'Plus I was asleep all afternoon.'

'That tanker. The one that went missing? Showed up off Cape Scott, drifting. Nobody on board. One lifeboat launched.'

She did remember the story. Her father was convinced it had been hijacked by terrorists and was carrying radioactive waste. 'That was months ago.'

'Yep. In the Atlantic. Now it shows up over here. Same name, Star of Whatever. That place in Russia I can't say. Somewhere Star. Same ship. Coastguard wanted the launch out to help look for the lifeboat but the launch is stuck down in McNeill. So. Yours truly.'

He waited in the doorway. The minute which was supposedly all he had was already long past, but he wasn't quite willing to go. It was as if they both knew there was something else to talk about but neither wanted to start.

'What happened to that mask?' Goose asked.

He thumbed through the wall. 'It's on my couch. I left it

in the car yesterday. I guess we'll look into it when things, you know. Power down a little.'

But Goose wasn't afraid to think about it any more. After all, she was the only one who knew, for sure, that Jennifer Knox had walked out of a locked cell in the back of the station; that Jennifer had gone paddling away from the land, alone, not looking back; that her coat had gone missing from her house before it burned and then had been found covering the marooned boy.

'It's a whale, isn't it? Orca.'

'The mask?'

'Yeah.'

After a long pause, he pressed his lips together, ruefully, and bobbed his head.

'Yup,' he said.

'You saw the mark,' she said. 'On the beach. Didn't you?' She traced the shape in the air with her palm, the wide shallow scoop, the impression of a massive body left like God's fingerprint in the pebbles. 'Didn't you?'

He broke away from her look and glanced at the clock. 'I got to run.'

She was expecting the phone to keep her busy. But it was a quiet morning, as quiet as if the fog were dissipating slowly to expose another uneventful Alice day.

The town, she thought, was holding its breath.

Jonas was supposed to take over the desk at two. She wasn't surprised when he didn't show up, given where he'd said he was going. She was glad of the chance to make up for some of the extra time he'd done yesterday.

She'd have done a couple of patrols just for a change of scene, but she didn't have a radio, so she sat by the desk. There were a few calls, routine things. The guy from the market came by in person to ask whether there'd been problems on the highway. One of his deliveries hadn't come in and he couldn't get hold of the driver.

Every half-hour or so she tried the computer. Most of the time she got the same result, the two words chasing each other across the screen in a dizzy blur. Sometimes nothing came up at all, as if the monitor were fried.

She didn't touch the TV. She didn't call anyone. The outside world didn't have anything to tell her; the fog was like a reminder of that. *Vous êtes ici.*

One of the officers from Hardy arrived late in the afternoon to take over. Lots of problems on the roads, he confirmed. Some big pile-up a hundred kilometres down the island highway, near Sayward, black ice on the steep climb there. They'd had to close the road.

'We're cut off,' he said, enthusiastically.

The remnant of the morning's fog was now no more than the usual forest-hugging pencil-coloured cloud, but darkness was coming in its place.

She was going to stop for a while at Traders to refuel on coffee and a doorstop sandwich. The place was unexpectedly crowded, though, and everyone wanted to talk. Getting away was less complicated than she'd at first feared once it became clear that the person they really wanted to talk to was Jonas. They were quite ready to believe that she didn't know anything. She was still a down-islander, or an off-islander, or even a kind of foreigner. Most of them were there because the mill had cut production for the day, leaving them with nothing to do.

She drove over Thirty towards Hardy. It was true, she thought to herself, that she didn't know anything. But she knew what she'd seen.

She had a while before her overnight duty began. The sensible thing would have been to rest, but she still felt like she might never need sleep again. She parked at the hospital instead and went in to ask about the boy.

They wouldn't let her see him. He'd had to be sedated. They hadn't been able to get him to eat or drink, so he was on a drip. The doctor's main concern was how they were going to get rid of him.

'Do you have an ID for him yet?'

'Just that name,' Goose said.

He looked at his notes. 'Jia. Chinese name. There's probably ten thousand Jias in Vancouver alone. That number could be Los Angeles, too. I don't like to guess how many Jias there are in LA.'

'What number?'

The doctor snapped his notes away impatiently. 'Haven't you even tried it yet?'

'I haven't been directly involved in this case. Do you mean a phone number?'

171

'Hang on,' the doctor said, and left the room, returning a minute later with a small ziplock bag. 'I thought you people would have taken this away by now. The nurse found this in the inside pocket of his jacket.'

Inside the bag was a laminated rectangle the size of a business card, wrinkled and blotched, mouldy at the edges. She took it out and held it under the light. It had been written on in neat, fussy print. The letters were quite clear despite the fading and staining: *HOME NUMBER*, they read. The string of numbers below was a little harder to decipher, but far from obscure.

'It shouldn't take long to track him down,' the doctor said. 'Should it? I bet his mom did that.'

'What's that area code?' Goose said, squinting at the first three numbers. 'Oh one eight?'

He took a turn peering. 'That's what I thought at first. Must be eight one eight. That's LA. I checked.'

'Has someone tried it?'

'I'd say that's your job. You want to take this? We have his clothes too.'

She copied the number instead. Someone else would be responsible for the case; she'd leave the grumpy doctor for them to deal with.

'Oh one eight's not an area code,' he said, watching her make her note. 'It's probably an eight. Or I guess it could be a nine, there's that little bit there.'

'Or it's not a US Canadian number.'

The doctor obviously hadn't thought of that. 'It's written in English.'

Even the suggestion of a dispute about language raised particularly unpleasant spectres from her childhood. Her memories of the months leading up to her parents' divorce were of an insane linguistic retrenchment. She didn't remember the recriminations and insults themselves; she just recalled the horror of Dad refusing to say a word in French and Mom refusing (beyond the word *fuck* and its variants) to say a word in English. She promised the doctor she'd get back to him with whatever progress they made on identifying the boy, and made a businesslike exit. And it was indeed her intention to talk to whoever was dealing with the case as soon as she got to the station, because the doctor was of course right, she couldn't believe it would take long to track the kid down after he'd so conveniently provided them with his name and phone number, and she was eager – very eager – to know who he was and where he'd come from; but she'd barely walked in the door when Janice (who shouldn't have been there on a Saturday anyway) gave a flustered screech of relief at the sight of her – 'Marie!' – and sent her down to the dock to meet Jonas, and the coastguard vessel, and the ferry, which should have arrived at eleven o'clock that morning. 'Oh, those poor people,' she said, waving Goose outside. 'Those poor people.'

Twelve

THERE WERE NO people. The people had vanished.

A young coastguard officer met her at the ferry dock. The two of them put up a police line across the off ramp to keep the small but intensely agitated crowd away from the vessel, and stayed ashore to protect it while his colleagues and Jonas worked their way through the ferry, looking for some clue to what had happened. He told her the story while they waited.

Coastguard had made contact with the ferry early that morning, as soon as the navigation markers in the Passage failed. Their own satellite navigation had gone down not long afterwards. In the fog there'd been nothing they could do except cut speed to a crawl and use charts and compass reckoning to try to work their way into the Passage, looking for a safe harbour. The last they'd heard from the ferry was the captain announcing that he was going to assist a small craft in distress. He'd thought it might be the lifeboat from the *Irkutsk Star*. The airwaves were full of confused shipping; they'd lost touch with the ferry until Jonas radioed in to say he'd found it off course, drifting, idling, dangerously near the islands at the entrance to the Queen Charlotte Strait. By early afternoon the fog had cleared enough for them to make their way to the spot. They went aboard and found no one. No crew, no passengers. The manifest was in the purser's office; twenty-six truckers and forty-three other travellers had boarded the ferry in Prince Rupe for the overnight journey. Their coats and magazines and snack wrappers were spread around the seats, their cars and trucks and campers were in the vehicle hold, their change was in the cafeteria till. They themselves were gone. The young officer was visibly shaken as he described it.

'Lifeboats?' she asked.

'Not touched. The alarm didn't sound. It gets logged automatically. It's like they all just . . .'

Just what? She tried to imagine what it must have been like for Jonas, first aboard.

'. . . Jumped in the sea. It's like . . .'

He couldn't say what it was like. He was surprisingly fresh faced for a coastguard but he had the look of someone who'd been digging bodies out of the rubble of an earthquake. She looked at the ferry, a disproportionately large silhouette in this town where everything that wasn't a parking facility was on a reduced scale. Its lights were on. Its engines rumbled contentedly. The coastguard guys had brought it in themselves.

'Fire?' she suggested.

'That's the first thing you check for. We went all over the engine rooms. Nothing. No problems.'

The peculiar restfulness she'd enjoyed all day was bleeding out as the invisible sun went down. The usual evening murk was spreading quickly.

'Freaky,' she said.

He nodded vigorously and gestured towards the clump of spectators gathered beyond the tape. 'We're going to have to tell them something soon. Some of them are family.'

Oh God, she thought, *please let them not make me do that just because I'm the woman*. 'What have you said so far?'

'Emergency. Accident aboard. Investigating. That stuff.'

A shout came from the bright open maw behind them. Another uniformed man stood at the top of the off ramp, motioning to his colleague.

'You better stay here,' the young officer said, and went to answer.

As soon as they saw she was on her own the crowd began to call to her. She clenched her jaw, took a few deep breaths, tried to remember her training, and went to say what she thought she could say. She saw the emotions on people's faces, written as plainly as the most compulsive emotions always were, the ones no one could do anything about: shock, fear, grief.

Everyone was still talking all at once and she'd barely begun to prepare the ground when a woman pointed over her shoulder and said, 'There's someone!'

They all fell silent, Goose with them as she turned to look. The front of the ferry was open, a wide gate in the increasing darkness, and a few figures had gathered there, among them (she saw) Jonas, bigger and sturdier than the rest. All were in uniform except one, a long-haired thin silhouette whom Jonas seemed to be guiding by the shoulders. A blanket had been wrapped over her shoulders and her head was bowed; she went unsteadily, in small shuffling steps. An older woman, it looked like, except that her hair was very dark, and (Goose now saw, as the group came slowly down the ramp, into the brutal glow of the dock's lamps) extraordinarily long, reaching to her hips.

'Maculloch?' It was Jonas, shouting. He was too good a pro to call her *Goose* in front of a crowd.

'What?'

'Clear those folks back, would you?'

Everyone started yelling. Fortunately for her they weren't angry yet; they were still at the stage of stunned pliability. She kept talking as she cleared a route to the patrol cars, always slightly more loudly and sharply than anyone else was talking, always pushing a little more firmly than anyone else pushed. It was only difficult for the first little while. As the group led by Jonas came closer the anxious crowd fell silent again, one by one, and a collective look came over them which Goose could not identify at all.

Jonas was escorting a painfully thin, painfully hunched blind woman. She clutched the blanket they'd given her tight at her neck, and her head stayed bowed so that her lank and matted hair covered most of her face, but her skin was so pale that the blot on that face was unmistakable, the thick band of black between white forehead and white mouth. A scarf or blindfold or bandage was wrapped over her eyes.

'Easy,' Jonas was murmuring. 'Eaaasy. OK. Nearly there now.' The crowd had fallen so quiet everyone could hear every long syllable, and every shuffling footstep as well. The blind woman wore dark boots. She was not old.

Jonas raised his head to Goose for a moment. He looked like an entirely different person: stricken, exhausted.

'Hold the fort,' he said, nodding back towards the ferry. He shepherded the woman into the back of a patrol car and was gone.

It was some two hours before relief arrived; Cope himself and one of the corporals. The crowd had gone by then. She'd had to stop a couple of people who'd tried to force their way aboard. The senior coastguard had come out and given a statement to the effect that everyone known to have boarded the vessel was now considered missing. There'd been a very small, very ineffectual riot immediately after that. It kept her warm, at least. Once they'd all gone it was just her on the tarmac under the lights, the air like stop-motion spray against her skin.

Cope rolled over and stood beside her, looking at the ferry. From time to time they caught sight of the coastguard guys working their way from deck to deck, shining torches into the cabs of the trucks. The corporal, whose name Goose couldn't remember, came to join them.

'Good job, Maculloch.'

'Thank you, sir.' She wasn't sure what Cope was referring to.

The sarge sighed heavily. 'What a day. What a goddam

day.' He kicked a stone across the empty queuing lanes. 'Anything I need to know about?'

'I don't think so.'

'All right. That's one piece of good news, anyway.'

'Is the passenger all right?'

He frowned at her.

'The passenger, sir. Jonas escorted a woman off the vessel.'

'We don't know if she's a passenger or not. Hasn't said a damn thing. She might be a deaf mute stowaway.' He tugged to loosen his collar. 'Sitting there like a hunk of wood. Gives me the creeps. You know what, Maculloch, you ought to try. Use your woman's touch. Or maybe she speaks French.'

'Try what?' She hoped he was joking.

'See if you can figure out who she is, what the hell she was doing on board that ship.'

'I thought Jonas . . .'

'Yeah. You'd think, wouldn't you? I mean, who wouldn't talk to Jonas?'

Jennifer Knox. Goose felt a chill.

'Is she in the station?'

'I didn't know what the hell else to do with her. Christ. I'm glad I'm not on duty overnight. Who's on tonight?'

'Me, sir.'

'Oh.' He looked away. 'OK. Well, just remember that woman's a suspect. Until we have any information suggesting otherwise.'

'A suspect in . . .'

'Christ, Maculloch.' He waved an arm at the bulk of the

ferry. 'This. Whatever this is. We've got eighty-odd people unaccounted for and one person at the scene.'

'A blind deaf mute?'

'You know something, Maculloch? My tolerance is running a little low right now.'

'Sorry. I guess it just seems weird.'

'You think? Anyway. Weird or not, as of right now we've got jack else to go on, all right? So let's try and make sure she doesn't up and go walking out of the station on your watch. Hmm?'

For a moment she was too angry to speak. Whether he was joking or not – and now she thought he wasn't; now she thought his gruff banter was really just bullying, plain and simple – she didn't care.

'Can I go, sir?'

'You do that. Go get some coffee. And have a good night.'

'Thank you. Oh, sir?'

'What?'

'I was sorry to hear about Fitzgerald.'

The sarge looked away. 'We all were.'

'His dad thinks the girl put a curse on him.'

'What?'

'It's nothing. Goodnight.'

She was off duty till ten. Enough time to cross back over to Alice if she'd wanted to, but instead she got hot drinks and cold food from one of the malls, drove a mile or two out of town, and sat in her car by the side of the road. People had stopped her in the mall. One half-toothless old guy as good as chased her down the dairy aisle. 'Is this the big one?' he kept asking. 'Are we done for?' Strange, she thought, how the town somehow went on functioning in its sad and boring way at the same time as people started to go crazy. There were women in the market with kids sat in the seat of their trolleys, and they were buying tacos and baby formula, and the town's teenagers were still out on the sidewalks walking or skateboarding up and down in their little packs the way they always did, while at the same time the fuel truck hadn't arrived and things they all took for granted suddenly couldn't be counted on and the ferry had turned into the *Mary Celeste*. Canada, like everywhere else, had secretly found it difficult not to laugh at the Brits. England! Of all the people in the world you'd have picked to go collectively insane, the corgi-loving tea-drinking stiff-upper-lip Brits would be at the very bottom of the list. But now she thought she understood how it might have happened, how everything could simultan-eously be normal and . . . not. She'd do her shift and then go home and (fingers crossed) sleep and get up and brush her teeth the next morning, and then she'd do whatever the next thing was, maybe unpack the last few boxes, and then the next, and so on, whatever else might be happening out there in the darkness and the fog.

Wouldn't she?

The Hardy detachment of the Royal Canadian Mounted Police consisted of fifteen officers. Three of them were on duty that evening; herself, Kalmykov and Wardley. It was the first time she'd done a shift in Hardy. It was much more like an office than the Alice station, which was for most practical purposes an extension of Jonas's living room. It smelled of uniforms and cleaning products. The light was harsher. The sarge's office at the back was glassed in, half hidden by cheap blinds, like a crummy executive bolthole.

In a deep chair in his office sat the blind woman, back straight, head bent slightly forward. Wardley leaned against the counter next to Goose and stared at her through the blinds.

'She's hardly moved.'

Goose didn't want to stare but couldn't help herself. The office door was closed. The woman couldn't possibly hear them, or (of course) see them; the chair she sat in was turned away, so they were looking at her in profile, and her witchy hair hid most of her face; nevertheless, Goose couldn't shake the feeling that the woman could feel their tactless scrutiny.

'She'll take a drink now and then.' Someone had put a coffee and a couple of cookies on the corner of the desk by the chair. 'That's about it. Except if you put your hands near her face, then she'll move. Oh yeah.'

'Who tried that?'

'Paul. He wanted to get a better look at her, get a photo for ID.'

'Did we get one?'

'I think so. The camera's still in there. And I don't mind saying, you can get it yourself. OK, look, here she goes. Watch this.'

The woman reached for her drink. Her hands were pale and bony and not so much wrinkled as shrivelled, as if the skin had shrunk in the wash. They closed around the mug, held it, lifted. She tipped her head down and instead of drinking sniffed the coffee. Goose thought she saw her nostrils flare.

'Watch what?'

'I don't know.' Wardley was almost whispering. 'It doesn't look right when she does that.'

Blind people were supposed to have their other senses highly developed. There was something too intense about the way she held the mug under her nose, very still, as if the question of whether she could drink it or not was a matter for careful meditation.

She opened her lips, bent a little more, and was about to sip. She stopped halfway through the motion, her bottom lip just touching the edge of the mug. Goose suddenly felt as though she were watching some weird piece of abstract theatre, the kind of stuff Annie's friends were into.

'See?' Wardley said. He was whispering without knowing it. 'See what I mean?'

'Anyone found out anything yet?'

'Paul said the ferry stopped to pick up a boat. Get this. That was the last they heard from it.' Wardley looked at Goose significantly.

'He thinks . . .'

Wardley nodded. 'They pick her up in the sea somewhere. Next thing anyone knows they're all gone.' He pointed at the door to the sarge's office. 'I locked it.'

She'd been thinking she should go in and at least make her presence known, maybe offer the woman a pillow, make a bit of an effort. Now that the sarge had decided to treat her as some kind of suspect, the woman was presumably going to spend the whole night in the office. Goose looked unwillingly at the almost white lips poised at the rim of the mug and then turned her back.

'By the way,' Wardley added, 'you get the desk.' Which was protocol; technically she was junior to both him and Kalmykov, so she'd be the last to answer a call. But he said it with unnatural relief.

Half an hour later and she was on her own. She didn't know what counted as normal here in Hardy, but it seemed like it was a busy night. She tried to keep tabs on where her colleagues were but the radio was cutting in and out.

At least the mainframe was functioning here. She made herself stop looking over her shoulder and settled down at the computer. She went through the security procedures and got into the shiny new Missing Persons registry. It was evident from talking to Wardley that no one had yet made any effort to identify Aitch Jia. He and Kalmykov had barely even registered that an unidentified juvenile had been rescued the day before. They'd had other things to occupy them in Hardy, clearly.

She hadn't used the registry before. It seemed like searching by surname ought not to be too complicated, but when she entered JIA she ended up with more than a thousand results. She tried again. Frowning, she browsed through a couple of the results. They didn't seem to be case files at all, not even the sketchiest outlines of case files. Beyond the names the fields were mostly blank. There were over seventy H JIAs. It looked more like the census than a missing persons registry, so much so that she logged out and back in again in case she'd opened the wrong database by mistake. She hadn't. It seemed the RCMP software had in its wisdom declared that every single person in Canada was missing.

She searched MACULLOCH.

And there she was. Name, address (the one from Victoria), date of birth. No more details. She had an unpleasant sensation at the back of her neck as her eye strayed to the 'Date Missing' box, as if she was afraid she might not find it empty, but it was blank.

She logged out again. If in doubt, she thought, try the internet. The RCMP had just spent God knows how many million on their database, but it looked like she'd be just as likely to get a result for nothing. If the kid had run away or disappeared there was every chance Google would be able to tell her about it. Everything that happened left its more or less indistinct footprints in the internet somewhere. She opened a browser. The unreadably bland mounties' home page popped up, ready to keep the population of Canada docile by the sheer anaesthetic power of bureaucratic prose. She went to a search page and tried again: H JIA.

Again, there were hundreds of results. Hundreds. This time, though, they weren't the wrong people.

She read, and read. There were pictures too.

'Sarge?'

'Hello?'

'Sarge. It's Maculloch.'

'Oh, Christ. Don't tell me.'

'I'm sorry to bother you, sir.'

'Well, you've bothered me now. Let's get it over with.'

'I found the boy. The kid Jonas and me brought in yesterday. I have an ID for him. Sir.'

A heavy silence.

'Is this important now, Maculloch?'

'He's from England. He went missing from,' she checked the screen, where Horace's face looked back at her, wearing the forced and mirthless half-smile of seventh-graders in school photos all over the world, 'Falmouth, south-west England, three months ago. That's where all that trouble started. He went missing that day.'

More silence.

'It's definitely him, sir. He had his home number in the pocket of his jacket, it's the right area. And the jacket's his school uniform. I'm looking at it right now, sir. In a photo. His name's Horace. Horace Jia. It was a big story.'

Still the sarge didn't answer, though she could hear him breathing.

'He's twelve years old. Thirteen in a month.'

'You're looking at what photo?'

She knew by his tone of voice that she shouldn't have called. 'His school photo. It's the mugshot they released over there.'

'This is on the internet.'

'That's right, sir. I'm looking at a page from a British news service. There are lots of others.'

'What'd you use, freaking Google?'

'It's him. No possible question.'

'This is the same place people said they saw that flying thing, right?'

'I checked the BBC website. Plus the national papers, a couple of them carried the story.'

'You know what, Maculloch? I'm sitting here trying to think of a reason this can't wait till tomorrow.'

'He's a twelve-year-old boy. He's been lost for three months. I've been watching the video clip of his mother's appeal.'

'OK, I have an idea. You deal with it.'

'Sir—'

'You get hold of the police over there. With their damn stupid hats. Tell 'em you found this kid in Hardy. You explain it to them. By the way, you might want to remember they're kind of busy with people rioting in the streets and such, but hey, I bet they'll be delighted to hear from you. Oh, and it's, what, seven a.m. there? But go right ahead.'

This is how people do it, she thought to herself. This is what you do: you put off thinking about a lost boy appearing after three months on a tiny island on the far side of the world, because you've had a long day, you're grouchy and tired, you just want to go to bed. That's why things appear to go on as if they were the same as always.

'All right. Thank you, sir.'

'Maculloch—'

But she had hung up.

* * *

It was the same day. How come no one had pointed that out before? Or perhaps they had. Somewhere in the nightmare babble of the internet, in among the millions of insect voices all chirping simultaneously across the dark cave whose limits none of them could guess at, someone – perhaps a few people, picking up the idea from one another in random conjunctions of bored accidental clicks – had probably noticed that the day Jennifer Knox had (or hadn't) pushed her brother down the stairs and stopped talking was the same day that it had started snowing in the south-west extremity of England and people had (or hadn't) seen a gigantic black flying beast circling overhead. But why would Goose have cared about the coincidence before? Why would she care now?

Because, she thought. *Because . . .*

There was no reason she could put into thoughts. It was like being in the fog; but the fog held snatches of voices.

She looked over her shoulder. Her breath caught.

The woman in the sarge's office had turned in her chair. Her sightless face was directed towards Goose.

A car door banged outside. She heard scuffling. Kalmykov came in, steering a big shouty handcuffed teenager. Goose didn't realise how fast her heart was beating until she got up to help. For the next few minutes the station was blessedly full of yelling and banging and paperwork. She threw herself into it energetically, so energetically that the shouty teenager dialled down to a more respectful volume much faster than he'd perhaps expected to. They got him into a cell, where he went very quiet indeed.

'Shame they can't all be like that one, eh?' Kalmykov

nodded towards the office. 'She doesn't seem to be any trouble.'

Goose laughed nervously and didn't look. Her ears were singing. *The boy was a whale.* The thought kept passing through her, a weird thought from somewhere else, like a direction-less noise floating in fog. *The boy was a whale, then he became a boy. It was Jennifer's coat.*

'Who's been looking at junk online on company time?' Kalmykov was in a good mood. They all complained about the busy nights afterwards, but while it was happening it was actually a lot better than sitting at the desk or cruising around at random in a patrol car. He leaned over the computer. 'Hey! This isn't porn! What are you, Goose, some kind of weirdo?'

Wardley came back. The two of them came and went. Goose stayed at the desk, hoping she'd be needed outside as well. She wasn't. She tried not to let her look stray to the office, not too often at least. She saw that the woman had drawn up her knees under the blanket and was sitting curled tight in the chair.

'Think she's asleep?' Wardley was also trying not to look, and failing.

'I hope so.'

'You been in there?'

She shook her head. 'Going to leave her alone. Who's coming in at two? Thorpe?'

'Thorpe and Turner.'

'She can be their problem.'

'Oh yeah.' Wardley gave up trying and stared through the

glass and the blinds, as if hypnotised. 'Oh yeah. Someone else's problem. That's the idea.'

Midnight. Wardley went off duty. Kalmykov was out. As if by instinct she could feel the town settling down, giving up, going to sleep. It was something about the rhythm of noises from outside. The passing of cars up the block became rare enough that she noticed each one, consciously: *there's someone out late.* The shouts of macho laughter from the park down the block stopped altogether. Two hours in the silence, she thought, as the clock ticked by. Kalmykov radioed in a couple of times but he was less cheerful now things were settling down. Another night, then another day.

Things could change, though. Things could be different, utterly different, overnight. 1 December. She faced the screen, her back to the office, reading, clicking. She leapt from point to point in an unreasoning nebula of information, cold and distant spots in a universe of dark matter. *'Someone must have seen Horace that afternoon,' DCI Franklin said. The devil is growing more brazen which is a sign the end time is closer, see all the things which are happening in Cornwall they are not natural. A twelve year-old boy has gone missing from his home in Mawnan Smith. Rescue efforts have been hampered by the extreme weather. What do they mean state of emergency, this is a free country last time I checked, we are not living in a police state. Mrs Jia had to be physically supported as she read the appeal. Lol i bet that bird ate him lol. West Cornwall police have been overwhelmed by emergency calls as the bitter weather contin-ues. These are NOT RUOMOURS hundreds of people have seen it how would you fake ALL those videos anyway???*

It was him. There was no point trying to doubt herself. It

didn't matter that it couldn't be him, not according to any sequence of events she could imagine. There was a limit to what she could imagine happening, what anyone could imagine happening. She'd already met that limit. It had faced her in the cell in the station in Alice, looked at her eye to eye, before going out and disappearing into the fog. (To the island, to the whale, the mask, the boy.)

She looked at the phone number.

Protocol told her to leave it alone. The proper course of action was to get in touch with the authorities over there and leave it up to them. She checked the clock. Eight hours' difference. It was half past eight in the morning in England. The authorities might not be in their offices. There might not even be any authorities any more. It was too late for protocol, too dark, too quiet. But the sun would be up there, on the other side of the world.

She worked out the numbers for an international call. They were supposed to log things like this. Janice would be mildly cross, in the morning. (Janice, the morning, the sun up: she couldn't imagine any of it.)

The station was completely silent beyond the hum of the lights. She listened to the hiccupping double tone. Stop-start, stop-start. When she was little, calling her grandparents in Scotland, she always used to think it meant something was wrong on the line.

A click.

The funny echoey silence.

'Hello?'

'Hello?' a voice answered, hesitantly.

Goose sat up in the desk chair, swivelling. 'Hello? I'm sorry to bother you so early in the morning.' She listened to herself sounding like a policeman. 'I'm calling from Canada. Officer Séverine Maculloch of the Mounted Police. May I confirm who I'm talking with, please?'

After a pause, the voice answered, doubtfully, 'You're somewhere else?'

The voice's intonation was almost comically British, neat, small. She sounded like a child.

'In Canada, yes. I have some information which may be important. Is this the Jia household?'

Again the person took a while to answer.

'Are you to do with Horace? Where are you? I was trying to stop this thing making a noise. My friend's asleep.'

There was a small noise behind her. Goose swivelled around, the phone still at her ear.

In the office, the blind woman had risen from her chair. She let the blanket fall behind her. Her clothes were mouldered and torn.

She stepped without uncertainty or hesitation towards the office door.

'I,' said Goose, her hand suddenly tight on the phone. 'I need to talk to an adult. Can you do that for me? Can you get an adult? What's your name, by the way?'

The blind woman put out her white hands and spread shrivelled fingers against the glass. Her head turned to face Goose: straight to face her.

'Get her where? I don't understand where you are,' the child said. 'My name's Marina.'

Part II

Thirteen

'**M**ARINA?'

No answer. No running footsteps upstairs, either. He saw her shoes in the hallway, though, and the only marks in the grainy snow outside the front door had been made by small animals, or were his own.

'Marina!' She'd left the door unbarred again. He pulled it shut. The noise rolled ahead of him, expiring in the house's empty passages. He edged forward in the gloom, holding a canvas bag to his chest. His shoulders ached from carrying it. There were no easy journeys any more, not even bringing the shopping. 'Marina?'

He stepped on something yielding. It crunched. He jerked his foot away. As his eyes accommodated to the shadows he saw a small brown dead thing on the hallway floor. A songbird, mangled. The cat had broken off its head.

The house was freezing, as usual. There was still plenty of wood in the stable barn after all these bitter weeks but

– because – she wouldn't use it. He'd start a fire in the main room, he thought, once he'd rested his arms.

He carried the bag towards the light at the far end of the hall, calling up the stairs. The sloping field beyond the window caught his eye. It had been white for so long he'd forgotten it could ever change its face. Now it was mottled with grey slush and pocked all over with shallow bullet holes, the impact craters of sleety rain.

'I brought some food!'

He set the bag down in the kitchen. There were plates on the floor, scattered with peelings and wilted leaves. Feathers and tiny bones. She and the cat ate together, both half wild. The larder smelled of staled milk. He poured the four-pint bottle he'd brought into a clean jug and tipped the remnants of the last one out of the window, under trickling eaves. He unwrapped the cheese and left it in paper on a shelf, promising himself he'd watch her eat at least a few bites later. Everything else he left in the bag while he went to find her.

The cat hopped soundlessly down the stairs, meeting him halfway. It was looking lean, too, but at least it was happy to see him.

'Marina? Where are you? It's me. Owen.'

He hoped she might be asleep, for once. Since she'd been on her own, six or seven or eight or however many weeks it was now – the calendar, like a lot of things which before the snow had felt as ordinary and inevitable as oxygen, no longer seemed much use as a way of describing the world – he'd had no first-hand evidence that she ever slept at all. But all the beds were empty. All the rooms, too. She must have gone out somewhere barefoot.

(He had a sudden memory from the previous summer: Marina sitting on the front step in sunshine, laughing at something he'd said while she bent forward to lace up her shoes, suddenly almost pretty in a way that wasn't quite childlike any more, and he noticing that and being struck by the unwanted thought: *how much longer can this go on?*

Not long at all, it turned out.)

He was about to go back downstairs when a draught surprised him. She'd left a window open, then. All night, probably. Though the snow had begun to thaw at last, the nights were still icy. He followed the trickle of cold air. The cat overtook him, lolloping ahead and disappearing around a narrow side door. With that, he realised where she was hiding.

'Marina?'

He hadn't seen that door open for years, so long that he'd forgotten it wasn't just a cupboard. Behind it was a flight of tiny twisting stairs. The chill spiralled down them. He put his head around the first corner and called up.

'Is it all right if I join you?'

No answer. He sighed, ducked, squeezed himself into the ascent.

A hatch-like window under a cramped gable led out on to the roof of the house. The cat's tail brushed out ahead of him. He'd lost weight himself or he doubted he'd have been able to wiggle after it. Lean months. People like him, comfortable English people, had lost their collective memory of such times. The myth of perpetual abundance had stopped being a myth. This is how it is, they'd thought, and how it always will be: always more than enough.

Not for the first time he wondered whether everything that had happened was really surprising at all.

The back of a hooded head stuck out on the far side of the peak of the roof. She was looking northwards, perching on the slates. They looked too steep and brittle for him. There was a low parapet around the roofline but he still felt queasy, high up and out in the open. He kept his feet on the frame of the midget window and held on to the gable as he stood straight. The cat came marching along the ridge of the roof and nudged at his hands as if it thought it might be funny to try to push him off.

'Hello,' he said.

'Hello.'

'Aren't you cold?'

'Not really. You always ask that.'

Now that he was standing, albeit precariously, he could see over the top of the roof. The trees at the edge of the garden screened the house, but she was high enough here to see partly over and partly through their bare tops, across the river valley to the fields around the church on the opposite bank. The clusters of tents stood out against the snow, strips and squares of colour. Some of them had collapsed, some blown down to join the spackling of litter pinned against the lower hedges. Through the knotted treetops they could just about see a couple of people moving around the camp.

'I brought some fresh milk for you. And a few other bits and pieces.'

'Thank you.' She still hadn't turned around.

'I'm sorry I haven't been able to come for the last couple of days.'

'It doesn't matter.'

'Doesn't it? But I'm sorry anyway.'

Now she twisted her head around. The baggy hood still hid her face. It was one of the jumpers Gwen had knitted for her, more like a woolly sack than a garment.

'I'm not,' she said. 'I told you, I don't mind.'

She turned back northwards, to watch her tiny fraction of the larger world.

'Do you want to come in for a bit?' he suggested, cautiously.

'I don't know. I don't know what I want. I don't know if I want to do anything.'

'Oh, Marina.'

'There are less of them than there used to be. Fewer. Do I mean fewer? They must have finished whatever they were doing.'

His back was beginning to stiffen. It was still cold – always cold – and he was standing awkwardly. Once upon a time, small imperfections like that had been worth thinking about. Whole lifetimes had been spent mitigating them; millions of people dedicating their existence to pursuing the absence of discomfort.

'How long have you been coming up here?'

'I don't know. Some days.'

'You've been . . . careful, haven't you?'

She didn't answer.

'Marina?'

'No,' she said, 'I haven't.'

She was well enough hidden where she sat, he thought. Screened by the trees, camouflaged against the slate and stone of the old roof. But still. He ought to try to talk to her about it.

'Would you look at me? Please?'

'If you like.'

She didn't look any worse, really. She'd always been very thin and she'd never been particularly clean or tidy. A couple of weeks ago (was it?) she'd got annoyed with her hair growing long and cut it herself, with the iron shears. The result – a ridiculous crop halfway between do-it-yourself punk and tufted duck – didn't help, but if he tried not to get distracted by it, or by the radiant unhappiness of her expression, he had to admit she looked no less healthy than usual, not that *healthy* was quite the word.

'You look awful,' she said.

He had to laugh.

'I'm not very good with heights.'

'I only just discovered you could open that window.' *Only just* could mean the past few hours or the past few years, in Marina's language. Of course, he thought. For as long as she's known, any day of each season has been much like another, until . . . this. 'Daddy and Gwen always said it was stuck.' She pushed her hands deeper inside their opposite sleeves.

'I imagine they didn't want you exploring out here. It could be risky. These tiles aren't meant for walking on.'

'It's just more lies.'

A helicopter whirred over the horizon, angling west to east. He met her angry look. He'd never had children of his own but he'd spent plenty of time talking to teenagers in the parish.

'No one can tell the truth all the time. Especially not to children. It doesn't mean they didn't—'

'Don't say it.'

His fingers were beginning to sting from gripping the stone. 'All right.'

'Don't say that to me again. Ever.'

'I'm sorry.'

'I'd never lie.' If he'd had any grief left over after the past three months he'd have been heartbroken listening to her. She sounded just the same as the girl he'd watched grow up, and yet not the same: her impulsive simplicity had turned into the twisted shadow of itself, a determined bitterness. She seemed ten years older. 'I'd never tell anyone anything I knew was wrong. If a child ever comes out of me I'll always tell her the truth. I'll promise her as soon as she comes out. "I'll never lie to you and I'll never go away," that's the first thing I'll say.'

'Marina—'

'Don't!' It was a tight scream. The ring of trees echoed it for a dull instant.

The helicopter drifted nearer. Its monotone buzz broke into a *chop-chop-chop*. He waited as long as he could before speaking again.

'We ought to go inside.'

Around the church, a couple more people appeared out of their tents. The church bell began to ring.

'I know you're very unhappy.' He spoke as calmly as he could. 'But things could get much worse if someone saw you and decided they wanted to find out who lived here.'

'There's nothing wrong with them. I've been watching. They just go in and out of their little houses.'

'People have done terrible things.'

'Where?'

'Lots of places. You'll just have to believe me, Marina. I know what could happen.'

'Are these things worse than what everyone did to me?'

The bell in the church tower kept ringing, though it didn't look like many of them were left to answer it; as she'd said, they were mostly gone now. The helicopter veered in their direction.

'If you don't come in soon,' he said, 'I'm afraid I'm going to have to try and fetch you myself.' A useless threat, he suspected, looking at the age-smoothed slates, but just as he was wondering whether he'd have to give it a go anyway she hitched herself back and swung her legs over the top of the roof. She had thick green socks on. They must have been her father's.

'You sound like you're talking to Grey Mouser. My bottom's getting sore anyway.'

Downstairs, he began laying a fire in the living room. Its chimney was the likeliest to spread at least a suggestion of warmth through parts of the floor above. She followed him unenthusiastically. Everything in the house was out of place.

She'd dropped things wherever she'd tired of them. When she peeled off the hooded jumper she looked like a mournful scarecrow.

And yet – he noticed it as she stood behind him, watching his efforts with matches and kindling – and yet for a painful moment he felt the tug of her. His heart thumped in warning and his hands trembled. The pyramid of twigs he'd been working on collapsed.

'You needn't bother,' she said. 'It'll just go out.'

He forced himself to concentrate on his hands. 'Not if you keep an eye on it. A couple of logs every few hours and it could go on for ever. There's stacks of wood.'

'I'll just leave it after you go.'

'Well then.' He propped the last sliver of wood up and struck a match, cradling the flame. One of the lasting benefits of his training in the priesthood, it turned out, was that he'd become good at patience. The terrifying irrelevance of everything else he'd spent so much time learning and thinking about was largely balanced out by the fact that patience, his only surviving asset, had turned out to be the one thing he and everyone else needed most. He remembered learning that at root it was the same word as *suffering*. They meant the same thing. 'How about keeping it going for Grey Mouser? She must like it.'

'She doesn't need us to look after her. Anyway, it's getting warmer. The snow's beginning to melt.'

The wood caught quickly, as it always did. Magic. The fireplaces drew and the walls stayed sound, the well was always sweet, the teenage girl standing behind him was a siren's child. That was the world now. He'd had years to try to get used to it and never managed. What must it be like for everyone else?

He stood up and faced her. The little sting inside him pricked again. A siren's child, and she was growing up, growing into herself. *Don't touch her*, he told himself. He clasped his hands behind his back to make sure.

'There. That's that done. I'll put a pot over it, shall I? I brought some things you can boil up. They're all in the kitchen. And you'll have hot water.'

She crouched down and scratched the cat's head as it rubbed around her legs.

'I'll eat it,' she said, sounding all at once much more like the Marina he remembered, hesitant and eager to please, 'if you stay and make it.'

His heart sank. 'I'm so sorry,' he said. 'I would if I could.'

The glimmer of eagerness flickered out. 'Never mind.'

'Honestly. I wish I could stay all day. I come as often as I can.'

'You needn't come at all.'

'Please don't be like that, Marina.'

'That's a stupid thing to say. Gwen always said how stupid it was.' She'd finally started talking about Gwen in the past tense. '"Don't be like that." You only have to think about it and you can see it's stupid.'

Patience. Suffering. 'It's quite difficult getting food at the moment. If I stayed here, I wouldn't be able to get to other people.'

'Yes, I know. All those other people.'

'You understand. I'm sure you do.'

'Just go away, Owen.'

'Marina, please.'

'Sorry. I didn't mean to be rude.'

'You can be as rude as you like. I just wish you'd stop being so unhappy.'

'I don't mean to be unhappy either. I'm not doing it deliberately.'

'Yes, I know.'

'I'm not being deliberately lonely. I didn't choose for Daddy to drown. I didn't ask everyone to go away.' The urge to step forward and hold her hand was like a gale blowing at his back. 'I never decided to be here all on my own.'

He waited a moment before saying, very gently, 'He'll come back.' She spun away from him. 'I promise.'

'"Promise",' she repeated, savagely.

'He will. You know he will.'

'Horace hasn't come back. Gwen's not coming back. Daddy's never coming back. Why should I think Gawain's coming back either? Because he *promised*?'

She was framed by the light of the window. Her shoulders were quivering. Outside, past the thawing field and the black woods below, the wreck at the mouth of the river was an ugly silhouette, the radio mast leaning high over the water like a gibbet.

'I can't say anything to make it better. But it doesn't mean that everything will always be this way. He'll come back when he can. We just have to try and wait.'

She went over to the window and stared out for a long while, as if looking through the bars of a cage.

'Why won't Horace come?'

Owen was glad she wasn't looking at him. 'It must be the weather.' He wasn't much of a liar, but Marina wasn't sophisticated enough to hear the strained lightness in his tone. 'This winter's driven almost everyone away.' He'd never had the heart to tell her that Horace had vanished too, believed lost in the snow. 'He probably had to go with his mother.'

'Go where?'

'Wherever they could. Somewhere it didn't snow and people can still get around, get things they need.'

'He never came to say goodbye. I think he just forgot all about me.'

'It's a hard journey when you can't cross the river.'

'Oh, that's right.' She pressed her nose to the glass. Her tone was as cold, as brittle. 'My mother would have killed him.'

He thought it best not to try answering.

'That's what she does, isn't it? She drowns people.'

The fire simmered, hissed, popped. He knew silence was probably best, but he couldn't stay much longer and he hated the thought of leaving her like this. Whatever she was, half of it was just a thirteen-year-old child alone in a huge cold house.

'Marina. Please listen to me quietly for a moment. You could walk down to the river any time you like—'

She rounded on him, eyes wet with desperate rage. 'Shurrup!'

Who'd taught her to say *shut up*? It could only have been

Horace. 'Maybe you wouldn't feel so lonely if you just went to talk to her once. Even if you shouted at her, showed her how you're—'

'Shurrup! Shurrup!'

Patience, patience. 'She loves you.'

'I don't care!' The house echoed back her shouts in the form of a miserable fading whine. 'I don't care, I don't care!'

'All right. I'm sorry.'

'No you aren't! You just want to make me do what you want.' Her eyes were shining. Water-eyes, whirlpool eyes. 'That's all anyone ever cared about. No, shurrup. I don't want you to talk to me any more. I know what you'll say. Lock the doors. Stay inside. Eat hot food. Go to your mother. I won't do it any more.' She banged her little fists on the back of a chair. 'I won't! I want you to stop coming. Go away!'

Let her vent, he thought. If anyone had a right to their grief and anger this winter, it was her.

She flopped down into the big chair and covered her face with her hands. He knew he'd have to go, very soon. The impulse to go and touch her hair in comfort was almost unendurable. It might only be months before he'd have to do as she said and stop coming altogether. Misery was stripping childhood from her shockingly fast.

'Sorry,' she mumbled, picking at her sleeves.

'Poor old Marina. It's all of us who ought to apologise to you. It'll be all right once Gavin comes back.'

'Gawain,' she corrected, in a whisper.

* * *

The thaw was bringing floods. Meltwater coursed off the moors and the heathland. Frozen deep by months of unremitting winter, the ground was too hard to soak it up. It crammed into the valleys and became a rampant brown froth, tearing at bridges and pylons, covering roads with upended trees. South-west winds lifted moisture from the ocean and emptied it over the peninsula. Stunned into life by the violent spring, clumps of blackthorn bloomed like a white rash.

'Here again, child?'

She climbed down from the bars of the gate at the sound of the voice behind her, placing her feet carefully on the cattle grid. It had been buried in snow so long she'd forgotten it was there. A hint of the evening sun glinted from under hanging western clouds, making the wet world shine. She squelched across the slush-topped snowpack to the bizarre sculpture standing alone near the gate. There was a kind of hollow at its base where her back fitted neatly. She pulled her father's old coat down far enough to sit on and wriggled herself in, tugging her knees up.

'Sing to me,' she said.

'Not now,' the green face above her said.

'Why not?'

'I should speak solemnly this evening. I watch you at the gate and would ask why you stand there so, but I fear your answer.'

She curled up a little more tightly and listened to the dripping and the birdsong.

'Is it true you can't lie?' she said, after a while.

'Am I myself, or another?' Holly answered, imitating the pitch of her voice. 'Are you the daughter of earth or water?'

Again Marina was quiet a long time. She loved the smell of wet bark and the music of Holly's voice, but it always surprised her how cold she was.

'So tell me why I have to stay here. If you can't lie.'

The voice above her ahhhhed, a long sliding tone.

'I cannot,' it said, softly.

'I knew it.'

'You know so little. The world is wide, child.'

'I can't stand it any longer. Just waiting. On my own. I'd rather something bad happened to me.'

'You will not wait long, then.'

'I don't mind. At least it would be . . . Something.' She'd raised her voice resentfully, expecting contradiction, but when Holly finally answered it was in a tone almost rueful.

'You are free,' it said.

Marina peered up and saw the face bent over her, its red unblinking eyes.

'I wish I knew how to set you free too,' she said.

'Ah, child. You were better to stay bound as I am. The world is as wicked as wide.'

'Don't you get lonely?'

'I am not as you are, half-girl. Holly is not half made of wishes and regrets.'

'Then you don't know what it's like. You don't understand what it's like for me here.'

'You are water as well as flesh, child. You can choose

peace, if you wish. You may sit by my roots and hear me sing and no harm will come to you. I cannot be other than I am, but you are free to choose.'

'That's right,' Marina said, eyes on the gate. Owen had chained it shut and nailed plywood over its bars. 'I can do what I want.'

'And have done to you what you do not want.'

On the inside the bars were like a small ladder. She'd perched halfway up them quite a few times now, looking out along the empty alleyway of white running left and right between its neatly parallel hedges: the road outside Pendurra.

'It doesn't hurt me any more,' she said. 'I never used to be able to go by the gate. I couldn't wear Daddy's coat before either, it's got this lining that used to make me tingle. Those things don't bother me now.'

Holly watched her, unreadable.

'Why is that? Why is it different?'

'This is an altered world,' Holly said. 'It can no longer deny you.'

'Yes.' She nodded to herself. 'That's what I thought. I knew it was wrong that everyone tells me I have to go on like I used to.'

'You will not heed me,' Holly said. 'You choose wishes, and regrets.'

'Would you try to stop me? If I climbed over the gate one day?'

'If I could halt you, child, I would hold you here beside me, each of us forever fixed. But I am ward, not gaoler. Your will is your own.'

'Why? Why would you do that? No one ever tells me why. It's just the same as everyone else. Daddy, Gawain, everyone, they all say I have to stay here, it's so important, I mustn't ever go anywhere except Pendurra, but none of them tell me why and then they all went and left me on my own.'

'You wish to learn why?'

'Yes.' She sniffed, wiped her nose on a cuff.

'No wonder, then, that you will not be satisfied.'

Marina was going to protest, but found she couldn't think of an answer. The gleams of watery sunlight were swallowed by the west. The snow took on its twilight plumage, feather-grey.

'Can you sing now?'

The dryad sang.

Fourteen

THE BELL ACROSS the river rang for a long time that night. Lying in her bed she heard a faint impression of faraway clamour. She opened the bedroom window and sat on the stone sill, where she'd sat hundreds of thousands of times. Everything she did, everything in and around the house, had gone stale. The nights were the worst. At night she felt suffocated by the dreadful changeless repetitions of her life, the places she'd sat in and the steps she'd taken and the things she'd touched, all hundreds of thousands of times. At night she was also smitten with appalling memories of the few days of sudden change, when horror and despair had come unannounced to the house. When she did manage to sleep she had awful dreams. And when she woke up the very first thought she had was that she was facing another day on her own, again, hopeless, the hours already wasting away towards the next installment of nightmares.

The distant noise sounded like people shouting to each

other in the night while the bell rang. They must be the people she'd been watching from the roof for the last however many (too many) days, little specks and blobs scuttling around their miniature coloured houses. Owen called them 'pilgrims', a word she loved; it tasted of her favourite kind of books. They were there, he said, because it was where Corbo had been seen. People kept trying to make them leave but they wouldn't go. The sight of Corbo had sent people into a kind of madness, he said, though he couldn't explain it. If she'd known earlier she would have asked Corbo to go and talk to them and find out what they wanted, but Corbo was gone too.

She felt a little tremor of hope. Were they shouting because they'd seen him again? And if he'd come back, then perhaps Gawain had come back too.

The sound of their voices was so small and muffled it was like the noise the ships sometimes made out at sea, but she was astonished to be hearing it at all. People, out there in the world, their mouths making sounds that reached her windowsill. How close they must be, really! Over there where they were was also where Horace lived with his mother, and Horace came all the time, just because he felt like it, as easily as she might walk from one side of her house to the other. How close it must have been for him; how easy!

Used to come.

He wouldn't come in the morning. Nor would Corbo, nor would Gawain. She'd stopped hoping many days ago, weeks ago.

She closed the window and went back to lie on her bed. She wasn't sleepy.

As the next day began – a gusty, showery early March day – she went down to the kitchen as soon as there was enough light to see by and began putting things in a jute bag. She wasn't really thinking about it; she just knew she couldn't endure another night awake, deserted. Gwen used to take her out towards the headland for picnics sometimes, in the old days, so she packed the bag with the kinds of things they used to take on those expeditions. Some things to eat, some extra layers in case she got wet or the weather changed, a book. She was going to put on her small shoes like she would have for a picnic but they turned out not to fit very well. She must have grown a lot since the autumn. The bigger ones took much longer because they laced right up her calves. She heard drizzle spattering in occasional squalls against the windows so she took her father's coat with its pull-up hood even though it was far too big for her. Gwen always used to carry the bag but she'd have to do it herself now. Grey Mouser was off somewhere chasing things to eat. She left the front door open for her, slung the bag across her chest and walked up the driveway.

Holly watched her as she came past the lodge. Only her head moved, neck turning slowly. Marina decided not to come within reach of her limbs just in case. Near the beginning of the snow, Owen said, some people had climbed over the gate and come down the driveway. He'd told Marina that Holly had made them go away. Later she found out the truth: Holly had killed them.

'Goodbye, then,' Marina said, stopping a few yards away. 'So you choose your human half.'

She was never quite sure what Holly was talking about anyway. She'd been glad of the company occasionally, but most of the time she just liked it when Holly sang to her, even if it made her cry. She couldn't think of anything else she'd miss, except maybe Grey Mouser.

Having Holly watching her made it easier to keep going. It would be embarrassing to have packed the bag and got to the gate and end up stopping there. She walked up to the cattle grid. The space beneath it had sunk deeper as all but the last of the snow melted. It had become a pit, clogged with leaves and fragments of broken branches; it yawned up at her with dark strangeness. She wondered whether climbing over the gate would make her die. No more nights awake, then, fighting off the memories and dreading the nightmares. Being dead was a bit like being asleep with only good dreams, Gwen had told her once. There were times she'd wanted that kind of sleep so badly she'd twisted her fists into her pillow and pushed it in her mouth to stop herself screaming.

The only thing that happened when she climbed to the top bar of the gate and swung her legs over was a luminous voice calling behind her.

'Fear men,' it said.

She decided it would be best if she didn't even turn her head.

There was a road beyond the gate. She'd always known that, but she'd never known what it was like. Immediately above its surface it was like anywhere you walked, scattered with twigs and streaks of mud and snow, but the surface itself was almost like a floor, hard and uncomfortably smooth. It went west and east. East would have been towards the sea. She walked along it a few steps the other way. The whole world seemed to unhinge itself. The hedge on her left lowered and a horizon she'd never seen before appeared behind it, enclosing a shapeless chasm of unknown things, everything out of place, wrongly arranged. Her legs went weak and she squatted down on the damp tarmac, shaking, her breathing shallow and fast.

Later she went on another thirty steps, pushing her legs as if she were climbing stairs. The road tilted up and the trees on her right, the Pendurra woods, stopped being there. In all her life she had never been above everything before. There'd always been the valley, folding her and everything else in. A wave of vertigo broke over her. She clutched hard on the strap of her bag, as if it was the only thing keeping her from flying off the ground and disappearing like a wisp of pollen into the enormous sky.

More distances appeared, other expanses of things. They looked a bit like things she knew, backdrops of uneven hills, hedge-bordered and wood-fringed fields, but they *weren't* the things she knew, they were sickeningly strange. There were little buildings scattered like accidents, stark and weirdly shaped as though parts of the houses they belonged to had been cut off. All of it moved when she moved, things appearing and disappearing as if they were made of cloud.

She came to a thing she recognised from illustrations in books: a signpost. It was much taller than she expected. The hard surface she was walking on grew extensions like a branch, splitting into three. Between them was a car that wasn't Gwen's, one of those things she'd learned to fear touching so long ago that coming upon it unexpectedly and out of place gave her a throb of instinctive dread. The words on the signpost, though, were familiar. They made her think of voices she knew, Caleb's way of saying 'Saint Anthony', Horace speaking the word 'Helford'. From here she could see glimpses of the river in the valley below, so narrow and strangely shaped it was almost impossible to know it for the same river and the same valley. Across the river was the place with the bell and the pilgrims, which was where Horace lived, and also the person Gawain had said he was going to see before he went on his long journey. The name of that place wasn't on any of the signpost's four sternly lettered arms, and she couldn't see the tower of the church any more.

There was part of a house down the hill to the south. It looked like a toy house, like the houses in cartoons in magazines, all flat and plain. There were words painted in wobbly, smeary, washed-out white streaks on its roof. The bottom three-quarters of them were hidden by the near hedge but you could still read them: *FORGIVE US*. Someone, she thought, must have gone up there with a ladder and a paintbrush. Someone she didn't know, someone *else*. Other people must live inside that house.

There were four directions: back the way she'd come,

down closer to that house, down the other way towards the river, or on westwards. She thought for a second of standing in the river up to her ankles on a grim December evening. The memory rose like bile. She scrunched up her eyes and fists and hurried west.

She came to a tiny house beside the road, just one room with no door and a bench inside. It was cobwebby and musty with damp. Words had been written inside it too but she didn't understand them. There was a kind of big poster behind a screen of spotted and mouldy glass. It had more writing on it, and a picture, like part of a cartoon. It said not to litter, but she didn't think the message was for her, and the house and the road outside it were filthy anyway, not just with mud. She'd seen coloured bottles and boxes and bits of things she couldn't name poking out of the wet heaps of snow or drowning in puddles of water as brown as her coat. All these words seemed wasted. There was no one anywhere to read them. Earlier on she'd seen the top of some kind of car moving over a hedge in the distance, and heard its sound, a bit like the sound some of the boats on the river used to make, but otherwise the only moving things apart from her were the birds, the trickles of rainwater around her shoes and the clouds.

The bench in the tiny house was made of slats of wood. Exactly half of them were broken (she counted). She sat down and felt the relief of walls close around her, keeping the strange expanse of the world at bay. She got her book out and read for a while.

* * *

It occurred to her that it was actually quite like reading.

When you opened a book, especially if you hadn't read it before, you were somewhere else, somewhere you knew hardly anything about, wondering what would happen. Everything was strange and surprising.

She knew how to start a book, she thought. She'd done that thousands of times.

Not too far past the tiny empty house with no door she came to another crossroads and another signpost. This one was piled around with a slumped pyramid of unnameable things, like a compost pile except made with discarded dead rather than living matter. From two of the signpost's arms hung crudely stuffed sacks draped in ragged clothes. Going closer after a long and wary pause, she saw they had heads too, smaller sacks stitched on top of the big ones. They'd flopped over like the heads of the dolls Gwen used to make. A hat was still just about attached to one of them, dangling feebly, a soaked and misshapen piece of felt. She didn't like them. She wasn't sure which way was which but she ducked down the road to the right because neither of the sack-corpses was hanging from the arm which pointed that way, and because the road there was the narrowest, sheltered by high hedges and overhanging trees. Lots of branches had fallen. She had to clamber around them sometimes as if she was walking in her own woods.

She kept on taking steps, like turning the pages in a book. Sometimes you turned the pages more slowly, sometimes faster. It began to feel as if it was happening by itself. It was more like being inside than outside. The hedges made walls like the long upstairs corridor, and from time to time they were broken by gates like windows, letting her see to one side or the other. As in the corridor, some of those windows looked out into the open, others into groups of buildings like the stables with no house attached, jumbled and empty. One of the gates was closed with a chain and hung with a painted board: *KEEP OUT WE ARE ARMED WE SHOOT FIRST*. She hurried away from that one. It wasn't so much the message that alarmed her as the presence of writing in the emptiness, as if she'd gone out of her bedroom and found the print of an unknown shoe right by the door.

Not long past the closed gate she heard the noise of water running ahead. The green-walled corridor bent steeply down. The sound grew louder and coarser and then she came to a place where the road was gone. Dirty water surged over its edge, racing as fast as if it were being poured out of a bucket. An uprooted tree had wedged itself in the shrubby tangle at the bottom of the slope, choking the flooded stream into ridges and eddies of perpetual angry motion. A boy – she thought it must be a boy; it happened almost too fast for her to see – started up like a surprised bird from one of the boughs of the fallen tree, dropped himself lightly into the water and vanished.

The brief flicker of movement caught her by surprise, but she barely had time to be startled before it was gone. She looked around, at a loss.

'Hello?'

There might have been another skip of dappled shadows

among the half-drowned branches; she couldn't quite see. The boy, if it had been a boy, had dived away as shy as an animal. He must have been a very good swimmer, she thought, to have disappeared so completely in the noisy turbulence.

She waited a while but no one came out to talk to her. The waiting gave her time to wonder whether she ought to look for another way to go. She could see where the road continued, though, up the other side of the small steep valley beyond the stream, and the idea of retracing her steps felt wrong, like turning pages backwards. It might make time run the wrong way too, sending her backwards in her own story until she'd be stuck at Pendurra again, abandoned and desperately unhappy and with nothing to do but wait for the next dreadful night alone. So she took off her shoes and socks and skirt and put them in the bag, hitched up her shift to her waist and felt her way carefully into the water. It tugged at her ankles and then, fiercely, at her calves. She couldn't see where she was putting her feet. She felt the hard surface of the road come to a crumbled stop under her toes. The next shuffling steps took her into mud and stones and brought the stream suddenly up around her thighs. She could tell what it wanted, all of a sudden: it was trying to push her down to the big river below. She resisted. She wasn't a child any more. She steadied her look on the rising road ahead and kept her footing. The deep part was only a handful of small steps across. Her feet found the broken edge of the road again and she clambered swiftly out, breathing hard.

Her shift was all wet around the hem. She always had to

change her shift if it got damp, but of course she didn't have another one to change into. She looked up at the sky. The early morning drizzle had gusted away and the air felt fresh and sharp. She decided the best she could do would be to hang the damp undergarment over a branch for a while until it was at least comfortable to walk in. She wrapped herself in her father's coat and sat down by the water's edge while she waited for the shift to dry.

She was going to read, but she discovered as she opened her bag that she was hungry. A moment later and a series of thoughts worked their way through her for the first time that day: if she ate the picnic now, what would she eat the next time she was hungry? If she finished the book, where would she find another one? How would she wash and dry her clothes when they got smelly? These ideas were so peculiar they almost made her laugh. Where did the road go? Would the next road be different? What would happen in an hour? In two hours? At bedtime?

With the exception of a few unthinkably hideous days at the beginning of that winter, so alien in the memory that they didn't feel like part of her history at all, Marina could not think of a time when she hadn't known what was around the next corner and how the rest of the day would unfold. There was food, there was shelter, there was sleep, all as permanently fixed as the architecture of the house she lived in. These things happened in their natural order like the sun tracking westward.

Sluggishly, she tried to grasp the idea of eating something else, sleeping somewhere else. Those thoughts were like wet and heavy clay. She chewed a corner of cheese. She got the cheese from the larder; that's where it always was. It was there because people brought it. But now she wasn't anywhere near the larder, no one knew where she was, the place she was sitting in didn't have any sort of name and there didn't seem to be any people anyway: what, then, would happen, when she'd eaten it all?

She was wrestling with the peculiar inert weight of this question when she thought the noise of the stream changed, its undertone roughening. She looked up and around and then heard the yapping of an animal. The sounds separated out. It wasn't the water at all: something was coming growling down the road on the far side of the flooded stream, the way she'd come, some kind of car.

A whispery voice close behind her said, 'Hide yourself, half-sister, or follow me to your mother.' She spun around and saw the boy standing in the stream. He'd snuck up on her without a splash. He was wood-brown and wearing no clothes; a mop of hair slicked over him like mud. He didn't wait for any sort of answer but ducked and then somehow dropped or fell back into the current, going down out of sight as easily as a pebble sinking. The car noise became abruptly louder. The roiling of the stream had masked it until it was very close. The yapping was louder still, horribly loud, like someone shouting in a small room. Someone did shout then, a man's muffled yell: 'Shut up, you!' Unable to think for surprise, Marina stood where she was. The front of a dirty blue car bigger than Gwen's came pushing around the last corner before the stream, wheels crunching and snapping the woodland litter on the road. Behind its smeared window Marina saw a face, a face she didn't know. Another face poked out of one of the back windows, a pointy black and white face she recognised as belonging to a dog. The dog barked wildly at her as if trying to throw its head off its own shoulders. Its paws pushed at the top of the window below its neck. The car ground to a stop.

'I said shut it!' She saw the man reach back and aim a slap at the dog. It retreated from the window, still barking, going in circles in the back of the car, clattering so loudly she could easily hear it over the noise of water and engine. She couldn't stop looking at the man's face. He looked like neither Caleb nor Owen nor her father nor Gawain; he didn't look like anyone. He was someone else, an other person, with no name, no place: he was like one of the stuffed sacks hanging from the signpost, an inexplicable baffling copy of the idea of a man, except talking and moving. 'Down! Stow it!'

The dog noise subsided. The man opened the door of his car and climbed out, staring at Marina. She looked around for the boy, wondering whether the two of them knew each other. It felt unlikely, and the boy was nowhere to be seen. For the first time the instruction he'd given her sank in. *Hide yourself.* Where? She felt instinctively that she'd have liked it better if she was hidden, if the man with his own strange face wasn't looking at her, but it was too late for that. She'd have started walking up the road except that she didn't have her shoes and socks on and her shift was still hooked over the point of a crooked branch.

'All right there?' the man said.

'What?' How could he be talking to her when she didn't know who he was?

'I said, you all right?'

Something about the way he spoke made her think of Horace, who used to skip some of the letters as if he was too impatient to say whole words.

'Me? Yes. I got a bit wet. And I was hungry so I thought I'd . . .' She couldn't finish the sentence. The dog had gone into another doggy frenzy. The man banged on the back door of the car with his fist, shouting at it again.

'He don't see too many people in the roads,' he said, turning back to her. 'Where's your mum and dad?'

'I don't know where my mother is.' The stream whistled and clattered steadily but she only had to raise her voice a bit. 'My father's dead. She killed him.'

The man's clothes, like his car, were a faded and dirty blue. He stuck his hands down in pockets, rather like Caleb used to do, but somehow more heavily. Lots of things about him were heavy.

'Brought you down here with them,' he said, 'did they?' He pushed his lips together in what looked like it might have been disappointment. 'Left you on your own. Typical.'

She wasn't sure what he meant by the first bit but she knew the rest was right. It must be obvious to other people that she'd been deserted, or perhaps everyone just knew. His look kept dropping down to her bare legs, as if even his eyeballs were heavy.

'I'm just drying off,' she said.

'You got somewhere to go?'

'What?'

'Who's looking after you? You got someone? 'Course you don't.' His voice dropped to a half-mutter; he'd given up trying to converse with her and was addressing himself instead. 'Soft in the head.'

She didn't like the way he looked and now talked at her. When she talked to the people she knew she could feel herself reflected in them, but with this man it was like she wasn't really there. They had nothing to do with each other and shouldn't be having a conversation at all.

'I'll just put my shoes and socks on,' she announced, and sat down on the road. Putting socks on damp feet was always a struggle. She had to wiggle her knees and lift her feet up.

'Where're you off to, then?'

An answer popped into her head. She said the name of the place where Horace lived, him and the woman Gawain had taken the mask back to. 'Mawnan.' It hadn't occurred to her until then to ask herself exactly where she was going. There was no *where* out here beyond Pendurra. She was just walking away from her own misery, so that something else could happen to her, something involving the people she knew coming back and everything being all right again.

'No good going back there. They all upped sticks and gone. Won't be any of your lot left by tomorrow. Hey. You hear me? You won't find no one there. What's your name?'

'Marina.'

'That's nice. Hey. How about you come with us? That's an idea. We can look for mummy. Eh?'

'No,' she said, 'thank you.' She started on the other sock.

'It's all right. Just drive around till we find mummy and then she can take you home. Nice and warm in the car. You like doggies? Want to see Alfie?' The dog broke into hysterics again. 'Shut up!' When he shouted at the dog she could hear in his voice that he wanted to hurt it.

'I'm not cold,' she said.

'Come on now. Can't go wandering around on your own.' The man took a couple of steps towards her, the stream curling over the tips of his boots. He beckoned. 'You'll be all right now. I've got some food. Eh? Food?'

She pushed her feet into the shoes, which were at least dry. She decided not to say anything else at all. They didn't have anything to talk about. She pulled the lacing tight and knotted it hurriedly, stood up and lifted her shift from where it was hanging.

'No you don't,' the man said, and came a couple more steps towards her, as if he'd failed to notice the torrent between. He sprang back with a snarl. 'Oi! Aren't you listening? I'm trying to help you!' He'd never said that. She started up the slope without saying goodbye. The dog pushed its head out of the open window and yapped at her back. She heard the man bang the car door behind him. Its engine roared. The yapping turned into a mad avalanche of barking. She looked back, alarmed, and saw the car charge forward into the water. Its front slumped abruptly and nosed down into the deep stream. The engine sputtered and stopped. As she hurried away she left the car tilted and half overrun like one of the river wrecks. The man and the dog were shouting at each other inside, their voices blended into a single barrage of rage.

Another high crossroads, four unknown names on the sign-posts, a confusion of fields and valleys and buildings and stripes and smears of lingering snow in every direction, nothing to distinguish any of them. However far she went, they only seemed to rearrange themselves like the bits in a kaleidoscope. Her feet told her she'd walked a long way, probably as far as from the house to the point and back, and yet she hadn't seemed to get anywhere at all; she was just shaking the bits around.

Without her shift on the coat chafed. She'd been hurrying to get away from the car and the shouting man. She started to feel tired and a bit uncomfortable. Normally when she got tired and uncomfortable she just stopped, but when she tried to sit down and read she found she couldn't concentrate.

She thought seriously about going back. She thought about what a relief it would be to stand inside the gate of Pendurra and have everything she looked at, in every direction and in every detail, fall back into perfect changeless place, so perfect that when she closed her eyes for a moment and thought about it she could see the outline of each individual tree in her mind's eye.

Then she remembered how unhappy she was. With that, an unexpected thought came over her.

She realised that actually, now, she wasn't unhappy, not at that moment. She was a little tired and quite uncomfortable and more than a little frightened, but she wasn't unhappy. Not at all. The misery was back behind her with all the other things that stayed in place.

She heard the barking of the dog again, quite far away. She put the book back in her bag and carried on the way she'd been going.

At the bottom of the next dip in the road the flood was a kind of lake rather than a stream. The woods were thicker and taller here. A pair of ducks circled around the shallows. Some unfamiliar things occupied the water as well: three big cylinders of rusty metal and a decaying soggy lump which Marina couldn't work out at all until she saw the shape of a withered head and resolved it into some long-drowned animal. The rain had started again, plinking through the bare trees and making circle patterns on the water. She didn't mind walking in it but she didn't know where to put her shift so it would have a chance to dry out. Or rather she did know: you hung it up on the rack in the kitchen. But there was no kitchen.

She waded through the flood, which turned out to be deeper and faster moving than it looked, though still easy enough for her to manage. Then, since there was no point stopping to let things dry when it was raining, she wiped her feet off on her shift and got back into her still slightly damp socks and shoes and went on. The light had changed, not just because of the showery clouds. It was more spread out, higher overhead. With a small shock she realised time was passing. Despite the fact that she was wandering in this non-world where nothing was properly itself, the morning had, in fact, become the afternoon, as if everything was normal.

Her road ended. It did so by emptying into another road, a much wider one, with much lower hedges on the sides. She stopped at the junction, halted by a new kind of uncertainty. It hadn't occurred to her that the road would stop. She was just getting used to it. She'd assumed it was the one taking her wherever it was she was going, leading on towards whatever was going to happen to her.

Only at that point did it strike her fully that she was *lost*, that she didn't know where she was, that she was a point in space with no knowable relation to any other point.

She sat down to calm herself and tried to organise what she knew of the world. She'd looked at maps: ones that showed everything, like the big globe on its lovely noiseless axis in her father's study, and ones that only showed a few things. She knew that the sea was to the east, that the river ran east and west, that the church tower with the ringing bell and the field of straggling pilgrims was across the river to the north. But she could see none of those things, the river, the sea, the church, not even a hint of them. The sky told her west was sort of ahead of her but that didn't help her with *here*, wherever here was. Here there was no north or south or east or west at all. Here was just a floating somewhere or other on which she was drifting like a castaway.

She began to feel much more afraid.

She chose one direction along the new road. It was much worse to walk along. Its width was unfriendly; it made her feel small, like an ant crossing a path for people. After a little while she saw a house right by the road, right on top of it, walls and windows overlooking where she was walking. She stopped at once, turned, and went the other way. The same thing happened, though now it was a different house, but still unmistakably a place for people to live. The windows were evenly spaced rectangles like wide sad unblinking eyes, like a drawing of a house in a book. One of the huge-wheeled tall cars she knew they used on farms was leaning into the hedge opposite it, at an angle which suggested it would have a hard time getting out. She'd seen things like that at a distance already, houses, farm machines. She hadn't yet seen them close. Their strangeness loomed huge. She turned away again, went back to the junction and sat down in the trickle of rainwater flowing over the surface of the road, feeling hopeless. She looked back down her road, the one she almost liked now. It was like a string attaching her to Pendurra, the gate, Holly, the house, the cat, the fire.

Then she remembered the man and dog and their car, stuck now in the middle of it, snipping the string.

The problem of what she was going to do became immediate. What was she going to do *now*?

Now, like *here*, had nothing to it; it was empty; it was like reaching for the banister in the dark and finding nothing. She felt her breath coming faster. The rain intensified. Its noise in the branches mocked her with phantom familiarity: *I am a thing you think you know.*

After a while she decided she ought to try finding a sign that pointed to where Horace lived, or a person who knew where he was. Horace had always loved to tell her things about the world, before he'd stopped coming to see her (without even a goodbye). Though she wondered now whether all of it had been lies, like the other things people had lied to her about, her father and Gwen telling her they'd always love her and look after her, Gawain promising he'd stay with her always. Gwen had always told her the world was full of people, so many that the number of them was actually impossible to think about. Where were they? She thought there were supposed to be cars in the roads and dwellers in the houses. She'd read about them. Owen had talked about everyone else having to abandon where they lived because of the snow and not having any food or warmth, but most of the snow was gone now. There must be someone who knew where she was supposed to go next.

She went back on to the wider road and walked along it again until she reached the less tiny of the overlooking houses. She watched it for a while, looking for firelight in the windows, or smoke from the chimney, but it was as quiet as a doll's house. She went closer, step by slow step. The strangeness of it, the differentness, seeped out of its stones. They were yellow-brown like stream pebbles, the wrong colour for a house. The wood of the window frames was rotten and the windows themselves were sheets of flat darkness. She made herself walk in front of them. Beyond the house a gate opened off the road into a sort of courtyard, like the stable yard but smaller and with the stables open sided and haphazard. The side windows of the house were cracked with patterns like spider webs. Filthy greying snow filled the edges and corners of the yard. In the middle of it was a pile of charred things like an oversized half-finished campfire. The charring spread out from it too, burnt scraps and fragments stuck in the snow or glued by damp to the buildings or snagged in the hedge by the gate. One of them caught her eye: a shred of paper with a picture on it, blackened and sodden and caught in the twigs but not yet completely erased. She noticed it because she saw a glimpse of a crumpled face. It pricked her eye with a minuscule jab of recognition. She bent down and poked at the scrap where it was buried in the hedge. Part of it disintegrated limply at her touch, but she was able to straighten it enough to see the face fully. In that ocean of difference she identified it immediately as the remains of a thing she'd seen before. Gwen showed it to her sometimes: the rectangle of blue-green coloured paper with swirly patterns and portentous words and a big number five and the head of the old woman who was supposed to be a kind of pretend queen although she didn't look even slightly queenly, despite the crown.

Marina didn't like to think of when Gwen might have come this way, or why someone might have set fire to her piece of paper with all the other things. She didn't like to think about what had happened to Gwen at all. Even starting to remember it hurt her, a very particular kind of pain, an involuntary twist and wrench as if the bad memory was a small beast that had taken up residence in her guts and attacked her unless she pretended it wasn't there. She walked faster, leaving the empty house behind. The rain drummed an insistent rhythm. Her wet feet were beginning to rub.

Descending steadily, the new road went under taller trees. The familiar smell of wet oaks and alders swamped her so intensely that she wondered whether her path had turned her around and was about to deliver her back to the Pendurra woods. She pulled the hood of her coat forward to keep the rain out of her eyes and trudged on, glad to be going downhill, until an abrupt whoosh of heavy wingbeats made her look over her shoulder. A pair of swans came flying over the brow of the hill behind her and wheeled down behind the trees ahead.

Only then did she realise she'd been led to the bank of the river.

The road kinked around a steep corner and went right down to a creek mouth, a wood-fringed pocket of flat water opening out on to the tidal expanse beyond. She knew it was the river, the same one, even though it was far narrower than she'd ever seen it before and the shape of the land on the far bank was all wrong too. The differences melted away in face of its serene certainty. The water she was looking at through a screen of trees was flowing slowly seawards and would pass under the lookout where she'd sat a hundred thousand times, and then around the headland where she'd been on a hundred thousand walks and picnics. It was as familiar as a face.

She stopped and looked away, balling her fists in the pockets of her father's coat.

For three months she'd refused to sit at the lookout or walk to the head or go anywhere in sight of the river.

Her heart was beating hot. She looked behind her, back up the steep hill. Apart from the rain and the thudding in her ears everything was calm.

She remembered how the other road had always gone down and then up, dropping to the swollen streams and then climbing away from them. She told herself it would be all right, this one would be the same. She made herself look across the ribbon of water. Nothing stirred. The upended bows of two or three sunken boats stuck up out of the water, but otherwise nothing disturbed it but the pecking of the rain. She put her head down and carried on.

She followed the road to the edge of the creek. It turned sharply there to cross the inlet before rising away from the bank. There had been a bridge at the crossing, a stone hump barely wide enough for a single car. She saw the arc of stone lying cracked and sideways in the water. The road tipped up into empty space. The bridge had washed away.

She walked right up to the crumbled lip. The creek seethed below her, milky brown with the earth it dragged away for drowning. It had come far up over its banks; she could tell that by the trees that must once have overlooked it but now stood feet from dry land. The broken edge of the bridge on the other side might as well have been the far bank of the river itself, for all the chance she had of crossing. The road had led her nowhere: a dead end.

The rain gained a voice.

'Marina!'

She whirled around. Out in the river a white shape was gathering, a shape that made her heart stall. A white body came gliding up out of the water, cresting it like a swan.

'Daughter!'

It rose like a wave, effortless and fast. It seemed to be made of the marriage of rain and river. It held out its arms. The beast woke again in Marina's stomach, seized something tender, and bit. She doubled over, dropping to her knees.

'Child, my child! Marina!'

She shut her eyes tight. She heard the voice coming closer but couldn't look, or wouldn't.

'Dear heart.' The voice was so like the rain, full and hollow at the same time. 'What possessed you to try your luck in this world of men and women? Come to me now. Come, be safe.'

She bit her lip to stop herself moaning aloud at the suddenly ferocious pain.

'Marina? Won't you even look at me? Can you still not forgive me?' The voice was close below now. It had turned soft. 'But here you are. You've come at last, beloved. Thank you. Look at me now. I want you to see my promise. I'll do nothing to hurt you again. I'll keep you with me always. Child, poor child, was there no one to tell you you can't live in the wasteland? Take my hand, Marina. Come. Open your eyes.'

Marina opened her eyes.

Her mother was standing at the edge of the flooded creek, white and green like another half-drowned willow. The rain smoothed over her as if there was no difference between its substance and hers. She seemed to be flowing down into the water where she stood, at rest yet in motion like the river itself. She held her arms out, white fingers taut. She was perhaps three of those arms' length away from where Marina crouched on the broken road.

'I waited for you every day.' Her words dribbled over Marina and puddled away. 'I know how hard your sadness must be and I waited to comfort you as a mother should. Every day, dearest child. And not one day would you come to me. You've been cruel.' At the word *cruel* Marina twitched, plucking the soggy cuffs of her coat in her fists. 'I was wild with fear for you. We wrecked every vessel that approached your shore. We drowned every man. It was all to keep you safe, dear heart.'

Marina could smell her now. It was an old, mysteriously familiar smell which had once made her happy, the particular tang of pebbles in running water. She and Gwen used to sit beside the stream, counting things and making paper boats.

'You're growing into my daughter. I can see it in you. Men can see it. They will love you, and not know why, and want to hurt you for it. Your time has come to leave them behind. Everything will be well in the water, dearest. No one will injure you again. You and I will love only each other, always.' Swan-graceful, swan-smooth, she slipped along the water. Only her ankles now made eddies in the flow. She held her arm up. 'Come.'

'Don't touch me!'

Marina sprang to her feet. Her fists trembled beside her. She screamed again. 'Get away from me!'

'Daughter—'

'How can you call me that?' Bending at the waist as if she might spit at her mother, she hammered her hands against her own thighs. 'How can you even speak to me? How dare you?'

The wind gathered and began to moan.

'I don't want to be your daughter. I don't want to be anything like you!' Swanny stood frozen in the water like an alabaster offering. 'How can you call me cruel? Me? Me?'

'Marina.' Agitated wavelets ruffled the river. Slanted by the sudden gust, the cold rain spattered into the girl's eyes. 'Spare me.'

'You're nothing to me. I wish you were dead like everyone said. I wish Daddy had killed you! Shurrup! Go away!' Stumbling, she spun around. The road skirted the edge of the riverbank; she blundered away from it, heading into the trees. There was an overgrown track there, rising away from the mouth of the creek. It was little more than a trough of leaf-strewn black mud but it was earth, it was under cover. 'Don't say anything!' She lunged towards the track, half blind with tears, her limping steps like furious punctuation. 'I'll never come near the river again! You'll never see me again! Never, ever!' The gnawing misery down in her core twisted and writhed and wrenched as if it wanted to slay her through sheer despair. 'Never! Never!' Behind her, in the river, an awful howl was rising. The abrupt wind bent and clattered the trees. 'I want Gawain!' She couldn't stand up. She ran hunched as if about to drop on all fours. 'Gawain!' Her feet sank in the mud but she drove herself on blindly, caring only that she was going away from the river, away from everything that lived in it, everything that had died in it. Weeks of pent-up grief burst out in a flood. 'Gawain!' she cried, but even his name only fed the terrible memory, the one she was no longer strong enough to fend off. She saw it behind the veil of tears which had turned the world blurry: coming scampering back to the cove, steering the wooden box so carefully in her two hands, proud of herself for having spilled hardly any of the well water at all, and then looking up and down and up the shore again in the fading light, her father gone.

Fifteen

HOURS LATER, MARINA dragged herself out of the darkening wood into a patch of open space sheltered by lines of cypress and yew. She was black with mud from shoes to thighs and all up her forearms. She'd fallen many times, and sat crying almost as many, hugging the jute bag to her chest, too broken to bother pushing herself farther along the forest path, until the tears ran out and there was nothing else to do. The track wound a long way through those woods, always ascending and always soft and heavy underfoot. By the time it came out at the bottom of what had once been a garden she was so exhausted she could have dropped on the grass in the rain and gone to sleep with only the coat for covering. There was a gap in the wall of yews, though, with a set of stone steps leading up, and beyond them a low building with an overhanging shelter. She saw and heard rainwater spilling down from a broken gutter.

She limped up the steps into a ruined square of converted

farm buildings. The bowl of the fountain in the middle of the square still held a well of snow. She stepped around broken glass and flowerpots and a stack of green plastic chairs tipped across once-neat rows of box and lavender. She could still smell the box, but the lavender was dead, twisted clumps the colour of bone. Wires drooped from a tall pole at one corner. She put her mouth under the spout of rainwater and drank; then she took off her coat and shoes and socks and stood under it, scratching at herself until most of the mud was gone from most of her skin. The door to one two-storey brown building across the square was open a crack. It was warped and jammed; she had to bang it with her palms to get the crack wide enough for her to slip in. The room beyond was a shadowy mess of things ransacked and upended and abandoned. She found a checked tablecloth. It smelled of stale water and mould. She wrapped herself up in it, lay down on a patch of rug in a corner and curled herself tight as a cat.

The rain eased. A fresh evening wind came up out of the south-west and swept the last of it away. Gaps opened in the clouds. While Marina slept, the descending sun found one of those gaps. For the last few minutes before dusk its light streamed slantwise across the freshly rinsed country like a volley of golden arrows. They poured in through a defence-less window and stung the sleeping girl in the face.

The first few times she woke up it was quiet as well as completely dark, the silence almost as perfect as the darkness. There was just the far-off sound of water running for her to listen to. She could almost have been asleep on the floor of her own bedroom, except the smells were wrong.

Then, one time, different noises happened. Scrunching and scraping, like Daddy and Caleb coming back inside late, their footsteps rough in the gravel below her bedroom window and their conversation too quiet to hear properly. She heard whispering as well as scrunching. Not Daddy and Caleb, because they were both gone and she didn't know where she was.

Glimmers of white light appeared in a window, too small and high up for her bedroom windows, and in the wrong place. For a second the square of dirty glass flared bright as the beam of the lighthouse across the bay.

There were people outside, with torches. She recognised torchlight. Gwen used to walk back to her house with a torch in the winter evenings. Marina wasn't supposed to touch it.

The people mumbled to each other. One mumble sounded a bit like Caleb, but the other was completely different, and even the one that sounded like Caleb wasn't right. They were other people, people she didn't know about.

'You have a look in there,' muttered the slightly Caleb-like voice. Marina was completely awake now. The torchlight fixed on the jammed door. A white sliver came through the crack, lighting up a crazy arrangement of objects and shadows. She felt her heart beating very fast.

'What about you?' The other voice was much thinner and higher.

The light swung away, leaving her in blackness again. 'That was the shop, over that way. I'll have a look in there.'

'I'll come with you.'

'In a bit. You see what you can find in that one first. It looks like where they lived. Might have left stuff behind.' Back came the torchlight.

'By myself?'

'I told you. I can't fit.'

'Let's break down the door, then.'

'Don't be stupid.'

'It's not stupid.'

'You want someone to hear us? In you go and have a quick look, go on.'

'You said there's no one here, Dad.'

'What's wrong? Scared?'

'I don't want to go on my own.'

'Could have thought of that before you said you wanted to come. It's too late now to mess around.'

The two of them scrunched closer, double torchlight wobbling all around the slender crack of the open door. Marina burrowed herself behind a toppled chair.

'Please, Dad.'

'What are you so bloody frightened of? You can bloody well stay at home from now on if you're going to be like this. Get in.'

'Can you wait right outside?'

'No I bloody well cannot wait right outside. Next time I'm letting your sister come. You're more a baby than she is.'

One of them banged against the door.

'Shhhh!'

'You said no one's here!'

'Could be anyone about, couldn't there? What did I say right at the start? You keep bloody quiet!' There was a scuffle, and an angry whimper. 'Don't forget upstairs too. There were six or seven of them, must have had a few rooms. Check them all, right? Properly now. If you're out in less than five minutes you'll have some trouble.'

Marina held herself completely still. The room darkened again, because someone was squeezing themselves through the door. She could hear them breathing. Then, a moment later, the torchlight was inside. It swept shakily around.

'There's nothing in here, Dad,' the thin voice called, so close it could have been on top of her. Its owner shuffled around on the far side of the tumbled chair. 'It's all just junk.' A girl's voice, squeaky and nervous.

'Stop bloody shouting! Upstairs. Five minutes. Every room, all right?'

'All right.'

'See? Nothing to be scared of.'

'Stay there.'

'Come over when you're finished. I'll be looking in the shop. Five minutes. I'm counting.'

'Dad! Stay there!'

The outside steps scraped away.

'Dad!' said the close voice. 'Dad!' The whisper hissed with fear.

'I hate you,' it went on, a bit later, now a shaky mumble. The light began to sway around the room again, poking into corners. 'Hate you. Hate you.' The girl moved deeper into the room. She was still breathing too fast. 'No one's here. I'm not going. Stupid . . . stupid . . .' She pushed at something, another chair maybe, making it grind against the floor. 'Stupid junk. I hate . . .'

Marina sat unmoving, listening to the mumbling and the shuffling. The taint of strangeness so close to her almost made her choke. She felt she ought to say something, but how could she, when she had no idea at all who this other person was? The stranger went upstairs after another minute or two. There was some hesitant banging and scraping above, feet moving back and forth for a while, and then the almost-familiar sound of creaking stairs again.

Marina stole a look from behind her chair. The staircase was down a short corridor on the far side of the room. She saw the light coming down it and, before the torch swung straight along the corridor and made her duck out of sight, glimpsed the person who held it: a girl smaller than herself, with anxious eyes and a half-open mouth.

The other girl had stopped whispering. She came back close to where Marina was and then squeezed herself out the jammed door.

Marina couldn't think of anything to say or do, and couldn't possibly have got herself back to sleep, so she sat in the darkness, feeling for her bag. By touch she itemised its contents: book, piece of hard bread, onion, shift, extra socks, cabbage leaf, extra skirt, half-chewed length of salsify. The shift was still damp. She felt around for a surface to hang it over. She couldn't find her shoes or jumper or coat, until she remembered taking them off before washing herself under the gutter outside. Would they still be there where she'd dropped them? That was how it worked in the places she knew. If you put something down in the hallway or the kitchen or under one of the garden trees, it would stay there until you picked it up again, unless Gwen or Daddy or Caleb tidied it away. She had no faith that it would be the same here. The world around her felt shapeless and loose, liquid not solid.

The voices with their torches came back. Even before they were close enough for her to distinguish words, Marina could tell their tone had changed, whispery excitement now instead of anger and fear.

'Here,' said the father's voice, when they stopped outside the jammed door.

'Won't that make a lot of noise?'

'Never mind that. Only way to break it. Make sure you don't hold back. Once or twice really hard and the lock'll snap just like that. Don't go tapping it like a girl now. Hold it like this. Then you give a proper whack with the hammer.' One torch swung up and down. 'Proper whack. See?'

'What if it doesn't break?'

'Wedge this in, nice hard whack there, it'll break in one go. Easy.'

'Yeah, but—'

'Just give it a go. That's a girl. A proper go, now. Then you tell me what you find.'

'Is there going to be food?'

'Food? No. Not in a bloody filing cabinet. Least I bloody hope not. This lot were such bloody freaks, who knows what they did. Probably just papers and such.'

'Why can't we leave it, then?'

''Cause it's locked. See? You don't lock something if it ain't valuable.'

'Can you sell papers on eeee-bay?'

'We'll see, all right? Go on, then.'

'Wait here, Dad?'

'Right here. Hurry up. Proper whack, remember. Imagine you're hitting that teacher.'

The girl wriggled in through the crack again. This time she went straight upstairs. A few moments later, and there came a splintering metallic crack and a squeak of pain.

The father outside put his face to the opening and hissed, 'Amber?'

'Did it in one, Dad,' Amber shouted from upstairs, too proud of herself to whisper.

'Good girl. What d'you find?'

'Paper. Oh, Dad!'

'What?'

'Dad, come up here!'

'I can't bloody come up there, I can't get through the bloody door.'

'There's a box!'

'What sort of box?'

The girl came jogging down the stairs, torchlight bouncing. She hurried to the door. 'Look,' she said. 'It might be money.'

Something rattled.

'Give us the hammer and chisel,' the man said.

'I'll do it in here.'

'No you won't. Give us. Now.'

The girl squeezed out again. There was another crack, a tinny rattle, then a silence.

'Just more papers,' the man said, his voice flat.

'They look old,' the girl said.

'Official stuff.'

'What's that?'

'For lawyers.'

'Who's lawyers?'

'Doesn't matter any more,' the man said, and grunted a kind of laugh.

'Can we sell them on eeee-bay?'

'Will you shut up about bloody eBay? There's no more bloody eBay either. Here. What's this?'

'That's a Jesus.'

'We'll take that. Might be silver.'

'There's something else.'

Marina heard paper being pushed around. The people outside went quiet again for a few seconds.

'Acorn,' said the man.

'What's it made of?'

'What's it made of? It's made of bloody tree, it's a bloody acorn.'

'Can we sell it on . . . Can we sell it?'

''Course we can't, idiot. They grow, don't they.'

'Why'd they hide it in a box, then?'

'How the bloody hell do I know? They were all bloody nutters living here. Bloody Christians. Probably their holy acorn.'

'Should we take it?' Amber asked. 'If it's holy?'

Her father took a while to reply. 'What else d'you find?'

'Nothing.' She said it *nuffing*, like Horace did; Marina wondered for a moment whether these people might know where he'd gone, and whether she ought to go out and ask them. 'Just books and stuff.'

'What sort of stuff? I told you to have a proper look.'

'Just books.'

The man grunted. 'Might do for burning. All right. The good stuff's up in the big house anyway. Let's have a look. Come on.'

'What about that acorn?'

'Rubbish.' His voice was farther away already. 'You'd better learn what's rubbish and what isn't if you want to keep coming with me.'

'Dad! Wait!'

Then all she could hear was footsteps and mumbles, and then nothing except the steady clatter of the flooding stream. She worried for a while that she'd missed her chance to find out about Horace or the village where he lived, but when she tried to imagine feeling her way out from her dark corner and saying hello she couldn't do it. There was no background, nowhere to start. She'd hardly understood anything the girl and her father had said to each other. She knew all the words but they didn't add up, like a nonsense poem. Only the acorn stuck in her head. She curled herself up again, thinking of the word, *acorn*, a small, hard, solid living thing. She remembered what an acorn felt like in her hand, and in her head too: the wonder of knowing what grandeur lay hidden in a thing small enough to fit under her tongue.

She didn't remember it becoming light so she supposed she must have slept. She felt achy and tired and hungry, not at all the way waking up usually felt. She tried reading for a bit like she normally did in the morning before going down for breakfast but it didn't help. There was nowhere to go down to. There was no breakfast. She wasn't even wearing her pyjamas.

She did find her shoes and socks and coat and jumper outside, lying in a puddle. She wondered who'd have been stupid enough to leave clothes in a puddle, and why someone hadn't picked them up and put them away. It took her a few minutes to arrive at the idea that they were there because that was where she'd dropped them the night before; the night had come and gone and they'd stayed where they'd been put and now they were wet and smelly, especially the jumper. This kind of thinking – *this, then that, so the next* – was called *logic*, and she'd always liked it before, when she'd been doing maths or puzzles with Gwen. Now it seemed dingy and horrible. She hadn't meant to ruin her clothes, so why were they ruined?

Her shift had dried out a bit so she put that on instead, though it was getting smelly too. She had spare socks in the bag, and her shoes weren't too bad on the inside. There was a pickled onion left, going soft. She ate the bits that weren't mushy.

She wondered where to go to pee. The room was like a

room from a doll's house before you arranged it, or after Grey Mouser had stuck a paw in and knocked everything over. There was proper furniture, chairs and things, but lying around so you couldn't use any of it. A lot of it was sideways or upside down. There were pictures on the wall like pages from oversized books, big sheets of paper stuck on with tape or pins. She didn't recognise the places or the words on them, except for one which showed a sort of glowing sunrise over a mountain and had the words 'I am the RESURRECTION and the LIFE' printed along the bottom. That was a line from a book she'd read once. She remembered it because she'd had to ask Daddy what *resurrection* was.

Outside there were other buildings arranged around a square of mess. If someone had thrown together in one space the untidiest bits of the garden, the inside of the stable and the old office, added some other things that didn't belong and then poured water over the whole pile, they might have ended up with something like this square. A tall wooden pole was attached to the side of one building, and pieces of thick black cord trailed down from the top of it, snaking through the mess like the first abandoned threads of a giant cobweb.

One of the things by her feet was a battered metal box with a broken padlock. Sheets of typewritten paper were stacked inside it, and more stray sheets lay around, wet and disintegrating. She looked at them.

This, then that. All the things she sort of remembered from the night must have happened, here, where she was standing. She remembered the man and the girl talking about boxes and papers and breaking locks. The two of them had vanished as completely as dreams but their words had left traces behind, like writing: a box, papers, a broken lock.

She found a corner of the mess to squat in. From there she saw a proper house farther up the slope, tall, grey and rain-streaked. She walked up a sort of path towards it and came out in an area of leaf-strewn grass so wet underfoot that every step sucked at the heel of her shoe. The windows of the house were mostly broken. She walked around it a couple of times until something sank in. *No one lives here.* Some of the other things the man and girl in the dark had said came back to her, and she put the pieces together: *people lived here once but not any more.* It was the same as Gwen's house. Gwen had lived there once, when it had been neat and whole and warm; now it was wrecked and burned and Gwen was gone.

What had happened to Pendurra (she shivered and closed her eyes and made little noises between her clenched teeth to stop herself thinking about it) must have happened everywhere else too, then. Horror and ruin. Abandonment. Owen had been telling her stories like that but she'd only thought of them as stories before, if she'd even been listening.

The wind blew, and in a moment or two the sun came out, low in the sky, turning the wet world into a dazzle too bright to look at. It made Marina think about drying out her clothes, so she went back down to the messy buildings. Across the square from the one with the jammed door where she'd slept there was a windowsill and a patch of wall beneath catching the full force of the sun. She took her soggy jumper over and was arranging it to hang there when she happened to look in through the cracked glass above the sill. A man stood inside, looking back at her.

Marina froze.

The man wasn't like Daddy or Caleb or Owen, but he wasn't like the man who'd been shouting at the dog either; he was yet another person, different again. He had a strong face, and eyes that were hard to look at, intense and unforgiving. He was standing in a corridor which was dusty and dirty and cold looking but he himself seemed somehow bright and clear. Maybe that was because of his coat: it was as yellow as the sunlight. Or maybe it was just the way he was standing, still, arms at his sides, as if nothing could make him uncomfortable.

'Hello,' she said. She'd been standing holding her wet jumper for a while, and it felt odd not saying anything. The man didn't answer.

'Do you live here?' she said. 'Sorry.'

He opened his mouth. His teeth were very straight.

'I am,' he began. His voice was lovely, full, slow; he spoke as if reading aloud from a book, with that funny emphasis nobody ever used in normal talking. But he only said those two words. Perhaps he'd forgotten how the book started.

Marina felt awkward. 'I was just going to hang up my jumper here. In the sun.'

'The sun,' the man repeated, and took a step towards the window. He bent down and put his face to a gap in the glass. His skin wasn't speckly like grown-up skin, but smooth looking like her own, except browner, as if he'd been sunbathing. But it was definitely a grown-up face.

'To dry out,' she explained, wondering whether she was doing something wrong. She felt, suddenly, much younger. She had a memory she hadn't thought of for a very long time: she remembered how she used to be a little scared of Caleb, when she only came up to his waist. 'I'm going soon,' she said, looking away.

'You're lost,' he said.

She thought it was a bit of a rude thing to say, although as soon as he said it she knew it was the truth. 'I'm going to Mawnan,' she muttered, not wanting to admit he was right.

'You don't know the way.'

'I'll ask someone.'

'Ask me. I know the roads.'

'Do you? Is this your house?'

He smiled, very beautifully. 'No.' He disappeared from the window. She heard him stepping through clutter in the building, and he came out through an empty door frame into the open square. The sunlight seemed to gather around him. She felt thin and grubby, like another piece of the discarded wreckage underfoot.

'I just stopped here to wash the mud off and go to sleep. Do you want me to go away?'

He looked down at the mess, then bent and picked something up in his fingers. He held it up to the sunlight for both of them to see: an acorn. He smiled again, with obvious pleasure.

'Oh,' Marina said. 'Were you looking for that? Some people found it in that box in the night. They must have thrown it away.'

'Away,' he echoed again, though in his deliberate rich voice it sounded like two words, *a way*. 'I know the ways.'

Horace was always telling her that she didn't know anything. She'd always suspected it was something he did to make himself feel bigger and older and cleverer than her even though he was none of those things, not that she minded. She'd never guessed that it would turn out to be literally true: outside Pendurra she didn't seem to be able to understand anything anyone said, even when the words were as plain as anything.

'The way to Mawnan?'

'All the ways. All roads. I am . . .'

'I'm Marina,' she said, to fill what had become (for her at least) a rather embarrassing silence.

'You are double,' he said, 'and lost. I'll send you a guide. What do you have to offer me?'

'Did you say a guide?'

'Yes.'

'To Mawnan?'

'Wherever you're going.'

This bit she was sure she understood properly. 'Really? Now? Here?'

'Here,' the man said, 'and today.' He put the acorn in the pocket of his jacket.

'That would help,' she said. 'Thank you.'

'Thank me.' He made it sound like a command. 'And make an offering.'

She fingered the sleeve of her shift nervously. 'Do you mean give you something?'

'Yes.'

Once more she thought he was being rather rude. On the other hand, when he put it that way, so simply, she felt she didn't have a choice. It was again like when she'd been smaller and the grown-ups made things so just by saying them.

'I don't really have anything. Sorry. I only brought some clothes and food. And a book. There's a bit of cheese left?'

'You have your maidenhead.'

Half understanding, half not, she felt her face going hot. She looked away.

'Or there's lots of stuff here,' she mumbled, waving at the mess. 'I could try and find something nice.'

'There's no offering more precious,' he said, 'since it's only given once. I'll help you in return. You're lost, and alone, and I am the helper. Where I am, roads meet. Who do you want to speak with?'

'I'm sorry,' she said. 'I don't understand. I think I ought to go.'

'Come with me.' She looked back involuntarily and saw that he was holding out a hand.

'No.' She crossed her arms. 'Thank you.'

'This way.' He hadn't moved. The hand looked twice the size of hers.

'I don't want to give you that,' she said, her head bowed.

'Shall I tell you a story, Marina? Look.' His voice seemed to pull her chin up. His hand was flat now, and the acorn was resting on the palm; he'd taken it out without her seeing. 'A woman fled from me once. She took this, this seed. She fled by night, hiding. She fled here. She prayed for deliverance and hid, for two summers and a winter. In the next winter I came. I came, I fell on her as the sunlight falls on this wall. I am necessity. I am what happens. Come, then. Your tribute is accepted and I will give you what you want and need.'

'You're not a man at all. You're like my mother.'

'I am,' he began, closing his palm over the acorn: but instead of him saying anything else a bell began to ring.

It was startling enough to make Marina jump. It wasn't muffled and echoey like the bell in the church tower across the river; it was sharp, snapping on and off in a regular rhythm, and loud.

'What's that?' It sounded like it was inside one of the buildings, where she'd first seen the bright strong not-man.

'Someone calling you,' he said. 'Come and answer.' He turned and went back in the open doorway. She was relieved to see him go, and yet when she started moving herself she found that she was going the same way.

The building had a floor made out of hard squares stuck together. There were more chairs, thin metal ones, and other things like big white cupboards with no doors. There were boards with white writing on them but she didn't stop to look. The ringing was even louder inside, unpleasantly insistent and repetitive and shrill. It was coming from a corridor beyond the big room she'd entered. The not-man in the yellow coat beckoned from that direction.

'What's that?' She almost shouted to make herself heard over the sound. 'Can you make it stop? Please?'

'You can.' He was standing next to a dull yellow box

attached to the white wall of the corridor. The noise was coming from the box. 'When you answer.'

She stepped over a broken broom handle and icy puddles of fragmented glass. The yellow box had a handle on top. The not-man rested his big sun-browned hand on it.

'That's a . . .' She'd seen pictures. 'One of those things. It means "far-away voice".'

'A telephone,' he said. She knew the word, she'd just been too surprised to get it straight away. 'Answer.'

She remembered what you were supposed to do as well, from the pictures. 'You have to pick up that bit and hold it.'

He smiled encouragingly. 'Speak into the emptiness. And listen.'

'I don't want to.'

'Close your eyes, Marina.'

She did. It was as though sunlight had hit her full in the face; she had to.

His hand took hold of hers, shockingly warm and tight. 'Who is it,' she heard him say, 'you want most of all to talk to?' He moved her hand up and put it on a smooth dusty curved thing, pushing her fingers closed.

Daddy, she thought, with a dreadful lurch of pain. *Gawain. Horace.* No—

Eyes closed, she picked up the handle. The jarring rings stopped. There was a wonderful silence.

'Gwenny?' she said, cautiously. 'Gwen?'

Sixteen

*M*ARINA?

   'Gwenny?'

Marina.

   'Gwenny! I can . . . I can hear you. Where are you? I can't scc you.'

   Don't stop talking.

   'No. All right. I won't. I'll try, I'll . . . Can you see me? Can you really hear me? I've been waiting for you. I thought you'd never come back. Where did you go? Gwenny? Where are you?'

   Please. Don't stop.

   'Sorry. Sorry. I've missed you so much. Everything's been horrible. What do I do? Do I keep holding this bit? I still can't see you. Are you behind this wall? I'll come and find you wherever you are.'

   No. You mustn't do that. Don't come here. Whatever you do.

   'But where are you?'

There's . . . I don't know. There's dark water. Everything's on the other side of it. Stay away. Are you listening? Marina?

'Yes, it's all right.'

Just talk to me.

'You sound sad.'

We all get sad sometimes, remember?

'When are you coming back?'

I don't . . . Don't worry about that for now. Tell me something. What's something funny you thought of today?

Marina!

'It's all right! Sorry. I'm still talking. I couldn't think of anything.'

Tell me something you saw. Three things. We'll think of a connection.

'All right. Three things. Let me think.'

No. Don't stop to think. Let's not do that game. Tell me something easy. Tell me what you're looking at now.

'What's wrong? Something's upset you. Where are you?'

Anything. Something from the garden, or the house, it doesn't matter. Anything at all.

'There's a man here—'

Marina?

'Sorry. There was a man here, but he's gone. He was standing here a moment ago. I didn't hear anything.'

I love you so much.

'Don't cry, Gwenny. It's all right.'

I want to cry but I can't. Everything's dry. And dark. You mustn't come any closer. I mustn't let you talk to me.

'What happened? Gawain said you got lost.'

Gavin. No, I mustn't. You're just children. Leave me here, both of you.

'But where are you? I don't understand!'

It's so good to hear your voice. I love you so much I don't know how to tell you. You mustn't come any closer. Can you hear the water? Don't go near it. Let's say goodbye now.

'What? No. Just tell me where you are. I'll come. The man said he'd show me the way.'

Bye bye. Which language shall we use? Do svidanya.

'No, I'm not going. Don't go away. Did you get stuck in the chapel? It's dark there, and there's water. Is that it?'

The chapel.

'But the door's been open all the time.'

I went in.

'Gwen? Don't sound like that. Please, it's frightening me.'

And then . . . and then . . .

'Gwen?

'Gwenny?

'Gwen. Don't go. Not again.'

The box on the wall had instructions written on it, though she had to wipe away grime and dust to read them properly. There was a button it told you to press if you wanted to make another call. She pushed it over and over and over again.

She tried going round to the other side of the wall. It involved working her way through more rooms inside the building, past spilled and shattered things. All she found was confusing wreckage. She was becoming painfully hungry.

She sat down eventually on the floor of hard squares

beneath the telephone, clutching its silent handle to her chest, and cried until she could hardly breathe.

She had the idea of going around collecting things that weren't too broken or filthy so that she'd have things to give the not-man in case he came back again. He'd already told her there'd be a guide to Horace's house, but she was going to see whether she could change her mind and ask for help finding Gwen instead. She found a pile of the red-and-white chequered cloths like the one she'd wrapped herself in to sleep. Some in the middle of the pile were fairly dry. She found a shiny round tray, big enough to see her whole face in when she held it up in front of herself. On a windowsill in a small upstairs room she found a mug with a curly handle, painted with a picture of the big house up the slope as it must have looked when people still lived in it. Inside the rim were words going around in a spiral: TRELOW CHRISTIAN FELLOWSHIP. The picture was in summery colours, which seemed right for the not-man. She brought it down and put it on the telephone.

Her coat was dry enough to wear now, though it smelled of stale water and weeds, so she went back up to the big house and beyond into a patch of overgrown woodland bursting with the white froth of flowering thorn. Her father had shown her how you could pick the buds off the branches and eat them whole. Though it was still early for most of the trees, some were caught in a hollow out of the wind and had begun to sprout a few tight green pellets. She scratched her hands gathering them but she was so hungry she didn't care.

In among the ivy and rotting leaves she found a tiny clump of bitter sorrel, too small yet to be anything other than sour. She ate it anyway, down to the stem, and combed through the undergrowth with a wet stick looking for more.

The tumble of the stream was more muted here on the higher slopes where the manor house stood, and the wind had paused for once. She was working her way under knots of spiky branches when she heard a clatter and scrape from back by the outbuildings.

Someone was stepping through the mess.

She was halfway there before it occurred to her that it might be a different person again, someone else she didn't know. (She heard the steps again, something being kicked aside.) She'd been hoping and waiting for the not-man in his yellow coat but that didn't mean it was him. She slowed down and crept close against the unkempt cypress hedge which divided the big house from the barns, edging along it without a sound until she reached the edge. She peered carefully around.

Her heart leaped so high and hard it seemed to have torn itself loose.

A scrawny woman with long dark hair was pushing her way clumsily into the building across the courtyard. That particular kind of clumsiness was itself almost as familiar to Marina as the features of a face, but as the woman crossed the broken threshold she looked from side to side and Marina glimpsed her profile too, only for an instant and yet an instant was enough. She wasn't lost any more; the abandonment was over. She'd found Gwen.

Part III

Seventeen

SOME WEEKS EARLIER, a forty-three-year-old woman was cycling along the margin of a semi-suburban ring road on the western outskirts of London. It would have been hard to say which was more utterly joyless, the thoroughfare or the woman. Her bicycle was loaded with panniers front and back, making it sluggish in the contrary wind. She'd just switched on her lights when a mobile phone in the front pannier began to ring.

She let it go to voicemail. It rang again. And so on. After the fourth time she pulled up wearily and leaned the bike against a lamp-post. It was not quite twilight. Her thighs ached when she stood straight; she'd been riding for a long time. She unclipped the pannier and dug around for the mobile among the socks and knickers and dried apricots and energy bars, wondering why she hadn't turned it off when she packed it.

She corrected the thought quickly. There was a reason

why she always left the phone on. Just in case. Even after all these weeks, after a day short of eleven weeks (every one of them was notched on her heart), just in case. She extracted it with half-gloved fingers.

'Hello?'

'. . . Finally. Where are you?'

It wasn't the voice she'd been waiting for, hoping for, longing for. Of course not. It never was. She sucked in the chilly traffic-tainted air and thought about hanging up. She'd known, really, who was calling. That bludgeoning refusal to take no for an answer was unmistakable even in the guise of a ringing phone.

But then (she thought) it didn't matter how he took her answer this time. It no longer mattered what he said or did. (The thought was so astonishing it almost made her smile.) Instead of hanging up she held the phone a bit farther from her ear and blinked her eyes into focus, looking at a road sign in the middle distance.

'Egham,' she said. 'Nearly. Just outside Egham.'

'Oh. OK. And what exactly are you doing in Egham?'

'Just outside.'

'All right, then, what are you doing just outside Egham? What are you doing in the Egham environs? In fact, what are you doing anywhere other than here?'

At any moment, she realised, she could cut him off with the touch of a finger, as if dotting a crumb from the table-cloth. At any moment. And (here the astonishment swelled into outright incredulity) the only reason she wasn't doing so right now, the only reason she was submitting herself to the two-decades-old discipline of his meaty sarcasm, was that for all practical purposes she'd *already* hung up on him. She'd finally done it, that very morning.

She said, 'I'm just passing through.'

'Are you all right?'

'Yes. Fine. Sore bum, but otherwise.'

'. . .'

'How about you? Good day?'

'Right. I see your bike's gone. Tell me you're not thinking of riding all the way back from there. It'll be dark in an hour. How far is it? For God's sake. Egham, that's halfway to Windsor.'

'No,' she said. 'No, I'm not thinking of riding all the way back.'

'There's a station, isn't there? Staines, Egham, Virginia Water.'

'Yes.' He doesn't even know, she thought. He hasn't noticed. 'There's definitely a station.'

'Right, then. How long did it take you? You can't have ridden all the way there, it's bloody miles. You're only two weeks out of a cast.'

'Oh.' She checked the time on the phone. 'A few hours.'

'A few hours.'

'Yes. Three or four. Ish.'

'So the BT bloke showed up this morning, then.'

'The what?'

'The BT bloke. The one we've been trying to get an appointment with for weeks. Who you were going to wait in for. Instead of cycling to Egham. Nearly.'

'Oh yes.'

She sensed his tacit sigh, a quarter-part exasperation and three-quarters satisfaction at the opportunity to be exasperated. 'But you forgot.'

'Not exactly.'

'You know what? I'll wait in next time. If we can get an appointment again. It took me two hours to get through to them, and that was last week. But I'll take the day off work. It's only my career. At least it'll get fixed that way.'

'I wouldn't bother,' she said, after a small hesitation.

'Yes, I know you wouldn't. That why I'd better do it myself. In fact I'll start calling now, I might as well sit here on hold for however many hours. In the meantime, why don't you go find a train. I got some champagne for us.'

'I mean, you shouldn't bother, love. No need. He came last Thursday, actually.'

'Who did?'

'The BT man.'

There was something else in the silence now, mixed in with the usual weary-smug contempt: a pinch of genuine puzzlement. If this was a game, she thought – which at bottom it was, the twenty-year marital game, whose rules were made up as you went along but once made could never be changed or deviated from – he'd have been demanding a time out.

'I didn't tell you,' she added, feeling slightly delirious.

'I spotted that.'

'I felt a bit funny about it.'

'Right. So, let's start with . . . So the line's fixed? He figured out the problem? Has it been better since Thursday?'

'We had sex.'

'...'

'Or he had sex with me, anyway. It was more that way around. He was sort of . . . imperious.'

Even the silence didn't have anything to say now, so she went on.

'Which is why I didn't mention that he'd come.' She coughed. 'As it were.'

She could hear her husband breathing heftily.

'Anyway. I can't remember what he said about the line to be honest. I'm not sure he even did. Say anything about it. But he was down there for a bit so presumably he sorted out whatever was wrong. I suppose.'

She flinched when he started speaking again, before remembering that he was miles away. 'I'll tell you what. I'll come and pick you up. I'll leave right now. You head to the station and I'll meet you there. All right?'

'Really,' she said. 'Don't bother.'

'Don't argue.'

'I'm not arguing, Nigel. I'm telling you, don't bother.'

'You know what?'

'What?'

'Fuck it.'

She didn't answer. She found herself almost curious about what he'd say.

'This is pointless. Fuck it. I've had enough. I came home early specially but you weren't here and you know what my first thought was? Thank fuck. That's what I thought. I actually don't care any more. You can ride back or take the train

271

or take a tour of fucking Egham or do whatever the fuck you like. I'm going to drink this bottle of champagne in front of the TV and then I'm going to bed. Just fuck off somewhere so I don't have to put up with your miserable fucking face any more. Go and join the other wastes of fucking space. Or not. This is pointless.' She heard his mouth receding from the phone and pictured his hand moving to jab her into silence. He'd always liked to have the last word.

'Happy Valentine's Day,' she said, just before his finger hit.

Valentine's Day: the festival of unsigned letters, heartfelt and hopeless declarations, dutiful tokens, guilty gestures, presents silently inspected for double meanings. Something, people knew, had been sent to them, some mysterious unanticipated message; but was it welcome? And who was it from?

Woozy with the adrenalin of freedom, she cycled carefully. The phone was off. She didn't trust it to keep her location secret. She felt dangerous to herself, to others. As light left the sky and came down to concentrate in the flares of head-lights and shopfronts she found it harder to keep track of her route. She was looking for small blue signs, always bolted too high up or too far from the junctions they indicated. She was aware of swerving or slowing down in the wrong places to follow their directions.

She passed the train station. Staines, Egham, Virginia Water. Having admitted where she was, she thought she'd better pedal on a bit farther. It surprised her how much sitting down could hurt, but she ignored it. Physical pain had become an abstract thing to her, almost a welcome distraction, and anyway she was going to have to get used to days in the saddle. Her leg wasn't too bad. All that walking must have strengthened it gradually. Accidental rehab. They'd told her to go easy on it but even after Christmas when she was still on crutches she had to get out of the house, away from the phone and the computer, the message that never came, the answers she could never find.

Just give them time, her husband said. (Often.) *They'll call when they're ready. The police are right, there's nothing more you can do.* She almost loved him for his maladroit efforts to say something supportive. But she sat in front of the computer screen most nights, too terrified of her unhappiness to risk lying down in the dark, and might have done the same during the days as well if she hadn't forced herself out the door.

Clumping around on crutches had made her shoulders strong too. A few weeks after being hospitalised with a cracked shin she was fitter than she'd been since her twenties. She ate. She was constantly astonished at herself for being alive, for continuing. Every time she went out she stood by the parapet of the bridge or at the edge of the station platform and thought, Here I am, only a small act of will away from not having to remember or feel anything ever again; but, mysteriously, the step over the parapet or in front of the train never happened. Even now, cycling by the edge of the road, she wasn't quite sure what held her back from lining up an approaching lorry and timing her swerve so the driver would have no chance of braking in time. Perhaps she'd left it too late. Grief never got better, or so all the agony aunts and uncles agreed, but perhaps you lost the courage to rid yourself of it after the first few weeks. The window of opportunity might have closed while she was lying sedated and supervised in a hospital bed.

Or maybe it was that she still believed, even now, a day short of eleven weeks on, that one of those times the phone rang it wouldn't be silence on the other end, but . . .

The phone. The phone. Donor and withholder of miracles, oracle of her despair. Delivering its dreadful news on the last day of November, without warning, without possibility of reply. *Keep in touch*, people said, meaning *Use the phone*, but it wasn't like that. When you touched someone you knew they were there. Voices on the phone had exactly the opposite meaning: I am elsewhere. Not here, not with you. Out of reach. Gone.

Just remember what I said, OK? I'm not coming back. OK, bye then. Bye.

There was a particular hour – about this time, early evening – which she'd learned to anticipate. It was when the distractions of the day gave out, the long lonely night stretched ahead, and everything descended towards its unbearable worst. A sure sign of its approach was when she started remembering his voice on the answering machine. She slowed down a bit and concentrated on the biting soreness in her bum, and, when that didn't work, on the fact that she was no longer waiting at home going mad but instead doing something again, making an effort. When that didn't work either she dismounted. She happened to be adjacent to the gravelled and privet-bordered front drive of someone's stockbroker-belt mansion. She dropped the bike in the gravel, crouched beside it and screamed for a while. There were lights in the front windows but no one came out. Stranger things had happened.

She got as far as Windsor that evening. There was no particular strategy, beyond the vague idea that each day she'd cycle herself close enough to exhaustion to be able to sleep without pills. She'd even thought about not packing the pills. On reflection, that was the only aspect of the plan which was obviously absurd. Still, she was going to run out of them eventually, so it made sense to experiment with other ways of achieving unconsciousness, short of The Big One. She reserved the right to keep The Big One as Plan B, or C, or however far down the alphabet patience and ingenuity could drive it.

A fire was burning in a meadow by the river as she approached the town. Snatches of drumming came through pauses in the traffic. Students, probably, though she'd heard that all sorts of people were beginning to join in these gatherings.

(Her husband: *I don't understand why people can't just carry on like they did before.*

Her [angry, guilty]: *'People'?*

Him: *All right. You.*)

There hadn't been a specific moment when she'd decided she wasn't going back to work. It had been as completely obvious to her that she wouldn't as it had apparently been to him that, in time, she would. *We could always try closing our eyes and wishing really hard*, he said, *and seeing if the mortgage will pay itself.* The mortgage. The bills. The tick-tock of their enviable, affluent, suburban existence: salary comes in, expenses go out. *Tick*, we spend. *Tock*, we earn. *Bong*, we die. A hundred words left on an answering machine had smashed the whole mechanism to pieces, but he'd refused to notice, not even when the effects appeared to be spreading beyond the prison walls of their house, out on to the streets where impeccably ordinary people suddenly stopped clocking in for their daily labour or began throwing bricks at banks. Even in her well-heeled part of London a few youngsters and their allies had begun gathering on the common after dark, in the bitter nights around the new year, lighting a small fire or two. The police had put a stop to it. As she cycled towards the illuminated blob of the castle above the river she heard sirens. They didn't seem to be aiming for the little group in the meadow. Out here, maybe, there were things that needed stopping more urgently.

She found hotels around the castle, all either expensive looking or closed. She wheeled on at random. A petrol station at a nondescript roundabout ambushed her with a horribly vivid memory: she'd been there before. She'd stopped there to get a snack and a bottle of water more than once, on family excursions to the amusement park outside the town. If it had been December the ambush would have wounded her badly, but by now she'd been assaulted by pitiless memories and associations so often that they no longer had the power to stop her in her tracks. *All right, Mum, but can we get a Magnum on the way home?* She'd have said no. Her own voice was never in the memories – she was nothing to herself any more – but nevertheless she was sure her answer would have been no. It seemed like all she'd ever said was no. No you can't, don't do that, no you're wrong, no there isn't, no I can't see anything.

She found a chain hotel out towards the motorway. The boy asked her to pay up front. 'Sorry about that,' he said. 'It's just the way things are going.' She gave him cash, without protest. The room was so barren and bleak she didn't dare look at it. She left all the lights off, fumbling around in the near-dark to unplug the phone from the wall.

The silent calls had started not long after she'd been released from hospital.

'Hello?'

No response. Nothing, not even a hiss. She hung up, shivering, feeling weepy. She was shivery and weepy all the time in those days.

The second one was just a few hours later.

'Hello?'

Her husband was just coming home. She saw him through the window, loafing down the street with his homecoming gait, as if checking out each house in the cul-de-sac to see which was going to make him the best offer of dinner and bed. She hung up quickly and said nothing about it. She said nothing to him about anything, as far as was possible. They'd already had every fight there was to have, exchanged every mutually predictable barrage of detestation and blame, but it still felt as if the tiniest misplaced word or the most briefly unguarded tone of voice might trigger the whole thing again and leave her blown about by a tempest of hatred so furious she'd be wrecked by it.

The third time was two days later. Those first few times the calls only came when she was alone in the house.

'Hello?'

That afternoon was when she'd managed to get up the stairs for the first time, to the first floor where her son's room was. She hadn't been in his room since December, before her wild drive and the crash. Despite her pleading and her threats her husband had 'tidied up', as she'd known he would. Some things were moved. Some were even gone. While she'd been lying broken legged and drugged into oblivion he'd come in here and touched things, thrown things away. She was still weeping on the boy's bed when the phone rang and wouldn't stop ringing.

'Hello?'

Then and there she understood what the silence was about. She curled up, nestling the handset close to her mouth.

'Gav?' she whispered.

She was certain the silence was listening. It felt like a nothing that was somehow *there*, a presence at the other end of the line.

'Gav, love. I'm here. It's me.' She was suddenly terrified that he'd hang up on her. 'Please don't go,' she said. Like the gust of roaring air that preceded an onrushing train, she felt pain coming, fast. 'Please forgive me.' Even saying that much was too much. She started crying again, the kind of crying that was like being garrotted. She didn't stop until long after she'd dropped the handset to the carpet.

The next time, a couple of days later, she begged him to talk to her. 'Anything at all. Just one word. Please, Gavin. Please.' But he was determined to punish her. The silence was the worst possible reminder of his absence. *I'm not here*, it said, continuously. It was the same as the message he'd left. She'd played that message tens of thousands of times until it had stopped sounding like her boy speaking at all, until it was like the inscription on a gravestone. (Nigel had erased the message while she was in hospital. *It was only making things worse*, he said, *you know it was*.) 'I deserve it,' she told the silent caller. 'I know you're doing this to hurt me. It's all right, love. I don't mind. I just want to know if you're OK. Can't you just say that, and nothing else? Once? Please?'

The occasion that cured her of these agonisingly hopeless conversations with her missing boy was when one of the calls came in the evening, for the first time.

She couldn't get to the phone as fast as he could, of course. It took her twenty seconds just to get out of a chair and into her crutches.

'Stokes.' Her husband always answered the phone with this curt bark, a dog woofing his territory. Gets the other bugger on the back foot, as he put it.

'Who's there?

'Hello?

'Bloody nonsense.'

She gripped her hands together. If it turned out the silence would speak to him when it hadn't spoken to her, she knew she'd kill herself that very night. But he tossed the phone down with an irritated shrug. 'No one there.'

After a few more days of silent calls he complained to the phone company, and then the police. Equally useless, he said. *'Nothing we can do'? More like, 'Can't be arsed.'* One evening he began shouting at the silence. He went red when he shouted like someone in a cartoon. 'I don't know who you are or what you want or why you think this is funny but when I find you I'm going to . . . OK. I've got your number and I know where you're calling from so you'd better start watching yourself because I'm going to teach you a fucking lesson, I'll—'

'Stop it!' She screamed at him, banging both fists on the table, spilling coffee. 'Stop it! Don't talk to him like—'

He flung the handset at the sofa. 'You stop it!' He was red up to his bald patch. 'When will you . . . just . . . stop . . . being . . .'

They stared at each other, balancing on the very edge, again.

'Ah,' he said, in something nearer his usual register. 'I get it now.'

He took an invisible step back from the invisible precipice. He fetched the phone, carefully replaced it in its base, then sat on the sofa, rubbing his face.

'There's no reason to think it's him,' he said. 'Think about it.'

She started crying. She'd have given almost anything to master that reflex, to stop herself bursting into tears all the time like a particularly hateful spoiled four-year-old girl, but it had become as automatic as sneezing.

He sighed noisily, to show how much of a burden her unhappiness was to him. 'It's just some crank,' he said. 'Or a glitch. Probably a glitch. There's stuff like that going around. I don't think there's anyone there at all, it doesn't sound like someone not talking. It's probably a problem with the line. Just rings for no reason. I'll get BT to send someone round.'

She mopped up the coffee spill with her napkin, still crying.

'It's not him,' he said. 'When he's ready to get back in touch he will. You know that. I know that.'

She managed to gather enough breath to speak. 'You don't know anything,' she said.

'Here we go again.' She wasn't looking at him, but she could hear his eyes rolling.

'You've been in his room. You've thrown things out.'

'What the hell are you doing going upstairs?'

'You wouldn't tell me if he rang.' It was her worst fear. 'Would you? You'd do anything to stop him coming back.'

'Iz. Listen to me. You cannot haul yourself up and down those stairs. You'll break your neck.'

'I want to break my neck.'

'Oh, God help us.'

'I do. I want to.'

'Let me know when this bit's over.' He went to the kitchen. She heard unscrewing, clinking, pouring. She was shaking, staring at the invisible cliff, willing herself to go over it and fall and shatter. She felt like she was falling all the time but she never hit the bottom. Time went on. The awful evening continued, like all the other awful evenings. He came back in holding a drink, leaning in the doorway, looking patient, sensible, long suffering.

'I understand you don't want to hear it,' he said. He was the voice of reason. 'But this is what happened. Your sister spilled the beans, he flipped out, they buggered off together. You can tell me all you like that I don't know and I wasn't there and this and that and the next but I'm sorry, Iz, it doesn't change the simple fact. She had the brilliant idea that Gavin of all people was ready to hear that particular piece of news, and surprise surprise and knock me down with a bloody feather, he didn't take it too well. And it's just filthy bad luck that it happened to coincide with that, with that hoax about the bird and all that, which we both know is exactly, is *exactly*' – he had to speak louder and more firmly to keep going over the noise she was making – 'the kind of thing that Gwen *loves*, and it's even worse luck that every spotty leftie moron in the country chose the same moment to descend on Gwen and all the other morons and—'

She staggered out of the chair, reaching for a crutch to hit him with, missed, fell over, and knocked herself out.

The calls continued, day and night. Thanks to what he called 'pulling strings' a policeman eventually came, resulting in a conversation which if anything went worse than the one that evening. By steps that were gradual and somehow inevitable it progressed from the topic of nuisance calls and harassment to the whole sorry history of her efforts to locate her son and sister, including the official warning from the

Devon and Cornwall police after she'd threatened them with legal action and personal violence, and culminating with her mad wild drive south-westwards into the worst winter anyone had ever known and her humiliatingly predictable accident on an icy road on the flank of Dartmoor. The officer, very junior, very young, visibly terrified by the presence of a madwoman, strained so hard to be professional that it made her shame even worse, as though with every sentence it became more obvious that she belonged to a different category of person from him, the category it was his job to keep an eye on and (if necessary) lock up: the wrong'uns, the irredeemable. When he began to explain – forced calm, stumbling over words – the protocol for missing persons, as if she hadn't heard it a thousand times before, as if she hadn't spent whole days being fobbed off with *believed to be in the company of an adult relative* and *not treated as a criminal investigation until evidence arises to suggest otherwise* and *exceptional burden of cases at present* and *please try not to alarm yourself, Mrs Stokes* and *his message indicated that he intends to make contact in future so our advice is to wait however difficult that may be*, then she could no longer contain herself, and she metamorphosed into the harpy of grief and rage her husband found so deeply, deeply embarrassing. There was, of course, nothing the police could do about the calls, strings or no strings. Try British Telecom, the officer suggested as he fled.

She stopped thinking it was her boy calling. Harassment, creeping malice, prolonged cruelty: that wasn't him. When he wanted to make her feel bad his weapons had always been indifference or contempt. *Go away. Just leave me alone.* The blank teenager stare. He'd always hated the telephone anyway. He wouldn't have done this to her. He wasn't nasty.

She spent countless hours thinking about that. She searched her memory, looking for something to explain the in retrospect completely baffling imbalance between his lack of nastiness and how nasty they'd been to him. The more she searched the more astonished at herself she became. Was she uniquely evil? she wondered. How could someone as evil as her have got on in the world all those years, got a degree and a worthy job and a marriage and a house? Why hadn't she been blasted by divine judgement, or done away with by the first paladin of decency who'd happened to pass by? Or were all parents like that, without knowing it? She remembered lots of time spent agonising about whether she was a bad mother. How could it not have been obvious straight away how pointlessly vile she'd been? No wonder he'd run away with Gwen. Kind, sweet, silly Gwen. She'd run away from herself if she could. She'd run away from herself that very instant, if it wasn't for the fact that her tibia was cracked.

One evening, after her husband had picked up the phone and woofed and listened for a second and hung up, she said:

'Maybe it's Miss Grey.'

He went quiet in a different way from the usual. Nineteen years of marriage, and here was something a little bit new, a behaviour she couldn't interpret straight away. Perhaps, she thought, he's going to hit me. She'd felt it coming for a long time, like living with an incurable disease. He turned the page of his newspaper instead, deliberately, neatly.

'Good an explanation as any.'

'She might be missing him too.'

'Iz.' He tipped the paper down. 'I want to help you get through this. I really do. I want us to help each other through this. He's my son too, actually. I'm not having the best time either, actually.' He looked at her with intense, heroic sympathy, the look of a martyr. 'I honestly think the only way we're going to manage is if we try . . . If we stay . . .'

'Sane?' she offered, after a pause.

'Focused.' Ah, the vocabulary of the sports pages. He always fell back on it when he was trying for sincerity, or otherwise varying from his normal emotional range. Dislodged from his established territory of sarcasm or hectoring, his only lexical handholds were the clichés mouthed by the few people he envied (because they were good at what he wanted to be good at and as rich as he wanted to be). 'If we' – he meant *you* – 'can just try and focus on what we. Actually. Know. The facts. It's hard, I realise.'

'He might have been telling the truth.'

Her husband pursed his lips and angled the paper up again, shaking its corners.

'Don't you ever think it was odd?' This was another point she'd reflected on increasingly often. 'I mean, he could see we hated it, and God knows it didn't make him happy either, so why . . . Why did he carry on? If he was just making it all up?'

The front page, now raised to her eye, had a big picture of the young pilgrim woman who'd been on TV and who spoke so powerfully. Hair everywhere, a scarf that looked like it was knitted by her dotty grandmother, big untrendy glasses not concealing the passion in her eyes. Ruth, her name was: from a Christian commune, they said, though she wasn't preaching any orthodoxy now. *Spotty leftie moron.* The headline read: *Self-appointed Prophet Turns Sights on Money.*

'Well,' the voice behind the newspaper said, 'next time she rings you can discuss it with her yourself.'

She actually tried to, but she couldn't. Guilt choked her. She couldn't say the words again, *Miss Grey*, not even when she was all alone in the house except for the cavernous silence at her ear. Her lips closed to make the *m* and stayed shut as if glued. She was thinking of the months, the years, she'd spent devising strategies to prevent those two words being spoken in her house: talks with her husband that went on till midnight, talks in coffee shops with the two or three other mothers she trusted with the information that her son was delusional, talks with doctors, counsellors, a vicar. (A vicar!) When she was five she'd fantasised about waking up one morning to discover that she was actually a fairy. That was what it was like trying to persuade herself it might be Miss Grey on the other end of the line.

Whatever world her boy had lived in – a world where birds appeared in your bedroom and a knight in black armour carrying a spear trudged beside the car park on Wimbledon Common and people with the heads of animals waded through the river and an invisible old woman was your best friend – it was too late for her to pretend she lived there too. She tormented herself at night with thoughts of how simple it would have been. Gwen managed it, after all, apparently quite happily, with no harm to herself or anyone around her. Would it have been so bad? Where had it come from, this default assumption that thinking and talking like her younger sister would have made life ridiculous or impossible? Gwen seemed to get on well enough down there in the country doing whatever it was she did. Gwen hadn't ended up married to a person she didn't like, doing a job which ate so much of her energy that except on weekends and holidays the part of each day she enjoyed most was going to sleep. If she'd only been a little bit more like her sister, her boy would never have run away. But it was too late now.

Or so she'd thought.

The first appointment British Telecom could give them was almost three weeks away. Hopeless at the moment, they said. Problems in the supply chain, they said. Huge numbers of reported faults, unexpected staff shortages. Her husband raged and tried to pull more strings. They popped out and dangled limp in his hands. The calls continued, one every day or two. She got rid of the crutches and began to walk. To her eyes the outside world had a tinge of strangeness. Nothing felt quite real. The supermarket delivery van stopped coming. The company's software had caught the Plague. They had a name now, those mysterious inexplicable hiccups which manifested themselves in things which weren't supposed to be unpredictable: the Plague, capital P. Over prepackaged dinners he talked about how things were getting serious now, as if their lives before had been a kind of joke; this was oddly like the kind of things the spotty leftie morons were saying, though she didn't bother pointing that out to him. *Getting serious now.* It sounded about right to her. Now we've lost our child, now the thing I love most in the world has been torn away, now at last we get serious. Now we can stop arseing around. Now we get the message. But was it welcome? And who was it from?

On 9 February the phone engineer rang the doorbell. It was Thursday, and as far as she knew he wasn't due until the following Tuesday, but she was nowhere near caring about such details. He stood in the doorway as if he owned the place, smiled all the time (although it was a kind of inward Mona Lisa smile with no warmth in it) and kept his eyes on her. He smelled faintly of something almost like pipe smoke, something heady, burnt, bittersweet. His face was Middle Eastern but his voice was all England, bizarrely so, as though he was in fact a classical actor moonlighting for BT between jobs. She showed him where the phone line came into the house and he told her to undress. The whole process had a weird quality of fatefulness. Some script had been written and she had no choice but to stick to it. She wondered afterwards whether she'd in fact just been raped. No other way of describing it seemed appropriate, and yet there'd been no sense of violence, no aura of fear and shame. It had just . . . happened. She was turned so she didn't see anything. There was a nova of pleasure quite terrifying in its intensity, almost as if it wasn't *her* pleasure at all, as if she was merely hosting it. Then there was an aftermath of kneeling down on her own, staring at the floor, and then he might have said something about the fault being fixed.

She didn't say anything to her husband, obviously, not

even when there was another silent call that evening. He woofed, hung up, swore about bloody BT taking bloody ages to get their bloody act together. His heart wasn't quite in it. He was distracted. She heard him upstairs later on, talking on the phone with their financial adviser, self-consciously discreet mutterings about safe havens and getting assets offshore. Aftershocks of the alien pleasure rippled around her like reminders of catastrophe.

Around noon the next day the phone rang yet again.

'Hello?'

She listened for a while as she always did by then, thoughts of everything she'd failed to say in her life passing by in a pageant of misery.

'Lizzie.'

Her world stopped.

'Hello? Hello?'

'Lizzie. Can you . . .'

The voice was faint, remote, lost. It was the silence she'd been listening to for weeks compressed into the shape of a mouth and made to move.

'Hello? Hello?' She kept repeating it like an idiot, pulling the phone closer. 'Hello?'

'Lizzie. Speak to . . . Speak.'

Only two people in the whole world had ever called her by her secret childhood name. They'd come up with it because *Iseult* was hard for children to say and *Izzy* was what their parents used. Of the two, one was long dead.

'Gwen?' she said.

'It's not . . . I can't . . .'

She was crying again. This was the person she'd become, a dribbling shivering mess shaken at the whim of a huge cold hand. 'Gwen,' she repeated, or tried to. 'Where are you? Where's Gav?'

'No.' The voice sounded fearfully uncertain. The silence it had come out of squeezed around it. 'It's dark. Lizzie?'

'I'm here,' she said, between dribbles. 'It's me.'

'Talk to . . . Help.'

'It's all right, Gwen.' And it was all right, she thought; after ten unbearable weeks she had something at last. 'I'm here. Where's . . . Can I speak to him?'

'There isn't . . . No way up. Lizzie? Lizzie?'

'Yes. I'm here. What's wrong?'

'Help.'

'Where are you? Please let me talk to Gavin. Just for a moment.'

'Nothing's here.'

'Is he with you?'

'No. I wish . . . I . . .'

'Please. Just a word or two.' She felt a terrible desperation. If only she could stop the stupid, stupid crying. She couldn't hear what Gwen was saying any more. The voice was so far away, as if the line was coming from another world. 'My boy,' she said. 'I want my boy.' The phone slipped out of her fingers.

That was another bad evening, and a bad night. She became convinced Nigel had turned the phone off and kept going to check it. Her pathetic struggle to get herself out of bed and on her feet woke him up each time until he more or less forced her to swallow the oblivion pills. When there were no calls the next day she thought he must have sabotaged the line somehow. A neighbour found her trying to lift the manhole cover outside the house so she could check the wiring. She tried to get the police to trace the call, but the police had stopped talking to her. The neighbour wanted to sit in the house with her until her husband got home, and the only way Iz could get her to leave was by throwing things. She broke a pane of glass in the front window.

At about 4 a.m. on the Sunday morning she conceived the idea of bicycling to Cornwall.

It went through her in one magical tidal glow, like the hospital morphine. She couldn't think why it hadn't occurred to her before. After her first attempt to go and find Gavin and Gwen had ended in a wrecked car and a fractured leg, she'd somehow fallen into the assumption that she was powerless to try again. Driving wasn't an option. They hadn't bought another car because, her husband said, they couldn't afford to. Anyway she wasn't allowed to drive. Other obvious ways of getting to Cornwall had disappeared too. By the time she was out of hospital all trains and buses to the south-west had been 'suspended', in the hope of interrupting the stream of pilgrims and travellers and millennialists and lunatics flowing down towards the snowbound disaster zone. She'd always thought of it as the ends of the earth anyway, and yet – she looked at the map on the computer screen as if seeing it for the first time – it was only a couple of hundred miles away. Which was nothing, really. She clicked through maps of cycle networks. She used to ride for miles, when she was young and fit. She and an old boyfriend had cycled most of the way around Finland. A whole country. How could she not have thought of it before? The idea became thrillingly tangible. It brought her a feeling she hadn't had since the day in December when she'd at last accepted that the police weren't going to help her, and made the decision to go and look for Gavin herself. For the first time since the demented exhilarated hours of that midnight drive she experienced a sort of hope.

She had to wait for Sunday to pass, and then the Monday as well because her husband didn't go to work that day; there was a huge demonstration in the City and all the offices told people not to come in. The delay was useful. It gave her time to think about what she'd need, inner tubes and chocolate and wet wipes, and all the cash she could get out of the machine.

They watched the demonstration on TV together. His running commentary – why can't he ever just watch, she thought, amazed that it had taken her nearly twenty years to notice; why can't he ever just listen? – was all *morons* and *fantasists* and *look at those people* and *why can't they understand that X depends on Y and there'll never be any A without people like me doing B and C* and (when the window-smashing and the burning started) *maybe now they'll finally send the army in and sort these bastards out*; but now, with the thought of Cornwall so beautifully clear in her head, she found that she was suddenly seeing everything the other way around, the wrong way: a miracle *had* happened, all that video footage of the massive black bird thing wasn't a hoax, the suppressed BBC report had been the truth after all, Ruth the spotty leftie moron woman was right to say that people had to stop pretending everything could go on as it had before, the system of international finance really was a game of smoke and mirrors which would dissolve into nothing as soon as everyone stopped believing in it, and – most of all, most of all: she held this wrong thought tight to her heart as if only that warmth kept it beating – Gavin, her Gavin, had been telling nothing but the truth, all along.

Eighteen

IN THE MORNING her legs were almost too sore for her to stand. The nondescript grey stillness beyond the window of her room felt vaguely unsettling, as if the town was quietly anxious about something. She'd dreamed of Iggy, for the first time in ages. *I entrusted you with my child and look what you've done.* She often used to have dreams in which her long-dead twin came and took Gavin away, but this wasn't one of those. It seemed to her that Iggy had just come and stared at her while she slept, a ghostly visitation leaving a spectral deposit of guilt.

'Bike's extra,' the girl at the front desk said, as Iz hobbled stiffly out.

'Excuse me?'

'Ten quid.'

The girl couldn't have been older than twenty. A boy about the same age sauntered out from the back office. They both looked nervous.

'It's chained up outside,' Iz said.

'Still counts.' The girl wouldn't meet her eye. 'New parking fee. For bikes. We're supposed to charge for them now. Sorry.'

'Where does it say anything about a parking fee?'

'It's new,' the boy said, standing behind the girl's chair and opening his shoulders a little. 'Only ten quid.'

'That's ridiculous.'

'Cash only.'

She shook her head and turned for the door. The boy hurried out of the office to stop her.

'Tenner and you can ride away right now. OK?'

She'd never been mugged before, let alone by uniformed employees of a large hotel chain. She was so surprised she wasn't sure what to do. Her husband would have blustered and threatened and tried to maintain his masculine self-respect, so she took that as her guide and did the opposite. She was uncomfortably aware of how much cash there was stuffed in her wallet as she unfolded it, but the teenage extortionists seemed more tense than she was and might well have been relieved to be getting anything out of her at all.

'For your sake,' she said, 'I'm glad judgement really is coming.'

'It's a new rule,' the girl mumbled. 'Sorry you didn't know.'

As soon as she mounted the saddle she wished she could have stayed at least a few more hours before starting, but that was out of the question now. And, she thought as she rode off, standing on the pedals because her bum was too sore to sit on, there was one advantage to being robbed: on the off-chance that Nigel had pulled some of his legendary strings and got the police out looking, those teenagers at the hotel wouldn't be telling anyone they'd seen her.

She found the marked route out of town and headed westwards until she was clear of streets, then dismounted and walked. There was a biting wind in her face and her leg felt as bad as it had the first couple of days she'd been on the crutches. Aeroplanes took off close by, roaring unseen into low clouds, carrying away those who could afford to flee and had somewhere to go.

At a bench she stopped and sat for a while, stretching. Having her phone turned off made her nervous. What if he rang and couldn't find her? He'd told her that he'd come and find her one day: he'd promised. What if he came home and she wasn't there?

She weighed it up for a while, massaging her calves and thighs, and then dug out the mobile. When she switched it on it said:

Missed call Nigel (3)
Text Nigel (8)

She switched it straight off again.

By mid-afternoon, little ground made, she came through defaced industrial outskirts into Reading, where she sat in a café for three hours thinking about drowning herself. She watched other customers come in and out. None of them would look at her for more than an instant. The mirror in the hotel bathroom that morning had shown her a haggard wreck. She thought the other customers all looked suicidal too, except for the mothers with small children, who – though they wouldn't know it until too late – had a reason to go on living. Watching the children was a torture so intense it crossed over into a perverse ecstasy.

—*Mum? Do you want the rest of your biscuit?*

—*No, I've had enough.*

—*Can I have it, then?*

—*No you can't.*

—*Please?*

—*No.*

—*That's a waste.*

—*I told you, you can't.*

—*Can I give it to the bird?*

—*I said no, Gav. There isn't any bird.*

That wounded look on his little face: I don't understand what Mummy means. How could she not have grasped the meaning of that look? She'd seen it day after day. Why had she gone on saying no? Because saying yes would have meant admitting that he was ill; her little boy insane, aged four.

No wonder, she thought, that so many people had tried so valiantly to say no to all the things that had been going on for the past two months, the great black beast in the photos and the wobbly videos shot from phones, the unnatural and perpetual snow, the phantom emails and unaccountable glitches, all the things which by any standard of explanation had proved themselves inexplicable. And the ones who said yes instead had all driven themselves . . .

She'd joined the ranks of the mad. Whether she meant to or not. The other customers could see it, she supposed. Look, that thin woman in the corner with the hair all over the place and the crazed eyes, who's been sitting there not doing anything for hours: she must be another one of *them*.

She tidied herself up a bit in the café toilet before she went looking for somewhere to stay. It seemed sensible to go disguised.

It occurred to her the next morning that this was the first time she'd had two consecutive full nights' sleep since the hospital.

She felt – marginally – better. The aches and pains and blisters were an irrelevance compared to the gathering knowledge that she was doing something, going somewhere. She had a purpose. At the end of the day there would be fewer miles between herself and her destination.

Her bad leg was very shaky and the other one not much better, but at least the route was flat and the headwind had eased off. Brick terraces with their new infestations of weird graffiti passed by quickly, and she was soon out into those strange liminal spaces, beside tracks, under motorways, between towns, for which no use or name could be found. There were a lot of empty cans in the grass. The route took her along a puddled towpath, where some people on a canal boat cheered and shouted at her as she overtook them. Their faces were painted and they swayed like drunkards when they stood up to wave. A sign further on pointed out a connecting route to a train station. Theale, Aldermaston, Midgham. It was only half an hour from there back to the stop for her house, as though in two days she'd gone no distance at all.

She took the phone out again when she stopped to rest. The bench overlooked a pond or reservoir, a gloomy grey oval broken by islands of pebbly mud.

Missed call Nigel (7)
Text Nigel (9)

He hadn't given up, then. It made her feel she should try to go a bit faster. If he borrowed a car he could be here within an hour.

'Bollocks, really, isn't it?'

She looked up to find a younger man on the path ahead, hands in the pockets of an old grey overcoat. Its collar was turned up around a grungy scarf and a light beard. He walked bouncily, in a way that made her think he ought to have a mud-splattered spaniel running along beside him. He nodded towards the phone in her hands.

'Everyone spends their life attached to those things. Waste of time, innit?' He mimed hunching over a screen and prodding with thumbs. 'What's all that about?'

'I was just thinking that.'

He grinned. In my university days, she thought, he'd have been one of those people who protested outside branches of McDonald's. Happy vegan anarchists. Iggy's crowd.

'I used to have one myself. You think you can't do without it, eh? How did they get us all to believe that? Bollocks. Mind if I sit down? I'm not dangerous.'

'Be my guest.'

He sat on the back of the bench, mud-caked boots on the seat.

'Checking messages from the boss?'

'My husband, actually.'

'See, that's what I mean.' He shuffled forward a bit. 'You're actually, you know, married, but you've still got to have one of those things to talk back and forth. It's barking, when you think about it. I mean, why? People weren't like this when we were kids.'

She smiled. 'I'm much older than you.'

'Well, there you are, then. Even more so. You know what it was like, eh? I mean, you used to be able to go somewhere without, you know.' He did the wiggling thumbs again: air texting. 'Trying to be somewhere else at the same time. That's what it's all about, when you think about it. Bollocks. Know what I did with mine? My phone?'

'I can't imagine.'

'Chucked it in there.' He waved at the pond, and laughed. 'Splash. Gone. I'm serious. Best thing I ever did. Look at me. Don't I look like a happy chappie? Don't believe me, eh? It's true. Wade around in those reeds and you can get yourself a free mobile. Been there since Christmas, mind, so it might not be in tip-top condition.'

'That's the last thing I need.'

'See? You get it. I could tell soon as I saw you. I thought, she gets it. I swear, I feel a million times better since I chucked mine. You start noticing things again, yeah?'

'Being in the moment,' Iz said.

'Exactly! That's it. That's good, that is. Instead of being in a little screen. I like that.'

'They talk about it all the time in yoga.'

'Oh, you do yoga.' He sat a bit straighter. 'Well posh.'

'I used to.'

'Hard times, eh? Cutting back those little extras?'

'Sort of.'

'You think about what really matters, don't you?'

'Oh yes,' she agreed. 'You do.'

'That's why I interrupted you. If you don't mind me saying so. I could see you thinking about it.' One of his heavily nicotine-stained hands cocked finger and thumb to fire at her. 'I thought, *she* knows what's going on.'

'I wouldn't go that far.'

'It's what this is all really about, isn't it? That's what I reckon. Don't give me any of that religious stuff, eh? Sorry, no offence, that might be your thing, but . . .'

She shook her head.

'Yeah. Didn't think so. I mean, if it's God, right, then how come there's no message? The whole point with God is, Here we go,' he gestured to one side, 'you lot come with me to heaven,' and to the other, 'you lot are fucked. That's it. Job done. It's black and white, innit? Nah. Nothing to do with God, if you ask me. Not that you did.'

'I see what you mean.'

'It's more like,' he shuffled closer, 'the universe saying,

Hang on a minute. Yeah? Pay attention a sec.' He leaned right forward and opened his eyes dramatically. '"Wake up, people!" Yeah?'

'Yes,' she agreed, but she was thinking of a quiet voice, remote, frightened: *Lizzie?*

'I mean, the weather. The flippin' weather. How else would you get British people to sit up and take some notice, eh?' He chuckled to himself. 'You know they can't explain it.'

'The snow?'

'They've got billions of computers and radar and all sorts to do the forecasts. It's multimillion-pound, innit? Farmers, shipping, whatever, everyone's got to know the weather. But all that snow, right, it's not coming from anywhere. I mean, hello? Hello? Anyone think maybe that's a bit important, maybe? Like maybe we should turn off the computers for a bit? Sorry, madam, don't mean to shout at you. I should let you talk to your hubby.'

'It's all right. I'm trying to avoid him, actually.'

'Oh. Sorry. Like that, is it?'

'Very much so.'

The hands went back to their retreat in the frayed pockets of his coat. 'Not my place to say, but isn't that what we're talking about? Sorry for poking my nose in. But you find out what's important. Don't you? You chuck away all the nonsense and you decide what's really important in life.'

'What do you think's really important in life, then?'

'Haven't decided.'

'Very good.'

'Yeah. Crack myself up, I do. Where are you off to, then?'

'Oh. Just . . . going for a ride.'

'Good for you. See, don't take the phone. What's it for? There's trees, there's wildlife, there's . . . ducks, that's why you get on your bike, innit? Not to get messages from the boss and the hubby and the kids' school. It's bollocks. Chuck it.' *The kids' school.* She was already standing up and reaching for the bike, her hands shaking and her face hot. 'Go on, I dare you. You'll thank me for it.' She felt tears coming. She bowed her head, mounting quickly. 'All right. Off you go.' The phone was still in one hand; the handlebars wobbled crazily as she pushed away. 'Blimey. Sorry I spoke, eh?' She couldn't hear him. An acid flood of memory had unstoppered itself. She was hearing the school secretary's painfully professional voice. *We think it would be wise for him to have some time off. A few of the teachers have expressed concerns. Has anyone ever suggested this kind of evaluation before?* She pedalled furiously to escape the rush, ignoring the last shout from behind: 'Any chance of a shag?'

London's gravitational pull weakened as she pushed on west. Beyond the extended suburbs disguised as Berkshire county towns, padded out with half-hearted green interruptions on which no one had yet built rustically named roundabouts and three-bed semis, the last traces of the city faded from the landscape. Her route turned disobliging. It forgot about looking for parks and cycle lanes and well-marked flat backstreets. It became an afterthought, a few signs scattered over tangles of country roads which had never been meant to carry people farther than from farm to field. Chalk hills rose around her, funnelling the wind. It was much harder going.

Her wad of cash thinned quickly. She didn't want to use plastic in case it gave away where she was, but when she became desperate and tried anyway it turned out the card machines in the supermarket weren't working. *Asda's got the Plague*, someone yelled gleefully from the back of the queue. The next night she experimented with curling herself into a dry and sheltered corner around the back of a quiet petrol station, and was amazed to discover how cold the night was, and how full of imaginary threats. She lasted less than three hours before cycling towards the nearest glow on the horizon and paying far more than she wanted to for a room above a pub. The next day she risked using a cash machine, thinking she was far enough out in the country by now that Nigel wouldn't be able to track her even if he saw the transaction online and came straight here. The machine ate her card.

By elusive degrees the towns grew stranger. It was nothing she could pin down. She saw what she expected to see, pasty young mothers, men in work clothes looking at machinery, dog-walkers, pensioners, drab corner shops and low-rise schools, but something had changed, or was about to change. The patterns were out of kilter. The mothers weren't around the schools at the right times, or the men around the pubs, or the pensioners around the post offices. Everyone seemed wary of everyone else. And there were fewer of them, she was sure of it. She thought at first it was just an effect of the hours she spent alone in her strange bubble of sweat and weariness and the buzz of the chain and the hiss of tyres on the road, but the emptiness wasn't only in her. The winter skies swathed the villages in it, the wind blew it down every dead-end lane and across every unmowed playground. The world had had the stuffing pulled out of it. Its shape and its fullness were going. It felt limp. Almost ready for the tip, she thought; almost ready to be thrown out.

The weather turned against her as well. She rode west and a cold rain blew east, slowing her down, soaking through her gloves and down the neck of her top. Her clothes stank, her hands blistered, the withered muscles in her bad leg winced with every crank of the pedals. She'd thought that nothing as trivial as bodily pain would matter to her any more but she had to stop more and more often, and when she stopped she thought more and more intently about what it would be like to be dry, to be clean, to put her feet up, to have food waiting for her, to turn round and put the relentless wind at her back. Then she would remember all the things she'd done to earn her punishment.

—*Goodnight, Mum.*

—*Night night.*

—*Mum?*

—*What?*

—*Can you stay a bit longer?*

—*No. Night night. Go to sleep.*

—*Please?*

—*No. I can't. I've got a lot to do.*

—*Just five minutes.*

—*For God's sake, Gav. You're too old for this.*

—*I'm really scared.*

—*Scared of what? It's bedtime. There's nothing to be scared of.*

—Just a couple of minutes. Then I promise I'll go to sleep.

—No. No, Gavin, I can't stay with you every night for just a couple of minutes. You've got to get over this. You frighten yourself silly with these stories you tell yourself. You've just got to stop it.

—I'm trying, Mum.

—Oh, God. Don't start crying. Jesus. I don't have time for this.

—I'm sorry.

—No. You're not sorry. If you were sorry you'd stop doing it.

—I can't help it!

—I'm closing the door. I'll come back in half an hour to make sure you're OK. All right?

—Don't close the door!

—If you're going to cry like that I'll have to close the door. Dad and I have work to do.

—Please!

—It's your bedroom. It's your own bedroom. There's no one else here. No one can come in. All right? If you think there's anyone else in here then it's because you imagined it, you did, all by yourself. You're going to have to start learning to unimagine them. I don't have time to go through this every night. Night night now.

—Mum!

'I'm sorry,' she mumbled aloud, between gasps of effort as the hostile wind tried to stop her completely. 'I'm sorry.' She wondered sometimes what she'd say to him when she finally tracked him down. That was all it came down to. *I've made myself suffer as much as I can. I'm sorry.*

Signs told her she was not far from Bristol. Less than halfway there, and her cash was running low. Everything was supposed to be cheaper in the country but in the village shops they made her pay twice or three times what it said on the sticker even for a tin of fruit. One bristlingly irate lady refused to serve her at all. *I don't want your money. You can clear off. It's your sort's to blame for all of this. Go on. Clear off, or I'm getting my husband.* She'd snatched a chocolate bar on her way out and pedalled away from shouts and screeches and insults and threats, listening anxiously for the sounds of a car behind, but no one had followed. There weren't many cars on the roads anyway. She'd overheard someone ranting about petrol shortages that same morning.

In an area of exhaustingly tightly folded small valleys – there were snowdrops in the hedges, ignoring whatever had changed; to them it was just another season passing – she came to a place where the narrow lane was barred. Bright orange police tape was spooled across it. DO NOT CROSS, it said. A paper sign had been taped to a tree; the rain had smeared it entirely illegible. Two bulky concrete roadblocks sat under the tape. She ducked and steered the bike past them, then freewheeled down into the outskirts of a village.

The place was deserted. She'd become attuned to different degrees of background silence. The bike clicked and squeaked rhythmically, the spokes whirred, her own breath was a constant rasp, but when she was out of the wind and away from people those noises sharpened and drew somehow close. She rode through the village feeling as if she was miles away from the nearest dwelling. It had been a comfortable place once, but every house yawned with emptiness as she passed. She came to the bottom of the valley where the roads met. A helpful blue arrow indicated her way southwards. She was about to turn that way when it occurred to her that there might be a shop.

She'd already begun to fantasise about finding a village shop momentarily unattended. Five seconds to fill her pockets and she'd be out the door and riding away, no money spent and a day's calories in her bags. Or passing a shop in the dark, far from any houses, and seeing things behind unbarred and unwatched windows. Her pump was a solid aluminium tube. She was sure it would break glass. How hard could theft be? But here it seemed like she had a whole village to herself, a prosperous, *Telegraph*-reading Somerset village. She stopped and listened for a while. There was a steady racket of crows somewhere behind the houses. Their clamour reinforced the desertion; wild birds wouldn't gather so noisily when there were people around.

She turned the wrong way at the junction and rode slowly towards the village centre, watching for any signs of life.

She came, as she'd hoped, to a shop. It was as silent and as shut as every other building she'd passed. She felt all the windows looking down at her. She waited a long while on its doorstep before rattling the handle tentatively. When she pressed her face to the window she could see stacked shelves inside, biscuits and soup and plastic-wrapped bread.

She had the bicycle pump in her hand and was staring at the glass, breathing hard, when she caught the reflection of someone moving across the street behind her.

She swivelled around in abrupt shame, thinking to get straight back on her bike. At first she thought the person who'd surprised her was a pensioner in a black shawl, coming out of one of the humbler houses opposite. Then she saw a young hand feeling at the door, not coming out but trying to get in. What she'd taken for a shawl was a hijab. The person was a pudgy girl, badly dressed in a beige anorak and black leggings and cheap flat boots. She didn't seem to have noticed Iz at all. She fumbled slowly around the door of the house as if bewildered to find it shut.

As Iz watched, held in place by her reflex of embarrassed guilt, the girl backed away from the door and shuffled along the grassy verge to the next house. She stood in front of it for a moment and then prodded its door as well. She was facing away and half hidden by her headscarf, but even so Iz was touched by the peculiar hopelessness of the gesture. She couldn't have been older than Gav. Another lost child.

'Excuse me,' Iz said. 'I don't think anyone's here.'

The girl turned around slowly, looking dull and confused. 'Are you lost?'

The girl didn't answer. Her shoulders sagged and her mouth was half open. She was clutching something green and messy in one hand. It looked like a fistful of wilted salad.

'Everyone's left, I think,' Iz said. 'The police have closed it off for some reason.'

The girl stepped hesitantly closer. Her eyes didn't focus. She moved as if following the sound of Iz's voice, as if she was blind.

'Lizzie?' the girl said.

Iz dropped the bicycle pump.

'Lizzie? Is that you?' The girl shuffled towards her. 'Say something.'

Horrified beyond reason, Iz backed into the window behind her, stumbled, turned the corner and ran.

'Lizzie?'

There was only one way to go, a narrow street between empty white cottages. Her legs were used to pedalling and wouldn't run properly. She staggered away, bile in her mouth.

'Help,' the strange sad voice called behind her, still coming. 'Please.' There was a corner ahead. She ran around it. A fenced path went between the last house and an enclosed farmyard, ending in a gate with an open field beyond. Unable to think where she was going beyond the urge to get away, she stumbled along the path. A flock of crows rose up from the field ahead.

'Lizzie.' Or perhaps it was just the gargling of the crows; she didn't stop to look over her shoulder. She pushed through the gate into wet grass, looking around, thinking, *my bike, I left my bike behind*, and yet unable to turn back or even slow down. There were stones standing upright in the field, immense weathered red-brown fists and knuckles like petrified eruptions of the deep earth. Lengths of police tape were strewn around them in the grass. The view opened wider and more stones appeared, huge, some as tall as her and all a thousand times more immense. They seemed to be leaning in. She smelled a putrid and deathly smell. Something like a mound of abandoned bedding lay ahead of her, out in the field. Two more crows screeched up from it as she approached. When she saw that she wanted very badly to stop. She had to go back, to get her bike, to ride away. She looked over her shoulder involuntarily and stumbled in the long grass, spinning around. It felt as if the sky spun with her. The stones were a ring around her, and the pile of fabric lay in its centre. Not bedding, she saw, as she dropped to her hands and knees, but clothes, a mound of clothes.

Ugly flat boots.

Her gaze fixed on the boots and jammed.

The same ugly flat boots. Black leggings, torn to reveal glimpses of mottled white filth. Iz covered her nose and mouth with her hand as she got herself to her feet. The stench was death and rot. The ground seemed to be humming with a subacoustic groan, the voice of the assembled stones. Like an optical illusion falling into place, the reality of what she was looking at showed itself. It became booted feet, bloated legs, a maggoty corpse swathed in nylon and polyester and grime, a grimacing bloodless head half separated from the body by a long gash too revolting to look at. The hijab was still tied around the head. Iz reeled and turned and bolted. The chthonic rumble surged under her feet. Shadows fell around her as though the stones were moving. Her path into the field was a swathe of flattened grass. She followed it unthinkingly. No one was ahead of her or behind; the village was empty of all but its dead. She ran under the compulsion of absolute terror, stumbled across her bike and rode away out of the village and along the closed road until she had to stop to throw up.

Nineteen

S HE LOST HER way badly that afternoon and as dusk came found herself with no choice but to beg and bribe the landlords of a nakedly unwelcoming local pub for the use of an unprepared and unheated upstairs room. The thought of going on in the darkness looking for somewhere else was unbearable. She handed over most of her remaining twenty-pound notes. At least they let her wash in hot water. She barricaded the door to the room and lay on a mattress covered in a plastic sheet, listening to the grumbles of regulars coming up through the floorboards.

The next day she was puffing through a village when she passed a church with an open door. She hadn't seen the inside of a church for thirty years, but it suddenly seemed like the right place for her to go and take the step that needed taking. Some change had been completed, some accidental rite of passage. She didn't even know what it was, exactly. ('That's the point!' shouted the spotty leftie woman with the fiercely earnest eyes and the unfashionably lumpen glasses, standing on a stile to overlook her little audience and the cameramen behind them, all gathered in a snowy field. Her fervour made her shine for the cameras. *She can't get enough of being on TV, that one*, Nigel sneered. 'We don't know! That's the point! You can't talk about these things that way. It's not up to us to decide whether it's true or false. We have to stop thinking like that, before we do anything else.') She only knew that she'd arrived at the place of certainty where Gavin had lived all along. It had been so simple for him.

—*Who's that, Mum?*

—*Who?*

—*That man. The little one. No, you're looking the wrong way.*

—*Gav, love . . .*

—*He's gone now.*

Or:

—*Mum?*

—*Yes, love?*

—*If we go to Italy this holiday, will Miss Grey be there?*

—*Of course she will. If you want her to be. Don't you think?*

—*I don't know. Wouldn't she need a ticket for the aeroplane?*

She sat in a pew and apologised, out loud, for all of her forty-three years. She knew now what she'd say to Gavin when she got there and found him. There was no question of pleading with him to go back with her, no nonsense about wanting to be a family again. That lie was over. She'd go with him and Gwen, wherever they were, whatever they were doing. She'd drink herbal tea and meditate and wear crystal pendants, as long as they'd have her; and they would, because they'd see how sorry she was and how far she'd come. They'd know she meant it.

Some people came into the church and wanted to talk to her. They offered tea and biscuits – the fundamentals of the Church of England had survived even that winter – but she got up and left and rode away without a word. She paused only to rifle through the damp and stinking clothes in her panniers, pull out her powerless mobile phone and drop it in the nearest dustbin.

She went a long way that day. The last residues of doubt she'd been hauling along with her were shed. Like thousands and thousands of others, she'd achieved the full knowledge that there was no going back. Her face felt raw in the rushing air as she wheeled down the long flank of the Mendip Hills, down into the wide levels out of which the tor of Glastonbury rose like the pyramid of a green desert. From five miles away she could hear snatches of tinselly music, and see tufts of smoke and the encampments they rose from, tent villages lapping around the foot of the hill. She came across other people on the road, walking, cycling, a few camper vans. Some of them tried to halt her too, but she went on. Nothing could stop her now she knew what she was doing.

This must have been what it was like for her twin all the time, she reflected. She thought about Iggy constantly. She remembered feeling a kind of amused pity for Iggy's convictions. One week it might be wearing unbleached cotton to save the world; a month later and she'd be off to postcommunist Romania to volunteer in orphanages. Now, at last, she understood the pity Iggy must have felt for her.

How feeble her contemptible conventional sister must have seemed to Ygraine, fearless warrior of her own conscience. (They nicknamed her Xena at university: skinny, flat-chested, fox-faced Iggy. The incongruity was nine-tenths of the joke.) Iggy would have been in Cornwall days ago. She'd have pedalled from dawn to dusk. No: weeks ago, months ago. Iggy wouldn't have wasted time trying to deal with the useless police. She wouldn't have sat around picking the scabs of her grief, torturing herself in pathetic solitude. She'd have driven there straight away, without crashing the car. There'd have been no need for any of it, in fact, because Gav wouldn't have left her in the first place. She was his real mother, she'd have listened to him, he'd have loved her. He came from her, that was the truth of it. Pushing herself against the wind, legs hardening, blisters turning to tough calluses, Iz hoped that perhaps she was becoming a little bit like her sister. She was earning the right to be Gav's mother too.

The first soldiers she saw were at a supermarket on a ring road outside some substantial county town. An army jeep was parked by the sliding doors. Two young men rested their hands on weapons and ambled back and forth by the ranks of trollies. The shelves inside were more than half empty.

They'd heard about this in London. Radiating up-country from its epicentre in the far south-west, the mysterious disintegration of normal existence had been most of the news. Not just news: rumour as well, and myth. There were facts – the freakish weather, the outbursts of public disorder, the self-styled pilgrims, the state of emergency, the closed roads and helicopter drops and rationed goods, spotty Ruth delivering her strangely compelling open-air sermons to ever-increasing crowds. And then there were the things that didn't quite feel like facts. The persistence of the snow. The random nonsense email messages, the holes in web pages, other meaningless hiccups in the virtual world. The blurry photo of some black huge beaked thing on a woodland path. The video footage of something that might have been the same black thing, flying. The people who stopped showing up to work and the children who stopped going to school, as if work and school didn't matter any more. And then, as December turned to January and all those things showed no signs of being replaced by the next story as all news no matter how good or bad was eventually supposed to be replaced, there were the things no one could print or broadcast, things that were no more than intuitions, yet unmistakable and haunting nevertheless. The fraying of the order of things. The whispers of anarchy. The end times coming.

For Londoners like Nigel and Iz, supposedly protected by the charmed circle of institutionalised prosperity, all of these things happened *elsewhere*, in the not quite real realm of TV news. Londoners weren't choked immobile by weeks of snow or overflown by monstrous black birds. To them it had all happened at one remove, at least until it translated itself into the kind of existential crisis people like Nigel understood. The bottom fell out of the stock market, or the top of it was blown off, or its walls caved in: Iz didn't exactly understand its architecture. People like Iggy had always said it had no architecture at all. They said it had always been a thing of paper and breath and hope, and when enough people held their breath, down it came. But even that catastrophe was manageable compared to what they saw on the news. The collapse of imaginary value was, after all, a story with a familiar shape. It just meant that things were going badly instead of (as they'd always been promised) going well. The other kind of news, out at the margins of the country, was altogether different. It spoke not of things going badly, but just *going*. Going, going, gone. Off-white emptiness in the supermarket aisles, villages abandoned. Iz was seeing it now for herself, at last.

For the first time in months she smiled to herself. She was coming close.

She accidentally lost the signed route again as her legs began to give out. Backtracking through wet and over-grown lanes, the afternoon light thinking about fading, she passed a house she'd noticed earlier. It was set by itself in a small lank lawn near where the road crossed a stream. Beyond the bridge the lane twisted steeply up. She got off her bike to push, but instead of starting up the slope she stood looking at the house, thinking.

She waited for a few minutes and then squelched along its muddy driveway and rang the doorbell. The bell was a neat electric box and the door, like the window frames, was painted a trendy shade of rustic teal. A set of bamboo wind chimes hung near by. When no one answered, she poked the letterbox open and saw a spreading puddle of post on the mat within.

She did a circuit around the house. Now that she was looking properly, all the details reeked of suburban afflu-ence: wheelie bins with the name of the cottage painted on them, an elaborate squirrel-proof bird-feeder, a water butt attached to the downpipe from the gutters. Through a back window she saw vermilion cushions piled on a cream sofa. She knew from magazines and TV programmes that they weren't merely cushions: they were accents of bold colour. She was fairly certain that the only people who put accents of bold colour in isolated cottages in obscure valleys on the Somerset–Devon borders were people who actually lived somewhere else.

She wasn't sure how much farther it was to the nearest village or town. Anyway, she was exhausted, and so was her supply of money.

Iggy had always been the bad one. Iggy flouted school rules for the sake of it and dared their friends to steal nail varnish from Boots. Iggy grew her own pot. Iz felt she was about to cross into territory completely alien to her. She remembered her husband harrumphing at the TV news: *What would it be like if everyone decided to carry on like that? Do these people ever stop to think about that?* There was a terracotta straw-berry pot outside the back door, by the wooden wellie rack and the ornamental iron coathooks. As she picked it up she answered him silently: *This is what it would be like, Nigel. Watch.*

The shatter of glass was a surprisingly gentle sound, almost pretty. She used the base of the pot to clear splinters from the window frame. When she had a hole big enough, she went to get her bike from the road, threw the panniers in through the broken window, laid a wheelie bin down to use as a step, wrapped her hands in clothes and climbed in. Most of the glass fragments had fallen on the sofa. She pushed it out of the way and kicked the rest of the broken window under it.

She went to the front door to inspect the pile of post. The oldest mailings were from mid-January, more than a month ago. At the end of the school holidays these people had packed up and left. They'd tidied up, unplugged everything, put things in cupboards. She found food, wood, matches. There was no electricity but she'd seen a propane tank outside, and they'd left the instructions for the boiler in a purple ring binder labelled 'BOILER – INSTRUCTIONS'. There was a flap you could open to light the pilot light with a match. It was all ridiculously easy. *Anarchy*. At the cost of one smashed window she was dry, she was sheltered, she could sleep comfortably. There was washing powder in a cupboard in the laundry room. She filled a bathtub with hot water and spent the next hour washing all her clothes, and then herself, in someone else's house.

In the morning she went through the cupboards more systematically. Some were locked, but the keys were all in a kitchen drawer, each tagged with string and a label telling her which door it opened. She found lots of things she knew by now would be useful: a torch, batteries, dishcloths, a balaclava, gloves, a penknife, toilet paper, a lightweight coat, and – best of all – maps. There was a strange pleasure in the way books tumbled on to the varnished wood floorboards when she pulled the maps from their shelves. Every disruption of the house's obedient aspirational tidiness felt like an apology offered to Gav. *I'm sorry I cared about things like this. I'm sorry I cared about my world instead of yours. Look.* She picked up a mug of pencils and tipped them over the floor as well. *I don't care any more. See?* She rescued a couple of the pencils and snapped them before throwing them away again. She felt Gav smiling at her, like he used to in the days when he was still young and they went on expeditions together, before it all went wrong, so she went around the house looking for more things to break. She wrecked light bulbs, clocks, a brushed steel barometer, family photos on bedside tables; the tables themselves, once she abandoned her stupid restraint and attacked them savagely enough. *Do you forgive me now, Gav? You'll let me stay with you now, won't you?*

She didn't feel saddle-sore the next morning, for the first time. Drying herself after her bath the evening before, she'd studied herself in the mirror and thought she looked harder. The leg she'd cracked was still thinner than the other, but florets of muscle now bunched beneath its skin. She barely recognised herself.

The country was hummocks and hills again. Maps in hand, she abandoned the signed route and pressed on south and west as directly as the tangle of lanes allowed. Her panniers were heavily restocked and an icy drizzle blew against her on every ridge above every valley, but she went on steadily, knowing now that there were fewer miles ahead than behind. Late that afternoon she came to a hilltop junction where a bonfire had been lit in a field behind a roadside café. The building was dark and shuttered but its side door was open and there were voices inside, and from the field as well: woozy voices, laughter and delirious wailing. She hid her bike farther down the road and waited for darkness. Under its cover she walked back to the building and slipped inside. Within was the stench of spilled alcohol and the sweet reek of pot, and scattered blankets and bodies, four or five people sleeping or passed out under long tables. She found a corner to occupy. No one noticed her in the dimness, or if they did no one cared. More people arrived from somewhere as evening became night. The dance and sputter of firelight outside grew more vigorous. She heard tambourines, and more voices, shaky, glittering. She slept and woke alternately, or thought she did. Certainly she thought she was awake when she cloaked herself in someone's rough blankets and went out to watch the revellers in the field, all young, winding in and out of each other around the heat of the fire, dancing and chanting and rutting. Their eyes were glassy, their smiles limp; if they knew she wasn't one of them they never showed it, not even when she came right into the swaying throng. They whooped, sang, spun, fell over, dodging around her like a school of clumsy fish. A dark and antlered man walked among them, his hooved feet stepping to keep time with an invisible drum. She thought he carried a golden staff with a tip of horn, and touched it gently to the heads of the dancers as they passed him, or pressed it against the lips of those who lay drugged and drunken in the grass.

* * *

Near the southern edge of Exmoor she came upon the snow. At first she saw it only in north-facing hollows, or under the shelter of woods. Within a handful of miles it was dusted everywhere; another handful – painfully slow miles, wheels slipping, anything more than the gentlest slope unmanageable – and it was thick enough in the higher lanes that she had no choice but to get off and push.

She topped one of the endless exhausting small ridges and saw that everything to the west was white.

She put the bike aside, folded her arms, and stared into that sea of silence.

Here I am again, she was thinking. *I'm ready this time. Not like—*

'He's my son.'

'Mrs Stokes—'

'My son. He's my only child. He's just a boy.'

'Please, Mrs Stokes. I do appreciate—'

'Do you think I care? Do you think I fucking care? I don't want you to appreciate. Why haven't you found him? He's fifteen. He's a missing child!'

'I assure you, we're doing absolutely everything we can at this stage. Please. I understand this is a difficult time.'

'What are you doing? What *exactly* are you doing? It's been four days. No one's even rung me about what's going on. I've been waiting on the phone for an hour, an *hour*, and you can't tell me anything at all? How can you still have your job? How can anyone so fucking useless still—'

'Mrs Stokes.

'Mrs Stokes. Are you still there?'

'Yes. Sorry. Sorry, Superintendent, I'm just so . . .'

'There's no need to apologise. You're going through a traumatic experience. Believe me, the police are here to help you. We're doing our job. We're going to find Gavin. All right? We have a lot of experience of these situations. I can tell you, Mrs Stokes, based on what we know, it's very likely that Gavin will be in touch quite soon. Once he's ready.

'Mrs Stokes?'

'You're telling me to wait.'

'We'll absolutely be pursuing every possible avenue in the meantime.'

'You're saying I should just sit here. Aren't you? Do you know what it's like? Do you have children?'

'It's the best thing you can do. Believe me. In my experience these things are a matter of time.'

'I said, do you have children?'

'My family's not the issue here, Mrs Stokes.'

'I hope they leave you one day. I hope they die.

' . . . God. I'm . . . Superintendent?'

'Perhaps it would be best if we talked another time.'

'No. No, please, sorry. I've been trying to get through for days. Excuse me. I just . . . Is there anything you can tell me at all? I appreciate the conditions . . . I know the weather makes it difficult.'

'These aren't the ideal conditions for a missing persons investigation. But we won't let that stop us. Every missing child remains a top priority. Of course.'

'Yes. Thank you.'

'Well then. Thank you for your time, Mrs Stokes.'

'Wait. No. Just a moment. So you . . . you haven't found any more leads? There's no more news about my sister?'

'We're still pursuing our inquiries.'

'What about the post office? She must have been there over that weekend. I told you she got my letter. Doesn't anyone remember seeing her? Wouldn't that be a start?'

'My officers will be following up every line of investigation. Thoroughly.'

'Yes, sorry, yes. And the woman. Is there . . . What's the latest from the hospital? Do you know?' (*Rustling paper, voices off.*) 'Hello?'

'Excuse me, Mrs Stokes. I'm sorry to cut you off but I really must—'

'Please, just this one thing. The woman who left a message for my sister, the professor. Can you just tell me whether you've talked to her yet?'

'Madam. As I explained. We'll assemble all the—'

'You haven't. Have you? You haven't even spoken to her.'

'Excuse me. I'll contact you another time.'

'How hard can it be? How fucking hard? I might as well—'

'Listen. Listen very carefully. I shall say this once and then I shall hang up and continue working on the very large number of cases currently demanding my attention, including that of a missing twelve-year-old whose parent is at this exact moment outside my office. What we know for sure about your son's whereabouts is that your sister collected him safely from Truro station on . . . on Monday the 28th. We have his own evidence for that, and so do you, Mrs

Stokes, because he rang you to tell you so. We also know that . . . two days subsequently he rang you again, announcing his intention not to return home. Difficult as it may be for you to accept, Mrs Stokes, and I do understand that it's difficult, there is every reason to think that Gavin and your sister are together somewhere, perfectly safe. It's possible that Professor Lightfoot has some acquaintance with Miss Clifton which may be helpful in locating them, but Professor Lightfoot is currently in Treliske Hospital suffering from the effects of hypothermia and severe exposure and is unlikely to recover the use of her legs, so she's not best placed to assist us in an inquiry which, with the greatest respect, shows no signs of becoming a criminal investigation. All the indications are that wherever Gavin is, he's acting of his own free will and has never been in any danger. Believe me, Mrs Stokes, I know his decision is painful for—'

'"Decision"? "Decision"? It's my fault, is that what you mean? He's better off away from his horrible mother, is that it? Is it? You fucking bastard.' (*Click. Dial tone.*) 'You don't give a fuck. I'll make sure you're fired. You're finished. I'll see you fucking dead, I'll . . . I'll . . .'

—and then, some few unspeakable days later, the midnight phantasmagoria: lights on the motorways sparkling in her wet eyes, her own voice muttering and whimpering as the road howled below, desperation, urgency, hunger (she had barely eaten for a week). Turning aside at the blockade on the A30. Snowflakes glimmering in the impossibly narrow lanes. Driving dementedly, suicidally faster as she got more and more lost, the darkness of the great moor above her, pressing down, telling her she'd never get there, she was too late. The puddle of black ice. She had no memory of the actual crash but it must have come as a relief.

She thanked whoever it was who was watching over her that she'd remembered to pack wellies. There was nothing for it now but to walk.

Twenty

S HE SOON FORGOT that she was more than halfway there. The miles that had sped away under her tyres felt as remote as her childhood dreams of flying. She forgot that there'd ever been anything in the world except unremitting white. Where the surface of the snow had softened even slightly, or where its deceptively weightless accumulation had gone on perfectly undisturbed, the wheels of the bike sank far too deep to turn and she had to haul herself and her whole load along as if dragging them underwater. On the wider roads, the ones that followed broader valleys and connected villages and towns, she found parallel strips packed down hard by the tyres of tractors or cars. These were a hundred times easier to follow; but the broad valleys ran north-west–south-east, across her route instead of along it, and the villages, she quickly learned, were places to avoid.

She trudged towards one late that first afternoon and saw five or six people in the road ahead. They were standing around a makeshift sled, unloading plastic crates and split logs. They turned to stare at her as one.

'Clear off,' said a woman of about Iz's age. 'Go on.'

'Cheryl?' The man nearest her looked doubtful.

'Didn't you hear me? Back that way.'

Iz knew genuine hostility when she saw it. She thought of the supplies stashed in her panniers, and began wrestling the bike around without a word.

'It's a time for charity,' she heard the man say.

'Sod that. She can get her charity somewhere else, thank you very much. Somewhere that's got some left over.' The woman called Cheryl raised her voice at Iz's back. 'Wandering around looking for answers. Bugger off. All of you.'

'Don't try coming back,' another woman said, emboldened.

'The good angels are watching us,' the man muttered. He sounded full of shame.

'Doing a brilliant job, aren't they? Stop mooning after her like that and shift some wood.'

She was passed by tractors on the road two or three times. She thought they might stop and help, or at least ask her where she was going, but no, the hard-faced men and women who drove them wouldn't even look at her as she went by. Like the villagers, they took her for one of the pilgrims, one of the deluded or desperate thousands who had flocked to the south-west in the weeks immediately after the appearance of the winged monstrosity. Iz had seen them on TV too, of course, jamming the roads as the snow rebuffed them, battling on foot if they had the courage, camping in fields like fragments of an army in December retreat, turning to vandalism and theft as their progress failed. They'd mostly given up or been removed by now, so she thought. If there were others making the same journey as her she never saw them, though she was sure that no one with a need less than hers could possibly have kept going. There were many hours when she'd have given up herself if she'd had anything at all to go back to. When the lanes steepened and the snow was deep, half a mile was an hour's work. In the last week of February she gained barely forty miles as the birds flew.

Shelter wasn't a problem. There were abandoned houses and hamlets everywhere, and farm buildings where she could creep in under cover of darkness as long as she heard no dogs. The houses had already been broken into. Foxes had taken possession before her and snarled as they fled. They came back in the dark; she heard them scratching and whining beyond closed doors. Food was the challenge. When she saw a helicopter dumping supplies over the high villages between the Exe and the Taw she knew, if she hadn't known before, that the little cash remaining to her was worth nothing. The world of exchanging money for things had gone, as Ruth had prophesied. ('It's not *real*,' she shouted, pleading with her listeners, her passion making everything she said sound wonderfully obvious. 'There's no hope for us if we don't start looking at what's really here.' People had thrown banknotes on to campfires.) She melted snow in her hands to drink and hoarded her remaining supplies with obsessive exactness. From her days of not eating at all she knew how little she could survive on, but even so she might have stopped one day and not started again if she hadn't met with occasional unexpected kindness and luck. At one clump of dripping barns the farmer came out to call off her dogs and took pity on what she saw, returning with a plastic bag of soft potatoes and some strips of dried apple. And one evening Iz discovered, behind a broken gate and a driveway lined with fat-budded camellias, a house that had not yet been ransacked, perhaps because its last defenders had only recently abandoned it. She broke in and found packets of soup and drawers with things she needed, bandages, socks. The owners had left behind a lot of photos of themselves, on every mantelpiece and every window ledge. The girl had excellent teeth and impossibly shapely teenager legs. The two boys looked like half the children at Gavin's school, blond and louche, grinning the grins of children waiting for the future to drop all its satisfactions in their laps. The father and mother smiled breezily in every picture as if they never sweated and stank and shouted at their children, but Iz could see through them. She pressed her nose to the glass and looked into their eyes and saw him thinking about his thinning hair and his vanished ambitions and her hating her daughter for being so gorgeous. She saw all of it, no matter how well they thought they hid it. They hid the drink, too. She found vodka lying flat behind packets of rice on the highest shelf. When their lovely perfect children had finished gawping at internet porn or bitching on the phone about living in the country and had gone to bed, the parents sat downstairs and drank to save themselves from the horror of their days. The children would drink, too. Iz saw it all in their faces. The older boy already drank, and the girl did drugs, and the younger boy was a blond bully who liked making the quiet boys at school cry and would grow up and marry and hurt his wife for fun. When she was ready to leave, Iz piled all the paper and cotton she could find in a heap at the bottom of the wooden staircase and set fire to it. The house seemed reluctant to burn, but for a long time afterwards as she slogged away she could smell something bitter in the wind, and a smudge of smoke stained the grey horizon behind.

She breathed air so sharp and cold it was like swallowing ice. Then, one day, it changed; the wind became damp, salty, southerly. The sky changed too, turning whiter and wispier. By the afternoon there were spits of rain.

She had no way of knowing what day it was, of course. Nor did she know – though she might have, if she'd studied her maps – that on that same day she'd come over yet another level-topped rise and crossed into the watershed of the River Tamar. Least of all could she have guessed how long it would take her to cross the river and the forty-odd miles beyond, a distance to which three months ago no one would have given any thought at all, because three months ago forty miles was, literally, nothing, half an hour on the dual carriageway, a minor interval, a negligible gap between *here* and *there*.

She couldn't miss the tentative signs of a thaw. As the top of the snowpack lost its icy veneer, pushing the bike ceased being merely difficult and became impossible. She went back to the mouldering ruin she'd spent the previous night in and sat there until the next dark, waiting for the overnight freeze to resurface the lanes with a hard crust, but the cold stayed its hand that night, and the next. Dawn felt distinctly earlier. On the third morning it came accompanied by birdsong.

She abandoned the bike and set out walking, two of the panniers in hand. For a brief while it was actually better than struggling with clogged wheels. Then her arms began to ache, and then her hands, and then at the first gentle rise in the road her legs started burning as badly as they had when she'd set out from London. A few hours later she'd learned the new scale of her journey. No more measuring it out in miles; it was half-miles now, quarter-miles, the next turn in the road.

Even the smallest detour was now unthinkable. Villages could not be avoided if they lay in her way. Wherever she ended up when she ran out of energy would be where she'd sleep, one way or another. She inched towards the next place large enough to have its own name, knowing there'd at least be roofs and walls there, hoping to find them completely abandoned. Many of the villages were. She'd seen those pictures on the news too: stunned pensioners being coaxed into helicopters, rows of camp beds in school halls in the bigger towns along the main roads. But even before the village's church tower came in sight, she smelled smoke.

She slunk towards the jumble of houses and heard people moving about, talking. The sounds were strange to her. She'd lost any sense of kinship with people. She was an animal, she thought, a fox or a rat, coming stealthily in search of a dark corner to hide in and food to steal. With animal patience she waited until evening came on and then crept to the edges of the village. The smoke rose from a single building farther in, where the voices were concentrated. Whoever had decided to go on living here, they'd obviously gathered in a single house, sharing whatever warmth and company they had left. She stayed well out of sight until there was barely enough light left to see by and then stole to the nearest houses, trying doors carefully until she found a broken one, stepping quickly and quietly into the dim ruin inside. She felt her way to an upstairs room, closed its door behind her and crawled into the narrow space between bed and wall to sleep.

Bangs and whispered giggles woke her. She jerked upright, heart hammering, feeling cornered. Someone – more than one person – was coming in downstairs. She saw torchlight under the door. They knocked something over below.

'Shhhhh!'

More giggling. There were two voices, one male, one female.

'Upstairs.'

'What's wrong with the sofa?'

'Come on. Bloody hell, it's cold.'

'Shhh!'

'Who's going to hear us?'

'I don't know. Just be quiet, will you?' This was the woman, sounding breathless.

'I'm not going to. I'm going to,' he shouted, 'shout!'

'Shh! Danny!' Hysterical giggling. 'Don't!'

'"Danny!"' he mimicked. '"Don't!"' Squeaks of stifled laughter. A crunching bang.

'Ow. Bollocks. Why hasn't he set fire to all this yet?'

'Careful!'

'I'm coming in here tomorrow with an axe, I am. Chop it up. Look at that chair, that'd burn for hours. Where's the stairs gone?' The torchlight brightened in the landing outside the door. 'Here, give me that.' Giggling, thumping, a brief wrestle and a squeak of eager surprise. They went still for a moment. They were breathing hard enough for Iz to hear from her hiding place.

'Upstairs,' the woman said, 'quick.'

Iz started to feel for the clips on her panniers, wondering where the penknife was. The intruders clattered unsteadily up towards her, hurrying, the torch dipping and swaying like drunken moonlight. She squeezed herself tighter behind the bed. The door to the room banged open. Looking under the bed she saw two pairs of feet, one of them with dropped clothes tangled around the ankles.

'Come on,' the man said. His voice was thick.

'Urgh.' The woman stopped by the door. Her feet reeled away. 'What's that smell?'

'Christ!'

'It's disgusting!'

'Shit. Something must have died in there.'

'It's revolting.'

The torchlight bobbed around. 'Dead mouse. Probably.'

'Urgh. Don't say that. Where?'

'I don't know. Could be anywhere.' The light fixed on the corner at the foot of the bed, catching the bottom of one of Iz's panniers. The woman squeaked again.

'What's that?'

'What?'

'That black thing! It's a dead something.'

'Just some of Neil's stuff. Come on, downstairs.' The man's feet backed towards the door.

'It looked like something.'

'What do you mean, something? Oi, careful.' The woman had staggered against the wall. 'Pull your knickers up. Christ.'

'I'm trying.'

'Shit, that smell. I'm going to be sick.'

'Let's go somewhere else, Danny.'

'There's nowhere else. There's the sofa. This was your idea in the first place.'

'Yeah, well, I don't feel like it now.'

'You don't feel like it?'

'Not with a dead thing right there. It's horrible.'

'Let's just close the door then, all right?' The bedroom door slammed shut again. Iz took a deep breath. The voices stayed right outside, though, and now they were arguing instead of whispering. 'Downstairs. Are you coming?'

'It's still in there.'

'Christ, Tara. It's only a mouse.'

'How d'you know? It looked like a big thing.'

'What did?'

'Behind the bed.'

'There wasn't anything. Will you get your arse downstairs?'

'I'm not staying if I know there's something in there. I can't.'

'I don't believe it.'

'Danny, just go and look, all right?'

'You go.'

'I can't!'

'"I can't!"' he squeaked. There was no giggling now.

'What if it's one of those things?'

'What things?'

'Neil said there's things in his house.'

'There's no monsters in this village, you stupid cow.'

'Let me have the torch.' Clumsy footsteps and banging. 'I'm leaving. Right now.'

'Want me to look?'

'No!' A scream. 'Don't go in there!' The door swung open, light strobing madly as she tried to grab the torch from his hand.

'Thought you wanted me to. Eh?'

'Stop it!'

'All right, let's have a look.' The feet clumped towards the bed. 'Here, monster monster monster.'

'Danny!'

'Out you come, monstery. Let's have a look at you.' The light came looming over the bed. Filled with instinctive fury, Iz twisted up towards it as if to bite. The man made a sound like an aborted cough and fell back, dropping the torch. The woman screamed. The torch had fallen right by Iz's hand. She reached out quickly and switched it off. Now both of them screamed. She heard them crawling towards the stairs. She kicked out, making the bed scrape across the floor. The intruders shrieked and fell over each other and slid down the stairs in the dark, clattering and yelping their way out of the house.

It was perfectly quiet after that. Iz had almost fallen asleep when she had a strange dream.

'Tee hee,' a little voice whispered, somewhere close to her ear. Under the bed, perhaps. 'Hoo hoo hoo.' She heard a spidery scamper.

'Who's there?' Iz dreamed herself saying. She was too tired to move her head.

'Poo. Stinks.'

'Stinky,' agreed a slightly different voice. They sounded shrunken, as if heard through the wrong end of a telescope.

'Madam Stink.' A third voice, or maybe the first one again. Everything was blurry and sleepy and odd.

'Is it awake?'

'I'm awake,' she said, presumably wrongly.

'Made them scramble.'

'Scramble and tumble.'

'Ramble and scramble and rumble down stairs. Bangety bang.'

'No humpy fumbling.'

'Never again.'

'No more hump hump hump.'

'Shrivel up if he tries.'

'Make his sausage floppy.'

'Hoo hoo.'.

'All thanks to Madam Stink.'

'Hee hee. Scared them shitty.'

'Might never come back. Out of the house for good and all. Never never never. Woo hoo. Hail Madam Stink.'

'Hail.'

'Hail.'

'Owe her one.'

'One or two.'

'One.'

'Two. One for him, one for her. Two humpers tumbled and scrambled.'

'Takes two to hump.'

'Two, then. Owe her two.'

'Two lucky slices for the stinky lady.'

'What does it want?'

'What?'

'What?'

'What does it need?'

'A wash. Poo.'

'Soapy water.'

'Feather beds.'

'Snowshoes.'

'Wings.'

'Hope.'

'Going somewhere. Stinks of the road. Where's it going?'

'Gone to sleep.'

'I'm not asleep,' she said again. 'I'm going to find my son.'

'Sssss.' There was agitated scratching. 'Fibs.'

'Stinking fibber.'

'Hasn't got a son.'

'Hasn't got a daughter.'

'All dried up inside. Barren as bark.'

'On a humping to nothing.'

'Hump hump hump. No bun in the oven.'

'Not a bean.'

'Not a pea.'

'He is my son,' Iz protested, feeling hollow. 'He is. I love him.'

'Sssss.'

'Fib fib fib.'

'Two fibs.'

'No son no love.'

'Brazen.'

'Bold as brass.'

'Scratch one off. Lost a lucky slice. Liar liar.'

'One left.'

'None left.'

'One.'

'Two fibs. Two forfeits. None left.'

'Two or one.'

'Two. Lovey dovey. Love love love. Stinky fib.'

'Never loved him.'

'Shut him up.'

'Sent him away.'

'Spat on his dreams.'

'Squashed his squishy little heart.'

'All right. Two.'

'I did love him,' she croaked, in her dream. 'You can't say I didn't. I did the best I could.'

'Going to cry now.'

'Boo hoo.'

'Sniff sniff.'

'Madam Snivel.'

'Stinky Madam Snivel.'

'Snivelstink the Lying Lady. No lucky slices left for it.'

'Scared off the humpers, though.'

'True.'

'True.'

'Owe her that.'

'One, then.'

'One.'

'One lucky slice.'

'If it stops snivelling.'

'Better than humping.'

'True, true. Little sniffles.'

'Sleepy.'

'Long road.'

'Worn out.'

'Run down.'

'Could do with a slice of luck.'

'Listen.'

'Listen?'

'Stopped snivelling.'

'Stopped listening.'

'Went to sleep.'

'Whisper a secret?'

'Won't hear.'

'Which makes it a secret.'

'Keep schtum.'

'Silence is golden.'
'Mum's the word.'
'Who's it been humping?'
'Who stuck their sausage in it?'
'Stinks of it all over. Stinks of the road.'
'Tell it the secret.'
'Whisper the name.'
'Is it asleep?'
'No one's listening.'
'God of the Road.'

The morning came clear and therefore frosty, which made for easier going at first. She met two older men on her way out of the village. They eyed her bags suspiciously and asked where she was going in a tone which made it clear they didn't much care what she answered as long as she wasn't coming back. She thought they were more afraid of her than she was of them.

The map led her south-west. After another slow punishing hour or two she gained higher land again and stopped to rest her arms and take in the view. It was the brightest morning she could remember for weeks. Under the soft wet blue of the sky she saw what lay ahead: mile after mile of up and down, up and down, a wrinkled white sheet stretching all the way to the distant glittering swell of Bodmin Moor. A helicopter buzzed over the southern horizon; otherwise the scene could have been an arctic desert.

She came to one of the wider north–south roads, following the high ridge above the Tamar Valley. It was marked with the ribbed prints of tractor wheels. Ploughing had pushed high banks of snow to its edges, blocking the lane she'd walked up. She had to climb a crumbling wet wall before she could cross. She was gathering her breath and rearranging her soaked gloves and boots on top of this snow-bank when she heard a tractor approaching. It hove into view from her right, a dirty blue beast dragging a chained plank behind it, making a smooth flattened track in the middle of the road as it went. It had been days and days since she'd heard an engine so close. She pulled her panniers up beside her out of the way and waited for it to pass by.

It stopped next to her. She looked into the cab, where a bespectacled and messily bearded face stared back at her.

The engine cut off and the door of the cab screeched open. The driver leaned out, unfathomable amazement in his face.

He said: 'Jess?'

A hesitant smile creased his beard. He wiped his glasses with the sleeve of a grimy shirt, hopped down heavily from the step, and stared again. 'Oh my God. Jess. It's you. I don't believe it.'

Iz hadn't reckoned on encountering anyone resembling a normally approachable human being ever again. She reacted slowly. Her look of hesitant confusion must have been what the man expected to see.

'Greg.' He opened his arms. 'It's Greg. I know, I've lost thirty pounds. Hasn't everyone. And got new glasses. My God, I can't believe it's . . .' The smile broke his face wide open. He laughed in delight, crunched forward to climb the snowbank and before Iz could think what to say or do she was being bear-hugged. 'This is amazing. It's so good to see you.'

Very slowly, the significance of what was happening to her, of the name she'd been called, was seeping in. She made her arms close awkwardly around him in return.

'Hello, Greg.'

He backed away to look at her and take a deep breath. He wasn't used to her permanent stench of unwashed exhaustion. 'I thought it was you, then I thought it couldn't be. Praise God. What are you . . .' Transfigured with happiness, his face looked bizarrely childlike, a bearded ten-year-old, pink and innocent and hairy and grimy at the same time. He glanced down at the panniers. 'You haven't biked here? That's insane.'

'I cycled part of the way. Then I've been walking.'

'Walking? That's unbelievable . . . Listen to you! Look at you! OK, it's been fifteen years, hasn't it? That's actually quite a long time, isn't it? Would you have recognised me?' He fluffed his gingery beard. 'Satan's facial hair and all?'

'Never,' she said. She was smiling too, she realised, smiling incredulously at the sheer strangeness of the world.

'Of course not. God, I can't believe it. So, walked? From where? Where are you going? Are you off to join Ruth? No, wait, you left before she came, didn't you?' Without warning, his face fell. 'Didn't you? Sorry.'

Iz felt like her brain was ice-crusted machinery; she was having to chip at it to get the pieces moving. *Jess. You left.* She said nothing.

'Sorry. That was really tactless of me, wasn't it? Some things don't change.' He tried a faltering grin before looking away. 'Bad memories. Let's not talk about that now. It's just amazing to see you again.'

'Let's not.'

'Look, wherever you're going . . . Can I help? Do you need somewhere to stay for a bit? This can't be a coincidence. God meant me to find you. In the middle of all this . . . another minute and we'd have missed each other. Amazing. What can I do?'

Five minutes later she was wedged behind him in the cab of the tractor, ploughing down the high road, the truth of what was happening to her taking shape minute by unsteady minute.

She'd had a dream she remembered a little too vividly. Cruel voices had taunted her for not being Gav's mother.

Now she was.

The long journey had stripped her down, broken her, and remade her into her dead sister, who'd gone by the name Jess before she died, because Iggy was too silly and Ygraine was too posh. She was being mistaken for her twin. A complete stranger had looked at her and seen Gavin's mother. The unforgivable lie she'd told her boy for fifteen years was being reversed, unsaid, forgiven. It was a good thing the noise of the tractor made conversation impossible, because she found herself wanting to laugh.

Twenty-One

H E DROVE THEM into a narrow lane west of the main road. A few hundred yards on it began to descend. A beautiful wooded valley curled below them, trees lined with snow like something out of Narnia.

'Too steep for this thing,' Greg shouted over his shoulder. 'I leave it up here.' He hopped out to open the padlock on a barn door and steered the tractor in while she waited outside. He emerged pulling a children's sled. He tied the panniers on to it with bungee cords.

'The house is right down near the river,' he said. 'Half a mile. It's worse coming back up. Can you manage? What am I saying, you were always much more hardcore than me. You must have walked miles.'

Going down into the valley was like walking into another world, folded secretly inside the real one, which had in turn been ringed off from what used to be reality by the unnatural winter and the reports of monsters and marvels. They came to a cluster of stone houses with the usual broken windows and air of bleak abandonment. A hand-painted sign on a gate said TRAVELLERS WELCOME IN JESUS'S NAME. At the back of the hamlet, on a small rise overlooking the bend of the river, was a slightly bigger and much less damaged house among a scattering of outbuildings. It had once been a mill, Greg explained. A great round pierced stone was propped up near the entrance, mantled with snow. The river itself was visible only as a white channel between the trees, sinuous and unblemished, like a dream of a road.

The house itself was low ceilinged, white walled, cluttered like the inside of a tent, and almost colder than the air outside, but it was a dwelling, not a ruin; its chaos and mess spoke of being lived in.

'It's been just me since the new year,' he said, wiping off a chair for her with a plastic tablemat. 'Oh, of course, you wouldn't know. I got married. Three kids. That's them.' He pointed at a photo. 'I know, if it can happen to me it can happen to anyone, right? Sit down, I'll light the stove. Lil took the kids off to her parents in Leicester. This was no way for them to live. Jules, he's the youngest, he's not three yet.' He smiled vaguely at the picture, and then at her, as if she too were a representation of something he was missing. 'God. Jess. You're so . . . You sound different, do you know that?'

'It's been a long time.'

'You've gone quieter. Sorry, God, I'm embarrassing myself.' He went into a next-door room and started fiddling noisily with pipes and taps. 'It wasn't very tactful of me to start talking about the kids either, was it?'

'It's OK,' she called back. She stared through a dirty window at drifts of heaped snow, silently astonished at herself.

'So are you still in touch with any of the others? Katya? Steph?'

'Not any more,' she said. She could hear how the conversation was supposed to go. Impersonating her sister took no effort at all. She was talking with Iggy's mouth, the mouth that had first kissed her boy. 'What about you?'

'Not for years. You know how it is. It's funny, it was all so intense while we were there, and then you leave and . . .' He came back in, wiping his hands. A clogged and smoky smell followed him. 'And once you have kids your world goes like this,' he squeezed his hands around the cloth, 'you know? Oh. Oh God, I did it again.'

'No,' she said. 'It's all right. I have a child. A son.'

He blinked, suddenly shyly attentive. 'Oh. Nice. That's great. How old?'

'Fifteen last October.'

'Wow, fifteen. Oh, so he's . . .' The shyness turned into hesitant discomfort. 'When you left Trelow.'

Trelow. She'd forgotten she ever knew the name. Perhaps she never had known it; perhaps she was having Iggy's memories now as well as talking with her mouth. *Trelow* was what it was called, the place she shut herself away in when she came back from eastern Europe after finding God. Floor heaters and knitted scarves and prayer meetings and biscuits.

Perceptible warmth was coming in now, from the other room. Greg sat down in the only other empty chair, across the rickety table. 'I know, I said I wouldn't bring it up, didn't

I? I didn't mean to . . . Anyway, he's all right, your kid? Somewhere clear of all this? OK. Never mind, we'll change the subject. God knows I miss mine as well.' Iz didn't think she'd started crying; perhaps she just looked as if she was about to. 'My fault. We've all had to make hard choices since this began. Of course. "Who can endure the day of His coming? For He is like a refiner's fire." I think about that verse a lot.'

She looked at her hands, trying to imagine the way Iggy made choices. Nothing had ever seemed to give her a moment's doubt. Greg stared earnestly at her meanwhile.

'You haven't turned away from God,' he said, finally, 'have you?'

It was like being told off by a five-year-old. Iz found it difficult to hold back an unwanted smile.

'God turned away from me,' she said.

'No. Oh no. So many people are saying that and it's so wrong. It makes me so angry.' She'd never seen anything less angry than his rather sweet petulance. He'd obviously never encountered anyone like Nigel. 'God's giving us a new world, a whole new way of living, and people are saying he's abandoned us. Like they expect him to make things simple. You can't think like that, Jess. Not you. I can see you still live in faith. What else would you be doing walking all the way down here through the snow? That's . . .' He checked himself, leaning back in the wooden chair with its peeling grey paint. 'OK, look, I won't harangue you. Ha. That's a bit of a turnaround, isn't it? Remember how you used to sit me down and tell me my faith was weak?'

'Of course I do.'

'Used to drive all of us crazy the way you did that, but I still . . .' She saw him blushing. 'Anyway. Fifteen years ago, wow. Happy days. I miss Trelow, you know?'

'Me too.'

'Oh, I'm making tea, in case you were wondering. Old time's sake. No biscuits, though. The days of biscuits are gone.' She smiled with him, sharing whatever joke it was. 'I'm glad you remember it happily too. Such an amazing way to live. You know, it wasn't the same after you left.'

'Really.'

'Yeah. It was never quite . . . We still did lots of good work. Important stuff. But, you know, the feel changed. The group dynamic or something. Ruth kind of took over when she arrived. Anyway, after a couple of years I met Lil, so that was that.'

'Of course.'

'I've never been back. Funny. It was my whole world for four years. It still feels like this really important time in my life. But I've never wanted to go back. It's not even that far from here, but somehow . . .'

'Neither have I,' she said, after he trailed off.

He looked at her shyly. In the next room a kettle of water was beginning to stir.

'Is that where you're going now?' he asked.

'No.'

'No, of course not, there can't be anything left at Trelow by now. It's been terrible down there. Much worse than here, from what I've been hearing. But you're going on into Cornwall?'

'Yes. I'm looking for someone.'

'Ah. God. I still can't believe you actually walked this far. From, where was it?'

'London. I only had to walk the last few days.'

'Days!'

'I'm not sure how many. I lost track.'

He shook his head admiringly. 'You always were sort of unstoppable. They've been turning people back, you know. The army's on all the roads.'

'Not the kind of roads I took.'

He looked at the two panniers, and at the calloused stripes on her palms where she'd been carrying them by their awkward handles. 'Lugging all that. Someone's been watching over you, Jess. You may not realise it but there's no doubt.'

'Maybe you're right.'

'I know I am. So you got over that thing, obviously.'

She felt herself on shaky ground for the first time. She tried to look innocently uncertain.

'With going outside. Obviously. So that was a prayer answered, wasn't it?'

She wanted to mumble something non-committal, but he'd fixed her with an eager, cajoling look. 'I'm not sure what you mean,' she said.

He frowned. 'You're not telling me you only walked at night?'

'No.'

'So your skin's fine now. With sunlight.'

'Oh,' she said, trying to think of a way to change the

subject. She'd completely forgotten how to talk to people. 'Yes.'

He looked mournful, or perhaps disappointed. 'You prayed day after day to be saved from that. We all prayed together. Don't you remember?'

'It was a long time ago.'

'You don't want to give God the credit, do you? All right. I said I wouldn't harangue you. You'd probably rather be out by yourself in the snow than put up with that.'

'It's so good to rest a bit.' Warmth, proper warmth, was trickling into her, like forgotten happiness. 'Thank you.'

'No, no, this is wonderful. Seeing you. It's been pretty lonely, to be honest. I mean, I have the people I look after up the road, but coming back here every day . . .' He waved apologetically at the room. It was beginning to fill with a fine steam, beading on the window, furring the damp-stained walls, clouding the plastic tubs of toys stacked in the corner. 'It's very solitary. I never had that urge to be a hermit. Not like you and Steph.'

Iggy, she thought, *a hermit?* Iggy had despised people who hid away from the world. She'd burned with her sense of duty.

But then everything had changed in the last couple of years. Iz had been as astonished as anyone when she'd got her copy of the circular letter Iggy wrote announcing that she was going to live in a Christian retreat deep in the country, that she'd changed her name, that no one would hear from her. Being Iggy, of course, she meant it. There'd been nothing after that, not so much as a Christmas card. The next thing she'd known was two years later, the doorbell ringing at home one evening and her twin on the doorstep, wild and haggard and pale as death, and a tiny baby in her arms.

'You must be shattered,' Greg said. Iz realised she'd forgotten he was there. 'Do you want that tea?'

'Sorry. Yes. Please.'

'It takes ages to boil water. It takes ages to do anything, actually. It's all a bit medieval. It'll get there, though. I usually leave a big bucket of snow on the top every morning. So there's hot water by the afternoon. For washing and stuff.'

'Right,' she said, since he was looking at her expectantly again.

'So, um. If you feel like a bath . . .'

Hot food and water were pleasures so overwhelming they threatened to make her cry. The valley grew dark outside while the two of them sat at another table beside the range stove. The only light was the glow from the little chamber at its base where the wood burned. He hadn't bothered with candles or oil lamps, he said, since it was just him in the house after dark with nothing to do. They ate tinned beans and crackers. Everything came from the town down on the main road, he told her, but he hadn't been for more than a week and he'd given his rations of meat to the older people he kept an eye on in their remoter villages. He appeared not to have any notion what she'd been living on since her purchasing power ran out many miles and many days ago, and kept apologising for not being able to offer things she remembered as distantly as dreams: fruit juice, ham.

'You know,' he said. The speckled grime of his glasses had gone opaque in the faint gleam of ember-light. 'There was a rumour going around that you'd died.'

'Who told you that?'

'I can't quite remember. I think Katya said she'd heard something about it.'

'Well,' she said, holding a spoon close to her lips; even the warmth of the metal was magical. 'Here I am.'

'A lot of us felt really bad about it, you know. Not,' he added hastily, 'you being . . . I mean, of course, no one wanted to believe that. But about what happened. I think we . . . I remember Kat facing up to Chloë and Dave a few times and telling them we'd all gone too far.'

She said nothing.

'I know I felt the same way. I'm not making excuses, Jess. Honestly I'm not. I was part of it and I went along with it so I can't say I didn't mean it. But afterwards we didn't all feel we'd done the right thing. We talked about it. A lot.'

'There was always plenty of talking.'

He chuckled nervously. 'You couldn't have stayed, though, could you? Not making excuses again, but it wouldn't have worked, would it? I've done the baby thing myself a few times now. God. Imagine a baby at Trelow.'

If they hadn't thrown her out when she was pregnant, Iz thought, *Gavin would never have become my child. He'd never have had to put up with me. He'd have grown up with people who understood him and loved him.*

'I could have done it,' she said. 'I'd have made it work.'

He looked down. There was a long silence.

353

'Then I should ask your forgiveness,' he finally said. 'Maybe that's why God brought you here. So I can make up for it.'

Iggy too had that perpetual bizarre conviction that everything was about her. Iz felt a pang of her old irritation at the self-absorption of fanatics, but swallowed it down. It was a trace of her former self, and she wanted nothing more to do with that person.

'So. Do you forgive me, Jess? I'm asking humbly. I'll understand if you can't.'

She glimpsed her sister's unknown history like a ghost in the darkness of the house, waiting behind him. Why hadn't she ever wondered about it? Because there was a tiny baby to occupy all her attention; and because her husband broke off the conversation if she so much as mentioned Iggy's name.

Forget me. The very last words her twin sister had said to her. Her eyes were maddened; she kept glancing up at the night sky as if she was terrified that someone was watching. *Promise, Lizzie. Be Gawain's mother and don't let him know I ever existed. Don't ever talk about me. Forget me. Promise.*

'It depends what you want to be forgiven for. Specifically.'

'Were you a lawyer back there in London? Oh, all right. I know what you mean. Forgiveness is a selfish thing to want, isn't it? Anyway it's up to God to judge. But, look. I'm sorry I didn't stand up to them. I am, truly.' He tried for a moment to meet her eyes and failed. 'We had a meeting. Ha. Of course we did. You can imagine how it went. Dave and Chloë said you'd sinned and you should leave the fellowship.

All I'm trying to say is, I know now I should have been braver. Kat felt the same. So, that's it. I'm sorry. We were too quick to pass judgement. I was.'

'So now,' she said, stirring her small bowl of beans exquisitely slowly, releasing sensuous wafts of salt and sugar and MSG, 'you don't think I sinned?'

His discomfort, like his fervour, was endearingly hesitant. There was something not quite grown up about him: half man, half teddy bear. 'We were all so young. Weren't we? None of us had any idea about . . . Love. What Lil and I have, I know that's blessed in the eyes of God. Marriage is a sacrament, isn't it.'

'Marriage is hell.'

There was another very long silence.

'I'm sure you and your wife are very happy,' she said, eventually. 'Not because you're married, though.'

He poked around his bowl with the edge of a cracker. Every movement made soft murky shadows move. He seemed at a loss for words.

'It's so strange seeing you like this,' he said at last, not looking up. 'I know everyone changes. We all have. You, though.' He laughed in half-hearted amazement. 'Of all the people to lose their faith. I remember you arguing with Dave, saying we ought to be out preaching in the fields like the Methodists used to. Saying you'd be doing it yourself if it wasn't for the fact that you couldn't risk the sun touching you. I used to think how great you'd have been out there. Everyone would have listened.'

Iz could see all too clearly how Greg must have fallen in

love with Iggy. People tended to, the ones who didn't find her completely laughable.

'And instead it turned out to be Ruth. Who'd have thought. Shy little Ruth. You remember what she was like. God.' Iz was about to agree, glad of the change of subject, but fortunately Greg went on before she could. 'Oh no, of course you don't, she came after you left. But honestly. I remember her telling me she was trying to find courage to take the veil. Now look at her. Thousands hanging on her every word.'

The spotty leftie moron. Iz felt a dreamy bafflement that Ruth too was part of the shadowy story rising from its grave before her. She was tired. She wasn't at all sure who she was; she was hovering between her own identity and her sister's imaginary history, between the living and the dead.

'She's a powerful speaker,' Iz said.

'You've heard her?'

'On TV. Clips. She's . . . magnetic.'

'I don't get news any more. Just rumours. Everyone's talking about her, though. One of the old gents I look after calls her a prophet. I told him I used to live with her, that she left the top off the toothpaste and had a thing about headlice. And her surname is Shenley-Baverstock. Did you know that? We used to give her such grief about it. He doesn't quite believe me.'

'The newspapers call her a prophet too.'

'Do they?'

She couldn't actually remember. It sounded familiar. 'I think so.'

He slumped his shoulders. 'She's not preaching the gospel either, though, is she?' The look he gave her was almost pleading. 'She's not spreading God's word.'

'Not really. No.'

He put down his last cracker as if he was too distraught to eat.

'What happened to you?' he said. 'What went wrong?'

Abruptly, she felt the old misery sneak into the room. She'd eluded it for days, zigzagging through the lanes, but now it had caught up again. It began to sniff closer, circling her in the obscurity beyond the weak glow from the stove. Greg was too wrapped up in his own timid disappointment to notice.

'I did terrible things,' she said. *I'm sorry, Gavin.*

'Jesus's love doesn't change, no matter what you do.'

'I don't know about that.'

'Don't you? Really? Are you telling me you don't believe the promise of the gospel any more?'

'I'll never again,' she whispered, not to him, 'tell anyone that what they believe is wrong.' *Forgive me, Gav, love.* Gavin had inherited none of Iggy's fire and fury. Perhaps that was where it had gone wrong. If only he'd insisted. If only he'd shouted and argued like his mother would have, shouted them all down tirelessly and relentlessly until they all gave up and agreed with him. *All right, Gav, have it your way, your imaginary friend really is outside the back door, go and talk to her if you want, all right all right all right.* Then he wouldn't have had to run away.

'Wow. You really have changed, then.'

But she was suddenly tired of him, of everything. The dreadful ache found her and latched on. She said she had to go and lie down. The room he'd half-cleared for her upstairs had been the older children's bedroom, separated from his by a thin mould-spotted partition. She buried her face in the dank pillow the way she used to when she was trying not to wake up her husband with her nocturnal rituals of grief, but it was very quiet in that snowbound valley at night. He must have been able to hear her sobbing through the wall.

Greg was out all the next day. She slept through most of it, after being awake all through the night. At some utterly dark hour she'd been convinced her sister was calling again. *Lizzie. Help.* 'I'm coming,' she whispered back. 'I'm nearly there.' But when she woke in the daylight she felt in no hurry to leave. It was a delicious luxury not to stand up, not to have to carry anything, not to be cold and in pain.

Greg was out helping. That was how he'd decided to pass the trial he thought he'd been sent: looking after the weak and the old. 'Like we used to say at Trelow,' he'd explained. 'You bring what light you can to your corner of the world, wherever it is.' He was allowed to have diesel for his tractor on condition that he keep the road to and from Okehampton at least partly clear, and he was given food as long as he also took supplies to the remaining villages along that road where those who couldn't or wouldn't leave had gathered to try to survive the winter together. While he was gone, she lay in bed, wondering hazily how she'd ended up in that room with its peeling striped wallpaper and its shelf of painted model aeroplanes and its rectangle of glum light slowly crossing the carpet. She kept seeing and hearing other things, with the intensity of hallucination. Most of all she kept coming back to that Halloween night, her sister appearing out of nowhere at the door. They hadn't answered the bell at first in case it was kids demanding chocolate. She remembered the baby's quiet milky eyes, so strangely unconcerned that his mother was leaving him, that she was dying. She remembered Nigel giving in late that night, gruffly tender: *At least we'll be giving the poor kid a proper life. We can give him a proper name for a start.* He'd thought it would be like adopting a cat but with more paperwork. It was like that, at first. She remembered that winter, many nights blending into one in the recollection: she'd get up at some ungodly hour and go to him and find him awake and perfectly silent, perfectly calm, little head turned towards the window. *Wonderbaby*, she and Nigel called him. They sniggered at their exhausted friends with their clingy colicky children. Six years later her husband was slamming doors and saying *If only we'd never taught him to fucking speak.* Or was it her who said that? She was here in this bed because she was on her way to find him, and yet she remembered signing him up for every weekend activity on offer just for the sake of extra hours without him in the house. She remembered sitting at home on the sofa during those extra hours, thinking about the fact that she was legally manacled to a man with the sensitivity of a brick. She listened to her heart fluttering as she lay in the clammy bed and wondered what it would be like if it stopped.

'You don't look too good,' Greg said, when he came back.

'I'm all right.' She was still in bed, though.

'I should have tried to pick up some medicine. I can get some tomorrow. There's a chap farther up the road, I gave him a couple of boxes of aspirin the day before yesterday.'

She didn't feel ill, she just felt odd. This business of being transformed into a different person was very disorienting.

'I don't want to be a burden,' she said.

He laughed cheerfully. 'I've been wondering all day how to persuade you to stay for a while. Needn't have bothered, really. You're not going anywhere.'

'Why not?'

'You, madam, are sick.'

'I'm only tired. It's been a hard trip.'

'Do you have any idea what it's like west of here? Everyone's gone, except along the main road, and if they catch you anywhere near that they'll stick you in the back of an army truck and ship you back up to London. You'll need to carry a lot more than you've got in those two panniers if you're going to walk over the moor. I know you're a tough cookie, Jess, but you're in no shape to try that. Look at you.' He seemed pleased.

A useful side effect of appearing ill was that he didn't expect her to say much. He talked about what he'd been doing, and about what he used to do before the snow came and his family left, and about his family. He didn't wait for her to answer in kind, which was good, because she was increasingly hazy about which of her memories she was having and which she was only pretending to have, which family was hers and which her sister's. He was happy to leave her alone, or to pull up a plastic desk chair and sit across the room from the bed, hands in his pockets, chattering away undemandingly. He was, she thought, *nice*. She didn't realise you could lie in bed and talk or listen to someone nice; it wasn't a word you could ever have applied to her husband (she thought she remembered having a husband).

'So, you must have been married for a while? Back in London?'

'Hmm?'

'Based on what you said last night. It sounded . . . personal.'

'Oh. Yes. Yes, I was.'

'I'm sorry it didn't work out for you.'

'That's all right.'

'Lil and I have our ups and downs. It's hard with her being so far away. They used to bring letters down the main road but that all stopped a couple of weeks ago.'

'Can't you call?'

'There's no power. It's amazing what you lose without electricity. A chap up the road has a propane generator, I can charge up a phone on that occasionally, but I don't feel like I can keep asking.'

'Mmm.'

'To be honest I'm not sure . . .' He sniffed and reached out to pick up one of the painted models from a shelf, turning it around in his hands. 'Last time I called Jules cried on the phone.'

She didn't even try to work up some sympathy for him. What did other people's children matter, compared to her boy?

361

'Lil said I should join them there,' he said. 'In Leicester. Says.'

An icicle dripped outside, pinging every few seconds on an upturned bucket, like the tick of a clock slowed to a quarter speed.

'I know I should have, shouldn't I? But . . . my work's here.'

Food smells rose slowly from below. Cooking took hours, travelling took days. She listened to the world stalling. *Ping . . . ping . . .*

'Are you awake?'

'Mmm.'

'I should let you go back to sleep.'

'No, it's fine.'

'Ought to get some food down you, though. Are you hungry at all?'

'I could eat.'

'The thing is . . . You can't just do the easy thing, can you? This is a test. We agreed I was going to stay here as long as I was needed. Maybe if spring comes and they can get the power back . . . It's definitely been a bit warmer the last couple of days. Listen to that, that's something melting.'

They both listened. It was getting dark.

'Though Lil said things are getting difficult up there too. Everything's really expensive. Supply problems. And, you know, people just not going to work. You had that big march in London a couple of weeks ago, didn't you? Did you go?'

'Mmm. No.'

'I can just see you in there pitching stones at office windows. I heard it turned into a pretty big riot.'

'Yes.' She did remember. So had she been there? Or just watched it on TV? 'It did. They set fire to things.'

'God forgive them.' He put the model back. 'It's . . . You know the verse. Without vision the people perish. They know they want something different but they haven't seen the truth yet. False gods. It's all been prophesied. All they have to do is open the Bible and they'd know what's happening. God. To think that our generation would be the one to see this . . .'

She thought about telling him that he didn't know anything at all, but she didn't want to be hurtful.

'I said that to Lil. I mean, this is the heart of it, down here. This snow, and the angel appearing right over Trelow . . . She had to take the kids. They're too little still. But we should all have stayed if we could. Shouldn't we? I mean, this is where God touched the world again. Think of all the millions of people who wish they could be here.'

She shuffled under the clammy sheets. 'I don't remember an angel,' she said.

'You don't? I thought that was the one thing everyone knew about. That photo, and all the videos.'

'Oh,' she said. 'That.'

'You don't think it's an angel either.' His voice had gone flat.

'I hadn't thought about it.'

'It just means "messenger", you know? Everyone thinks it has to be white robes and silvery wings with a harp, but actually why wouldn't God's messenger to us be black? The world's full of sin.'

'That's true.' She'd spent hours, days, nights staring at

that photo, the slightly fuzzy picture apparently snapped on a phone by a man walking in the woods. Everyone in the world had see that photo. Unlike everyone else, though, she hadn't been staring at the black monstrosity facing the camera; she'd stared at the blurry image of the person with their back turned, blocking the monster's path. She'd convinced herself it was her son.

—*That's not one of the birds that can change, is it, Mum?*

—*I don't know what you're talking about.*

—*The ones that turn into people.*

—*Gav.*

—*What?*

—*Just . . . don't, please.*

—*Don't what?*

'It's frightening how blind people are. That's all been prophesied as well. You remember. A lot of people thought the angel was the devil. Or a pagan god. And then those terrible things started happening, the sacrifices in the stone circles. It's like the angel came to open everyone's hearts and all the evil started spilling out. I've got to stay. I've got to bear witness, you know?'

'Mmm.'

He went quiet for so long that she'd forgotten what he was talking about when he suddenly said, half strangled with embarrassment, 'Really I should go with you.'

She tried to lift herself up on her elbows to look at him properly. For some reason her arms didn't cooperate.

'No,' she said.

'I should be there. Right there. I think that's why God sent you here, to show me what I should be doing. You were always like that for me.'

We only met yesterday, she thought.

'All those pilgrims who went down there in the beginning, half of them were into black magic. Devil-worshippers. Really, can I let people like that be stronger than me? If no one else is going to bear witness . . .'

There was another protracted silence.

'Because you're not going to, are you, Jess?'

He sounded painfully tense. He must have spent the whole long pause gathering courage to say that sentence.

'What?'

'That's not why you're going there. Is it? You're not going to testify to God's word.'

She couldn't care less about his children, wherever they were, but the ruefulness right across the room from her was harder to resist.

'I'm a disappointment,' she said, 'aren't I?'

'No. No, no. It's so fantastic to see you, I'm so glad you're here. It's just . . . I can't see what's driving you. If you don't have faith any more. Which you obviously don't. I mean, I don't mind living like this, I don't mind being lonely and cold all the time and hungry and whatever, because, see, I know, I *know* this is what God's called me to do in this trial. But you don't . . . you don't have . . .' He trailed off again in mute frustration.

'Oh, I do,' she said. 'I do.'

She was ill, of course. As if her body had been hanging on through days of punishment until it was finally all right to give in, she collapsed. She sweated and dreamed waking dreams and could only crawl out of bed to pee in a bucket. She thought Gwen must have died and was calling for help from beyond the grave, and Gavin was alone in the snow somewhere with no one to look after him except the phone engineer with the beautiful voice. Greg came in and out, emptying the bucket, mopping her forehead and hands, rolling her carefully from one side of the bed to the other to replace the fever-soaked sheet with the one he'd hung up by the stove. He did it all with unfeigned cheerfulness. 'Just like old times. Remember how the pipes froze every January? Seriously, I miss that. Looking after each other was the best bit.' He was happier now he didn't have to be in awe of her. He was so happy it brought strange tears to her eyes when she thought about it. Nigel wouldn't have put his hands on a bucket of piss for anyone, unless it was a dare or there was money involved. She envied Greg. She envied Greg's wife. She envied her lost and dead sisters, and everyone who wasn't herself.

Some days later there came that utterly miraculous instant when she woke up and the illness was gone.

It was a late morning. The house was quiet. She felt rather than saw an ambience of thin sunlight. Everything in the room, the boys' toys, the patterns on the sails of the sailing boats in the wallpaper, looked clearer and sharply outlined. She sat up.

'Greg?'

Her voice sounded croaky, but it was definitely hers. She remembered how she'd got here and where she was going, and the extraordinarily lucky coincidence by which she'd been mistaken for her twin sister, sheltered and fed and given respite.

'Greg?' He must have gone out. He couldn't stay watching her all day, though he probably wished he could. Other people depended on him too. He'd left a cleanish towel beside the bed. (Bless him, she thought.) She daubed away the remnants of the night's sweat from her face and her hair, which was down past her shoulders now.

She remembered other things that had happened as well. Twice.

Twice, she'd heard a voice calling her by a name no one except her sister knew. There were other times she might have imagined it, but twice it had happened for sure: the recollections were as precise and solid as the objects on the shelves beside her head. Set aside all her sleeplessness, her despair, her exhaustion, her self-hatred, despair, anger, recrimination, hope, the whole mental blizzard she carried around with her, and they were still there.

How?

Answers do sometimes come dawning, but not in this case. There couldn't be any gradual understanding. No process of thought available to Iseult Stokes, née Clifton, could have led her step by step from that question to any kind of remotely acceptable answer. Instead she found the answer already there, not rising like dawn but clear as day.

It's—

—Mum?

—Yes, love?

—*You know magic?*

—*Yes?*

—*Well . . . How do they do it?*

—*I'm not sure what you mean.*

—*Magic. Like magic tricks. How do they work?*

—*Like card tricks, you mean?*

—*Yeah. Actually, no. I mean proper magic. Stuff that looks impossible.*

—*I don't really . . . I'm sorry, sweetheart. Can you give me an example?*

—*Like pulling a rabbit out of a hat. Not when there's a secret compartment. When you know the hat's empty, they show it to you so you can look inside and feel around so you know there's no trick.*

—*Oh, I see.*

—*So, how does that work?*

—*You mean how do they do it?*

—*Yeah.*

—*I . . . I have no idea. It's a secret. Apparently when you learn to be a magician you have to promise you won't tell anyone how it's done. Which makes sense, doesn't it? Otherwise it would spoil it.*

—*Spoil what?*

—*Oh, Gavin. You know. The fun. If you knew how a trick worked it wouldn't be any fun to watch someone do it, would it?*

—*But then—*

—*Anyway, you get on with your homework while I finish unloading the—*

—*But I mean, if it's a trick anyway—*

—*Gav.*

—*Then it's not really magic, is it?*

—*Of course not. There's no such thing as real magic.*

—*But then where's the rabbit come from? If you know there isn't a secret compartment.*

—*I don't . . . Look, Gavin—*

—*No, but if you know. If they show you the inside of the hat.*

—*Will you please not interrupt?*

—*Sorry, Mum.*

—*I already told you, I don't know. Probably it is a secret compartment actually, they just make it so clever that you can't see it even when you look closely. Or maybe it's hidden up your sleeve. I don't know, that's why people like watching magic shows, isn't it, because you can't figure out how they do it. Have you finished your homework?*

—*It's easy, Mum, it's only geography. So you know they do it?*

—*Do what?*

—*Do the trick.*

—*I don't see . . . Yes. Sorry. Yes, that's right. What's your geography this week?*

—*So it looks impossible but it isn't really.*

—*Gavin. What do you think 'impossible' means? Think about it. You can't do something if it's actually actually impossible.*

—*So it's not magic.*

—*No. Of course not.*

—*They shouldn't call it magic, then.*

 . . .

—*Mum?*

—*I don't want to talk till you've finished your geography.*

—*But I think I—*

—*I said. Not until after your homework.*

—*You'll be upstairs by then and I'm not supposed to go in your study.*

—*Oh for God's . . . All right. Tell me quickly.*

—*OK, what if, what if, OK, it just happened? Not in a show. 'Cos if it's a magician doing it you know there's a trick, but what if it wasn't, what if any old person took a bunny out of a hat. Like in Waitrose. Like they just did it.*

—*What do you mean?*

—*How would that work?*

—*It couldn't, obviously. No one can do that. Gav, I think I see what you mean now, sorry. You mean do things like that only happen in magic shows, don't you? You see, when a magician does it, it looks like magic, but actually everyone knows it isn't even though they call it that. It's just fun to watch. Even though deep down everyone knows there's no such thing. It's fun to pretend.*

—*I wasn't talking about pretending.*

—*Well. Never mind.*

—*I was talking about if someone did it and you knew there wasn't a trick.*

—*All right. All right. Then it would really be magic. Gavin, you're not concentrating at all. That colouring's not very good. Look at the edge there.*

—*Mum?*

—*Sweet Jesus. What?*

—*Would that be OK?*

—magic.

Iz prayed. Not in the sense of addressing herself to God: she didn't think God had anything to do with it, or if he did then he certainly wasn't going to do anything about it. But she did know that something entirely other than herself was at work in the unfolding of events, something out of her range. She tried to focus on that idea. She didn't bow or kneel because that would have felt like pretending. She did, however, close her eyes, to shut out everything which she'd formerly thought made up the reality of things, and in the no-space behind her eyelids she found herself thinking of Gav's Miss Grey, who had, after all, surely been real in this other, new way; so she prayed to her.

She spoke words aloud, because otherwise it was just echoes and half-phrases in her thoughts.

'Please let me find Gavin,' she said. 'I'm very sorry I spent so long telling him you weren't there. Just let me find him. I only want to say I'm sorry, I was wrong. I don't expect any more than that. But please let me have the chance to say it to his face. And to hold him. Once. Please.'

Truth is a rare beast, and when flushed from its lair a dreadful one to stand and face. The truth was that Gawain was thousands of miles away as Iz murmured her ineffectual prayer, every steady step he took stretching the distance further; and Miss Grey was dead.

Twenty-Two

'Hello there. Welcome back.'

'Hi.'

'Sitting up and everything. You'll be taking solid food next.'

She smiled.

'Feeling better?'

'Thanks to you.'

'All part of the service.'

'I'm so sorry, I—'

'Shh. None of that. You're a great patient anyway. Much better than having sick toddlers. You didn't throw up once.'

'I wonder what it was.'

'Fever, mostly. I suspect you were just worn out.'

'How long have I been in bed?'

'Four days. I think. It's amazingly easy to lose count. Don't ask me what the date is. The spring's definitely coming, though. There's a thaw on its way. At last.'

At last.

The map she'd taken from the first house she'd broken into ran out near here. While it was still light he spread out his own maps, clearing space by a window so they could peer over them together. 'Don't think this means I'm letting you go any time soon,' he said, the joke sounding far more nervous than it ought to have. 'So. There it is. You never told me exactly where you're going?'

She was so close. During the worst days, the couple of days after she'd had to abandon the bike, she'd forgotten that she was actually going somewhere. The journey had become its own endless purgatory. But now she was rested, her head was clear, she was going to get . . .

'There.' She drew a vague circle around the crook of land below Falmouth. 'Roughly.' She saw the word on the map, *Pendurra*, taunting her with its empty precision. They might not be there still. Or they might be cut off, alone, in trouble, who knew? The map couldn't tell her anything. But she'd get there, she'd see for herself what had happened. She'd find them.

It was a few moments before she noticed Greg was staring at her, not at the map.

'You told me you weren't,' he said. Under his gingery fringe his brow was knotted.

She looked at the map again, trying to hide her confusion, and saw it straight away. Just a hand's-breadth inland from Pendurra, another name off by itself in a patch of green: *Trelow*.

'Sorry,' she said. She could feel his eyes on her. 'I . . .' She tried not to let any of her own astonishment show. They couldn't be more than a couple of miles apart, the place Iggy had hidden herself in and then been expelled from and the place where Gwen lived. How could that be possible? Gwen hadn't gone to do whatever it was she did there until at least a couple of years after Iggy had died. Could it just be coincidence? Greg was waiting for her to finish her sentence. She tried to concentrate on assuaging his suddenly doubtful look. 'I didn't want to mention it at first.'

'Fair enough, I suppose,' he said.

What could she say to disguise the fact that she apparently hadn't even known where Trelow was? She avoided his eyes. 'There are still some bad memories.'

'I sort of knew. To be honest.'

'You did?'

'Well, where else would you be going? And. You know. I can see how you might have . . .'

He waited expectantly. He'd almost been embarrassed to look at her, before, but now she felt herself being scrutinised.

'Unfinished business,' she said.

'Exactly. No offence.'

'None taken.'

'Is it something you want to talk about? Can I help?'

She had no time to think about it. 'I'm looking for my sister,' she said.

'I didn't know you had a sister.'

'Two.'

'You didn't get on with your family, isn't that right? Remember that night we played Who Has the Worst Parents?'

She chuckled, a little uncertainly, but only a little; it wasn't difficult for her to imagine Iggy on the subject of their parents. 'Vaguely. Who won, again?'

'Well, me, obviously.'

She'd made a clear error, she could feel it at once. 'Of course. Sorry. I was just . . .'

'So what happened to your sister? May I ask? How did she end up at Trelow?'

'I'm not sure.' She knew she ought to change the subject, or get up and say she had to go outside, but she felt a reckless urge to carry on. Every time he started reminiscing about Trelow she felt he might be about to let slip something that would make everything clear. 'The same way I did, probably.'

'You mean she joined the community? I had no idea.'

'I don't know if she did or not. We weren't in touch. She might have.'

'You can't have told her about it?'

'No. No, of course not. I'm not sure what . . . Perhaps she just found her way.'

For a while she didn't dare look up at his face, but then it felt more awkward not to. He was still frowning, brooding.

'You never said anything about how you'd found us. I always remember that. That prayer, though. You remember? We always said it together every evening. You always squeezed my hand so hard at the Amen.' She'd run out of vague lies, but fortunately Greg began to recite a moment later. '"Thank you above all for leading us here to serve you." What was it we used to say? "All our separate troubled paths have come together in peace here.'" He looked at her expectantly.

She reached across to take his hand and squeezed it. 'Amen.'

'I always remember that.' His hand was hot and weak. He released hers reluctantly. 'It was very mysterious. Like your paths were particularly troubled. Gosh, Jess, you were so . . .' He laughed his short embarrassed laugh. 'And here you are again, out of nowhere. All mysterious and glamorous.'

'Glamorous? I peed in your bucket.'

'Seriously. You're . . . It's like you're on a mission. I feel sort of small.'

'I'd probably have died without you.'

He went as pink as raw meat. It was all too obvious that there was nothing he'd rather have heard her say.

They discussed the way she ought to go until it got too dim to see the map. He wanted to light one of his candles so they could carry on, but she wouldn't allow it, partly because he only had two left, and partly because the dimness gave her respite from maintaining her act. He said the only thing that mattered was avoiding anywhere there might be people. All the stories he'd heard were that Cornwall was lawless, beyond the three or four towns along the main road where the survivors had gathered, and even there the influx of pilgrims had brought on a chaos of overcrowding and disorder. The coming thaw might open the roads again, but he doubted that would mean things getting back to normal. He'd heard that Ruth's speeches were becoming more incendiary. (She remembered Nigel huffing at the television in fury. *That's right, tell them what they want to hear. Make it all sound so bloody simple. Rabble-rousers. You can't argue with people like that. They ought to get a sniper in a helicopter, best way to shut her up. Shit, there's the fucking phone again.*) There were marches in other towns and cities up and down the country now, marches that turned into riots, riots that ended in burnings. He'd been to Okehampton while she was ill, to collect his diesel allowance, and the talk going around the army kids who handed out the supplies was that Ruth was going to be arrested. All of it might have been no more than rumour, but the only safe option was to stay far from the road for as long as she could. The route he plotted out for her took her up on to the moor, where it had been hard enough for people to live even before the snow came and made it impossible. Once across it she'd have to turn southwards, looking for the open downs, passing through the valleys as quickly as possible, and, eventually, crossing the main road. He drew a zigzag line on the map in pencil, steering the remotest route he could find, picking out a crossing-point where the road was at its narrowest and far from any towns. When she lay down in the boy's bed that night she couldn't sleep for thinking about that line. It felt like a prophecy. I know the way now, she thought, lane by lane, turn by turn. I'm going to get there. *I'm coming.*

He insisted she keep the maps. The next morning he showed her into a chilly room at the back of the house and began pulling things out of a cupboard, a backpack, proper hiking clothes, thick-soled waterproof boots.

'Try them,' he said. 'You're taller than Lil but she's got

big feet. They'll be a lot better than wellies even if they pinch a bit.'

She looked at him. He'd gone slightly pink again.

'I can't do that,' she said.

'Yes you can. You've got fifty miles to walk. You need proper gear. Reminds me, I think we've got water purification tablets in here somewhere. Go on, try the boots.'

'They're your wife's?'

'She'd understand.'

'You know I'm not coming back, Greg.'

'You might. One day.'

'No. I'm not.'

'Doesn't matter.' He wouldn't look at her; he rummaged in the cupboard, pulling out a lightweight towel, a first-aid kit. 'This is just stuff. Sitting here. It ought to be used. You're going to need it.'

She didn't argue. As soon as she put on the boots and the backpack she knew they'd transform her journey. She understood what lay ahead of her now. When she'd set out she'd been mad with grief and hope, but the miles and days had beaten sense into her. With the kit he was offering she'd be dry, she'd be able to carry more than she needed. Ten miles a day, she thought. Five days. Five more days and she'd be there.

He'd hoarded extra food for her as well. She turned down as much of it as she dared, until he got angry, or as near angry as he could manage. He sat her down and did calculations with calories to prove how much she needed. She couldn't really explain that something else was fuelling her.

She was consuming herself as she drew closer to her boy. By the end, she hoped, she'd have got rid of herself completely. Gav couldn't hate her any more once she'd wasted to nothing. Greg wasn't to know any of that, of course. Eventually she gave in and accepted everything he pushed on her, just to stop the discussion.

She thought about leaving that afternoon while he was out. But they'd worked out the most likely stopping-points, and the first one was a full day's walking away; that, and she felt one more night's rest would help. She went out and tested her new gear, picking her way through deep snow beside the river. The bare trees glittered and dripped and the air felt almost humid. Even with the backpack loaded she felt so light she thought a gust of wind might launch her like a seed. The skin around her wrists was drawn tight to the bone.

In the evening Greg made checklists and ticked them off as he packed and repacked her supplies. She sat and watched him, seeing the sadness his efforts at brisk efficiency were meant to disguise. She observed it without sympathy. Perhaps he was grieving for something he hadn't dared say fifteen years ago, or perhaps because he still didn't dare say it now; either way it was a feeble grief, so trivial beside her own that she almost felt envious. She remembered how she herself used to spend pointless hours wishing she'd been brave enough to say no when Nigel proposed. As if that mattered now.

'Oh,' Greg said, straightening up abruptly from the table where he'd pinned his list. 'One more thing.'

His surprise was an act. She could see straight away that

he'd been thinking of this last thing all along and had only now worked up courage to mention it. 'I'm surprised you haven't asked about it already, actually,' he said, grinning awkwardly. 'Come on. Let me show you something.' He led her outside. It was dusk. Patches of clear sky threaded among banked and layered cloud were turning deep, deep blue. He went behind the house to a breeze-block shed built against the side of a crumbling stone hutch.

'I suppose you've forgotten,' he said, pulling open the door. She saw a lawnmower and a shelf with a rack of tools. He reached under the shelf and got out an old cigar box with a sliding top.

'I kept it in here,' he said. 'Hidden.' He opened the lid and gently extracted a small wad of tissue paper.

'There,' he said. 'You should have it back. After all this time.' He put it in her hand. It was hard to see his eyes behind the filth of his glasses and yet she could sense the embarrassed intensity of his attention.

'Thank you,' she said.

'Unwrap it,' he said. She hadn't even realised the paper was wrapping. She could feel no extra weight. 'It's still perfect. Or it was the last time I checked, which was, um, not long ago. Actually. Actually I come and look pretty often.'

She unpicked the wad of paper and found a dark smooth thumbnail-sized thing inside. She had to hold it up to the sky to be sure what it was: an acorn. An elongated, glossy brown one, its nubbled cap still tightly in place.

Greg watched her as if his future hinged on what she did next.

'You're right,' she said. 'I've forgotten.'

He seemed to go too still.

'Sorry,' she added.

'Seriously?'

'It's so long ago,' she said. 'So much has happened.'

'You gave me that,' he said. 'When we all decided to give each other something. Remember? It was Dave's idea. Come on, Jess.'

'Oh,' she said. 'Vaguely.'

He shrugged and slid the top back. 'Pretty funny that I kept it secret for fifteen years and you managed to forget the whole thing.'

'Remind me,' she said, but she was only half paying attention to him. She turned the acorn in her fingers. *This was Iggy's.*

'Dave did that thing? Surely you remember. We were all supposed to give each other something precious to us. To show we'd abandoned our personal things and become a community instead. Gosh, it can't have made much of an impression on you. Funny. I remember it so clearly. I remember you saying you didn't have anything, and we were about to give up because everyone had to do it, then you went up to your room and came back with that.'

Was this all she had? An acorn?

'I can't even remember where it came from,' Iz said. 'Did I say anything about it? It's all gone completely out of my . . .'

The stillness was heavy, thickened by the abrasive mutters of rooks coming to roost.

'You said it didn't look like much but it was the only thing

381

you had to give and I should always keep it hidden. So I did.'

'I'm sorry,' she said.

'I gave Kat that jade good-luck charm my grandpa bought in China. Just a piece of crappy tat. I felt like you'd given me some amazing secret. The way you came downstairs with it. Everyone stopped talking. Even Mac stopped talking.'

She rewrapped the acorn and zipped it into the pocket of her jacket.

'I should get an early night,' she said. 'I'll start early tomorrow.'

He closed the rickety door of the shed and put his hands in his pockets.

'I'm coming with you,' he said.

She had to bite her lip to stop herself smiling. *Oh, Iggy*, she thought. *I'd never have fingered you for a heartbreaker. I was the pretty one, remember?*

'You can't,' she said. 'You know that.'

'I can. I'm going to. You shouldn't go alone.'

'I have to.'

'Whatever you're doing,' he said, 'it's important. I can feel it. I want to . . . I'm supposed to follow you. I can tell.'

'There are people here who depend on you.'

'They can go to the camps in Okehampton. I've been thinking about it. They ought to have gone ages ago, they'd be much better looked after there. I've just been indulging them. And myself. I wanted so badly to be helpful, so I let their lives stay difficult so they needed me.'

'That's nonsense, Greg.'

'It's the truth.'

'This is your home. What about your children? Your wife?'

'They're not coming back.'

The rooks swooped and fussed overhead. It was dark enough for them to disappear completely in the shadows of the trees.

'Lil doesn't want me to join her either,' he said. His eyes had gone watery.

Ah, Iz thought. You think that's unhappiness. You think life has turned against you. You have no idea.

'I was ashamed to tell you. God forgive me. We're so stupid about these things. Or I am, anyway. You're not.'

'Let's go inside,' she said.

'She said . . . She says I've made my choice. Which is fair enough, I suppose. Though God, I miss the boys. But we all have to . . . we have to . . .'

She left him sniffling and went back to the house.

She slept poorly that night. She was slightly worried that he might try to come into her room in the dark. But no, she thought, as another chill grey morning trickled into the valley, he was too nice; he'd suffer, nicely, in silence.

It turned out he'd done his suffering downstairs, all night long. She found him at the table, looking dishevelled and blank eyed. His hands were clasped around a mug with a thimbleful of cold tea at the bottom.

'Couldn't sleep?' she said.

He raised his head to her.

'You're not Jess,' he said. 'Are you?'

She thought about sitting down, but in the end she just

stepped behind him and squeezed his shoulder, once, before starting to gather up her gear. His anxious preparations meant that everything was already laid out, packed, dry, ready to go. She'd have liked a last cup of tea since she wasn't sure how long it would be before anything hot passed her lips again, but it was a small thing, really.

'I don't know why it's taken me so long,' he said. 'Even tonight – last night – I didn't think of it until late. Even though you said. Sisters.'

Iz sighed a little, then sat down opposite him and started on her socks and boots and leggings.

'We were twins,' she said. 'In fact.'

'"Were"?'

'She died.' His shoulders sagged a little. 'Fifteen years ago. I don't know exactly what happened, but when you people drove her out she had the baby by herself and it pretty much killed her.'

His head tipped forward on to his arms.

'You've been so kind,' she said. 'Incredibly kind. I'll always remember you.'

'So.' He kept his back to her. 'Who are you really looking for? If she's dead?'

'We had another sister. Younger.'

'And she joined Trelow?'

'No. She lived near by.'

'Then you won't find her there.'

Lizzie, the voice had called, twice. *Help*. 'I will. Do you want me to give back these things? I have to take the boots and the backpack, but the rest—'

'No. They're yours.' He twisted around in the chair at last, desolation in his every movement. 'I still want to come with you.'

'No one can come with me,' she said.

He stood in the doorway.

'So.'

'So.'

He shrugged. 'Good luck. God be with you.'

'Thank you. For everything.'

He took his glasses off, polishing them ineffectually with his fleece jumper. 'I feel like my life just turned completely upside down.'

'My sister always had that effect on people.'

'Jess . . .' He squinted upwards, blinking. 'She was amazing. I had such a crush on her. I probably made that rather obvious, didn't I?'

'She had that effect, too.' Sometimes.

'What . . . What did actually happen to her? Before she came to Trelow? We all knew there was some big story. I've wanted to know for fifteen years.'

'I don't know.' Iz hitched the pack on her shoulders, adjusting the straps. 'She and I, we went our different ways. After university. It was after the Wall came down, she went to Romania. I think. She was going to save all those orphans.' And I met Nigel with the City job and the sports car and the wife he dumped because I was young and fit, and you despised me, and you were right, Iggy, you were right. 'She wrote to our sister from different places. Bulgaria. Greece.

She was travelling with gypsies, something like that. Then the next thing we heard she'd arrived in Cornwall and turned Christian.'

Greg winced.

'No offence,' she added.

'She was afraid of something,' he said. 'Jesus was her refuge. We all had our different reasons for ending up there but she . . . She was happy at Trelow, but it was almost like relief. Like she'd got away. She always said she felt safe with us.'

'That's good to hear.'

'I assumed it was a family thing.'

'We didn't reject her. She rejected us.' Us? Me. Mum and Dad too, but me, mostly.

'Was that true, that thing about her skin?'

'I don't know what you mean.'

'About the sun. Not getting the sun on her. No, I always thought there was something strange about it.' Her blank look had obviously confirmed a suspicion. 'It was more like she was terrified of the sun. Like a phobia.'

'Not that I ever knew.'

'She wouldn't go anywhere near direct sunlight. All summer long she'd only work at night. You didn't . . .? No. It never really made sense that it was a medical condition. She got twice as much done as the rest of us anyway so no one minded.' He laughed his weak, rueful laugh. 'She was amazing. When I drove around that corner and saw you . . .'

She had a sudden dread that his disappointment was a bad omen. She too was looking for someone lost, after all. She thought she'd better get away before he infected her.

'Good luck to you too, Greg.'

'Yes. Better let you go.'

Their breath steamed between them.

'Her real name,' she said, 'was Ygraine. Everyone called her Iggy.'

'Not surprised she changed it, then.'

She turned.

'Back up to the corner,' he said behind her, 'and then the other road leads over to the bridge.'

She raised a hand and waved.

Twenty minutes later, as she forced her way through deep undisturbed snow banked between walls of low stone, she thought she heard the waters of the Tamar trickling softly somewhere under their three-month mantle of ice.

She walked, rested, walked, hid herself and slept. Time passed in a slow trance of sweat and solitude, her breath the white cloud ahead of her, the blots of deep bootprints behind. She saw vehicles abandoned or burned, birds picking over things half buried in the fields, barricades of broken gates stacked between hedges. Now she was no longer dragging bicycle panniers and chafing in clammy clothes, her slowness was patience and steadiness instead of struggle and exhaustion. The ten miles she'd promised herself every day were a fantasy, but even the distance she managed around dawn and twilight each day marked out visible gains along the pencil line on her map. She stayed hidden during the full light, resting. Illness had sapped her. The slightest hint of the presence of another person made her take cover and wait.

But mostly when she walked it was through a wasteland, an obliterated kingdom.

On the third day the wind picked up, turned south-westerly, and took on the smell of the sea. It tore pale blue gashes in the clouds and let the sun in, so dazzling on the snow it was impossible to go on westwards in the evenings. The hedges sparkled with meltwater and she sank halfway up her calves with every step. Then the rains began.

A world of silence became a world of noise. It was as though the landscape she'd been crossing since entering the grip of the snow had been asleep and now woke up screaming. She sat out a whole day and night on a pile of tyres under the corrugated-iron roof of a dairy barn. The roof made a tinny thunder louder than she remembered sound could be. When the rain moderated enough for her to leave her shelter she heard the noises farther afield, a sound like a low angry wind from valleys below the moor.

That sound was water seeking the coast. She was lucky she'd reached higher ground before the melt took hold. The small streams draining the moor were overwhelmed. The ground beside them turned as porous as moss, shedding suddenly unrooted trees down to the valleys. Roads were buckling under the floods, bridges breaking. But in the open heathland where Iz was the slopes were still gentle. The meltwater around her boots was in no hurry yet.

Nevertheless, there were long hours when she could make no progress at all. Even the best gear couldn't keep her dry in that kind of rain. As her progress stalled she began breaking into the low-slung slate-roofed farmhouses that went with the decrepit barns. In one of them she found the farmer thawing too, going soft, hanging by a noose of tied sheets from a rafter above his staircase.

Wading as much as walking, she completed the half-circuit of the moor marked out by Greg's pencil, and looked down one evening across the valley on its western side. On the map, the river there was a tidy blue ribbon. What she saw instead was a great brown smear, churning and frothing at its nearer edge, dull and deceptively tranquil beyond that, making islands out of trees and houses and hedges. The flooded ground stretched all the way north to the sea.

It took her all the next day before she found a place to cross. Downstream of a half-submerged hamlet a huge tree had toppled over and jammed itself against shallow banks either side of the current. She picked her way along its trunk. The flood looked murky and sluggish from above but turned out to be savage at close quarters. While she stood clinging to a branch to catch her breath she watched flotsam spinning past. It was as though the sea had opened its throat to swallow the world, piece by piece.

She had to wade waist deep along the drowned lane beyond the river channel before it rose at last out of the floodplain into modest hills. After she'd reassembled the clothes she could still use, mopped out the inside of her boots as best she could and set off again, she discovered an astonishing change. The snow was all but gone; the floods cut her off from any risk of encountering anyone else; for the first time in weeks, she could go fast. Miles suddenly began to disappear behind her. She felt as light and swift as thought. She walked all day without noticing it. The drizzle cleared eastward as the evening came on, the cloud cover frayed thin, and an intermittent moonlight appeared around her; she kept on walking. After the punishing weeks of trudging through snow it was like a dream of motion. Halfway through that night she realised she was in ecstasy. The punishment was over: it was all easy now and she was almost there, ridiculously close. She thought she heard whispers echoing her footsteps, as if she were being shepherded along by good angels.

She slept the next day in a roadside bus shelter in the middle of nowhere and set off again as a damp dusk fell. Only the smallest traces of moonlight filtered through the clouds but that was as much as she needed. She came that night to the road she'd been so afraid to cross, the single main road running down the spine of Cornwall, linking this wasteland to the unimaginable rest of the world. Greg had warned her it would be patrolled and constantly travelled, and marked out one of the rare places where it was narrow enough that ordinary country lanes still fed in and out of it, but at three o'clock in the morning it was nothing, just another trickle of debris-spackled grey, though miles off to the west she caught a glimpse of the flare and sweep of headlights. When dawn began to break she unfolded the map and looked in giddy astonishment at the ground she'd covered. She'd come so far in one night she thought she must have made a mistake. There were perhaps fifteen miles to go.

As she rested the next day, holed up in what remained of someone's bungalow on the edge of a peculiarly dismal village, she heard an engine go by. The sound plunged her into an instant panic. She'd forgotten that the retreating winter had cleared the roads for other people as well as her. The thought of being stopped now was so hideous it made her take the penknife out of the pack and zip it in her jacket, right beside Iggy's acorn, so that she'd be ready to cut her own throat rather than be forced to turn back. She couldn't sleep. She kept trying to imagine herself walking into the house where Gwen lived, seeing her sister and her son there, right in front of her. She remembered that they almost certainly wouldn't be there, they'd have had to leave like everyone else; then she remembered that Gavin – no, Gawain, she should give him his own name now – wasn't like anyone else. She couldn't think at all. She wanted to start walking but she knew she had to force herself to wait for darkness, full night, when no one could possibly see her. She passed the time memorising every branching and turning of her route so she wouldn't even have to get the torch out to check the map.

Her food had run out so she ditched the pack, taking nothing but map and torch and knife and the clothes she walked in. It never occurred to her to wonder what she'd do the next night. If she'd reached her journey's end by then, she'd be all right, nothing else would matter; if she hadn't, she'd be dead. One way or another this was her last day.

As she crept out of the bungalow late that evening and set off southward, she heard the bells of Truro cathedral ringing to her left, and saw the clouds above the distant city lit up with reflected firelight. Two helicopters buzzed, harsh lights

probing like malevolent antennae. It all felt entirely disconnected from her. A few times she heard the angry buzz of a
car struggling up the clogged and slippery lanes, but never
coming her way. She stole along as quiet and invisible as any
nocturnal animal. There were wide muddy streams and
fallen branches and sinkholes and puddles deeper than her
boots, but she was carrying nothing at all now, and after
everything she'd been through it was easy, easy. She thought
she could smell the belated spring coming, nettles and ivy
and brambles uncurling again after crushing months.

As first light came she passed a gap in a wildly overgrown
hedge and saw the land steeple down suddenly beyond it,
dropping to a smooth darkness below: the estuary.

It was all she could do not to break into a run. Where that
same water she was looking at widened and approached the
sea, there was a house on the opposite bank: Pendurra. She'd
stared at the map for hours and hours. The precise contours
of that river were etched on her heart. Down there, out of
sight towards the sunrise, perhaps at that very moment, her
boy was waking up. She remembered what he looked like
asleep, on school mornings, in the precious moments before
she sat down on the edge of his bed to coax him awake.

It took a painful effort to make herself concentrate on
solving the last few miles between here and there. She
muttered aloud to herself, talking it through. Getting to the
other side of the estuary, that was the main thing. Which
meant going in the wrong direction, away from the sea, looking for a place where the valley became narrow. It would be
flooded, but that was all right. She'd find a way. Glints of

hesitant light were appearing in the crack of the horizon between the drowned land and the clouds. She had all day.

She kept to high narrow lanes, skirting the village where the first bridge had been. The line pencilled on her map took a wide turn around it, avoiding its prominent cluster of houses, but when she looked down the valley side she saw there was nothing to fear there. The village's position at the head of the estuary had been its ruin. The stream funnelled down into it from the hills, and like all the other streams it had turned violent. The village was a tumbled silted wreck, waist deep in water and choked with the carnage of houses torn open by the floods. No one could be living there.

Surveying the muddy destruction from her vantage point on a hillside above the village, her eye was drawn to what had once been a boatyard on its downstream side. Yachts were upended and tangled together as carelessly as toys, most of them three-quarters sunk. The thing that had caught her attention was a knot of dinghies, wedged between houses in what must once have been a pleasant creekside lane.

She spent a long time looking at the map, and looking at the abandoned boats, and thinking.

Eventually she made her decision and climbed into a field to walk down to the village. Every heartbeat felt like it might shake her apart. She wasn't sure exactly how fast the current pouring down the valley into the estuary would carry her but she knew it would be quick, much quicker than trying to find a crossing-place farther west and then turning and walking all the way back on the other side of the river. It might be an hour, or less. She might be minutes away.

She waded down the submerged street. She didn't care even slightly about keeping dry any more. She came to the group of three weed-streaked dinghies. They'd been lashed together; the ropes were now tangled around a bent lamp-post. Their hulls bumped against the walls of a house. They were carrying inches of fouled rainwater but that didn't matter either. A length of broken rotten wood bobbed inside one of them. It would do for a paddle. She clambered in beside it, kneeling in bilge. She looked at the way the current pushed around her and worked out which lines to free. The knots were too wet and tight to undo but that was OK, she had the penknife, though sawing through the rope was harder than she expected. Her hands were aching and blistering by the time she got herself adrift.

After that she needed to do nothing but sit and watch.

Twenty-Three

TREES WHICH HAD once overlooked the mudflats of a tidal creek now stood atop their own reflections, mirrored in a sheet of shallow water. She floated past them. This was the right way to finish, she thought. The journey which had been growing easier and easier as the snow melted and her pack lightened was now utterly effortless. The seaward current was its last benediction. She was, finally, forgiven. There were birds everywhere, egrets and cormorants and moorhens and swans, all untroubled by her passage. She was silent and full of grace, like them. The water became clearer. She was pulled around a crook of the estuary, a few dips of her makeshift oar enough to keep her in the current. The river met a tributary creek and widened. Though the sea was out of sight still, she smelled it, felt it.

Looking that way, she saw what she at first thought were other boats drifting ahead of hers like a ghostly escort. They weren't moving, though. As she slid into the wider reaches of the estuary she realised they were all wrecks.

Masts speared up from the surface at bizarre angles, some trailing bunches of sagging sail. She saw cabins of motor launches sunk halfway to their roofs, and rudders rusting on upended sterns. In the shallower water by the banks sailing yachts lay on their sides, exposing barnacled bellies. Her dinghy gathered speed as the creeks she passed fed the river current, pulling her into the graveyard. She leaned over the side with her rotten paddle and deflected her course a little towards the southern shore.

Eyeing the scattered wrecks ahead, looking for a clear course between them, she saw a body.

All that was visible of the boat was the flat top of what had once been its cabin. A bleached and naked corpse lay along it, half covered in feathery green seaweed. Iz felt a peculiar chill. She dug the paddle in to give the corpse a wide berth. As if the river had grown hands, it seemed to seize hold of the length of wood, tugging it down. She dropped it in surprise, looked ahead again, and saw the white body move.

What she had taken for seaweed was hair, vivid green hair. It framed a colourless face. That face was staring at her, watching her come closer. Her dinghy wasn't drifting with the current any more. It was being directed.

The body shifted, propping itself up on smooth white arms. Iz pushed wet hair out of her face. Cloudy eyes met hers.

—*Mum?*

—*What is it?*

—*That girl hasn't got any clothes on.*

—*Where?*

—*Over there. In the pond.*

—*Oh. There. Hasn't she? Maybe she's going for a swim. Don't start asking if you can too, real people aren't allowed to.*

—*Can we walk round the other way?*

—*What?*

—*I don't like the way she's looking at us.*

The naked white creature rose to her knees. The tips of her hair trailed over her hands into the water, fanning out in the current.

Iz thought: How beautiful Gavin's world must have been. Gawain's. Close up, the sea-woman was as lithe and silky as an otter, effortless as rain. Her lips, when they opened to speak, might have been carved from the inside of a shell.

'We should drown you with these others,' they said, in a voice that seemed soft and hard together, like wet stone. 'Weren't you afraid to cross my river? You've come far. I smell the dust of your journey on you.'

Abruptly, as if it had been something she'd been trying not to think about, Iz remembered how frightened Gav had often been too. Clutching her arm with his little hand, pulling her across to the other side of the road. Clinging to her in his bed, begging her to leave the light on.

'And grief,' the mermaid said. 'You reek of it. Did you come here to end your own journey? Is it that you want to drown?'

The bliss Iz had been floating on was draining away around her feet. She felt how cold she was, and how wet. A little puddle of misery began gathering beneath her.

'No,' she said. It was like trying to talk to Miss Grey. She felt ashamed to be speaking. 'Yes. I mean, yes, this is the end. No, I don't want to drown. Not now. I'm so nearly there.'

'None of these wanted to die either.' The head turned slowly, side to side. 'But here they lie, beneath us. People shun the water.'

'I didn't know,' Iz said. The mermaid's eyes were so terribly blank. 'I'm sorry.'

'You belong far from here.'

'I just,' she said, swallowing back a lump of desperation, 'want to go a little farther. Just to that shore.' She motioned towards the wood-fringed southern bank, no more than thirty feet away.

'You are the image of a woman I knew. What are you doing here? You've already seen death. You're half empty inside.'

'All I want,' Iz said, her voice beginning to tremble, 'is to find my son.'

Still kneeling, the mermaid swayed backwards, baring bone-white teeth in a sudden angry hiss. She raised a glistening arm and pointed accusingly. 'You have no son.'

'My boy.' Iz was out of the habit of crying. Her eyes began to sting. 'My child.' This was his world, beautiful and terrible; these were the creatures he lived with. She'd denied their existence for so long, but surely she'd suffered enough to make amends, surely. 'You can tell me about him, can't you? Please? You must know where he is.'

The white body rocked from side to side. 'Don't mock me with the shadow of a mother's grief. I have lost my own child, woman.' Her arms folded to cradle her belly. 'All these people drowned to feed my grief and it's still not enough. How dare you plead with me? I bore a daughter bloody and screaming. I suckled her. You have no child.'

'All right, then.' Iz felt her whole body shaking. The depth beneath her wasn't the mud-bottomed fathom of the river in flood any more. It was the yawning blackness she'd tried for so long to keep skating over, on the thinnest of ice. No forgiveness lurked in it. 'I raised him from a baby but I'm not his mother and he hates me. All right. Drown me. Go on. Pull me under. And if you see him, tell him I came all this way to say sorry. Isn't this grief?' She couldn't stop her hands quivering, but she thrust them into the slopping filth in the bottom of the hull and threw muddy water over her face. 'Really? Isn't it? Just kill me, then.' She reached out to the gunwale and began hauling herself over.

'Get back!' The hiss was so angry it made Iz lose her grip. She slipped and dropped in a wet heap into the bottom of the dinghy. The mermaid rose quickly to her feet and stepped lightly across, straddling the bow, standing over the wretched woman like a statue of victory. 'I have enough despair of my own to fill these waters. I won't have them polluted with yours. Go and die ashore. It was the once-boy you hoped to find, wasn't it? You're the picture of his aunt. Listen to me, then. His aunt is worse than dead, and he himself is gone. He sailed months ago on a stolen boat, alone. However far you've come to look for him, every step was wasted. He saved my child so I let him go, but now her heart is broken. I ought to have drowned him like all the rest. He's an ocean and more gone from here, woman. You'll never find him. We give our children our hearts and they tear them in pieces for us. Was that what you came all this way to learn? Consider yourself well taught. Now go and die on land, where I can't see you.'

Iz saw nothing of the mermaid's dive, nothing of the dinghy's sudden carom across the current into the marshy notch of land. She lay in the ankle-depth of putrid water like a twitching corpse. When her windpipe opened enough to make a sound she let out what was meant to be a howl, but even that was crushed almost to nothing and came out instead as a snivelling whine. She tipped herself out of the boat, expecting water, and found herself on saturated mud. Her hands were trembling fists; they punched convulsively at her own arms as if she could break herself. She fumbled at her chest for the pocket with the penknife but her jacket had fallen off somewhere. She crawled away from the river, afraid it would spit her out if she tried to drown. She lurched and stumbled through weeds until she chanced on a line of trees and a mud-choked lane leading under them, dark, shaded, out of all sight. A tree, she thought. No – she remembered a stinking body dangling from knotted sheets – a building. Any building. She dragged herself uphill along a narrow, hedge-lined, overgrown country road, a miniature of her whole dreadful pointless journey, mocking her with everything she'd suffered for no reason at all. The truth was terribly simple and terribly obvious. Gawain had always hated her, he'd left her, and he was never coming back. So straightforward, so clear, and so agonising, so intolerable. She scratched her cheeks trying to fend off the truth. The lane twisted up away from the river and branched. Along a side track littered with wet leaves and broken wood and glass she saw the outlines of a roof beyond trees. She hurried that way.

Buildings, walls and windows, empty, shattered, desolate; places like this had housed her for weeks and now this one could house her for good. She knew the routine. She trod through ruin, looking for a broken door. There it was, in a long single-storey building with cheap windows and broken outside pipes and a whole sea of detritus washed up outside it. She went in and looked around, saw roof beams over a dingy corridor to one side. She had to concentrate now, which was appalling because it felt like more steps in her journey and all she wanted was to get it over with as quickly as possible, for good. She started hearing Nigel's voice in her head. *You haven't actually thought about this, have you? Did it ever occur to you it might not be straightforward? It used to take professionals to do this properly, you know.* Shut up. Shut up. Only one way to shut him up. Sheets, she thought, remembering the dangling body. But wherever this place was it hadn't been a dwelling. It had shattered counters and stacked tables. She couldn't see very well because of the stinging in her eyes but she stumbled around and came across frayed and mouldering things that might have been tablecloths, it didn't matter. They were good enough to knot together. She yanked the knots hard.

She had to drag one of the tables into the back corridor so she could stand on it and tie the knotted cloths to the rafter.

That's right, she thought, as she climbed up. You stand on this and get the length right and then put it round your neck and kick the table away. *It's going to hurt, Iz.* Yes, Nigel, yes it is, but not for long, not every day and night like being married to you hurts and losing the boy you despised hurts, so just shut up and watch me. She measured out the length. Too short was better than too long; she might fail to break her neck but as long as her toes didn't touch she'd strangle. And too tight better than too loose, same reason.

There.

Perfect.

Perched up on the table, she took a few deep breaths, to concentrate. She tugged hard on the knotted loop to make sure it would hold.

She remembered the message on the phone.

Just remember what I said, OK? I'm not coming back, but one day I'll find you.

And this would be where he'd find her. The grimy grey corridor with the old yellow payphone in a niche. The heaps of rubbish and the smell of mould.

She had a sudden, overwhelmingly intense vision of the very last time she'd seen him, only an arm's length away but separated by the thick glass of a train window. Her husband muttering over his shoulder, *Get on with it, for God's sake, or he'll have fucked up our holiday before it even starts.* The grumble of the locomotive. The twitch of heavy motion. The angle of light changing on the glass, making him hard to see. 'Take care of yourself, Gav, love. I love you!' Maybe she saw his lips moving, saying he loved her back. Maybe not. Probably not.

And then gone, gone, and the secret of his last words to her gone for ever too.

How desperately relieved she'd felt, then. She remembered the thought like a scene, like a tune: Thank God he's gone. Had she actually said it aloud? No, but the words had formed in her more vivid than speech. *Thank God he's gone.*

'I'm sorry, love,' she whispered. She braced her legs to kick.

A small voice behind her said, 'Gwenny?'

A sliver of watery sunlight reached in through the broken window and slanted across her feet.

'It's me, Gwenny,' the small voice said. 'I'm here. You found me. It's all right.'

Part IV

Twenty-Four

THE WOMAN WHO wasn't Gwen sat on the floor beside the yellow telephone box, cradling the handle close to her mouth. From where Marina was watching at the entrance to the corridor she couldn't hear anything the woman had whispered into the telephone. She could tell what the last thing she said was, though, by the shape her lips made.

Goodbye.

The woman stood up unsteadily and put the handle back on top of the box. It settled into place with a click like a full stop. She stood like that for a long time, both hands on the telephone, her eyes – raw from all the crying – fixed on nothing at all.

Marina waited as long as she could and then scuffed her feet to remind the woman she was still there.

The woman looked up at her with an expression that made Marina wonder how she could ever have taken her for

Gwen. She looked broken, or haunted, or something else Marina couldn't describe, but definitely un-Gwenlike.

'Did it work?' she said, shyly. It had been her idea that the woman try using the telephone. 'He asked me who I wanted to talk to most.'

The woman who wasn't Gwen nodded.

'Yes,' she said. The crying had dried her voice out. Marina's was the same. They both sounded scratchy. For a long while they'd kept setting each other off, as if weeping was as contagious as yawning. 'It did.'

Marina went closer and held out her hand. She guessed it would probably start one or the other of them sobbing again, but the woman looked so desperately fragile she couldn't help herself. Calloused and filthy fingers met hers and knotted together.

'Was it Gwen again?' Marina asked. 'Did she say where we can find her?'

'No,' the woman said. 'Not Gwen.'

'Oh.'

'It was,' she began. The fingers gripped Marina's hand very tightly, and the woman drew in a long breath. 'It was,' she tried again, 'my sister.'

Marina frowned. 'You said you were Gwen's sister.'

'My other sister. My twin.' The woman scrunched her eyes shut. 'The one who died.'

The two of them stood outside, looking up at the pole with the snaky black wires dangling from it. Beyond the ruined buildings the woods dripped and sparkled with the lustre of sunlight after rain.

'They're all broken,' the woman said.

'So's everything,' Marina agreed, kicking at a fragment of coloured glass by her feet.

'Those are the phone wires. See? There's the box where they went into the building.'

Marina could only agree again. She hadn't yet worked out how to confess to Gwen's sister that she didn't really know anything about the world outside Pendurra. It had taken them long enough to get through even just a few of the things she did know; she'd had to say most of them three times before the woman properly understood, and as often as not one or the other of them had ended up bursting into tears before she could finish.

The woman took the mug that said TRELOW CHRISTIAN FELLOWSHIP off the windowsill again and turned it in her hands. She stepped through the junk to the box with its broken padlock and its scattered soggy papers. She knelt beside them, picking them up. Most were so wet they curled limp like cloth. She had to lay them out across her thigh.

'Iggy,' she whispered.

'What?'

The woman who wasn't Gwen looked up, pulled out of a reverie.

'It's such a long time ago now. You weren't even born. But here she was. This is the place. This is where she lived.'

Marina couldn't feel whatever emotion was making the woman's voice suddenly all hoarse and whispery.

'And those were her things,' she said, after a while. She didn't like it when the woman was silent for too long. It was as if she'd forgotten Marina existed. Gwen was never like that.

'Yes.' The woman ran a fingertip along the edge of the box, still not really listening. 'Yes.'

'Your sister.'

'Yes. My twin.'

'She's the one the man told me the story about, then.'

The woman turned away from examining the soggy papers to look at Marina.

'The same man?'

'Who took the acorn, yes. The other people took whatever else was in the box. If he comes back you can ask him.' She'd been going to say *we can ask him* but she felt much happier about someone else doing the talking.

'What was the story?'

Marina shut her eyes tight to help her concentrate. 'The man said she ran away from him but he found her. He made it sound like he might have hurt her. I can't remember exactly. He was holding the acorn while he said it, though. I'm sure about that. He said it was her seed. I remember that because I thought an acorn was a fruit not a seed. Then right afterwards he showed me the telephone.' She opened her eyes again. The woman who wasn't Gwen watched her intently.

'It was a story,' she added, nervously. 'That's what he said. But you could tell it had actually happened. He said that, too. He said everything he said happened. Something like that.'

The woman went on staring.

'She ran away,' she repeated at last, slowly, 'but he found her?'

'I think that's what he said. I probably wasn't listening properly. We could wait in case he comes back. Although I'm getting hungry. I ate all my food yesterday.'

When the woman smiled it was better than holding her hand, better than being hugged. It never seemed to last more than a heartbeat, but for an instant it made her feel as if no one had left, not Gwen, not Daddy, not Gawain.

'So did I,' she said.

Marina came closer and peered over the woman's shoulder at the papers from the box.

'Can we read any of it?' she asked. 'The ink's all gone runny.'

'Not much. The odd word or two. It looks like it might have been a kind of will.'

Marina was confused for a second before she remembered stories she'd read. 'Oh. When people give instructions after they're dead.'

'Exactly.'

'They're ruined now. I shouldn't have left them out here after the people broke the box open. I had no idea it was important.'

The woman leaned back and curled an arm around Marina's legs. It was like being hugged by Gwen's shadow; a faint copy of remembered love.

'It's all right, Marina,' she said. 'She wants us to find Gawain.'

Marina felt her heart twitch. 'Where does it say about Gawain?'

'No.' The woman peeled the sheet up and draped it carefully back in the box. 'That's what she told me.'

Marina still wanted to stay in case the not-man came back and made the telephone work again but the woman who wasn't Gwen pointed out that neither of them would last much longer with nothing but leaves to eat, and anyway it wasn't too far to where they were going. When she said that, Marina remembered how the bright not-man with the yellow coat had promised to send her a guide, and decided not to argue. She thought of what it had been like yesterday, on her own, baffled by the endless strange roads. Now she was with someone who knew the way everywhere. She didn't even have to explain about not wanting to go near the river. The woman said they'd go inland to get around it. Best of all, she was going to take them to Horace's village even though she'd apparently never heard of Horace (which surprised Marina: Horace had always told her everyone knew about him).

'We'll have to be careful,' she said. 'It's very close to Falmouth.'

'What's wrong with Falmouth? Horace says it's the most boring place in the universe.'

The woman who wasn't Gwen gave her another very un-Gwenlike look. 'Things have changed,' she said.

'Oh.'

'We should try and avoid meeting anyone. If we do, let me do the talking, all right?'

'Except Horace.'

'Yes.'

'Or the friend Gawain went to see. He said I'd like her. He said I ought to meet her some day.'

'But you never have?'

'Never have what?'

'Met her. The professor. What's her name, Hester Lightfoot.'

'No. She never came to our house. Hardly anyone ever did.'

'Gwen knew her, though?'

'Did she?'

'She must have. She . . .' The woman put her hands on her head and squeezed. 'Never mind. It doesn't matter. It's all we have to go on. You say that's where Gav went first, so we'll go after him.'

'He didn't say where her house was.'

'Oh, don't worry.' Her look went grim, as if she was remembering something painful. 'I memorised her address.'

Which turned out to be in Horace's village. Marina didn't say anything about it aloud, but secretly she was sure this was part of the not-man's promise. Everything she'd hoped to find when she decided to leave Pendurra had been waiting for her, all neatly packaged together. She'd just needed someone to show her the way.

It would have been better still if it had actually been Gwen. As they went along she couldn't help noticing the differences more and more. Walking with Gwen was as familiar and natural to her as breathing, and she knew what it was supposed to be like, interesting and cheerful. Gwen had always been chatting away about something or other. Gwen's sister went along quietly, in the kind of silence which said it didn't want to be interrupted. Also – and also unlike Gwen – she went slowly. She seemed terribly tired, like Daddy on one of his bad days. She leant on Marina some of the time, especially when they were going uphill. Marina carried the bag, slung over her other shoulder. There was nothing in it now except for her book and the broken box with the soggy sheets of paper. She'd given the woman her last extra pair of dry socks. But slow as they went, at least the woman knew the way, and she never halted in surprise or alarm no matter what they passed, though almost every corner brought them in sight of things Marina had never seen before. The only thing that made her stop was the sound of a car. Every time they heard it, no matter how distant, whether or not Marina thought it was actually just a momentary surge in the constant background grumble of running water, the woman took her by the arm and hurried her off the road, even if it meant standing in ankle-deep mud behind a gate until the sound went away again.

They toiled up one straight tree-shaded lane so laboriously that Marina wondered whether they might not reach the top at all, like in the puzzle about the arrow which never reached its target because there was always a bit farther to go.

'Sorry,' less-and-less-like-Gwen said, as if she'd been reading Marina's thoughts. 'I can hardly keep up. I think I'm going to have to stop soon. I walked all last night.'

'Stop where?'

'We'll find somewhere.'

Soon enough they came to a wide clearing of gravel and weeds beside the lane, at the back of which stood a small wooden hut with no windows. Marina went to investigate the faded words painted on its side.

'It says "Organic Farm Stand". Does that mean there'll be food inside?'

The woman had a way of looking at her that also reminded her of Gawain, as if they didn't believe what she'd just said.

'Not any more,' she said. 'If there was, someone will have taken it by now. Are you hungry?'

'Very.'

She hobbled over to join Marina by the hut. 'Let's see if we can manage one more day, all right?'

'We'll get there tomorrow?'

'Yes.'

Marina examined the tall unruly hedge behind the building. 'There might be the kind of leaves we can eat.'

'Leaves would be nice.'

'Maybe we can find roots and berries. I've read books where people eat those. Though it's too early for berries, and roots need boiling water.'

'There's always a catch.'

On one side of the hut was a cracked door with a fist-sized hole punched through it where the latch would have been. Inside was a dark dry space smelling of dust and cardboard and mouse droppings. Winter had driven away the mice, and the spiders too, though there were old cobwebs sagging from the roof. A heap of empty sacks filled one corner, leaking trickles of straw. They spread them over the floor. The woman slumped down on the makeshift bedding without even taking off her muddy top.

'Shouldn't you get out of your wet things?' Marina wriggled off her jumper and shift. There were hooks on the inside of the door to hang them on. 'That can't be comfortable.'

It was dim inside, the only daylight coming through the hole in the door, but she thought the woman was giving her that look again.

'I don't have any other clothes.'

'Nor do I. Don't you want to hang those ones up at least?'

'Aren't you cold?'

'No. Owen's always asking that.'

'Who?'

'Owen. Oh. One of my friends. He comes to the house from the village.'

'Does he?' The woman began tugging off one of her complicated boots. 'You didn't say you had a friend nearby. An adult?'

'Yes.'

'Maybe we should be trying to find him. Instead of trying to get to Mawnan.'

'No.' Marina squatted down abruptly. 'Let's not. He'd only tell me to go home. That's all he ever said. Let's go on, please. Horace will give us food. Or the lady Gawain was going to see, he told me how nice she was. You said it's not much farther.'

The boot came off with a squelching sound. A dark stain spread over the sacks.

'He might not be there,' the woman said.

'Who?'

'Your friend. Horace.'

'It's where he lives,' Marina said. 'He told me. I remember the name. I'm certain it's right.'

'Hardly anyone stayed in their homes. I've walked past hundreds of empty houses. The professor, Lightfoot, she almost certainly won't be there. She was in hospital. I can't believe they'd have let an invalid go home to this.'

'Why?'

The woman took a while to think about it as she worked on her other boot. 'The snow, at first. You couldn't get to the shops. Places were cut off. Then, I don't know. Freezing pipes, power lines down, things like that. Supply problems. Falmouth's on the coast, of course, so they could get some things in that way, but still. They'll probably be gone.'

Marina wasn't sure she understood, but this version of Gwen wasn't as easy to put questions to as the proper one. 'Horace wouldn't let things like that bother him,' she said, although she was thinking, *But he stopped coming to see me.*

'Well. That's good to know.'

'You said you'd take me there. You said that's where we're going.'

'We will. Yes. But.' She wriggled on the sacks, folding one into a pillow. She seemed almost too tired to speak. 'I've seen some terrible things on my way here. We might not find anyone there. Or it might be worse if we do find someone, the wrong people. You need someone to look after you properly.'

'I'm not going back to the house.'

'Marina.'

'No. I'm not. I'm never going to just sit and wait and be alone like that again.'

'I could come with you.'

'No. Anyway, Holly wouldn't let you.'

'Who's Holly?'

'She guards the gate. She already killed people who tried to come in. I don't know who they were. I'm sure she wouldn't actually kill you if I asked her not to but she won't let anyone past.'

'Is Holly your dog?'

'Dog?' Marina said, baffled.

There was a lengthy silence. Rain began to fall.

'I won't go home.' Marina pulled her knees up to her chest. 'Horace will be there, it's where he lives. Anyway, you're supposed to guide me. Or if you don't I'll find it on my own. I'm not a child any more.'

'All right.'

'Gwen wouldn't have tried to stop me. She always said one day I'd make my own way in the world.'

'Did she?'

'I've only just started. I'll learn what to do. If we can't find Horace I'll figure it out by myself.'

'All right, Marina.'

'But we will. He told me he'd always be my friend. Lots of times. It's just that he can't use his boat.'

'Marina?'

'What?'

'We'll go there. Together. Don't worry.'

A cold and calloused hand patted her foot.

The sacks were scratchy against her skin. Still, it felt good to lie down. The threat of more tears seemed to have passed. They lay together quietly while the rain strengthened, listening to its familiar monologue instead.

Later, the woman asked: 'Don't you want to try and sleep?'

'I'm too hungry to sleep.'

'I know what you mean. I had some nights like that until I got used to it. We'll find something tomorrow. Try not to think about it.'

'Is it always like this here?'

The woman rolled over in her nest of sacking and cardboard and straw and dirt. It was getting very dark outside by now, the clouds heavy and the evening drawing on. Marina almost couldn't see the outline of her new companion, only an arm's length away. 'What do you mean?'

'Living in houses like this. Being hungry. Daddy always explained that our house was different from everywhere else but I didn't think it would be like this. It's not like things I've read.'

'Oh. I see. No, this isn't . . . Everything used to be quite different. I used to . . .'

The rain drummed steadily above them.

'What?'

The woman sighed. 'I used to live in a normal house. Nicer than normal, I suppose. I used to be warm. Dry. Clean. Food everywhere. That's a strange thought, isn't it? You could just open the fridge and there'd be food in it. Or walk down the street and buy some. Beans from Africa or wherever, just down the road. That seems wrong, when you think about it.'

Marina was still trying to puzzle out what Africa had to do with it when the woman added, 'It's like a dream now. Forty-three years. Like I dreamed the whole thing.'

'Gawain said something like that.'

When the woman spoke again her voice had changed. In the dark, when she was just a voice, she wasn't like Gwen at all, not even slightly.

'What did he say?'

'That it would be like waking up from a dream. Or he said it would be like remembering something you'd tried very hard to forget.'

The woman didn't move or make a sound for a while, so Marina went on. 'I can imagine that. You know that feeling when you think of something you did or said once, really embarrassing or stupid things, and you have to make a little noise and sort of push them down out of the way again? Imagine if you couldn't. If they kept coming back up.'

At first she thought the pattern of the rain on the roof had changed, but after a minute or two she realised the new noise was coming from inside, from the body in the dark.

She shuffled closer and raised her head. The choked sniffs became a little more distinct.

'Are you all right?'

'No,' the answer came, in a watery broken voice she couldn't imagine ever mistaking for Gwen's. 'I'll never be all right.'

'What's wrong?' She patted around tentatively and found wet and greasy hair.

'Did he try to forget me?' A cold hand found hers and pressed it to a cold cheek.

'Gawain?'

'Yes. Gawain. I wasn't very nice to him.'

Marina found it strange being in the presence of someone else's grief. She'd always thought it was the other way around: children were sad and adults did the comforting. She couldn't work it out.

'I don't remember him saying anything about his pretend mother not being nice.'

The woman didn't answer again. Her stillness was terribly bleak. 'Sorry,' Marina added. 'You seem nice to me.'

'Actually,' the woman said, though it was more like a whisper. 'Let's not talk about it.'

So she didn't; but she kept her hand where it was. The woman shivered against her palm for a while.

'I'm so glad I found you,' she said eventually, in a proper whisper. Marina could barely hear it over the weeping of the sky.

'Marina?'

'. . . Mm?'

'Were you asleep?'

'Almost.'

'Sorry.'

'It's OK. I'm not feeling so hungry now. It goes in waves.'

'Can I ask you a question?'

'OK.'

'Do you know anything about God?'

Marina shifted. The padding of the sacks wasn't very thick and the floor beneath was hard.

'I thought that was all made up.'

'Oh.'

'Wasn't it?'

'I have no idea.'

'Horace can probably explain.' She'd been thinking about what his house would be like as she dozed in the dark. He'd never actually mentioned beds, as far as she could remember, but she felt sure it would have them.

'Was he the one who told you it was all made up?'

'I can't remember. I thought everyone just knew.'

Marina heard things being shuffled around near by. 'You were right, I should have taken the wet clothes off right away. I can't get warm now.'

'The rain's stopped, though.'

They listened together.

'I talked to my sister,' the woman said. 'On a broken phone. She died fifteen years ago.'

'What was she like?'

'Iggy? She was . . . Fiery. Passionate. She was always angry about something.'

'Not like you.'

'No. Not like me.'

'You're not at all like Gwen, either.'

'No. She was always so happy, wasn't she?'

'Not always, not really.'

'I think she was. Compared to most people. She'd worked out the secret of it.'

'She's not dead too, is she? I saw her drown, but it wasn't really her at all. She spoke to me through that telephone.'

'I was told she was worse than dead.'

'What does that mean? Who said that?'

'The woman in the river.'

Marina felt the bad memories rising, inching up like the tide.

'She's a liar.'

'You're her daughter,' the woman said, 'aren't you?'

'I never knew her. She went away before I could remember. Everyone told me I didn't have a mother.'

'Have you talked to people who've died before?'

'No. I never knew you could do that.'

Marina thought the woman had dozed off, but then she said: 'Neither did I.'

'I think it was the man I told you about. The one who took the acorn. I thought he probably wasn't really a man. He was the one who made me use the telephone.'

'That's why I asked.'

'Why what?'

'About God.'

'Oh.'

Marina was sleepier than she'd guessed. She felt it coming over her, reassuringly like the way it always had before. She remembered Gwen sitting in the chair with yarn and a needle at bedtime, fixing holes in Marina's jumper, laughing and calling herself *Sleep that knits up the ravelled sleeve of care*.

'She said Gav can make everything all right again. He has to give something back. That's what she told me to tell him. Then everything'll go back the way it was.'

'Who says?'

'Iggy. Ygraine. My sister.'

All these other people were going fuzzy in her thoughts.

'What's your name?'

'Hmm? Oh. Iseult.'

'Like in the story.'

'Yes.'

'We have a beautiful book with that story in it. I always loved the pictures of her. With her long red curly hair.' Now she was recalling Gwen's voice reading the thousand-times-repeated words while she lay in bed. *'In the faraway county of Cornwall, all surrounded by the sea'* – *That's not far away at all, Marina, that's where we live!* – *'there was once a castle all surrounded by the sea as well, and in the castle there was a king who loved to sail . . .'*

'Marina?'

'Mm?'

'That would be good, wouldn't it? If everything went back to how it was, like Iggy said? But with us all together?'

'Iggy's your sister.'

'Yes.'

'Who died.'

'Yes.'

'It sounds odd. I don't understand how you can talk to someone if they're dead.'

'Neither do I. I don't know very much at all, it turns out.'

'You're like me, then.'
'And everyone else.'
'Should we try going to sleep now?'
'Probably. Yes.'

Twenty-Five

MARINA WOKE MANY times in the dark, each time think-ing she must have been sleepwalking. She'd slept often enough in places other than her bed. They'd made camps in different rooms, sometimes in the stables. On summer nights they'd put her father's old tent up in the garden or out in the fields if the ground was dry. But now she woke not knowing where she was at all, not even sure she could actually be awake. When the first guesses at daylight eventually appeared around her and she saw that she was sharing a grimy smelly storeroom with a naked and grotesquely bedraggled version of Gwen, she had to recon-struct everything from the previous day piece by implausible piece, testing each memory carefully to see whether it bore the weight of actuality. *I'm not Gwen, no, I'm Gwen's sister. I came to find her and Gavin too. I'm his mother, not his real mother but he thought I was. Oh God, so they left you too. Yes, Gawain, yes, him, oh God. We'll go and find him together. You and I. Oh God in heaven.* She felt as if she'd perhaps gone to sleep and woken up inside a book, like Alice. But (as the light strengthened) there were the clothes hanging up, lined with drying mud, and (she sat up) there was the hunger too, waking up with her.

The woman – Iseult, like in the story, though her hair was dark and she didn't look like a princess at all – slept unquietly. Her lips twitched and made little sounds like seeds of words. Marina got up quietly and crept outside to pee and taste fresh air. The door creaked, making Iseult frown as if annoyed, but she didn't wake up.

The world looked a bit like one of Marina's own paintings of imaginary landscapes, all grey and murky blue because she always ended up getting the paints for sea and sky and grass mixed together. She was surprised again by how cramped it was. She'd always thought the world beyond the Pendurra gates must be vast, stretching off interminably like the sea, but the space behind the hut was hemmed in by shapeless walls of wet plant matter.

Something rustled among it, drawing her eye.

'Ahem,' said a muffled voice, from low down in the same direction.

Marina had been about to squat. She flinched instead, looking around.

'Ahem. Most rare and excellent lady. Were I practised in doffing, and had I cap upon my head, I would at this instant doff my cap. Oblige me by considering the act performed.'

She couldn't see anyone. The voice was apparently buried in the hedge. She leaned towards it nervously. 'Hello?'

'You might also honour me by taking a step in the

direction of the approaching sunrise. We small folk struggle to make ourselves heard over the longer distances, and it would be unseemly if I were compelled to shout.'

She looked down near her feet, where the voice appeared to be coming from. 'Who's there?'

'Now I've alarmed you. A woeful performance, I admit. A catastrophe of courtesy. May I entreat you in the name of your better nature not to show me a clean pair of heels at once? I confess that my address came off doltish, but I assure you, fine lady, it was long debated, and most sincerely meant.'

'I can't see you,' Marina said. 'Where are you?'

The matted base of the hedge rustled again. 'Conceal- ment is the safest habit, by tradition. Not to mention experiment. You'll forgive me if I decline to abandon it. However, I may inform you that you are facing me directly as we speak.' She squinted into the shadows. 'A gratifying arrangement, since it affords me full view of the gracious proportions of your person. The dawn itself acknowledges your loveliness. Or will, when it finally gets here.'

She looked back towards the hut. 'Gwen?' she called uncertainly, and then corrected herself: 'Iseult?' She remem- bered something about avoiding people. Intimidated by the breezy stillness all around, her call was hardly loud enough to carry to the door.

'What you can't see you fear,' the muffled voice said. It sounded like a jack-in-the-box talking with the lid closed. 'Just, politic, sensible. In this case, though, that same native sagacity will surely compel you to put your understandable anxieties aside. Merely consider: if I had intended you any mischief, would I not have perpetrated it some hours ago, while you slept in maiden innocence and defencelessness? You *are* maiden, aren't you? By the by? Since the topic arises?'

There might have been something more solid among the shadows and the wet grass, a small dark shape camouflaged by foliage. She crouched slowly, keeping her distance.

'Confessed, confessed,' the voice prattled on. 'It's an indelicate question. On nodding terms with vulgarity, if one were absolutely candid. What can I say? Fine speeches aside, I'm a vulgar fellow. There. Accused out of my own mouth. The shoe is tanned and stitched and fits me as snug as you like. Guilty. Still. Ahem.'

'I thought we were alone,' Marina said. 'Is that you? In the bushes there?'

'Shame mortifies me, good lady. Turn it which way I can, the meaning of your question remains obscure to my small wit. Assure yourself that I would reply in a snap' – something tiny clicked, like a dry twig breaking – 'if it were otherwise. Perhaps if you would deign to approach a little, as I suggested on—'

'I don't want to come any closer.'

'Ah. You are, if I may say so, categorical. Well. No doubt my voice will benefit from the exercise.'

'Are you one of the little people? Gwen said you were all in hiding.'

'The conversation is a rare honour, to be sure. I feel the privilege very deeply. Very deeply. Indeed, so sensible am I of the condescension you show me by prolonging our interview that it pains me to insist . . . to reiterate . . .'

Marina glanced over her shoulder again, remembering what Iseult had said about doing the talking if they met anyone. As she did so she noticed she wasn't even dressed.

'Oh no. I haven't got my clothes. Let me go and see if anything's dried.'

'No!' Marina had stood up straight; the flustered squeak stopped her. 'Hold your ground! Pardon an unvarnished negative, but no! Stand fast. Whoa. There.' Startled by the change in the voice's tone, she'd stayed where she was. 'So. Your, ah, modesty does you great credit. An underrated virtue. A, ah.' It seemed to be struggling to recover its fluency. 'A maidenly quality. One might say. A virginal attainment. But I, ah, we should both be the poorer were you to allow it to truncate our tête-à-tête. Fatally. A mortal blow, you see. Turn your back even once and we can speak no more. By what frail threads, and so forth. There, now. There. The crisis passes.'

Marina hesitated, feeling suddenly self-conscious. She crossed her arms over her chest.

'You mean you'll disappear if I turn round?'

'Crudely, yes. In a nutshell. So it might seem to a neutral observer, if one were present, which of course would be an impossibility, but let that rest.'

'I didn't know,' she said, not sure what to do. She wished Iseult would wake up. She was surprised all the talking hadn't disturbed her. 'I've never talked to anyone like this before.'

'Then I will redouble my efforts to leave you with only the happiest of associations when you reflect on our encounter in future years. And, on the subject of first occasions. Ahem.

On the matter of unprecedented conversation. May I refer my enquiry to your attention? Once again?'

'That must be why hardly anyone sees the little people any more. Is it? Gwen said it used to happen all the time, but then it stopped.'

'Gracious lady. The night wastes on. Time, though infinite, is paradoxically also short, and, to be blunt, getting shorter.' It was still murky overhead, but the shape hidden in the base of the hedge seemed to show itself a fraction more clearly. Its voice turned up a notch, rattling with impatience. 'At the risk of giving offence where none was offered, permit me to remind me of what you cannot have failed to note yourself, to wit, that in the course of our dialogue thus far you have presented me with not less than six questions, perhaps more if one were to relax one's grammatical precision a hair, the majority of which I have done my best to answer according to my best estimate of their intended sense. Whereas. Whereas I, you will recall, excluding merely rhetorical flourishes which not even the driest pedant would attempt to class under the heading of the interrogative, have limited myself to one. One merely. The singular. The bare minimum. One question, posed with the utmost simplicity. Unambiguous, straightforward of purport, admitting of only two possible answers, mutually exclusive, and neither taxing you further than a single syllable. Justice, sweet lady! Justice itself bids you recompense me with that syllable, before you enmesh me in extravagant discourses of a historical nature. Daybreak would be upon us before I'd so much as composed the preamble. Seize the moment! Redress the balance! Favour me with a solitary word! Speak!'

The voice had almost squeaked itself hoarse by the end of its outburst. Marina heard a hint of anger in it. She fell back a step.

'What do you want me to say?'

'By all that's green and grows in shit! Are you or are you not a virgin?'

She glanced over her shoulder again, troubled. 'You mean—'

'A virgin! A maiden! An unplucked flower. An unsullied stream. A white sheet. A corked bottle, a cold fish, an intact proposition, a what-have-you. Are you essayed? Are you broken?' Marina had an uncomfortably abrupt memory of odd conversations with Gwen, almost the only times she could think of when it seemed like Gwen wasn't saying what she really meant. 'Have you conversed criminally? Have you made the beast with two backs? Have you known boy, girl, animal or object inanimate? Sweet mother night, how hard can an easy question be?'

'I'm only fourteen,' she mumbled, edging away from the agitation in the voice. In the stories the fairies or little people or Sidhe turned nasty very quickly.

'You won't answer?'

'I don't—'

'You refuse? You deny even a yes or no?'

'I'm going,' she said, and made to turn on her heel, and couldn't.

It was as though her feet were fastened to the ground.

The wet leaves flapped and parted. It was still difficult to see, but perhaps a thing like a small animal stood up among them.

'Gwen!' she shouted, forgetting herself, and then, 'Iseult!'

'Now now. Don't alarm yourself.'

'What's happening?' She tried to pick up her foot, to take a normal step. Her legs wouldn't obey.

'I answered you as fairly as your questions admitted. You haven't answered me at all. Our conversation is incomplete, accordingly, and may not now be broken off until I am compensated. Rules are rules.'

'I didn't mean—'

'Never mind. Permit the condition of your hymen to remain veiled in the prudent mystery proper to maidens' matters. I'll take a better payment now.'

There was definitely something like a tiny bulbous man, strangely silhouetted, as if disguised by a cloak and hat made out of dust. His voice sounded sharper. The jack-in-the-box had been sprung.

'A keepsake,' he said. 'A memento. Some piece of you to call my own. There's a thing finer than all my fine words together. And afterwards we shall each reckon ourselves fairly dealt with and be on our separate ways. Though you might have selected your companion more wisely, I'll tell you that for nothing. To use a rustic metaphor, if you hitch your cart to a horse that's got nowhere to go, nowhere is where you'll end up.'

'Iseult!' she called.

'Precisely. Now, gentle lady. Here's a question worth its weight in cobwebs. What payment shall I exact? What, what?'

'Wake up!' Her mouth felt slow, treacly, like her legs. She

tried to bend down to fend off the advancing thing and found that she wanted to do the opposite, to keep as far away from it as possible.

'A toenail? A corn? A handful of down? But then, why set the sights so cravenly low? If ever there were an occasion for boldness, this, surely, were it. An eyelash? A tooth! A yellow tooth, for the pommel of my bodkin or the heel of my boot. Or! Or, or.' The voice paused for a deep inhalation. 'A hair! A golden hair, to wear around my waist. Wouldn't that be fine?'

'Help!' Marina shouted, her throat unclogging at last. She heard a shuffle from inside the hut. 'Out here!'

'Tsk, tsk. She wakes. More's the pity. Alas and alack and woe to us both, my hand is forced.' Marina flinched from a sudden sharp pain in her heel.

'Ow!'

'Marina?'

'Gwenny! I'm outside!'

'Stand down,' sighed the miniature voice. 'Your toll is paid. A satisfactory exchange. Though I, for one, will always wonder what might have been.'

'Are you OK?'

'I'm here!' Marina shouted, but already she could feel her legs thawing. She looked down and saw the blurry shape losing the little distinctness it had ever had. The voice was suddenly faint and tinny.

'A red pearl of your half-blood. I'll sip it from a silver thimble and toast your memory. Rare and precious, by the bouquet, though a smidgen too salty for the finest vintage. I blame the mother.'

'What's wrong?' Marina found she could twist around. In her panic she'd forgotten the name of the woman who stood looking exhausted and confused in the doorway of the hut, clutching a handful of dirty clothes in front of her. 'Is someone there?'

She backed away from the hedge, looking around. 'There was . . .'

'Is that blood? You've hurt yourself.'

She looked down and saw a red trickle.

'Let me see.' Iseult, that was her name. She crouched by Marina's foot. 'There's something in your heel. Did you step on something?'

'No. Did I?'

Iseult bent close and then carefully plucked a tiny spike from the wound. More blood beaded around it. She held it in her palm for them to look at in the spreading light.

'That's a hawthorn,' Marina said, taking it and rolling it in her fingers.

'Ouch,' Iseult said. 'It didn't go too deep, you should be all right. I had some bandages but they're gone like everything else. Let's see if we can tie something over it. Are you all right now?'

Was that all it was? Marina was about to say something else, but she felt embarrassed. She knew she was supposed to have let the woman do all the talking. Iseult was already distracted, back inside the hut, turning over Marina's shift, looking for its least filthy edge; she tore a strip from one of the sleeves.

'It should be fine,' she said. 'It's not dirty.'

But when they stopped an hour or two later to take their shoes off before wading a flooded channel, the folded wad of cotton was completely soaked with blood. They tossed it away so Marina could wash her foot in the cold water. Iseult wiped it with a broad blade of grass, frowning.

'It's so tiny I can hardly see it.' As they watched, a red drop bulged out. 'Must have gone deep. Does it bother you?'

'No.'

They folded a corner of Marina's bag and held it pressed against the pinprick for a while. It, too, turned gradually black.

'We can't stop,' Iseult said.

'I know. It's fine.'

'Your sock's pretty tight. It'll stop bleeding soon.'

The stream was at the bottom of lank and marshy fields. Iseult said it was the stream that fed the river that became the estuary; once they were across it they could turn east again and they'd only have a few miles to go, all along roads. But getting across was a long struggle. Where the water had burst its banks the mud beneath was deep and soft, and toppled trees made the channel itself a mossy, slippery labyrinth. Nevertheless they did at last reach the lane above the far slope, where they both sat down gasping. They took their shoes off to tip them out. From Marina's left one came a viscous red dribble. Her sock was soggy with blood.

Iseult watched Marina wring it out. Her face was blank with weariness.

'Let's get on,' she said. 'Let's just get there.'

It wasn't the kind of face you could confess anything to.

* * *

Iseult stumbled often as she walked. Her feet dragged. They heard the sound of a helicopter to the north, maybe more than one, though they walked under trees and couldn't see the horizon. She no longer bothered to shepherd Marina out of sight at every noise. She kept her head down. Sometimes when Marina looked at her she saw her lips moving silently and thought the woman was counting steps.

Once when they stopped to rest on a toppled stone they heard the churning of a car fighting slowly through the debris in the roads.

Iseult looked up.

'That's not far off,' she said.

Marina had peeled off her sock to see whether it needed squeezing out again. 'Should we get out of the way?'

The woman looked as if she'd do anything rather than stand up. 'Maybe it'll turn off,' she said. They were in a narrow and twisting lane. They'd passed a side road not long before but it was back down the hill, and retracing any steps at all had become a last resort. The engine sound was behind them, too, gunning angrily as it attacked the slope. It was obviously coming closer now. Marina stood up, one shoe in her hand, but there was no gate or gap in the hedge in sight. She looked at her companion, waiting to see what they should do.

Iseult closed her eyes for a moment and pushed herself to her feet. Instead of hurrying them away, she put an arm tight around Marina's shoulders, so tight she was half covering her face.

'Keep your eyes down,' she muttered.

The car was startlingly loud now, louder even than the telephone had been. It rounded the corner behind them a moment later. Her breath caught for an instant when she saw it. She thought it was the one with the shouting man and the frantic dog; but when its noise died abruptly to a coughing grumble and a head poked out to look at them, the head turned out to be different, yet another person, not even slightly like anyone she knew. She had a brief impression of a face as much animal as human, small and surprised, black circles around the eyes, before she did as she'd been told. The arm around her stiffened.

'Well met,' said a woman's voice.

'Morning,' Iseult said.

The other woman's voice chuckled in a way that made Marina think of Caleb. 'Need a ride?'

'No,' Iseult said. 'Thank you.'

'Is that your daughter? That girl should be inside.'

'She's fine.'

Marina heard another voice, a man's voice, from deeper inside the car. 'Engine's running.'

'Where you off to?' said the first voice. Marina couldn't help a quick glance to check whether it belonged to the small face.

'We're on our way to some friends.'

'Oh aye.' The woman leaning out of the car chuckled again. A woman, Marina now saw, though nothing like either Gwen or her sister. She'd smudged her face with charcoal, making those thick circles around her eyes. Her hair was tied up behind her. Two black feathers were stuck in the knot, crow's feathers. A dead crow had been tied to the front of the car, wings spread open and going ragged. The car itself was box shaped and mostly black, with a white cross badly painted from top to bottom and front to back.

'We don't have anything,' Iseult said.

'No one here's planning to rob you, dearie.' The car rattled heavily and its grumble stopped. Marina felt Iseult's fingers tighten on her arm. 'From up-country, are you?'

'Wild guess,' said the man. Marina couldn't see any more of him than a shape behind the car's smeared and spattered front window. Iseult's shoulder nudged at her head. It took her a moment to understand she was supposed to look down.

'Look like you've had a hard time of it,' the black-eyed woman said. 'Just the two of you, is it?'

'We're OK.'

'Your girl's bleeding.' Marina was staring at her feet. She watched as a tiny zigzag of blood spilled through the dirt and on to the grass, making a drop as bright as a ladybird. 'Hey. What's your name? Are you hungry?'

At the mention of food Marina couldn't help herself.

'My foot doesn't hurt at all,' she said, looking up. 'But we're very hungry. We haven't eaten for a day.'

She felt Iseult's grip go hard as wood. There was a peculiar extended pause, like when she and Gwen did one of their plays and one of them forgot the next line.

'Nicely spoken girl,' the man said. He'd leaned across to the woman's side of the car, and Marina caught a glimpse of a face with a beard that was frizzled and rounded, not long and straight like Caleb's.

The woman smiled, which made the marks around her eyes look like a mask with a woman's face half-hidden beneath it. 'Sounds to me, dearie, as if you might have bitten off more than you can chew. Eh? Trust me, you're not the only ones. Here, Tam, don't we got plasters in the box still? These two are on our side, obvious enough.' She dug around in the car for a moment and then handed a paper bag out towards them. 'Here you go. Up to us to look out for each other now, isn't it?' She shook the bag. It made a whispery rattle. 'Raisins,' she said. 'Not the freshest but they'll do. Go on.'

'I don't have anything to give you,' Iseult said.

''Course you don't. Did I ask you to? The days of everything having to be paid for, that's all finished now, isn't it? Go on. Your girl's half starving. Chew slowly, makes 'em last.'

Iseult didn't say anything, so Marina ventured a hesitant 'Thank you'.

Both people in the car laughed for some reason.

'Well brought up too,' the man said.

The woman shook the bag again. 'Want me to drop this in the road?'

Iseult uncurled her arm and stepped forward. 'I don't mean to be ungrateful,' she said. 'We've had a difficult journey.'

'Hop in, then,' the man said.

'No.' Iseult snapped the answer back almost before he'd

finished speaking. 'We're all right.' But she took the paper bag from the woman, to Marina's intense relief.

He banged something shut inside the car. 'Can't find the plasters,' he said, leaning farther across the woman. 'Want me to have a look at that foot? It'll get infected if you let it go like that.'

'Thank you again,' Iseult said. Her voice was empty of any warmth. 'Leave us be, please.'

The black-eyed woman shrugged. 'Suit yourself. Girl must have got her manners from dad, eh?'

'Hey,' the man said. Marina had her eyes down again but she could tell the voice was aimed in her direction. 'You'd like a ride, wouldn't you?'

She was astonished by how quickly Iseult moved. She was wrapped up in her grip again within moments, and this time Iseult stood between her and the car. She could feel her companion's heart beating against her, hard.

'We'll make our own way,' Iseult said. 'We're very grateful.'

'It's not right to leave the girl like that,' the man said.

'Not for us to say, is it?' the woman answered. The car clicked and began rolling slowly forward. With a terrible grating gargle its engine started again. 'If we all make it as far as London maybe we'll see you there,' she called over the noise. 'Remember who gave you something for nothing.'

Iseult didn't let Marina go until the sound had gone faint in the distance ahead.

'Who were they?'

'I've no idea.' Iseult unwrapped the paper bag, very carefully.

'You didn't want me to say anything, did you?'

The woman sighed. 'It's all right. They've gone.'

'Weren't they helpful? Those look all right to eat.' The two of them stared into the bag. Marina dipped her fingers in.

'Just take one,' Iseult said. 'One at a time. Make it last, like she said.'

The raisins had withered as dry as mouse pellets, but their rank sourness spread through the mouth like nectar. They ate them in turn, one after another, until there were ten or fifteen left, when Iseult closed the bag firmly.

'For later,' she said.

'How much longer do we have to go?'

'Four or five miles from here. We should start seeing it on the signposts soon.'

Iseult was like Horace, full of mysteriously absolute knowledge about things. At the very next meeting of lanes, the letters and number were there on a sign, pointing ahead, as if she'd conjured them up just by talking about them: *MAWNAN 4*. To Marina their appearance was miraculously encouraging, but Iseult stopped by the sign, frowning, twisting the ends of her hair in her hand. She looked so unwilling that Marina began to feel doubtful herself.

'Isn't that the right place?'

Iseult looked around as if trying to peer over the horizon. 'I'm just worried about what we're walking into.'

'Where?'

'See that?' She pointed between bare tree branches. 'That's smoke.' The grey sky was darker and heavier in that direction. 'And the helicopters keep buzzing around. They're nearer now.'

'They go back and forwards a lot. I used to watch from my roof.'

'I keep wondering what that woman meant about getting all the way to London.'

It seemed obvious enough to Marina, but she had a feeling she'd done the wrong thing when the people with the raisins had driven by, and didn't want to start talking about them.

'The back was full of jerry cans,' Iseult said. 'Did you notice that? And the way she'd dressed herself up, the way she talked. She made it sound like she was on a crusade. I watched people like that on the news, before.'

Now Marina was thoroughly uncertain again. 'Oh,' she said.

'I'm afraid we've made a bad decision,' Iseult said, quietly. 'Still.' She reached out and squeezed Marina's hand briefly. 'No going back now.'

Marina was more worried about the way the lane curved and dipped and then settled into a steady downward slant. Each time they'd gone over a crest in the road before, they'd been able to see glimpses of the river off to their right, safely distant, but now the lane was pulling them back towards it. The sign had told them which way to go so it wasn't as if there was any choice, but as the steady descent continued she became more and more anxious, and finally asked Iseult.

'There's a longer way around,' the woman said. 'I thought about it. But we're in no shape for a detour. Why are you worried about the river?'

'I don't want my mother seeing me,' Marina answered, eyes fixed ahead.

Iseult didn't answer for a long while, and when she finally spoke it was in what Marina had come to think of as her other voice, as if she was talking to someone completely different about some entirely unrelated subject.

'The river barely touches the village down there,' she said. 'It's at the end of a little creek. We can skirt around.'

'You've been there before?'

'No. I spent hours looking at the maps. Memorising them. Hours and hours. They were all I had to look at. I wasn't as wise as you, it never occurred to me to bring a book.'

'If you're sure.'

'Fairly sure. Trust me, I don't want to see your mother again either.'

Houses began to appear by the road, strange small ones like almost life-sized doll's houses, or like copies of pictures from books and magazines. They had cars in front of them, and weeds in front of the cars. Some had messages painted on the roofs or walls, obviously meant for someone other than her and Iseult. A couple had pictures, birds with their wings spread painted clumsily in black, or they might have been supposed to be dragons. They reminded Marina of the dead crow on the front of the car.

Iseult noticed her looking at them. 'That's because of the flying thing, I assume,' she said.

'What's the flying thing?'

'You must have heard about that. It's why so many people

came down here at the start of the winter. You know. The big black bird thing. In all the pictures.'

'Oh,' Marina said. 'You mean Corbo.'

Although the scope of Iseult's knowledge was amazing, there were surprising gaps in it, like in Horace's: things she didn't seem to know anything about at all. She halted in the road and turned to stare at Marina with an expression of naked astonishment. It was in that silence that they both heard, muffled but distinct, the sound of a short burst of laughter farther down the road into the village.

Iseult reached out and grabbed Marina as if something was about to attack her.

'What—'

'Shh!'

They stood still, listening hard. After a moment there came a muted fragment of conversation, and some scraping, something heavy being dragged along the road. It sounded like two people, a man and a woman.

'It's—'

Iseult put a hand over Marina's mouth, then a finger over her own lips. She leant in to Marina's ear.

'Whisper,' she whispered, and slowly withdrew her gag.

'It sounds like them again.'

Iseult nodded.

'What should we do?'

They looked back up the road behind them. It had felt gentle enough coming down. From the bottom, it suddenly appeared steep and painfully long. Marina could almost feel Iseult wilting as she contemplated it.

'They seemed all right,' she whispered, 'didn't they? They gave us those raisins.'

Iseult waited a while before turning to her. They heard snatches of chatter again.

'You're right,' she said. 'But. Look at me.' Marina obeyed. Up close, Iseult looked simultaneously more and less like Gwen. The outlines and proportions of her face and the colour of her eyes were almost exactly the same, but a completely different person was looking out of them. 'Don't say anything at all unless you have to. And try not to look at the man. At all. That's very important. Understand?'

She nodded, frightened by Iseult's sudden intensity.

'It'll be fine.' The woman gave Marina a quick cold kiss on the cheek, took hold of her around the shoulders again, and they went on down.

The two people had left their car with its dead crow and its white cross at the side of the road. They were farther down among the houses, which crowded close together now, each staring at its neighbours with the blind eyes of broken windows. They were doing something with the cars in front of the houses, something which involved attaching lengths of dirty orange tubing between a hole in the side of the car and a plastic can in the middle of the road. Marina did her best to look only for moments, peeking out from under her messy fringe. She noticed both of them were wearing clothes like Caleb's, waxy coats and rubbery boots and big thick gloves like gardening gloves, although whatever they were doing it clearly wasn't gardening.

'Look who's here,' the man said. Standing out on the road

he turned out to be very tall, and younger than she'd guessed when he was mostly hidden behind the filth of the car windows.

'Made good time,' the woman said. Sweat had made the charcoal rings around her eyes blur and run. 'Must have got a burst of energy off them raisins.'

'They were good,' Iseult said. 'Thank you again.' Marina was instinctively slowing down. Her companion pushed discreetly, keeping their slow pace steady.

'What're you doing down this way? I hope your friends weren't supposed to be here. This is a proper ghost town.'

'Just passing through.'

'Are you now? Good luck with that. Road must be six feet under.'

'We'll find a way around.'

'Very determined, ain't you? How's the small one doing? You all right under there, me love?'

'Mummy told her not to talk to strangers,' the man said. He sounded amused, or at least so Marina thought; listening to these people she didn't know was confusing and taxing. What they said kept sounding for a moment or two like the language she recognised, but then the sound would go wrong, or the feeling of the words would escape her, as if she were playing a guessing game rather than actually hearing someone speak.

'Very wise. And Mummy won't go telling strangers about what she seen here, will she?'

'All we want to do is get where we're going.'

'Same as us.' The woman guffawed, setting her hands on

her hips. She was tiny, barely taller than Marina, but there was a mysterious largeness about her, as if her presence used up some of the surrounding empty space. 'We got a bit farther to go, though, so we need to carry more fuel.' She tapped one of the plastic containers attached to the cars with her foot. 'You'll appreciate how that is, I expect.'

'Of course,' Iseult said, elbow nudging Marina forward. 'Good luck to you.'

'Offer of a ride still stands,' the man said. 'Long as you don't mind waiting while we finish up here. And if you're heading Truro way.'

'Or beyond.'

'Thank you. But no.'

'Where are you headed, then?'

Marina felt Iseult hesitate. They'd almost reached where the woman stood. Out of the corner of her eye she saw the man watching them very closely.

'I'd prefer not to say.'

'If it's back to Mawnan, don't bother. Police came in early this week and cleared everyone out of the fields.' The woman stepped back into the road as she spoke, blocking the path without giving any sign that she'd intended to. Iseult stalled, and Marina with her. 'Probably they was just waiting till they could get the paddy wagons in. Rounded up half your lot and took them off God knows where. I heard they put up a bit of a fight, though. Some of your folk found their way to Truro. Surprisingly handy around the barricades, weren't they, Tam?'

'No one's left in Mawnan?'

'None of your people.'

'We're not pilgrims.'

'Oh? Well, forgive the mistake, dearie. You've got the look of someone who's lived in a tent for three months, if you don't mind my saying so.'

'Got the sound of them too,' the man called Tam said, strolling into the road as well to double the barrier in front of them – more than double, since the feathers in the woman's hair barely came as high as his breastbone. 'Oh, I know. I found those plasters. Let me hop back up to the car and get you one.'

'There's no need.'

'Won't take a moment,' he said, and jogged past them. Iseult started to walk again, but the small woman leaned in close to them, lowering her voice.

'You should join us, dearie. Don't mind the make-up, we're harmless really, long as you're on our side. You and your girl won't last long just the two of you. If you've come from the west you won't have heard the worst of it. See that haze?' She jerked a thumb over her shoulder at the sky. 'That's Truro burning. Did you hear they took Ruth?'

'We've seen worse.'

'Have you, though? I doubt it. Worse is just beginning. There's thousands of us who've had enough. We're on our way to London to get her back, and no one's stopping us.'

'Excuse us,' Iseult said, and steered Marina around the woman.

'That girl don't look too willing. Is she yours? Hey. Is this your mum?' Iseult hugged her more tightly and kept going.

'No use going down there, dearie, creek's right up over the road. There's a way round behind the houses. Let me hear the girl speak for herself, now.'

They stopped. Iseult let go of Marina's shoulder and turned around.

'I never said she's my daughter. I'm taking her where she'll be safe.'

'Is that right, dearie?'

Marina realised they were all waiting for her. She turned too and looked up. The tall man strode back into view. She met his eye, only then remembering that she wasn't supposed to.

'We're going to find Horace,' she said, suddenly nervous. 'Or the woman who lives in the same village. This isn't my mother. I won't go with my mother. I told her that already. I'd rather go with Iseult.'

There was an expectant silence, but she didn't know what else she ought to say. She began to wish they'd gone the long way round.

Iseult came beside her again and took her hand, still looking at the others.

'You see,' she said, as if something else had happened which only the three grown-ups had observed.

'Poor child,' the black-eyed woman said, shaking her head.

Tam strode forward. 'Come on, then,' he said. 'Let's have a look at that scratch at least. Pop that boot off.' He was about to crouch in front of Marina when Iseult stepped between them, again startlingly quickly.

'I'll do it,' she said, sharply.

Tam paused, shrugged, and handed her the plaster. Marina had never used one herself before but she'd seen Caleb sticking them on often enough. She sat on the road and started pulling off her shoe.

'Not here,' Iseult whispered, but too late; Marina already had the shoe off by then. As she tipped it up in her hands, a brief red stream dribbled out of it on to the road. Her sock was a dark wet mess.

'My sainted aunt,' the small woman muttered.

'Right,' Tam said. 'Let's get this sorted out.' He sat on the road and beckoned. 'Here, give us your foot.'

Iseult dropped to take hold of her so swiftly Marina thought she'd tripped and fallen. 'Don't touch her,' she spat, and wrapped both arms around Marina's shoulders, hiding her face.

Tam held his hands out. 'All right, keep your hair on.'

'What's wrong?' Marina whispered, as quietly as she could. Iseult didn't answer.

'Needs a wash,' the man said. He pulled a clear plastic bottle out of the pocket of his coat. 'With clean water. You can use a drop or two of this. What'd you do, step on glass or something?' Marina knew now not to answer. She could feel the tension in Iseult's arms.

'Shall we do the plaster?' she whispered, cautiously.

Iseult's grip relaxed. Taking that as encouragement, Marina peeled off her sock. Blood made her fingers sticky. The man held the bottle towards them; after a pause, Iseult took it and poured out a capful, wiping the wound clear with her hands.

'That's it?' Tam said. 'It's less than a scratch. Shouldn't be bleeding like that.'

Iseult still said nothing. She fumbled the paper off the plaster and patted the skin dry. While she was attaching it, Marina saw the man do a strange thing. He picked her sock up very quickly, put it against his face for a moment and sniffed. The furtive gesture was so surprising that Marina forgot she wasn't supposed to look at him. He flashed her a strange look as he hurriedly put the sock back on the road again, wiping his fingers, only a second before Iseult reached around to collect it and wring it out.

'She can't wear that,' Tam said.

'We need to go,' Iseult murmured to her, and stood up.

'Child needs proper care,' the black-eyed woman said. 'We've got field hospitals in Truro. Good people there too. We got hold of medical supplies. Come with us that far at least. No one'll stop you going wherever you want after.'

'Marina,' Iseult said, 'put your shoe back on, please.'

The woman shrugged. 'Have it your way. Come on, Tam, we're wasting time on these two.'

'Marina, eh?' the man said. 'That's a pretty name.'

Iseult looked frail beside him, exhausted and ragged and small, but her voice had a dangerous edge. 'If you could show us how to get around the flood,' she said, 'we'd be grateful.'

'Would you? Easy enough.' The woman pointed. 'Between those two houses, round the back of that far one, you'll see a big alder down across the stream below. Looks muddy on the other side but you've obviously been through plenty of mud already.'

'Maybe we shouldn't let the kid go with her,' Tam said. 'Someone ought to be looking after her properly.'

'If you lay a finger on her,' Iseult said, 'I'll scratch out your eyes.'

'Oh aye?'

'Try me if you like.'

Marina became horribly aware of the background sounds, the muted angry rush of the stream behind the houses and the far-off ebbing whicker of a helicopter. The whicker grew rapidly into a heavy throb. All of them except her looked upward.

'Leave them be,' the small woman said. 'We got more important things to be doing. They're all mad anyway, their lot. Praying for salvation, pssshh. If we want a new world we got to go out and grab it ourselves.'

Iseult pulled Marina up to her feet. 'Come on,' she said, gathering her around the shoulders again. In a whisper she added, 'Don't look back.'

'Nothing's going to change if we just hide away.' The woman's voice rang behind them. It was a strong voice for such a small person. 'What are you waiting for, another sign? One wasn't enough for you? Waiting for someone to come and tell you what's happening? I'll tell you what's happening. The old powers came back for us, now all we got to do is lay hold of 'em.'

'What does she—' Marina began, in her quietest mumble, but Iseult cut her off.

'Don't talk. Don't look up. Keep going.'

Only many minutes later, when they were back on the lane again after crawling over a broad trunk and fighting through a pocket of swampy scrub, would Iseult allow them to stop. She bent, catching her breath. There was a canopy of tall trees overhead and more houses around them, half overgrown with ivy and bramble like dirty miniature versions of Sleeping Beauty's castle.

'I don't think they're following,' she said.

Marina assumed it was all right to talk again. 'Why were you so angry with them?'

'Was I? I just wanted to get on.'

'They gave us food. I bet they'd have let us have some of that water if you'd asked. And the plaster.'

Iseult looked at her for a moment, then just said: 'Let's go. Look, there's the road up the valley. Just ahead.'

'They were helping us.'

'It doesn't matter whether they were helping us or not. I should never have let us do this.'

'Do what?'

'Come this way.'

'What?' Marina strode faster to keep up. 'We have to. You said so yourself.'

'You can't be around people, Marina. Didn't you ever wonder why they kept you out of sight all that time?'

Marina was shocked by the sudden bitterness in her voice. For a dreadful moment she was reminded of when Gwen had turned, become the opposite of herself, that unspeakable nightmare day. 'It's not my fault! No one ever gave me a chance to try. You wouldn't even let me say anything.'

'It's not what you say. Or do. It's who you are. I should have known last night. I could feel it. Even in that filthy little shed when we could hardly see.' She glanced at Marina's stricken expression, and relented. 'You're right,' she said, more gently. 'It's not your fault. You wouldn't understand. But listen to me. Whether we find your friend or not, whoever we find or don't find in Mawnan, we need to get you back to your house. Your dog can tear my head off if it wants to, I don't care. As soon as we can, we're going there. Tomorrow. We're not taking any more roads either, we'll find a way across the river.'

Marina had been holding her hand. She let go as if Iseult was aflame and stopped dead.

'No.'

'I'm afraid so.'

'No. You said not. We agreed. Not going near the river.'

'I was wrong. Come on.'

Marina followed so she could keep protesting. 'I won't.'

'When we get there, when we find somewhere to rest and eat, I'll try and explain what will happen if you don't get back to your hideaway as soon as you can. For now, if we meet anyone, *anyone*, you mustn't let go of me. Not even for a second. All right?'

Fuming at her betrayal, Marina shook her head.

Iseult turned wearily away. 'Let's hope we get lucky and don't see anyone. I'll be more careful now.'

Twenty-Six

THE FIRST PEOPLE they came across made no sound at all. Marina and Iseult had arrived at a barrier of felled trees in the road. The raw stumps in the hedges were still caked with congealed sap. Beyond the barricade a tall white car lay on its side, its windows smashed, and beyond the car were two men smashed as well. Marina wondered what they were doing flat and motionless among the chipped wood and dead leaves on the road when they obviously needed help, until it struck her that they were dead. Dead like animals, empty bodies sprawled by her feet. Their bloodied faces weren't faces any more, just parts still stuck together, skin and jelly and bone. The tang of sickly burning in the air was heavier. It smelled like smoke, but without the warm sweetness of wood. They'd walked up from the secretive valley of the estuary into open fields. From there the thick haze to the north-east was visible as a thing with its own shape and presence, squatting like the shadow of a cloud over a quadrant of the horizon. Sometimes when they paused to rest they heard suggestions of a distant clamour, as if that cloud had a voice. Iseult looked increasingly anxious.

'We can't turn back,' she said, as much to herself as to Marina. 'We'd starve.'

Marina would have refused to turn back anyway. They passed another signpost: two miles. But she was no longer thinking of how surprised and happy Horace would be when they found him. Something felt wrong. None of this looked like the world he talked about when he came to visit.

The hubbub became more distinct. Iseult stopped again.

'Can you go any faster?' she said.

Marina's feet were aching and hunger was trying to tug her stomach out through her backbone. She hurried nevertheless. Iseult had gained a desperate energy from somewhere; Marina had to force herself along to keep up. They came to a junction. The narrow littered lane they'd been following emptied suddenly into a space so wide Marina could scarcely believe it was a road at all: she could have lain herself across it six times. The sign pointed right and said *MAWNAN 1*. But the noise they could hear came from the right too. It sounded almost like the wild chatter of the overflowing rivers, except that it hummed instead of whispering: a stream of voices. The helicopter was closer too. Marina looked the other way and saw it growing big in the sky, droning, floating towards them, a fat stag beetle thudding its jaws as it flew.

Iseult hesitated at the junction as if unsure which way to turn. The rumbling from both directions grew louder. Marina had a sudden image of the world folding in from each end, being torn up and crushed together, with her in the middle. She put her hands over her ears.

Iseult took her thin jacket off. She surprised Marina by giving her a sudden tight hug, and then surprised her even more by pulling the jacket down over her like an execution-er's hood.

The next minutes were a bizarre and terrifying dream. Iseult's voice came to her, close by her ear but muffled: 'Just keep going. Keep going.' She felt herself being pushed along. All she could see was their feet. 'Keep going. We'll be all right. Stay hidden.' But above and around Iseult's voice a great pandemonium of noise was gathering and spreading, a bedlam. The sky began to pulse. There was a sudden star-tling massed shout, people Marina couldn't see all speaking up at the same time.

'Who's that?'

'Someone's hurt.'

And then Iseult's voice, right above her, shouting too, shouting at someone else. 'Let me through. Let me through!'

'What's happened?'

'That's a kid.'

'Head wound,' Iseult shouted again. Everyone had to shout. The sky was being hacked by relentless blows. 'My daughter. Let me past!' They swerved and all but stumbled. Marina pressed her head against Iseult, trying to hide from the dreadful overhead crescendo, and did her best not to trip. She was being pushed and squeezed. Without being able to see she knew all of a sudden that there was a crowd around her, people in unimaginable numbers.

'Bastards!'

'She all right?'

'Let them past, it's a kid!'

'Food,' Iseult shouted. 'Has anyone got anything to eat?'

They bumped and shuffled. Marina felt things brush against her, other bodies. The sky became a blanket of vibrating noise, smothering her, so loud she could feel it in her clenched teeth. Then a voice tore out of it, a huge monstrous distorted voice like a mouth made out of a metal drum. It spoke in lumps of slow speech. *GO – BACK – TO – YOUR – HOMES*, it said, as if it had found Marina's secret fear inside her and dragged it out to write it in vast letters on the bottom of the clouds. *I – REPEAT – GO – BACK – TO – YOUR – HOMES – ESSENTIAL – SUPPLIES – WILL – BE – DISTRIBUTED*. 'This way, this way,' Iseult kept saying in her ear, though the only thing keeping her going was the constant pressure of the arms around her. She had to keep moving her feet just to stop herself being pushed over. The crowd around them jeered. *WE – ARE – DOING – EVERY-THING – WE – CAN – TO – RESTORE – POWER*. 'And we're doing everything we can to overthrow it!' someone near by screamed: there was a huge laugh and a discordant cheer. 'Can anyone spare food?' Iseult yelled. 'Anyone. Please. Oh, thank you. Bless you.' *I – REPEAT – CLEAR – THE – ROADS – AND – RETURN – TO – YOUR – HOMES – A – STATE – OF – EMERGENCY – HAS – BEEN – DECLARED*. A chant was gathering strength on the ground, the bedlam of voices coming together, saying *Down* some-thing, *Down with* something, like a spell to make the helicopter fall. Iseult was also shouting all the while, begging, cajoling people out of the way. Then suddenly it seemed like they were going faster and the throng was behind them, and Iseult's voice was close to her ear again, saying, 'Well done, we're all right, we're almost there,' but her arms kept the hood clamped over Marina's head and the welter of angry noise still filled the air. Marina had a sudden and sickeningly eager longing for the silence of sleep, of deep water. Running footsteps passed by, with a quick exchange of conversation ('You all right?' – 'She'll be OK' – 'Are they fighting?' – 'I don't know, they're just back that way, is there somewhere we can get food and water?' – 'Ask in the church'). Shutting her eyes helped, but she couldn't shut her ears. Without meaning to she began to whine, drowning out the babel with her own voice. Iseult stroked her arm as she pushed her along and tried to murmur something through the hood; Marina didn't hear it. Someone else came running past. Everyone in the world was here, she thought. All those empty houses, the people had all been sucked out of them and thrown into this one place. She should never have come. She thought of her home, bare feet in empty corridors, motes of dust falling slowly in front of familiar windows whose view never changed.

She noticed after a while that her feet had stopped.

She heard the noise she was making, suddenly. *Ahh ahh ahh ahh ahh.* It sounded horrible. She made it cease. Iseult's whisper appeared in the space it had vacated, saying, 'Shh, it's OK, shh.' There were no other voices. The shouting crowd was gone. The rumble in the sky had receded as well and turned back into a helicopter, the far-off throb she recognised.

'You're OK. They're gone now. OK? We're here, we made it. Marina? Do you want to see?'

Iseult wasn't pushing her any more. Her grip eased. She lifted her jacket away and put it back on while Marina accustomed herself to the daylight.

'Here.' She handed Marina a couple of small biscuits.

The road they were in was lined on both sides with more of the miniature houses, as if using them for hedges. Each one was different, the confusion of shapes and colours almost as bad as the massed and mangled shouting of the angry crowd. Iseult saw her cringing and held her close again, steering her towards the closest house, a dirty white box behind a screen of straggling bushes. 'Number thirty-six,' she said (and now Marina saw a tile by a door with that same number written on it). 'That's it.'

'That's what?'

'Eat. It'll make you feel better.'

Marina nibbled a biscuit. It was intensely salty, deliciously so; she gulped the rest.

'Slowly.'

'Where did these come from?'

'Someone gave them to me. I've got some bread as well. We're all right. And that's the house. Here we are.'

'Which one?'

'Lightfoot's house. Gav's friend. This is where he told you he was going first.'

Marina knew with complete certainty that Gawain was not here. He'd never be in a place like this.

'The houses don't look abandoned either,' Iseult went on.

461

'Not all of them. A lot of people must have stayed in this village. Look on the doorstep.' Marina did, though she didn't see why she should until Iseult explained. 'Mud. From shoes. Someone's been going in and out.'

'What should we do?'

Iseult straightened and took a deep breath. 'Let's try knocking.'

This meant squeezing past the wet bushes and banging on the door and calling. They tried that for a while. Everything else had fallen quiet again around them. While they sat on the doorstep, Iseult shared out the bread and the last of the raisins. A bucket under the gutter was half full of rainwater. They drank some of it, scooping with their hands. It was strange to be sitting without getting ready to stand and walk again. The idea that they'd arrived where they were going was hard for Marina to grasp. Nothing seemed to have changed. She was if anything even more tired than she'd felt before, and eating a few salty mouthfuls had only made her hungrier.

Iseult must have been thinking something similar. 'We'll give it a day,' she said. 'We'd better find somewhere to sleep. If she doesn't come by tomorrow we'll go.'

'Go where?'

'Home.'

'We should find Horace instead.'

Iseult shuffled closer to her and took her hand. 'Marina.'

'What?'

'Your friend Horace . . . That's Horace Jia, isn't it?'

'His other name? That's right.'

'The Chinese boy.'

'His mother's from China.'

'I'm afraid,' Iseult said, weighing out her words cautiously in a way that made Marina think of her father, 'we won't find him here.'

Marina felt like retorting *How do you know?* For some reason, though, she just stared at her hands in her lap.

'You haven't see him since the snow began, have you.'

She shook her head.

Iseult spoke gently now. 'It was on the news. I watched his poor mother. He went missing early on.'

Marina didn't say anything. She felt stupid. She felt like she'd always known that something had happened to Horace. Otherwise he'd have come to see her, no matter how busy he was or how difficult it was to go anywhere in the snow.

'He and Gav,' her guide went on, 'on the same day. I was so angry with him. I didn't even know who he was but I thought, Why is that boy the one everyone's trying to find? Why is his mother the one who's crying on TV?'

'So he's lost too,' Marina said, dully. Of course he was. Him and everyone else.

'He is,' Iseult said, picking up her hands and squeezing them. 'But we'll find them. My sister said.'

No one came to open house number thirty-six. After waiting a while they went inside the house on the other side of the road, so they could watch across the street. They didn't use the door, which was locked too. Instead Iseult led them around the back of the house, into a tiny wet space with a washing line and brambles, and broke a window with a slab of slate fallen from the roof. She scraped away the glass carefully and then reached in and undid the latch.

'If these people come back they'll get a shock,' she said, as she swung the window open. 'But I doubt they will. Not if there's some kind of mad war starting.'

'It's all right for us to rest inside?' Marina peered in doubtfully. She saw a tiny room full of ugly coloured surfaces squashed too close together.

'Yes. It's fine.'

They climbed in. Iseult went first, sweeping bits of glass away, and then helped Marina after her. Now she was the doll in the doll's house, surrounded by all the doll's-house furniture that was too close together, sofas and chairs made out of scraps of patterned cloth or smooth and faded like old toys. She felt as though anything she touched might break, but Iseult walked through the rooms as though it was where she'd always lived, opening doors, looking behind and under everything. 'Neat and tidy,' she said, as if the state of the house annoyed her. She went up a set of narrow walled-in stairs and came back down a minute later with a yellow towel and some black socks.

'You can clean up your foot a bit,' she said, handing them to Marina. 'There might be some water in the toilet cistern. It must have stopped bleeding by now. I found a box of plasters anyway.'

Marina didn't want to sit on any of the chairs, so she found a space on the floor, which was like a towel itself, pale blue and slightly fuzzy. She eased off her shoes while Iseult went on looking around in other rooms. She knew there was still a puddle of blood in the heel because she'd been able to feel it while she walked. Some of it spilled out; the floor soaked it up like cloth, leaving a dark blot. The plaster was wet. As soon as she peeled it off a red bubble swelled up on her skin.

She wiped her foot with the dry towel, wondering whether she ought to tell Iseult about the little man in the hedge, and how she could do it without mentioning his embarrassing question. Dried blood had crusted all over her like another layer of old mud. The black socks were very thin, and very perfectly stitched, without any sign of patching or holes. They looked a bit small for her. She unrolled them to check, and saw labels sewn around their tops with a name printed on them:

H JIA

They sat on the narrow staircase together, the woman higher up. From there they could watch the road and the house opposite through a small square window beside the front door. Whenever someone passed, Iseult leaned forward to put her fingers over Marina's lips, though they were talking almost in whispers anyway. It happened only a handful of times before the afternoon became evening and it was too dark to see; solitary people going one way or the other, usually carrying bags, one pushing a squeaky wire cart whose tiny wheels kept catching in cracks in the road. A couple of cars came crawling and bumping along.

The rest of the time they talked.

Or rather Marina did. She started by talking all about

Horace. She kept thinking of different things to say, and they all got mixed up in the wrong order, and so she ended up telling Iseult all about Holly as well, and then about Corbo, and then about Gawain, because Iseult wanted to know about everything he said, everything he'd done, no matter what order she told it in. It was her thaw. For the weeks of winter since Gawain had left she'd wrapped herself in painful silence. Now, suddenly, sitting in Horace's abandoned house, she began to flow again. She found herself wanting to tell things she hadn't even let herself think about before, about Gwen, about her mother, about Daddy choosing to die instead of going on looking after her. Iseult listened quietly in a way that reminded her very much of Gawain. Neither of them started crying. It wasn't like that now, for some reason. There were a lot of things the woman didn't understand the first time, or even the second, but Marina didn't mind explaining again. For the first time that day she was comfortable. They'd found clothes she could wear, a sort of padded coat and a pair of trousers which fitted her at the waist though they only came down to her shins. They'd shared out the last bits of food Iseult had been given. She answered all the questions and told the woman everything she could think of. It turned out to be a relief, shucking off her stagnant misery like her wet and filthy clothes.

'Shall I tell you something now?'

Marina hadn't noticed they'd stopped talking. She'd almost fallen asleep without knowing it. The house, Horace's house, had gone nearly dark and the comfortable feeling had spread all through her.

'I think,' Iseult said, not waiting for an answer, 'it was you I came all this way to find.'

'You said Gwen never told you anything about me.'

'I didn't know it was you I was looking for.' This was Iseult's proper voice, not the other one. It wasn't warm like Gwen's, and Marina could hear its edge of suffering, but there was no distance in it, nothing kept back. 'I think I had to let go of everything else before you could come along. You know what I was about to do, don't you? When you found me. Perhaps that's how far you have to go before something like this can happen.'

'Like what?'

'Meeting you. A miracle.'

She's tired too, Marina thought.

'I didn't deserve Gav,' Iseult said. 'But I'll try and deserve you.'

'The man who did the telephone said you'd be my guide.'

'Did he? Then I will. That's what I'll do.'

'He must have meant we'd find our way here. Do we stay here now? What do we do tomorrow?'

'We'll see if we can find the professor. Though I don't think we will. But it doesn't matter. I know where we're going now.'

'Where?'

'I'm going with you. I'll take you home.'

She was about to argue but something stopped her: a hand in the dark, coming to rest on her shoulder.

'I shouldn't have come looking for Gav. He told me not to. Simple as that. He left a message for me, did he tell you?

He said wait for him, that he'd find me one day. And he said not to worry. I should just have believed him, shouldn't I? I should have just listened. I ought to have learned that by now. He was right and I was wrong. So, let's do that. All right? We'll wait for him together. If he told you he'll come back then he'll come back. He wouldn't have said it unless he meant it. We won't mind waiting, will we, you and I?' The cold hand patted her. 'We'll go together. You won't be lonely any more and nor will I. We won't be hungry. Winter's over, things will grow again. I'll get you everything you need. I promise I will. And you can show me everything. You'll do that, won't you? I want to see your house. I want to see everything you told me about. I'd like to meet your friend Holly. Remember how you thought I was Gwen, when you first saw me? That's how it'll be. I'll be like Gwen was, I promise. And then one day Gav'll come back, and you and I will be there waiting for him, and then everything will be all right.'

It took Marina longer to get to sleep than she expected. Iseult insisted that she use one of the beds upstairs, though she'd have preferred to curl up with the woman down in the room with the broken window. 'No one'll get past me,' Iseult said, with her grimmest and most determined look, the one you couldn't argue with.

She was used to lying in bed by herself in the dark, entombed in unhappiness. After the last two nights of exhausted and uncomfortable sleep among strange smells and surfaces, it was peculiar to find herself back in a lightless bedroom, even though the bed was the wrong texture and size and she could somehow tell that the walls were all out of place even without being able to see them. In the perfect darkness her two days' journey felt as if it could have been a sleepwalk. She half expected dawn to come and reveal that she'd never left Pendurra at all. But she knew that wasn't right. There was something absolutely unlike her own room, even in the dark, a difference more certain than the odd stickiness of the sheets and the springiness of the bed and the window being in the wrong place. It kept her woozily awake until at last she realised what it was: not the smell, not the rub of the pillow, not the unfamiliar angles of the invisible walls, but the absence of misery.

She woke in silence.

'Iseult?'

She sat up, pushing the blanket away. There was a big dark stain by her feet, damp to the touch. The fresh plaster she'd put on the evening before was soggy. She wiped her heel on the sheet and tiptoed downstairs.

The woman lay in a messy heap. The clothes she'd been wearing were in another heap by her head, not much messier. She'd wrapped herself in a blanket with a flowery pattern. She slept with her mouth slightly open and was making funny scratchy snoring noises. She looked silly, the way everyone did when you caught them asleep. At peace, she went back to being very nearly Gwen. A rinsed-out morning smell came in through the broken window. It must have rained in the night. They'd put a kind of saucepan out on a windowsill upstairs to catch dew. She went back up to check it. It was full to the brim. She brought it carefully in, cupped her hands, splashed her face, and drank.

On the small dresser by the window where she'd put the saucepan down there was a hand-sized statue of a fat bronze smiling man and a black telephone. Iseult had told her the man was a lucky god.

The telephone began to ring.

Part V

Twenty-Seven

GOOSE COULDN'T TAKE her eyes off the woman's hands. She wanted to, very badly. She'd rather have looked at anything else in the world. The hands were pale and withered and their nails were long and yellow and crooked like an old man's teeth, but it wasn't just that. It was the way they moved. The woman had a thick black blindfold knotted over her eyes like the image of Dame Fortune turning her unforgiving wheel, and yet her hands moved with perfect certainty. They moved to the handle of the sarge's office door.

Sitting at the duty desk, holding up the phone, Goose watched the handle dip and then straighten. The locked door rattled, once.

'What did you say about Horace?' said the voice in Goose's ear. 'Hello?'

One of the hands made a fist and knocked on the glass partition.

Tap tap tap

'Is he there? Have you found him?'

The voice was bright and eager and thousands of miles away. Only a few metres across the station a blind and silent head turned slowly and pointed straight at Goose. Its thin lips drew back for a moment to show the teeth, then fluttered, then made a half-pout: mouthing three syllables. The withered fist repeated its summons.

Tap tap tap

'Uh,' Goose said. 'That's correct.'

'You've found him! Is he there? Can I talk to him? Please?'

'He's, uh. In hospital. Will you excuse me for a minute?'

'Where's the hospital?'

'Just up the road.' She could have sworn the hideous blind woman was seeing her and talking to her. The three syllables looked like *SéVerIne*. 'I need to, uh.' Goose swallowed. 'Step away from the phone for a moment. Don't hang up. OK?'

'Hang what?'

'Don't hang up the phone. I'll be right back.'

Tap tap tap

'Hang it where?'

' . . . Can you stay right where you are for me? Just like you are now?'

'I think so.'

'Great. Hold on. I'll be right back.' She put the phone down and raised her voice. 'Here I go. Wait right there.'

'All right,' the phone squeaked. For an eerie instant it seemed like the half-witted child with the ridiculously fruity accent was actually inside it, an incarcerated pixie. Goose steered around the desk, wiping her hands on her pants, and unlocked the door to the sarge's office.

The head that turned its simulacrum of a stare on her was like a disarmed medusa. The wide black bandage turned it into an eyeless mask tasselled with tentacular hair that snaked halfway to the floor. All the woman's clothes were black too, faded and shrivelled like decaying fruit, the knee-high boots tinged green with rot. She smelled only of old fabric and salt. There was no odour of a body at all.

'Can I help you, ma'am?' Goose heard herself say.

'No, Séverine,' the mouth said, in an English-accented voice hollow and soft as wind. 'But I can help you.'

'What the fuck.' Goose's hand went to her hip. She felt hot and cold at once, cheeks burning, a sudden chill at her core. 'Who the fuck are you?'

'I am the answer to all your questions, Séverine.'

'Who told you my name?'

'No one. I know you, Marie-Archange Séverine Gaucelin-Maculloch. I've been waiting for you.'

'Like hell,' Goose said, stepping back and reaching for the door. She gripped the handle, ready to slam it closed.

'Tell Marina,' the thing in the shape of a woman said, 'that Gwen is here.'

'What?'

'The child. A third of the world away. The longer you leave her, the more anxious she gets. She's afraid you've abandoned her as everyone else has. I know, Séverine. I know where the shaman girl is, too.'

Goose threw the door shut hard enough to rattle blinds

475

against the glass. The blindfolded thing didn't flinch. She patted her hip again, looked down and saw she had no weapon. She stared around the station. Blank screens stared back at her from empty desks. The clocks read forty minutes after midnight. Her head was buzzing with something she gradually identified as catastrophic terror.

'Hello?' chirped the pixie in the phone. 'Where are you?'

She stumbled around the desk and grabbed it. 'Marina?'

'Oh! I did what you said.'

'What the hell is this?'

In the doubtful silence that followed, Goose saw the handle of the door to the sarge's office turn again. She'd forgotten to lock it. The blind woman pushed gently with her corpse's hands, swung it open and stepped out.

'Are you dead?' the girl's voice asked, hesitantly. 'I thought hell was . . .'

The phone had chained Goose to the spot. Or perhaps it was fear. She watched the shipwreck-woman step deliberately closer, walking without need of eyes.

'Marina,' Goose whispered. She didn't mean to whisper but her throat was as tight as a tourniquet. 'You're Marina, aren't you?'

'I told you that.'

The woman's boots tapped on the floor.

Tap tap tap

'Who's . . . Who's Gwen?'

'Gwen!' The voice almost split itself open with eagerness. 'Did you say Gwen? Is she there too?'

The woman came to the far side of the desk, halted, and

reached out an arm. The eroded sleeve of her coat hung from her wrist in a cobweb of frayed threads. She held her hand open for the phone.

'Hello? I can't hear you any more. Hello?' The voice danced at Goose's ear. 'Where's Gwen? Are you in that place with the dark water? Can I talk to her again? Hello?'

The darkness where the eyes should have been was looking at her. The medusa head was perfectly still.

'She's . . .' Goose croaked into the phone. 'She's right here.'

Helpless as a child, she passed it over. It emitted a pixie whisper, shrunken and faraway.

'Gwenny?'

The long-nailed hand closed around the phone, lifted it, found a button and pressed.

A dial tone whined.

'Shit.' Goose pushed herself off the desk to her feet, fists balling. 'Why the hell did you . . . Give me that.'

'I can't help that child.'

'I said give it to me!' The number was still on the desk. Suddenly too shocked and angry to be afraid of the grotesque hand, Goose wrenched the phone back and stabbed out the digits.

'No one can help her.'

'Shut up!' She tried again. Her fingers stumbled over the keys. 'Why the hell did you do that?'

'That's thousands of leagues from here, Séverine. What has anything so distant got to do with you? Talk to me.'

'I said shut up!' Down the phone she heard a long bleating tone, a busy signal perhaps, or a wrong number.

'I can show you where you want to go.'

'You can go to hell.' Maybe she'd hit the wrong buttons. Or maybe the phone had broken, another connection snapped.

The blind woman spread shrivelled fingers over the surface of the desk. They stroked, gently, side to side, caressing the varnish with inexplicable slow intent. 'There's only one girl you have to find, Séverine.'

'Actually.' Goose dropped the phone. 'You can go straight to the cells. Right now.' She came quickly round the desk, behind the woman, ready to clamp her and march her. She was itching to do some damage. Then she saw the knot that tied the bandage. It crouched like a burrowing animal in the rank tangle of her hair. Quite suddenly Goose found she couldn't touch her. Her own hands had rebelled. She put all her panicky rage into a yell. 'Move move move!'

The woman didn't move.

'And who will tell you where to go?' There was a terrible slithering emphasis on the word *you*.

'Cell!' Goose shouted, leaning as close as she dared. 'Go!'

'North of here,' the strange voice began, 'there's an island. There were houses there, long ago. They and the people who lived in them fell into ruin. The shaman girl has gone to open them again. While you and I stand here she's asleep by their hearth. I can hear her dreams, Séverine. I can follow the sound of her like a thread in the maze.' She lifted her hands to her temples and touched the bandage, fingertips brushing over it with the same sinister softness. 'Night or day is all the same to me. I can lead you to her.' Slow as a dancer, she turned around to present Goose with her sightless face. 'Find us a vessel, and I can guide you there now. Tonight.'

Goose stepped back.

'By tomorrow night,' the mouth beneath the blindfold said, 'she'll be gone.'

'You're talking about Jennifer,' Goose said.

The mouth ignored her. 'Already she's closing the ways in and out. The passages obey her. Tomorrow people will be afraid for more than their money. I can hear riot brewing. You'll be besieged, Séverine. This is your last chance to find the girl. I am your last chance. Tonight.'

It was like having a staring contest with the night itself. Goose tried to square up to it and felt it slip away and around her, soft and immense.

'No freaking way,' she said.

After a handful of long seconds the head bowed a little, the mask-face turned away, and the boots tapped back towards the sarge's office. They didn't miss a step. The woman went back in, closing the door carefully behind her, and sat herself in the same chair. The mug of coffee was still on the table beside it. She extended one finger and began tracing around the circle of its rim, around and around and around.

Goose waited for her resolution to come back. Once she knew what she was doing again she lunged for the door and locked it.

She sat back at the desk, breathing hard, staring at the scrap of paper with Horace Jia's home number written on it. She pressed the numbers into the phone again, double-checking. The only answer she got was the mournful electronic bleat. Busy. Line closed.

A couple of further attempts later the radio beeped and crackled.

'Goose?'

She twitched at the disembodied voice.

'Goose? You there? Kalmykov.'

Of course it was. Calling in from the patrol car. She blinked as she picked up the radio and steadied her voice before she answered. 'Yep. Maculloch.'

'Hey,' Kalmykov said. 'Goose. Loosey Goosey.'

She glanced towards the office without meaning to. Behind open blinds and glass walls the thing which knew her name sat quietly, waiting. She looked down hurriedly and saw the boy's number again. The boy who'd been a whale and then a boy again, crossing the world's oceans to arrive here. In the little town he'd disappeared from, they said, a revolution had begun.

'What's up?'

'Jack. I'm bored. Got the highway closed but no one's coming by. How's the station?'

'Quiet.'

Kalmykov sighed noisily into the radio. 'You too, huh. Hey, we got a while till Thorpe and Turner take over. How about I come on back to the station and you can jerk me off?'

Goose looked around the chrome and plastic of the station as if seeing it for the first time. The duty rota pinned to the board, promising day after night after day. The red and white flag her mother had tried to teach her to resent. The photo of the prime minister looking like a waxwork, or vice versa. The laminated sign Janice had taped to the inside of the counter: *REMEMBER TO SMILE!*

'Joke, man. Joke. Jesus. Lighten up a little, will ya?'

She reached around the back of the radio and pulled a wire. It was satisfyingly difficult. She wrenched viciously until the wire came out of its socket with a gasp of smeared static from the speaker.

Everything went completely quiet. She thought about the silence in the cell, the silence in the file, the silence of the mask.

'All right,' she said to herself. 'We're done here.'

She went to unlock the door.

Downtown Hardy teetered on the edge of ghost status even in the middle of the day. After midnight and out of season, every whisper of life was sucked out of it. The area by the dock was wide black tarmac and empty windows. A single tall light overhung the ramp and the pontoons. Jonas's boat was shadowed down among barnacled pilings. Low tide. There was no wind in the bay for once. Offshore, nothing interrupted the darkness, not a speck, not a glimmer. When Goose tried to think about what she was doing, her inner monologue answered like a glitchy file, looping the same two seconds over and over while the rest of the information buffered and failed to arrive: *This is crazy. This is crazy.*

'This is crazy,' she said. 'I can't take a boat out there. No way.'

The tap of boots on the wood of the dock behind her dragged to a stop.

'Look at me, Séverine.'

'No thanks.'

'Do you imagine darkness matters to me?'

She didn't answer that. The steps came up close behind her.

'By tomorrow nightfall you'll have all your questions answered. Unless you turn back now.'

'Why should I believe you?'

'Because I cannot lie.'

Goose snorted. 'Everyone can lie.'

'Not I. Nor can I make you believe me. Turn round and go back if you wish. Whatever you do will be what you choose to do.'

When she examined herself she couldn't find anything that felt like choice in there. The bit which made decisions had gone missing.

'What happened on that ferry?' she said. 'There were supposed to be eighty-plus people on that boat. Where did they all go?'

'That would be more than eighty stories to tell, Séverine, even if I knew them all. Midnight is long past. The girl will wake at dawn and leave the island.'

'Sounds to me like you just dodged the question.'

'If you like.'

'Are they dead?'

'Everyone's story ends in death.'

'That's not what I asked.'

'It's the best answer I have. Are you afraid of me, Séverine?'

Oh yeah. 'No.'

'I can't hurt you. You see how weak I am. I'll guide you, but your hand will be on the wheel.'

'So is that your name?'

'Which name?'

'What you told me to tell the kid. Gwen.'

There was a long pause behind her, long enough to become unpleasant.

'What do you think?' the voice eventually said.

She didn't want to think. She couldn't imagine it would get her anywhere. She clattered briskly down along the pontoons to Jonas's boat. For a moment she was worried she wouldn't be able to find the key, there were so many upturned buckets scattered around the cockpit, but it was under the first one she kicked aside. She didn't wait to watch the limping whispering thing with wet black snakes for hair climb aboard. She zipped up her regulation coat, pulling the high collar up to her chin, yanked in the fenders and started the engine. It was astonishingly loud in the deserted night. She glanced up at the ghost town, expecting to see Kalmykov or Cope or one of the others racing down the hill, lights flaring, coming to rescue her from throwing away her career and presumably her sanity as well, if not her life.

'OK,' she said. 'Now what?'

The thing had sat itself in the stern. It smiled its warped smile and pointed into the absolute black.

'North,' it said.

Reason told her the landscape was still there like always: the hemlock and spruce and cedar forest on either side, the open bay ahead, the twenty-kilometre width of the Queen Charlotte Strait with its diminished backdrop of mountains. She'd never felt more alienated from her own reason. A white running light mounted on a pole above the cockpit shone ahead, illuminating a few metres of restless polished black, and that was it. Apart from its dislocated sloshing and its tang of salt and cold, the rest of the world ahead of her was a void as absolute as interstellar space.

She set the throttle to a crawl. Rocks, floating deadheads, the shore: any hazard could be anywhere. The single light would give her barely any warning of what lay ahead of the bow.

'This is ridiculous,' she said. 'I can't do this. How the fuck am I supposed to helm?'

'Listen to me. I won't steer you wrong.'

She spun the wheel, bringing the boat around to face the dock again. 'No way.'

'Starboard a touch. There is a buoy.'

'What?'

'Starboard.'

Goose jerked the wheel as an object drifted into the puddle of light in front of the bows, a floating drum with a loop of rusty metal. 'Shit.'

'It's your choice, Séverine.'

'What, you're going to sit back there and be, like, Go left, Go right?'

'Yes.'

'That's retarded. Why don't you steer yourself?'

'This is your journey.'

'Like fuck it is.' She was angry and frightened. This wasn't how she usually talked. She hated the sound of it, swearing and snarling like those teenagers pumped on alcohol and confused historical grievances who kept the detachment busy on Friday nights.

'You hold the wheel. Look at yourself.'

'We're going back to the station. And this time you can knock all you like, my friend. You're staying locked in there.'

'Then we'll each be back where we were. Séverine, do you really think that nothing has changed? Do you really believe that tomorrow will be just another day?'

'Here's an idea. Why don't you shut up?'

'Because silence will give you no answers,' the voice behind her said. 'You know that already. Remember the shaman girl.'

The shape of the dock was hard to see from the water at night. Dark spaces beneath it blended with the water. Goose put the motor in neutral. She looked up at the barren town. The flashing lights of a patrol car appeared up the hill.

Shaman girl? Shaman was a word from picture books, or museums, or an online game she'd played for a few weeks once: a pretend word, a not-in-real-life word.

The patrol car swung around the roundabout by the motel and began dropping down into the town. Kalmykov, she guessed, wondering what was going on at the station and why he was getting no answer on the radio. If he looked down the hill he might see the light of the boat bobbing beyond the dock. He'd be curious about who was going cruising in the middle of the night.

'So you're telling me Jennifer Knox is a shaman?'

'Séverine,' the hollow voice at her back answered. 'Why do you ask me, when you already know the answer? There's only one question you should ask yourself. Do you dare look for her or not?'

'Oh, you dare me. That's impressive.'

'What else is holding you back but fear?'

She had no answer to that. She was thinking of Fitzgerald's father on the phone, distraught. *Says she put a curse on him. Says she gave him the evil eye.* Of course she did. And she sprang the lock of the cell at the station in Alice, she did that too.

'This,' the voice said, 'is the moment when you must choose.'

Goose saw the patrol car disappear behind the house below the station. In a few seconds, Kalmykov or whoever it was would find her gone.

'All right,' she said. She nudged the throttle forward and tugged the wheel around. 'Let's go.'

She wanted her silence to be sullen and determined. In fact it was terrified, a clamp-jawed, white-knuckled silence. As a child she'd had an incommunicably dreadful recurrent nightmare in which she'd been a tiny dot in an infinite nowhere, a shrunken point of consciousness which was the only thing there was. No words could explain how appalling this dream was. She didn't try going to her parents for comfort; she just shivered upright in her bedroom, forcing herself to stay awake in case it came back when her eyes closed. For years she'd forgotten about it. Now it was back with a vengeance. Within a few minutes the boat had become a solitary comet in a black void. She followed the murmured instructions from behind her unquestioningly because without them she'd have imagined herself about to steer off a waterfall at the edge of the world. 'Port . . . There . . . To port a touch . . .' Only the straggling pinpricks of Hardy's lights behind her assured her that she wasn't going round in circles. She tried not to look over her shoulder, though, because every time she did she saw the thing sitting there, slightly bowed, its face a glimmer of pale skin split in two by a band of darkness, the rotting black clothes cloaking the rest in shadow.

Hardy shrank behind them until it became a smudgy galaxy fallen to the horizon astern. The invisible sea stirred as if their passage had woken it up. They must be approaching the mouth of the bay, Goose thought. To the west was the ocean, then, squeezing its thinnest whitecapped tendrils down the strait. She didn't want to ask more questions if she could help it, but the thought of entering the Inside Passage in complete darkness made her desperate.

'So how far are we going?'

'I don't know the future.'

'I'm asking where this island is.'

'North of here, and a little west. At this speed, some hours' journey.'

'Has it got a name?'

'Many. It would be better to go faster.'

'You're kidding me.'

'Do you want this journey to have been for nothing?'

'You know what I want, my friend? I want you to stop with the suggestions.'

'Once the girl wakes I can't hear her. She may leave the island.'

'I'm not going any faster than this. Anything could be out there.'

'It will be a long dark passage, then.'

'What's the matter? Are you cold?' As always on the water, the wind felt sharper and the Arctic closer.

'Yes. I feel cold. Very cold. Flesh feels so much, doesn't it, Séverine? When the spray strikes my skin I feel that too. The boat vibrates under us. It's exquisite, isn't it, to be alive? Steer to starboard. A little only. There. Now there's open water ahead.'

Just don't say anything, Goose told herself. *Don't even look round.* She began to think about something else she could do. Instead of going any farther she could turn around and push the thing overboard. After that she could set the throttle to Jonas speed and point the bow at the knot of faint light they were leaving behind.

'You're afraid of me.' Its voice slithered like the water under the hull. 'I feel that too.' Do it now, Goose thought. Just a couple of steps to accelerate, then hit hard and low. She knew how to tackle properly. 'I won't harm you. You're far stronger, Séverine. There's nothing I can do to you beyond what I promised, to take you where you want to go.'

'So you keep saying, my friend.' Why couldn't she stop talking? 'What about you? Huh? What's in this for you?

What are you doing here anyway? What's your game?' It felt as if the cold was forcing her teeth to rattle out questions. 'Where did you come from, anyway? You've got an English accent. The bad guy's always got a fricking accent, you know? Jeez. How the hell did I end up like this? I thought it was going to be boring up here. Nothing ever happens up-island, that's what they told me. Shut up, Goose.' Better to imagine that there was nothing in the boat with her at all. Don't even think about it. She pushed her lips shut. Her eyes were watering with the salt air and the strain of concentrating on the patch of emptiness beyond the bow.

'Starboard again,' the voice said, after a little while. She nudged the wheel clockwise.

'Farther. There's a log. Good. Now, to port.'

Had she really chosen this? It couldn't be right. There must be some alternative path, she thought, not this dark parallel universe but the authentic normal one, in which she was Constable Maculloch of the RCMP 'E' Division who ticketed drunk drivers by day and Skyped her friends in the evenings. Where had the switch happened? There must have been a step she'd taken, once, a wrong turn somewhere, or how else could that world now be so infinitely far away? She searched her memory of the last few days but couldn't find the moment of her error. As far as she could tell she'd only been doing her job, carrying along sensibly enough, until, that night, or maybe before, it had so happened that her job had stopped meaning anything, and so had the word *sensibly*.

'The girl brought these fallen trees down to fill the waterways.' Refusing to turn around, Goose could hardly tell the difference between her own thoughts and the whispery voice behind her. 'She made the sea rise and break the booms. She was the one who doused the lights and silenced the bells. Her dreams are all of what belongs here and what doesn't. Everything seeks its home, Séverine. Everything seeks its proper place. You've all made your home in a many-sided chamber of mirrors. You live among phantoms of yourselves and don't know where you are or which is truly you. I can feel the aura around you. All those other places and other lives. Ghosts, echoes, shadows. Voices from the far side of the world. Images of bodies without flesh. Don't you long to return to the world, Séverine? To feel what's really here?'

Don't say anything. Don't say anything at all. Just keep going till it gets light. She tried not to shiver. Her mouth wouldn't stay sealed. Under her breath she began to recite her long-neglected rosary, *Je vous salue, Marie pleine de grâce, le Seigneur est avec vous . . .*

She felt it before the thing in the stern spoke: a subtle settling of the motion beneath the boat, a hint of invisible shelter windward, and a suggestion of wet bark thickening the sea air.

'Close now.'

She couldn't guess how long it had been. A lifetime. She'd been remembering things, odd and startlingly vivid details, no rhyme or reason to them that she could tell. Her favourite shorts when she was seven. Insults inked in bathroom stalls at the Depot. Crying the first time she caught a fish. Being groped on the bus at the corner of Saint-Laurent and

Villeneuve. The cover of a cheap comic lying on Annie's unmade bed.

'A compass point to port, now. There are shoals.'

Shoals?

Perhaps she'd been half asleep. Her feet were numb from hours of standing. The droning chug of the motor and the soft chop of the sea were equally unchanging, hypnotic. Now the sound had changed a fraction. Windless open water had the rhythm of someone breathing in their sleep, unrushed, lots of pauses; now there were tiny agitations to interrupt it. Somewhere, waves were coming up against rock. The difference came from no particular quarter. It was like a circle of whispering creatures out in the dark, edging cautiously inwards.

'Too far. Starboard.'

This is crazy. Shallow water, in the pitch black? She reached for the throttle. Her fingers wouldn't bend properly in her thick gloves. The chill had rusted them. She tapped the stick back into neutral. The motor sighed into a soft idle as if relieved.

'Séverine.'

She didn't turn around. She hadn't looked back for a very long time. She spoke towards the cone of light ahead.

'No way I'm going close to land in the dark.'

'There's nothing to fear—'

She raised her voice. 'No. Way.'

'The boat's adrift. You're in danger.'

'I'll get the anchor. If I can find it under all Jonas's crap.' She rubbed and stretched her legs and stepped out of the cockpit.

'There is a channel. Straight, between two smaller islands, and deep at this height of the tide. I'll steer you through.' Goose ignored the voice. She'd almost forgotten what it felt like to make a simple decision. Navigating an offshore island group in the dark? Excuse me? She pushed a couple of crates aside with her toe and saw the anchor locker under the seat in the bows. A little light came on inside when she opened it. The chain was neatly looped. Trust Jonas, she thought. He was only shambolic on the surface.

'I can stand at your shoulder. There will be no mistake.'

'Oh yeah. I'd just love that.' She heaved the anchor out and slotted the chain through the bracket at the bow.

'Don't stop now. Not when you're so close. Séverine.' But she'd already dropped the anchor down into the black. The chain paid out noisily for only a couple of seconds before it went slack. Shallow water already. The sound under the hull changed again; the sea protested softly now, finding itself resisted. She wiped the gauges clear of condensation and checked the battery charge and the tank. Both were healthy. With plenty of diesel to spare she decided to leave the outboard running. Its mechanical grumble was like a second anchor, something to cling to against the whispering pull of the sea. She settled herself into the seat, folding her arms, keeping her eyes on the light ahead.

'It would be better,' the voice behind her said, 'to find the girl asleep.'

'Oh yeah?' Goose swivelled the seat from side to side, working the feeling back into her numbed feet. 'Better for who?'

'For you.'

'Is that so. Because, you know. I'm wondering.'

'I can't lie to you.'

'You seem in an awful hurry, my friend. I'm wondering what that's all about. Anyway. I'm in charge here, like you said.'

'Do you dare force the girl, if it comes to that?'

'Oh, excuse me. Is that what's bothering you? Yeah, actually. I think I can handle a sixteen-year-old kid.'

After a long silence, the voice said, 'There is so much you don't know.'

She couldn't stop herself turning angrily. There it was, bowed head all but invisible in the near-dark, as though it hadn't moved at all since they'd left the dock at Hardy. Only the white hands stood out, spread over the seat like a pair of dead starfish. 'You're so right. Which is exactly why we're going to wait now till I can see what I'm doing. That's what you're really worried about, isn't it? You know what? I reckon when daylight comes you're going to have to get back in your freaking coffin. Am I right? Are you going to turn to a puff of dust at sunrise? Huh? I don't know what you are and I don't want to know. Here's what I know. I know I'm not running aground in the middle of the Inside Passage in the dark. This isn't even my boat. For all I know we could be anywhere. It's, what.' She pushed her thick sleeve up to check her watch. 'Maybe a couple more hours till it gets light. Then we'll see who's been telling the truth. OK?'

The head lifted. Goose realised her hands were clenched and her heart was racing. The bleached starfish spread their withered limbs and slid gently over the seat, back and forth, back and forth.

'I fear nothing,' it said. Its voice did not change at all. 'I hope for nothing. I am indifferent to dark or light. The million million manifestations of the world all touch me with equal weight, Séverine. Each one is so full. So . . . perfect. I cannot grasp this mystery of *desiring*.'

Her own sweat was turning clammy above her collar. She shrugged her neck deeper into the jacket. If it had moved towards her she'd have thrown something. She was tense all down her back and shoulders, braced for contact. If it had even begun to stand up she'd have pulled the fire extinguisher from its clips and hurled it like a bomb. But it merely caressed the dirty padding, with a lover's delicacy. Nothing else in the boat moved. The hands swayed as calm and gentle as weeds in a pond.

'If I went to sleep,' Goose said, once it seemed like nothing else was going to happen, 'would you still be there when I woke up?'

The head bowed again, falling back behind its own screen of shadows.

'No,' it said.

Twenty-Eight

S HE JOLTED UPRIGHT. The spasm made her neck sting. The rest of her felt as numb as meat. An armada of dreams capsized and sank in an instant, leaving no trace. The sea where they drowned was a deep murky blue. She looked up to the surface, far overhead.

The blueness righted itself and became air. She rubbed her neck and stared around. An indigo world had whispered itself into half-being. The sea was purple-black, the wide bowl above it a few shades less dim. A blot of land nearby was a remnant of the night suspended between them.

She was alone.

Not entirely alone. A grey spot winged above the island group. It mewled a high tremolo: an eagle.

Goose looked around, shocked that she'd fallen asleep. She remembered telling herself not to, pushing herself upright in the chair. How could she have let herself drift off when she knew she was being watched by . . .

By . . .

She wrestled with the conviction that she was still dreaming. She made herself stand up and walk around the boat. The anchor chain scraped and creaked. She was cold to the marrow.

No one was aboard with her.

Take the boat away and the dawn gathering around her could have been ten thousand years old. The mutter of the outboard and the lurid red and green and white of the running lights suddenly seemed intrusive. She switched them off, her fingers clumsy in thick gloves. At once an oceanic immensity of wilderness enveloped everything, too raw and vast for habitation. The only sound now was an ambience of gentle white noise, air and water at rest, like the dawn breathing. The eagle vanished against a darker line on the horizon. That long smear could have been either side of the passage, the mainland or the great island. She might have looked at the gimballed compass beside the wheel to find out but she didn't want to. There were no charts or directions, no comings or goings. Everything was unnamed. A directionless breeze sent wavelets to brush against the hull. Their unstopped sibilance was the sound of her mother tongue, saying *vous êtes ici, vous êtes ici*.

She began remembering how she'd got there. It was a complicated effort. She seemed to have come loose from reasons, causes, effects. She couldn't find a good way of thinking about what she was doing on Jonas's boat far out in the Passage in the very early morning. She remembered Jonas; she remembered Jonas escorting the shrivelled-looking blind woman with the grotesquely long hair off the abandoned ferry; she remembered the same woman sitting in the stern of the boat, saying things that sounded more like incantations than words; all of it seemed to belong to another dimension, dream or theatre or fiction.

The nearby land was becoming solid. Light spread and sharpened the edges of its silhouette. She began to distinguish the shoulders of rock which separated one solid mass from another. The nearest was no more than a bare reef draped in kelp. Beyond that were tree-crowned hummocks, and a longer grey wall behind, a larger island still murky with distance.

What am I doing here?

Might as well ask that eagle. Or the reef. They weren't doing anything here, or not the way the question meant it. They just . . . were.

Jennifer. She was looking for Jennifer. That was right, wasn't it? She was looking for Jennifer because it was her job. She'd told her boss she'd find the kid, she was a mountie and the mounties always got their man. She had a duty of care. The girl was a vulnerable minor. Due in court. Due at the juvenile facility over on the mainland. Et cetera. Procedures, protocols, obligations.

She remembered that Jennifer had shut her mouth to that whole world. She remembered the girl sitting in the cell, looking at her, mute. Then the girl had walked out of the locked cell and disappeared into the silence.

This silence.

Goose knew then that what she really wanted was to find out what the silence had to say.

Back in the world she'd stepped away from, flights were cancelled. Traffic had stopped. The navigation lights were all switched off. The ferry had turned into a ghost ship. The TV wasn't working. The internet had failed. Voices from the wrong places came and went on the radio.

Instead of all that, then . . . what?

This, she supposed. She rubbed her arms briskly. This: daybreak in solitude. Sounds and colours unchanged since before there'd been people to hear and see them. She didn't doubt that Jennifer was here. Where else would she be? There were no due dates here, no court orders, no decisions made by legally constituted authorities. No papers. Zero megabytes. No words.

No place for herself either, Goose admitted, reluctantly. Hunger and cold were her prompts. She'd have to go back to Hardy, or whatever was left of it. Still, at least she could bring Jennifer with her. Not to the station, though. Not to be arrested or institutionalised or whatever. There'd be no more cells or court orders. She'd put the kid up herself if she had to, or maybe Jonas would. Jennifer had spoken, that night when it all began. *Shouting*, the file said. *Crazy stuff.* But it wasn't crazy, of course, and everyone would have to admit that now; or at least if it was crazy, that didn't stop it being true. They'd all have to try listening to her, instead of just yelling at her in the wrong language.

Starting with me, Goose thought. I'm here because some kind of undead ghost freak thing with an English accent sat in the back of the boat and told me where to go, unless I imagined it all, which maybe comes to the same thing anyway. I've got to be ready to hear some pretty crazy stuff.

She didn't bother checking the compass. It seemed unlikely that it would be reliable, and anyway, if she wanted to find out where she was, why not just look? She knew how the Passage ran, a wide-mouthed funnel with its open end to the north-west, the coastal range walling it on the mainland side. It was only a few weeks to the equinox. The dawn light would be spreading from the south-east, then. She turned a full circle anticlockwise and saw where the horizon brightened above a thin blur of forested land, and then where it rose into snaggle-toothed peaks, and then where it was serenely empty, sea and sky touching like watercolour paper peeling back from an ink-dark block. South-east, north-east, north-west. Hardy lay somewhere to port and astern, then, hidden in its bay for now but easy to find if she simply turned the boat around and motored down the Passage along the southern shore. There wasn't another vessel in sight. Here, one of the world's busiest marine highways, and the only thing she could see travelling it was the eagle again, gliding towards the islands ahead.

She followed its flight, watching as it banked and vanished into the dark outline of the larger island. A spot of incongruous colour caught her eye by the shore beneath the trees. Yellow.

She was looking down a channel between outlying rocks. Shadows made it hard to see but the daylight was strengthening steadily. There was definitely a brushstroke of unlikely yellow there, as alien to the grey-blue world as she and her boat were. She saw the way it sat above the waterline like a lurid instance of the ubiquitous stripped logs which decorated every shore along the Passage. She made the connection: the kayak. What was his name? Mr Hall's kayak. (The scowling boy inside the house. What were they doing now, she wondered, while she was out here in this gigantic silence? Was it beginning to sink in there, too?)

An idea occurred to her.

She went forward and pulled up the anchor. She had to take her gloves off to get a proper grip, and the chain was rough and painfully cold. After she'd stowed it she had to sit on her hands for a few minutes before she could manage the key and the throttle. When she did finally get the motor going the noise and the petrol smell and the froth behind the propeller embarrassed her, as though she'd caught herself taking a spray-can to the dawn.

She eased the boat forward nevertheless. From the length of exposed rock at the skirts of the small islands ahead she could guess that the tide was a good metre below its highest point, but Jonas's boat drew very little, and the water was icily clear; the channel didn't look too risky. She noticed that she was almost deliriously relieved to be trusting her own eyes and making her own decisions. Whatever had happened to her in the night, the dawn must have banished it. There'd been a lot of bad nights recently. Even in her dingy apartment in Alice, surrounded by nothing more sinister than packing boxes, things could turn wrong quickly; even lying awake in her own bed had sometimes felt like being afloat in a black ocean. But when daylight arrived you could always see straight again: the despair turned out just to be tiredness, the bad thoughts just distractions. Whatever had haunted her this past night, the main thing about it now was that it had disappeared.

The islands grew tall in front of her, trees crowding together on their shelves of rock like survivors on an insufficient raft. Dead wood tumbled over the edges, weathered and rotted into twisted arabesques. In their lee the water turned perfectly calm. She saw the sea floor rising beneath, but the gap was wide and deep enough. She steered through into a sheltered bay ringed by shoals and the low promontories of a more substantial island, draped with bunchberry and salal as well as the tight-packed evergreens. The kayak had been drawn up above a small arc of slate-coloured sand. Behind the scent of damp forest Goose caught a momentary smell of smoke.

She cut the engine and raised the outboard. Every noise was magnified by the stillness but no one had come running yet. If Jennifer was awake by her fire, perhaps she was deep in the trees, or perhaps she didn't care. That was the advantage of her idea, Goose thought, as she stripped off jacket and gloves and watched the bow drift towards the sand. It would make any negotiation a lot simpler.

She took the bowline and waited till the drift brought her close enough to jump ashore. Solid ground jarred her for a moment and her legs were briefly unsteady. She looped the line around a spur of beached wood and went to fetch the kayak. Jennifer hadn't bothered to turn it over. The paddle was tucked down in the cockpit, washed by a small puddle of seawater and dew. Rather than dragging, Goose heaved the boat up to her shoulder and carried it back across the beach. There was no question of jumping now but she didn't mind getting her feet wet, though the first trickle that came in through her boots was astonishingly cold, bitter enough to make her swear between clenched teeth. Nor was there any question of being discreet. The only way to get the kayak into Jonas's boat was to reach up and tip it in. It clattered down on to the plastic tubs and other assorted junk he apparently needed for his fishing trips (*That's not junk, man, that's equipment*). A pair of ravens flapped out of the trees, annoyed by the racket, and began spiralling upwards. Goose waded back to the beach, untied the bowline and clambered back aboard. The stern had come round and was scraping gently against shelving rock. She used the kayak's paddle to push out away from the shore and then sat down to get her boots and socks off before her feet froze.

The island undergrowth crackled. She was drying her feet on one of Jonas's rags when the girl stepped out of the trees.

Their eyes met, as in the cell. Her look was the same, Goose saw. Jennifer was wearing the same clothes too, donated, probably, from some charitable collection in one of the various hospitals and holding pens she'd been shuttled among: a hooded athletic sweatshirt in burgundy, grey sweatpants, old sneakers. She had the hood up, which made her look even more like a seal, round headed, wide faced, with big dark silent eyes. The only thing that was different was that she'd acquired some kind of necklace from somewhere, the pendant a plain brown ring hanging from a grey chain.

'Fancy meeting you here,' Goose said. There was no need to raise her voice.

'That's my kayak,' Jennifer Knox said.

Goose was so surprised that the surprise was for an instant indistinguishable from fear: a sharp cold shock. She stood up.

'Well, hey. Nice to hear your voice.'

'What are you doing with my boat?'

The shaman girl sounded just like any other grumpy teen-ager. She came down to the wet sand. The sleeves of her sweatshirt were too long. She pulled them down over her hands, her fists improvising pockets.

'Technically,' Goose said, trying to keep the nerves out of her voice, 'I think this belongs to a George Hall. Of Tsakis Road, Rupert. You know Mr Hall? Fat little dog? He got it for his kids. The kayak. Not the dog.'

The girl stared. Her face was young, a girl's face, healthy and fresh the way only teenagers could look, but the way she stared made her look ten years older, or a hundred.

'You're that cop.'

'Officer Maculloch. I'm glad you remember. Though I probably just got decommissioned, so why don't you just call me Séverine. Though actually everyone calls me Goose. Long story. Did I tell you that already?'

'What are you doing here?'

The boat was barely drifting at all, sheltered from any wind and out of the pull of the tide. What little lazy momen-tum it had was away from the beach, which made Goose feel a little more secure. She propped her arms on her hips and tried to smile.

'It's time to go home, Jennifer. I thought I'd come and fetch you.' She patted the wheel. 'Easier than paddling all the way back, eh?'

The girl's face was a mask, a smooth coppery mask.

'Not, like, your actual home,' Goose went on. 'Obviously. Because you set fire to that. Right? Didn't you?'

Hands still curled in the sleeves, Jennifer folded her arms.

'No one was hurt. You'll be glad to hear. I guess.'

This was what Goose remembered from their few minutes' encounter in the back of the station in Alice: the way anything she said to the girl just bounced off.

'OK,' she said. 'Look. Actually I don't care about what happened with your house. Truly I don't. I'm sorry I brought it up, eh? That's all finished with now. I'm not trying to arrest you, nothing like that. No more cells, no more hospitals, no more lawyers, whatever. Promise. I didn't come here as a cop, I came here as me. You understand? Come on, Jennifer, talk to me.'

'How did you follow me?'

Goose picked up the paddle and corrected the boat's drift, nudging back towards the beach. 'You know,' she said, 'it might be easier to talk on board. While we head back.'

'I'm not finished here.'

'Oh. Well. How much longer do you need?'

'It's not your business.'

She dipped the paddle again, keeping the bow straight. 'See, the thing is, Jennifer, I've got your boat.'

The girl didn't answer.

'Mr Hall's boat. Or let's call it yours, doesn't matter, I'm not accusing anyone of anything. I took this one without asking too, now I think of it.'

'You better bring it back, then.'

'Oh, I'm planning to. Oh, wait. You mean the kayak.' It sat awkwardly along the gunwale, stern tipped up, a big yellow plastic prize catch. 'I'll be straight with you, Jennifer. This is kind of why I took it, eh? I mean, I could have come ashore and done the whole heavy cop thing, but, you know. No one wants that. So you finish what you need to do, and I'll wait right here with the kayak, and whenever you're ready you come on aboard and off we go. How's that sound?'

'Do I have a choice?'

Goose tapped the kayak beside her. 'I guess you don't, really. Sorry.'

The girl turned her head abruptly, as if she'd heard something unexpected. 'You here on your own?'

Goose spread her arms. 'Looks like it.' Her heart was going faster than it should have been. There'd been no sound; she was sure she'd have heard anything near by.

'How'd you find this place? You shouldn't be here.'

Goose concentrated on holding an unthreatening smile. 'You know what? We both have a lot of questions. There's a ton of stuff I'd like you to tell me about. Like the last time we met, for starters. I spent quite a while running around looking for you after you walked out the station, you know? So. If you're ready, I'll paddle over, you can hop on in, and we'll talk. I have to say, it's great that you're talking to me like this. I've got to think that's a good sign, eh? It's going to make things much easier.'

The stare was wavering. Jennifer stepped back from the water a pace. She pushed back her hood and glanced around the bay again.

'I hate to say it, but you probably shouldn't take too long deciding. I'd kind of like to get started back. You know. Breakfast.'

The girl's hands popped out of their sleeves. She lifted the chain of her necklace and tucked it down inside her sweatshirt.

'If I have to,' Goose said, 'I'll come and get you. But I'd prefer not to.'

'You'd dare touch me?' It wasn't the usual empty bravado of pumped-up teenagers squaring up to the cops; Goose would have recognised that. Jennifer seemed genuinely incredulous. 'You gonna lay a finger on me? You heard about the other cop yet?'

Goose gripped the wheel to hold herself steady. 'Fitzgerald?'

'You put your dirty white hands on me, they'll start stinking so bad you'll want to cut them off.'

'Jennifer.' Goose's smile disappeared. 'Give it a rest. I'm not the bad guy here. I just want . . .' What? 'Come back. Talk to people. I'll help. I understand why you wouldn't say anything before. But look, you're talking now. Right? I'm listening. I'm not going to let anyone lock you up or make you go back to your mom. Nothing like that. I know you didn't push your brother downstairs. Whatever you've done, I know you've done it for a reason. Everyone treated you wrong, I know that. But you're talking to me, right? So you know I'm OK. I've . . .' For an instant she saw what

Jennifer's silence was like from the inside. There were certain things you couldn't say: she felt the impossibility on her tongue. 'I've seen some things,' she finished, lamely.

'Talking with you's like talking with nobody,' the girl said, matter-of-factly.

'Jeez. Thanks.'

'Who'd you bring with you?' Jennifer edged towards the water again, distracted. She shouted something Goose didn't understand, in another language perhaps. From high in the upper air the call of the ravens answered, another language again.

'No one,' Goose said. 'Just me.'

'Bring the boat.'

'You're coming? Great!'

'All right. Come on.' Jennifer's stare had gone the way of Goose's professional smile. She looked her age again, a girl on a beach, worried she was going to be left behind. She craned back to look at the ravens, who were still circling each other, rising, already impossibly high.

'Here. I'll toss this to you.' Goose clambered around the crates to the bows again, coiled the bowline and threw. 'Easy. Whoa there.' The girl had yanked the bow in hard. 'Got to spin it side-on. Walk along that way.' Goose leaned over the side with the paddle, fending off against the cracked rock below. 'There we go.' She was going to paddle a little closer to the sand but Jennifer didn't wait, didn't even roll her sweatpants up, let alone stop to take her shoes off. She splashed in up to her knees and launched herself at the gunwale, spreading her elbows across it, thrashing the water as she tried to pull herself over. 'Easy!' Goose reached over to haul her in by the waist. They ended up in an untidily intimate heap among the crates.

'OK.' She straightened herself out, leaned over with the paddle again and pushed away. 'That worked. Kinda.' A couple of shoves and a couple of backstrokes and the boat was moving away from danger, spinning slowly as it went. 'Welcome aboard.'

Jennifer sat down in the passenger seat, hunching morosely.

Goose pulled in the bowline hand over hand, quietly pleased with herself. Though she was past the stage of knowing what to expect, her plan had gone about as well as she could have imagined. If she'd had any expectations, they certainly wouldn't have included a Jennifer who was not only reasonably cooperative but reasonably communicative as well. Though there'd been plenty of stuff in the file testifying that she was basically a good kid; but that was before she'd become—

The shaman girl. The phrase spoke itself in her memory in a horrible dry voice; the *r* in *girl* not sounded, in the English manner, turning the word cold and sinister.

Goose sat in the bows, the safety of the windscreen between her and the girl, while she forced her feet back into her boots. The damp lining was horrible but still better than open air against her skin.

'Jennifer?'

The girl glanced up, plucking hair away from her cheek.

'I just want to make something clear to you.' There was

the weight on her tongue again. She tried to think her way around it. 'There's a lot of stuff I don't understand, but I know it's . . . different now. OK? So anything you want to tell me, I'm not going to try and tell you you're wrong, you're crazy, whatever. We were wrong. Weren't we? The rest of us.'

Jennifer looked like she could have been modelling for a statue: Teenage Sullenness.

'So.' Goose shrugged. 'That was it, I guess.'

She'd never have expected the girl to answer, but Jennifer surprised her.

'This was a place people lived, once,' she said. 'The biggest house was my people's. The orca house. Over on the far side, where the long beach is. Where's your house? Where do you belong? You don't even know.'

Goose looked at her. She couldn't see a shaman girl. All she saw was another stroppy kid.

'That's what all this is about?' she said. 'The old you-stole-our-land stuff? Jeez.' She stowed the coiled bowline, more neatly than Jonas would have bothered to. 'That's kinda disappointing.'

'It's nobody's land.' Jennifer clasped her hands over her breasts, a strange gesture, almost religious. 'It never belonged to anyone. The Band talk that way 'cause they don't know any better than you. My mom, she don't belong here. Or anywhere. She don't know how to live, don't matter where she goes. Get drunk, watch TV, have babies.' She spat another word Goose didn't know: it sounded like a curse. 'Yeah, you were wrong. You and everyone else.' For a moment her voice made flat echoes ring from the wave-smoothed shoreline.

'Were we?' Goose said, moving Jonas's crates back out of the way. 'Is that so? And you're going to fix it?'

Jennifer said: 'It's gonna fix itself.'

Goose thought of the couple she'd met that foggy morning in Alice, running away down-island because they were afraid of living by themselves with no TV. She thought of the failed bank machine, no longer translating digits in an account into money for the wallet. She wondered what they'd find when they got back to Hardy.

The wind was gusting up a bit. They were still sheltered from it, but Goose could hear it in the trees, and see the grey sheet of the Passage beginning to wrinkle into dark lines. A rough crossing would be no fun in a boat this size.

'Well,' she said, squeezing behind the passenger seat to take the helm again. 'Let's go back and see, shall we?' She pressed the switch to lower the outboard.

There was no response.

She pressed it again, clicking it back and forth. '*Tabarnac,*' she growled, jiggling the key in the ignition. The battery gauge caught her eye. Its needle showed zero charge. Less than zero: the needle was slumped against the edge of the dial as if it had broken. The fuel gauge was the same. It had been showing three-quarters of a tank maybe half an hour ago. Now it showed nothing.

'Crap.' The boat was spinning unhurriedly, drifting closer to one of the small islands. She jabbed at light switches. None of them worked. The key clicked back and forth without provoking the smallest response from the motor or any of the electrics.

'Great. That's freaking great.' Goose thumped the dashboard in frustration. 'Must be some kind of battery thing.' A broken connection was the best she could think of. She looked at the scattered boxes and spools and weed-streaked fenders covering most of the boat. 'Where the hell's the battery?' There'd have to be some kind of hatch in the hull, she guessed, probably in the stern. She tried the key a few more times. 'Come on. Jeez, Jonas. Trust you.' On the coldest winter mornings back home it would sometimes take a while for the car to start. She remembered sitting in the back with Tess, watching their parents stomping around the hood in their snow jackets, getting angrier and angrier, first with the car, then with each other. But on those mornings you could at least hear the ignition trying to turn over. The boat wasn't making any noise at all. It had gone dead as driftwood. '*Tabarnac!*' She kicked it.

'You shouldn't have come here,' the girl next to her said, not smugly; she sounded tense.

'Why don't you shut up for a bit, OK?'

'Something bad's come with you.'

'Here.' Goose picked up the paddle of the kayak and put it in Jennifer's hands. 'Here's something useful you can do. Make sure we don't run aground while I get this fixed.' She began kicking her way through the junk in the stern. The girl got to her feet, too slowly. There were shallows beneath them; they'd drifted out towards the channel between the rocks. The black bulk of a drowned log came into view near

511

by. 'Don't just stand there!' Goose grabbed the paddle, leaned over and shoved them clear of it. 'All right. Sit down. Let me.' The tide was ebbing, slowly enough as far as she could tell; still, she didn't like the idea of losing depth in the channel. Better to get out into open water before seeing what she could do with the electrics, she thought, especially if the kid was just going to be a pain in the ass. She went forward and sat with her legs over the bows. From there she could just about paddle the boat, though it was as unwieldy as trying to row a bathtub. A faint current helped, the tide draining out of the bay. Her back ached as she bent, dug the blade in, pushed. She noticed how hungry she was, and how stiff. The steel blue of dawn had turned into the inevitable grey day. *Shouldn't have come here.*

'Oh,' Jennifer said, behind her. 'I get it.'

The stern was swinging the wrong way. Goose battled the paddle sideways. The water beneath would have been no more than waist deep if she'd been standing in it. 'Shut up.'

'That looks like hard work.'

Goose didn't have the breath to shout. She tried to ignore the girl. They were abreast of the outer island. A cliff-rooted pine jutted out overhead at a ridiculous angle, doomed to end up among the fallen wood, though its losing battle might go on for decades more.

'You're not going to make it the whole way.'

'Shut your freaking mouth, you freaking witch,' Goose said, very quietly, between breaths. The rocky bottom fell away suddenly and the sea became a dark opacity. She clenched her teeth and gave a few more powerful strokes, propelling them away from the bare shoal to starboard, then sat up, putting the paddle aside, feeling her back. The boat yawed abruptly. She looked around. Jennifer had stood up and was trying to lift the kayak.

'What the hell are you doing?'

'Leaving.'

'No freaking way.' Goose swung her legs inboard. The kid wasn't strong enough to get the kayak up. Goose got a hand on it before she could move it more than a couple of inches and shoved it back, hard.

Jennifer turned on her. 'You can mess around with the motor all you like. It's not gonna help. I get it now, I get what's happening. You people, you always wanna go faster, don't you? Gotta have your cars and your boats and your planes. Gotta be able to get away, get somewhere else. You can't do that around me. You know what happened? I called the killer whale to me.' She reached inside her sweatshirt and pulled out her necklace, the plain brown ring looped on a chain that had gone the dull speckled green of tarnished silver. 'From the other side of the world. He didn't get on some plane. He came the way a whale's supposed to come. This is what he brought me.' She clutched the pendant in her fist. 'This makes everything the way it's supposed to be. No motor's gonna speed this up. If you wanna take this anywhere you're gonna have to do it yourself, the way a person's supposed to. That's how I came here. That's the way you should have come too. You screwed up. Gonna be a long paddle home.' She pointed across to the distant southern landmass. 'Or you can let me go my way, then you can go yours. Quick as you can, A to B. Hurry hurry hurry. Get it over with. And you're wondering why you don't belong anywhere.'

Goose's fingers were beginning to tingle. She'd always hated the ones who yelled back. They never made any sense either: they were drunk, usually, and crazed with their stupid pride, their desperation not to give in to the law even when she was hauling them into the station and filling out the charge sheet. They always had to have the last word. She breathed carefully, concentrating on keeping her temper.

'I've got to take a couple of steps back here,' she said. 'Did you just say you broke my boat? Jonas's boat? You remember Jonas. Officer Paul. He drove you up that morning. He's a pretty nice guy, but he's not going to be happy with you if you messed his boat up. Is that what you just said?'

The girl turned away. 'You don't get it,' she said. She braced her girl's hands inside the cockpit of the kayak and started trying to lift it straight again.

Goose leaned her full weight on it. 'I found that kid. That boy.'

Jennifer dropped her hands to her sides and went still.

'What was his name? Horace something Chinese. Him and the mask out on Masterman Island, and your coat. I found him. What'd you do, leave him there on his own? He could have died. Is that what all your this-is-how-it's-supposed-to-be bullshit's about? Leaving a kid to die?'

Jennifer looked for all the world like a tenth-grader being told off at the front of the class.

'I know he was a killer whale too,' Goose said, without

even stopping to wonder how she could be saying such a thing. 'I know that. But when I got to him you know what I found? A kid who couldn't speak and couldn't move. That's what he was on that island. I looked him up. He's been missing from his home for three months. His mom made a bunch of appeals. You can see them on YouTube. A couple of times she tries to say his name and she can't, she chokes up so bad she can't breathe. The cop has to lift her up from the table and make her take a drink of water, and she spills it down her coat because she can't open her mouth properly, she's shaking so bad. You look at her face and you think she's a hundred years old. That's his mom. Is that what you mean by everything being where it belongs? Huh? Jennifer?'

She'd tried to keep her temper but she'd ended up almost shouting. The girl wouldn't look at her.

'Sit down,' she said. 'Stay out of the way. Oh, and forget the kayak. Actually.' Goose had left the paddle leaning upright in the cockpit; now she took hold of it, held it straight like a javelin, pointed up and out with her leading arm like she'd been taught and flung it from the boat. She had strong shoulders and good technique. It went spinning and arcing a long way, landing with an ugly splash. Jennifer had made a small motion as if to stop her, but far too little and too late. 'There. Now, why don't you shut up for a bit while I check the battery. You went all that time without saying anything, you should be able to keep quiet for ten minutes.'

The girl put her hood up, tucking in her chin, and sat down. Her fingers went to the necklace, spinning the pendant around its chain. Goose took a few moments to flex the anger out of her hands, and then kicked her way through Jonas's crap to explore the stern.

She found the hatch by lifting the seat across the back of the boat. The battery was in a watertight compartment beneath. Sheathed rubber cables connected it to the outboard and the fuse box. She saw no cracks in the rubber, no loose cabling, none of the scum or froth that would have suggested a leak. Everything was as shipshape as the anchor had been. Jonas let everyone think he was a slob, but she knew better. There was even an inspection certificate, neatly slid inside a plastic folder taped to the lid of the compartment. She unclipped the cables and wiped the connections, though they weren't particularly dirty, reattached them, and tried the key and the switches again. Nothing.

'You're gonna have to go fetch that paddle,' Jennifer said.

Goose sat down in the seat next to her, rubbing her cheeks. She was beginning to feel seriously uncomfortable. The chill wasn't too bad for the time of year, but she felt the bad night catching up with her, and her stomach was pinching and growling. It had been a while since she'd gone this long without coffee, too.

'Say what you said again,' she said.

'What?'

'You know. About how you can only go as fast as you're supposed to go, all that crap.'

'You still think it's crap? Can you see anything wrong with the boat?'

'OK, so say it again. The boat was running fine an hour ago. What happened?'

Jennifer shook her head. 'You're not listening.'

Which was true, when Goose thought about it. Wasn't that the problem all along? Hadn't she promised herself, that morning, as she watched the dawn begin, that she'd listen to the kid?

She sat for a while, trying to remember what Jennifer had just told her, thinking about it.

When she'd finished, she stretched slowly, rolled the lingering stiffness out of her neck, and stood up. Casually but carefully, she positioned herself behind the girl's seat.

'You going to fetch that paddle now?' the girl said, still hunched in her hood.

'Nope.'

Goose whisked her hands down over Jennifer's shoulders, grabbed the necklace chain and pulled it off. The girl had time for no more than an ineffectual spasm of her arms and a sharp and angry scream before Goose bunched chain and pendant in one hand and threw them out into the grey chop. They disappeared with barely more splash than a drop of rain.

The first note of rage gathered in Jennifer's throat like muted thunder. As she rose to her feet it became a howl. She turned on Goose with murderous eyes and roared wordlessly at her. The howl cut off suddenly, leaving them face to face, breathing hard. The girl's face had turned as ferocious as the orca mask.

'You're gonna die alone,' she said, 'and in pain.'

Deep inside her, Goose felt a light go out, or a small door open on to a long dark passageway. She faced it down.

'OK,' she said, as calmly as she could. 'Let's try the outboard now.' She could tell from Jennifer's look that she'd been right. *No motor's gonna speed this up*; whatever the deal was with the kid's necklace, that was the problem with the boat. She didn't understand it, of course, but it wasn't about understanding, it was about listening. She made to step around the girl, reaching for the dashboard.

Either anger made Jennifer quick, or Goose had relaxed a fraction too much. The girl spun round, pulled the keys out of the ignition, and held them up over her head.

Be calm now, Goose told herself. She'd done what she needed to. Time to defuse the situation. 'Give me those, please.'

Jennifer backed a step away. Her eyes were so dark they were as good as black, like Jonas's.

'OK,' Goose said. 'Think about it. I've got to have the keys, right? One way or another. So, why don't we do it the easy way.'

Jennifer cocked her arm. Goose lunged at her. Jennifer thrust her free hand out, fingers spread, a gesture so heavy with fury it stopped Goose in her tracks.

'You lay a finger on me and you'll rot,' the girl said.

Just a punk kid playing tough, Goose tried to think, as she'd thought a hundred times before, rounding up troublemakers on the night shift, but she couldn't make herself go any farther. While she hesitated, Jennifer twisted her torso and threw the keys out into the sea.

In quick succession, Goose thought

—*crap*

—then: *she throws like a girl*

—then *crap* again (as the little metal shrapnel dropped down to the water)

—then: *now we're really screwed*

—and then: *oh, Jonas. Trust Jonas.*

She grinned.

The Vancouver Canucks emblem on Jonas's key chain was made out of foam. Of course. Every fishing boat had a float on its key chain. You'd have to be a lot dumber than Jonas Paul not to have one. It bobbed around barely ten metres away. A small smooth-topped reef was just breaking out from small waves beyond it, emerging as the tide fell.

'All right,' Goose said. 'So I guess that makes us almost even.'

Jennifer slumped down on to the seat in the bows, covering her face with her hands.

'At least you get to see me swim for it.' Goose didn't much like the idea, but by this stage she hardly cared. Get her hands on the keys, get back to the boat, get back to Hardy. Whatever was going on there at least she'd be able to dry out, warm up and eat. She stripped off jacket, boots, pants and sweatshirt, trying to ignore the cold. Having some dry clothes afterwards would be the main thing. She could mop herself off with the sweatshirt when she got back and then wrap herself in the rest. She couldn't bring herself to strip off undershirt, knickers or bra. Maybe they'd keep her a fraction warmer for a few seconds, who knew, but the thought of going into that grey sea naked was intolerable.

She denied herself hesitation. She told her legs to jump

and they jumped. Salt and cold hit her together, the base elements of a brutally alien world. She closed her eyes and put her head down. Six frantic strokes later she took her first breath, a shocked gasp. She shoved hair out of her eyes and looked for the bobbing float.

A wild screech broke behind her. She flinched, imagining an eagle plunging, but it was Jennifer. The girl had sprung to her feet and was shouting, twisting in panic. Goose couldn't see what had frightened her, if anything. Her eyes stung with the salt. Small waves slapped over her mouth. Straightening herself to look, she kicked against limpet-crusted rock. Her feet were too cold to feel pain. She saw the keys a few strokes farther off, took a deep breath and kicked out again. The shoal rose abruptly under her. She felt for handholds among fissured stones, distracted by the girl's screaming. The current had pushed the keys over the reef. It was too shallow to swim here so she hauled herself up on to a shin-deep platform of stone. Coming out into the wind made the freezing wet almost unbearable. She turned to shout at Jennifer, patience snapping: 'Will you shut the f—'

Another body had risen from the water.

On the far side of the boat, on a small promontory of shingle reaching out from the last of the islands, a drenched black figure was unfurling itself from the sea, water oozing from mouldering clothes and gorgon hair. The wind gusted sharply, and Goose felt her palpitating heart seized by a grip of ice. Jennifer stretched her arms out towards the monstrosity, yelling. It drew itself upright on the shore. It had arms too, and hands, withered white hands, salt-scoured and leeched of warmth. Goose wiped at her eyes to see what those hands held as they lifted skyward. Something small, looped on a silvery thread. The chain caught a gleam of tarnished daylight.

Jennifer went suddenly silent. The gust redoubled at Goose's back, but the chill in her spine had come from inside.

The twice-drowned thing shuffled slowly around and raised its head.

There was just a moment, the interval of a breath, when Goose had time to think to herself, *The bandage is gone*, before she saw what it had for eyes.

She lost her footing. Caught by the reef, a wave crashed over her, into her nose and mouth. She choked but couldn't turn away. The spots of lurid fire held her blurred gaze like twin beacons. Everything else was grey and salt and cold: only the drowned revenant's eyes burned with ghastly unlife. It braced its hands over its head in triumph, the silver necklace chain strung between them, and snapped it. The ring quivered for an instant in empty air, a speck against the clouds behind. A skeletal hand caught it and slipped it on.

An anguished wind howled. The keys, Goose thought to herself, for want of anything better to think; don't let them blow away. Otherwise, otherwise . . . She was shivering with cold compounded by dumb dread. She saw the float and dived again. Whipped to anger, the sea smacked against her flailing arms. She swam in a frenzy, feeling herself going numb in soul as well as body, horror as overwhelming as cold. A white-capped crest picked up the keys and flipped them near her hand; she kicked and clutched and grabbed them, and couldn't remember why she wanted them, what she was doing in the water, shivering and tiny, an atom in the deadly vastness of the ocean. Her arms and legs were turning sluggish, heavy, dead wood. She was struggling to stay afloat. A single desperate urge overtook her at the expense of everything else, the atavistic compulsion to get her feet on solid ground: she drove herself back to the reef, scratching ankles and arms as she beached herself on it, clutching an outcrop of rock, hugging it, sobbing, gasping at the inhuman cold. The shoal behind her lifted the swell into breakers and threw them over her head. She spat phlegm and water. *Ah non*, she was thinking, *ah non, pas moi, pas moi.* She remembered the boat, salvation. The keys were still in her fist though she couldn't feel her fingers. She remembered the thing, the demon, the undead, its whispering voice in the dark: *everyone's story ends in death.* With a dreadful effort she pulled herself higher and made herself look over the rising sea. Everything froze; everything turned to an arctic blank. The wind had driven the boat away twice as far as it had been before. 'Jennifer!' she screamed, and threw herself towards it, forgetting to take a breath. Waves lifted her and sucked her under. She surfaced, coughing, blinded by spray and salt and terror. What if *it* was swimming beneath her? She kicked out again, not knowing what she was doing. When the sea let her force her head up for a moment she saw the boat, no closer. It was only a moment. Her legs were losing strength. The dark beneath her was wrapping feelers around her ankles and beginning to pull. She tried to call out again and a mouthful of ocean slapped itself down her open throat. In a terrible instant she saw herself as if from the eagle's view, swimming weakly until she sank; the horror of it was too much to bear. She poured her desperation into her limbs and made them fight towards the only solid thing she could see, the bleak hard angle of the reef, until her feet scraped rock again. *Qu'est-ce que j'ai fait?* She looked at her fists, close to her eyes. Empty. The key chain had slipped out of her fingers. Empty. She stared at them again as if the mistake would correct itself. *Pas moi.* No keys, and the boat drifting farther and farther away. Her arms wouldn't let go of the rock, as if they'd made their own decision that all that mattered was that she was alive, now, anchored in place, not about to drown. She hugged herself tight to it and tried to look for the float. Waves were curling higher than her head; they pushed her weakening torso as if she were limp kelp, scraping her over the rock. A single explicit thought loomed up like the black-clad corpse from the sea: *la mort.* The end. She would die, freeze and drown, unless she, unless she, unless . . .

Dry land wasn't far. She could see it. When the vicious spray let her, she could see individual trees shaking their tops in the sudden wind. Out of the water. Her story contracted to that single point: she wanted to be beyond the sea's reach, otherwise it would have her, and then no more Goose, no more story. She tried to steady herself and time a few deep breaths to match troughs between the breakers. She became aware of her existence balanced on the point of a pin. Struggle in the water for the keys, struggle to reach the boat, or force herself across the fifty metres of tossing grey to the nearest of the solid islands? It didn't feel like a choice. Only one end was in sight. She gritted her teeth, gulped air and let go. The first wave rolled her over, capsizing her, blotting out all sound for a second beyond the weird hushed wallowing of underwater currents. She kicked up against rock, found air, glimpsed for a moment the crown of trees marking safety ahead, and began windmilling her arms.

It was a contest of effort against pain. She knew all about those. She'd won hundreds of them. She won again, eventually. There was even a strangely sweet moment when she knew she was going to win, when she came into the lee of the scattered landmasses and felt the sea calming, and looked ahead as she took another painful breath and saw the evergreens filling most of her view. She emerged out of the wind, dragging herself on scraped and bloody hands and knees until the numb hooks of her fists were tearing at leaves and bark. She collapsed in a hollow among driftwood above the top of the tide, and lay there, alive, not finished, listening to herself breathing; alive, cold to the bone, hungry, all but naked, and utterly marooned.

Twenty-Nine

IT RAINED A tantrum: violent and short. She cramped herself beneath a contorted overhang of ancient dead wood. Everything afterwards smelled of pine.

After the storm the sky seemed brighter and farther away. Later on it flaked apart and the sun came out.

Her undershirt had been scratched to shreds. She peeled it off and discarded it, a heap of artificial seaweed. She could hear the wind still but not feel it. Her little hollow was sheltered, and faced south, into the strong light. The stripped and barren wood warmed fast. She pressed her back against it. She couldn't remember the last sunshine she'd seen. It turned the world as bright as a postcard and fell on her skin like an eager lover.

A while later she found she could sit up. Her hands could flex. Her heartbeat was thin and rapid, but it no longer felt manacled by chains of ice. The sun had risen higher. One long flat stone near her hand was actually warm to the touch. She clasped it between her feet until they stung.

Across ten kilometres of glittering water the low top of Vancouver Island was a finger's-width of fresh green. There were roads there, and people, and phones, connections: Highway 1, stringing the whole of Canada together. A little later still, when the yellow warmth had gone deep enough that she could stand and walk, she made a circuit of the island where she'd landed. She had the mysterious feeling that somewhere on it she'd find those things, Canadian things. A secretly hidden well-stocked marina, perhaps, or a solar-powered emergency phone with a connection to the coastguard. It seemed necessary, somehow. The idea that she was cast away on a tiny speck of untouched and unin-habitable rock in the middle of the Inside Passage was peculiarly unthinkable. It could only be a bad joke. There were places where she had to climb up through narrow defiles in cliffs and skirt the prickly undergrowth of the trees, but she went all the way around the island until she reached her little sun-washed haven among the fallen trees again, having found nothing, of course, but what was actually there.

She found herself hoping for things. A spring of fresh water. (She pecked rain from tiny crevices like a bird.) A passing boat. No, a passing helicopter. No, Jonas arriving in his boat, with a big smile, a thick blanket as big as a comforter and a bag of warm almond croissants from Au Pain Doré. It was the kind of hope which hurt, physically, the kind that makes you short of breath and sick to your innards.

That finished, eventually. Afterwards she had other thoughts, involving things like bird's eggs, or actual birds killed by well-judged stones, or rubbing sticks together, or piling up stones to make a cairn visible across the Passage, or lashing logs together with seaweed.

Other kinds of things, too: what-ifs. These were also exquisitely painful. If she hadn't thrown the stupid paddle out of the stupid boat, so she wouldn't have had to swim to get the stupid keys. If she'd made herself swim after the boat instead of to dry land. If they'd asked someone else to come and replace Fitzgerald instead of her. If she'd never listened to the thing from hell, if she'd stayed at her post. If she'd just ignored Kalmykov. How many times had she, a fit young blonde woman in the police force, ignored or shrugged off that sort of crap? A hundred? So why not a hundred and one?

All that finished too, so then she thought about dying.

For some reason she'd never expected the thought of it to be so frightening. It had always just seemed like one of those things that happened (to other people, that is). It was going on all over the place. She'd assumed that when her turn came it would feel ordinary, unexceptional. Instead it turned out to be like the worst fear she'd ever had magnified by a factor of a thousand. She'd do anything not to die. If God came out of the sea and told her she could live but a hundred happy children would starve in her place she'd have wept with gratitude and said *yes, thank you, let them starve, save me*.

She remembered the way her grandmother's old TV used to turn off. No remote or anything: you pushed in the knob, *snick*, and then the screen shrank suddenly in on itself to a point of light, and then, *wink*, nothing. When Goose thought of that she gibbered in terror. She pulled herself into a ball and fell on her side in the sunlight and her mouth went *ahh non, ahh non, non non non*.

Some inward voice told her that she ought to be ashamed of such cowardice. (Her mother?) The accusation felt weak. Shame needed witnesses. Shame was public. She was alone. The island didn't care about courage or cravenness. It didn't care about her at all. It had no interest in providing her with food or means of shelter or escape. It didn't want to listen to her memories or her complaints about unfinished business or the things she wanted to say to the people who'd miss her.

There must be something I can do. Dying was ridiculous, impossible; it couldn't happen. So, something else. It was just a question of figuring out what it was.

The problem was that she was so weak with hunger she could barely think.

She narrowed it down to three things: food, warmth, escape.

Like a juggler's batons, they refused to stay in her grip together. She had to toss one away to grab another. She could maybe try to find two small logs to lash together with the remains of her shirt, and float out on the raft when the tide began to rise to fill the Passage, letting the current carry her south and east, maybe lying flat on her stomach and paddling with her hands; but she'd have to start right away, while there was daylight left, because soon she'd run out of energy, and then it would be night and she'd be naked at sea in the dark. Or she could look for something better than seaweed to chew on, maybe gather enough to get her through the day, but then she'd still be stuck. Or she could stay here in her suntrap where it was pleasant to soak up warmth, and be comfortable, and starve while she hoped for something else to happen. Or make herself some kind of shelter so she'd be warm through the night, which would give more time for the miracle to come along. It was the age of miracles, after all. She'd seen a demon on the neighbouring island: why not an angel on this one? *N'ayez pas peur, Séverine.* Choral music and harps.

She noticed the sharp-edged shadow of a branch above angling differently across the shoreline. Lengthening, just a fraction. Pointing, cruelly, towards the water. The sun had started its descent.

Her hands began to shake.

She remembered Jennifer saying something about the larger island, people living there, a house, a hearth. She thought she remembered catching a faint whiff of smoke. (Jennifer. Why couldn't she have left the girl alone? Why couldn't she have done what Cope had made it so clear he wanted her to do: colluded with her boss's neglect, pretended the whole damn thing hadn't happened? She was a junior officer; she was trained to do what her superiors told her to do. Why? Why?)

She scrambled around to the side of her island that faced into the bay where she'd come with the boat. It was in the shade. As soon as she wasn't feeling the sun on her skin she was assaulted by clutching, withering cold. She looked across the small expanse of calm water, wondering whether it was shallow and still enough that the suddenly glorious day had warmed it a degree or two. Maybe it wouldn't be too bad. Thirty seconds, max, then out again on the shingle where Jennifer had pulled up her kayak, and she could race around to the south-facing shore and get herself warmed up again. If only she wasn't so hungry. Her limbs felt like sticks.

Am I making a good decision? she thought, as she shuffled down to the edge of the tide. Mustn't make bad decisions. Hungry and panicky and tired. Think. But don't think too long, because the sun's going down.

She clenched her hands into fists and ran in. As soon as the ice of the water hit her she had her answer: *this is stupid. You can't get cold again.* Too late. She'd told herself not to stop so she didn't stop. She hopped from submerged rock to rock until she could plunge in. The cold hit her breasts and belly and crotch. She swore breathlessly and swam hard, keeping her head up because she couldn't bear the idea of submerging it. She swam badly, horribly, like a novice, like the kids she'd laughed at in school swim lessons. (They were all somewhere now with food in their stomachs and roofs over their heads, and she was going to be dead by the morning. Ha ha ha.) She staggered out on to the hard beach, still swearing. Her body temperature had plunged. She found she couldn't swear properly even through clenched teeth. Her jaw was shaking too violently. The sun, she thought, the sun. She turned left. This island was wooded closer to the shore but the tide was still low enough to leave eaves of rock above the water. She limped around until she was out of the shadow of the trees and spreadeagled herself over sun-warmed stone. She felt small breaths of air over her back, hints of the sea breeze: each one was like being doused with ice shavings. She remembered thinking, just an hour or two ago, that whatever she did she mustn't let herself get cold again. How had that just happened? How had she voluntarily immersed herself in North Pacific water, knowing she had nothing to dry herself on and no clothes at all beyond her soaked underwear, nothing to cover even a patch of her body? She huddled herself close, waiting for the sun to work its magic, imploring it.

A shiver attacked her. It wasn't like the shiver of fear or the tremble of a draught. It was a different beast entirely, a thing with an iron fist and a will of its own. It rattled through her as if it had determined to shake her loose from her. *That's enough of you.* It took over her muscles and turned them against herself. She whimpered in helpless pain until it let her go. Clothes, she thought. Blankets. Quick. But there were no clothes or blankets. She got to her hands and knees to crawl somewhere where the mild caress of wind couldn't touch her. It hit her again, dropped her and doubled her up. It was like retching, an irresistible exhausting grip. In the middle of it she thought, very clearly – perfectly clearly – *C'est ça.* This is it.

She struggled nevertheless, as living things will. When the shiver subsided she inched herself up towards the undergrowth, looking for some kind of shelter, but the forest was cool and soaked with fresh rain on top of its own permanent damp. Her truant muscles were barely capable of moving her at a crawl. Farther along the sunny slope of rock a long white log lay beached. She was halfway there when the breeze crawled over her naked flesh again and another spasm of shuddering took hold, curling her up but denying her rest, racking her from top to toe. She tried to tell herself to fight but she had no weapons. The shivers were an enemy within. It was all she could do to keep breathing, long shuddering gasps through rattling teeth.

The sun began to go down.

Within a few unspeakable hours the entire world had reduced itself to a square metre of rock. Her chin was tucked to her chest, her ankles locked over each other to squeeze in the last fraction of warmth, her arms bent foetal. She breathed in small soft huffs. She waited to fall asleep permanently. From time to time she caught herself sliding to the brink of it, dipping a toe in the dark, but it would only happen when she wasn't watching. There'd be no one to watch. Her body pushed in on itself, groping for a comfort which wasn't there.

She was too tired to be frightened now, and too cold. She'd given up. She'd stopped thinking about moving. If she admitted the slightest cranny of air into her cocoon the feverish shivering would follow it at once and savage her up and down.

Night fell patiently, as always, drawing the blinds gradually. The scoured stone under her eyes turned from yellow-gold to grey.

A few flutters of grief came with the thought: *I'll never see anything else again.* Some of the multitude included in that *anything* swam up before her mind's eye. There was less pain there than in the compressed misery of her flesh, though. The shivers squeezed like an old mangle, spread her flat and empty for the coming night to get to work on.

Not too much longer, she hoped.

Death came when it was fully dark. It arrived with a swish of surprised air, and then scraping footfalls, *tchok tchok tchok*. She stirred at the sound. Only the smallest tremors quivered through her now. She felt the dullness of relief. She must have dropped over the elusive edge at last, fallen accidentally into a final delirium. If her eyes were open they were looking through its veil. They saw a delicate glimmer over her tomb of rock, a mild failure of darkness, like the most tentative echo of moonlight.

Death moved to stand right over her. It was shapeless and fully black.

'Someone here,' it said.

Death bent. Its breath was a warm gust.

'Not her,' it said. 'Wrong girl.'

The brush of warmth passed. With a feeble ache of disappointment Goose saw Death retreat from her, returning some of the wispy starlight it had blotted out. Its outline wavered, making a stiff rustle.

'Too late,' Death said, in its skeletal voice. 'Missed her.' It withdrew farther. The unbearable cold came back and pressed in. She tried to move her lips to plead with Death not to go; impossible. Something else answered instead, another shape forming and approaching, not Death itself but Death's unknown and unexpected companion. The shape came close and bent over her with no sound at all, since Death's companion was a barefoot boy.

Part VI

Thirty

MARINA HAD BEEN told to stay right where she was, so that's what she did. She was careful not even to shuffle her feet. It wasn't helping. The telephone had been quiet for a long time now.

'Hello?'

Where the peculiar voice had been there was now no sound at all. She must have made a mistake. There'd been a thing she specifically wasn't supposed to do, something about hanging. Hanging upside down? Could she have done it accidentally? But how, without even moving? She hadn't even wiggled the telephone in her hand, until her elbow had started aching.

'Gwen? Gwenny?'

Horace had always told her she didn't know anything but she didn't see how this could be her fault. The voice had said it was coming right back. She'd waited, like it said. And waited. And waited. She'd waited so long her feet were hurting from standing still and the wet trickle dribbling from the plaster on her heel had made its own miniature swamp on the floor. Something had gone wrong. There must be something else she was supposed to do. Cautiously at first, then desperately, she shook the thing she was holding, pressed it, squeezed it against her mouth, her ear, her chest. Nothing she did made anything come out of it. It was just a thing among the houseful of weird things, as silent as the fat lucky god.

Where had the voice gone? She furrowed her brow and tried her hardest to remember what it had said (it was so difficult, though, with her painful confusion getting worse the longer the silence went on, and the tormenting feeling that some kind of chance was drifting away, some door closing). Horace was just up the road. Horace was in a hospital, which explained why no one had seen him. Gwen was . . . And the person who was talking about them was . . .

Marina was standing by the window overlooking the street in the upstairs room. The window was still open from when she'd fetched the saucepan of rainwater in from the sill. A rumble gathered outside and a few moments later a big car came up the lane from right to left, all dirty white walls rather than windows. It came slowly, crunching over the sticks and empty bottles and scraps of wet plastic in the road. Instinct made Marina shrink away from the window, though not before she read the word POLICE printed on the car in big black letters.

At once her memory was jogged. The voice had said something about the police. Was that it, then, going up the road, to where Horace was? She leaned out of the window, still holding the phone. The big white car had already passed the house: she couldn't see anyone inside. She put the telephone carefully down on the dresser and ran lightly downstairs. Iseult was still asleep and snoring on the floor. Marina didn't want to lose time waking her up; she slipped on her shoes and shift, stained and tattered but dry, and levered herself as swiftly and quietly as she could through the empty pane of the broken window. She could still hear the car grunting away down the road. Otherwise everything was very still. The morning was on the way to being foggy without having quite got there. She skipped around to the front of the house, thinking to wave at the car before it disappeared.

She stopped before reaching the road.

Someone else was there. A man was standing just outside the open door of the house opposite, examining her from among the brown wreck of its front garden. Taken aback, Marina dropped her eyes at once, remembering Iseult's face at its fiercest, telling her not to talk to anyone.

'Are you lost?'

The car noise was fading into the distance. Marina was about to retreat back out of sight behind the house when she remembered how careful Iseult had been about making sure no one saw them go in. She didn't know what to do.

'What is it?' another voice called from somewhere behind the first one, inside the house.

'Kid on her own. Looking for someone.'

Several different half-recollected instructions and

prohibitions jostled each other. Confused, she stayed rooted to the spot at the edge of the road.

'Is empty house.' The second voice said it like that, missing out some words and pronouncing the remaining ones oddly. 'All these houses empty now. Except this one. Are you looking for the professor?'

Marina looked up in surprise. Two men were studying her now. The house across the street on whose threshold they stood was the house she and Iseult had been going to, she remembered, and the woman they'd been going to see was called Professor. The man she'd seen first was the nearer of the two. He hid behind round-lensed spectacles like Owen's and a wildly unpruned beard. The other man stood on the doorstep behind him, leaning out of the house to look. He was shorter and sharper. His face was like a hunting bird's except pale instead of dark. His eyes were icy and he had straight hair that was almost white. They were almost as unlike each other as they were unlike anyone else she knew. Neither voice could possibly have been the one she'd heard on the phone.

'Professor left weeks ago,' the sharp-faced man who left out words said. 'Before new year. Others all gone too now. Are you left behind? Who are you looking for?'

Iseult had told her not to say anything to anyone, not to look at anyone, but she hadn't told her how to do it. Was she supposed to stand with her mouth shut until they went away? She didn't know. She did know that they'd knocked on the door of the house across the road just yesterday, though, and that the woman called the Professor was one of the people they wanted to find.

'Yes,' she said. 'Please. We wanted to see the woman who lives there. Do you know where she is? Or Horace, he lives here too, or Gawain, he—' The bearded man turned to his friend so sharply Marina was sure they'd recognised something she'd said. 'He came here. Didn't he? Do you know? Please. We've come such a long way.'

'Did you say—' began the bearded man, the nest-brown tangle around his mouth twitching, but the other man put a hand on his shoulder and stepped in front of him.

'You know Gawain.' His strange voice said it *Gah-van*, halfway between *Gawain* and *Gavin*, as if he wasn't sure which was right. 'Man with mask.'

A spark of hope kindled, lighting a sweet flame. 'Yes! Of course!'

The bearded man muttered something to his friend, who nodded. 'You should come,' he said.

'Where?'

'Inside.'

'He's there?'

'There is message from your friend.'

The bearded man beckoned, crouching slightly, the way she would have herself if she'd been trying to get Grey Mouser in through a door. 'It's OK,' he said, unnecessarily: of course it was! A message! They'd come to the right place after all.

'Where?'

'Come,' the blond man said, eyes narrowing keenly. 'I show you.' She crossed the road quickly. Up close the men were bigger than they'd seemed. Both smelled of unwashed clothes and coffee. The bearded one's hands twitched at his sides.

'Hi,' he said. 'Yeah.'

Marina stopped a pace or two away. The other man motioned towards the open door behind him with slender and dirty fingers. She looked inside over their shoulders but saw only dimness.

'Or maybe I bring outside?' he said, smiling as oddly as he spoke. 'Is better light. You know where he is now, this Gawain?'

She hesitated, momentarily confused again. Wasn't it the two men who were going to tell her where he was, not the other way around?

A muffled shout came from behind.

'Marina? Marina!'

Iseult must have woken up. 'Oh,' she began, half turning, 'that's my—' and got no farther. A hand closed over her mouth, another pulled her around the waist, and too quickly for her to register any of what was happening beyond the stink of man-flesh in her nose and the brute force propelling her, she was bundled into the waiting house. The door clicked shut.

The two simplest freedoms, to move and to speak, and she had lost both.

This had never happened before, in all the life she was willing to remember. It came as an existential shock.

Not that Marina didn't know about brutality. There was no sweetness about her innocence: on the contrary. She had grown up far more intimate with the raw harshness of things than most children. Until the beginning of that winter, when the world stirred from its centuries-long coma and began to remember that its nature was double like hers, she'd been completely untouched by all those discreet mechanisms which insulate us from the real. No out-of-the-way slaughterhouses and supermarket packaging hid the fact that someone killed the meat she ate. No underground pipes brought warmth generated hundreds of miles away when her house was cold. No phantasmagoria of imaginary lives was pixellated and projected on mesmerising screens to displace or blot out the slow immediacy of her own. The part of her that belonged to her mother couldn't tolerate such things. She hadn't been able to touch plastic or nylon or tarmac. She couldn't eat refined sugar or hydrogenated vegetable oil or sodium hexametaphosphate. Everything that was needed to keep her alive she saw with her own eyes. She watched it growing and dying. She knew how to twist the necks of birds and gut fish. She watched Gwen's cat toying with a field mouse and never thought of cruelty, any more than she'd have sentimentalised the aphids which ladybirds gobbled from their garden roses. It wouldn't have occurred to her that she was entitled to a life where violence only happened somewhere else.

But she'd never felt the fact of it, the actual weight of it on her own body. Neither her father nor Gwen nor Caleb had ever touched her in anger. (It could have been that as well as loving her too much they knew enough to fear her mother; but Marina didn't know about that, not yet.) She couldn't comprehend what was happening. She heard Iseult outside in the street, shouting her name louder and louder, a horrible edge of panic in the sound sharpening each time. So all she had to do was jump up and open the door and say *It's all right, here I am*, but instead of that a big hand was pushing all over her mouth like the opposite of a kiss, its fingers were clamping her jaw tight shut and there was a muscling heaviness wrapped all over her back.

Her eyes were wide open.

She was in a gloomy place of hard surfaces and scattered disordered things to do with eating. She saw plates and forks and bowls and packets illustrated with pictures of food, all of it in chaos. Everything screamed its wrongness but she couldn't even scream with it.

A hot mouth breathed right by her ear as though trying to worm inside. More than anything she wanted to twist away from it, but the hand stopped her even turning her neck. The meaning of being weak and small became starkly clear, a totally new kind of knowledge, worse than the worst surprise. She couldn't do anything. She might as well not exist at all.

The bearded man crept in and out of the room. He and the one who was holding her kept whispering things to each other, as if she wasn't there, as if they hadn't noticed that she was trapped and half suffocated.

'OK, she's gone. Out the village. South.'

'What about the police?'

'No sign.'

'Is woman coming back?'

'I'll look outside.'

'No! Not yet.'

'I reckon she's gone.'

'Wait longer.'

'Can she breathe like that?'

'You think I kill her? Go watch next door.'

'Can't hear anything any more.'

'One minute. Then open door.'

Things like that. The heat of the body behind her was making her hot too. She couldn't help breathing in the stench of the hand. She gagged and tried to cough but the hand shoved the cough back inside her.

'Shit, Pav, careful. That's her neck.'

'You want she scream? You want police come?'

'They're long gone. No one's about.'

'How do you know? Who's watching?'

'Can't we just tie something round her mouth? Shit. Hey. You won't scream, will you? Understand?'

'What are you, moron?'

'I'll check the street now, OK? It's totally quiet.'

'Window first.'

Things like that.

It wouldn't have occurred to her to scream. In her world there had never been any strangers to come when they were called. When the hand finally freed her mouth and the contagious weight behind her loosened, she just stood, gasping.

'Good, good! Sensible girl. Nice and quiet.'

The room had a stale metallic reek. Though the brutality had withdrawn she could feel it thick in the air, waiting.

She held very still, as if any movement might bring it toppling on her.

'How about sitting down?' The bearded man stood in the doorway to the other room, the one they'd pushed her in through. He gestured nervously towards a stool.

'OK,' the other man said. 'We go outside very soon. We go find mummy. Yes? My friend went to tell her you come soon.'

'Yeah. That's right.' When the bearded man pushed his lips closed his mouth vanished altogether. His eyes had already gone. The window was shaded by a roller blind and his spectacles reflected its rectangle of grubby light back at her.

'I like kids like this. Not noisy all the time.' The blond man patted her on the shoulder. She flinched. 'Hey. It's OK. Nothing to worry about. Good girl.' His hand tried to rest on her arm. She whimpered as she twisted away and screwed her eyes shut.

'Shit. You freaked her out.'

'What?' The blond man started talking far too loudly for a small room. 'No, no. Girl knows we don't hurt her. Yes? Maybe frightened a little bit, OK. Sorry. I worry mummy doesn't let us talk to her even though we have message from her friend. Hmm? But is OK now.'

'Yeah. Just want to talk, that's it. Hey, what's your name?'

As well as the men's there were three other faces in the room, Marina saw, when her eyes opened again. The two gentle ones were in a picture on the wall, one caught in the act of whispering to the other. The third was flat, almost featureless, and looked like it was made out of black stone. It lay on a table and stared vacantly at the ceiling.

'Go on. You can tell me. I'm Jon. What are you called?'

She realised she was free to move now but when she glanced around she could see nowhere to go. The man called Jon blocked the whole of the doorway where he stood. There was another exit on the far side of the table, leading to a narrow curving staircase, but the smaller man was between her and it.

'Look what you've done. You scared the shit out of her.'

The sharp face pinched with momentary anger. 'Shut up.'

'Ah, fuck. Look. She's fucking pissed herself.'

The blond man looked at her feet, spat a word she didn't understand and crouched by her shoes. He poked at her ankle with a finger. She jumped away from the touch and bumped into the bearded man, who grabbed her shoulders. 'Stand still, will you?' The weight of his grip shrank her. 'Disgusting.'

The other one sniffed his finger.

'Not piss,' he said. 'Blood.'

Her shoe was soggy inside. A dribble of liquid oozed over the back. The man was feeling her leg now, up inside her shift.

'Not woman time,' he said.

'Great. You hurt her.'

'Sit down.' After a moment he dragged a stool across the floor and pushed her into it. Her body had turned into a kind of toy, like one of the dolls Gwen used to make for her with their sad floppy heads. She couldn't do anything with it. The blond man pulled her shoe off. A dark spill gobbed out of it. He jerked his hands away in revulsion and made a snorting noise. 'Get a bowl,' he said. He pulled a handful of tissues from inside his jacket and wiped her ankle.

'What'd she do to herself?'

'Bowl,' the man by her feet repeated, still mopping away blood. In the dull light she saw her own skin pale for a moment. A tiny dark bulb appeared there a second later and began to grow.

It did something to her memory. It brought things back into order, things that had happened to her.

'I have to go now,' she said, and stood up.

The blond man looked up, surprised, and then grinned. 'See? I told you she is OK.'

The bearded one had opened a cupboard and was pushing things around in it. 'What's wrong with her foot? Looks like she lost a fucking toe.'

'I can't see. Small cut maybe.'

'So. Goodbye, then.'

'No no no. Sit down.'

She turned to the doorway. The bearded man dropped something in the cupboard and hurried to block it again. She walked up to him.

'Excuse me,' she said, remembering her manners. 'Please.'

He just looked at her. The tip of his tongue fidgeted around his lips.

'You forgot message,' said the other one.

She could tell, somehow, that the one called Jon wasn't going to move out of the way even if she asked him again, politely. No one had taught her what happened in that situation.

(Not yet.)

'It's important,' the other added. 'You help us understand it. Then you go. We take you to mummy.'

There was a sort of thinness about everything they said to her, as if the words were stitched together in their mouths and sent out like sails in her direction, rather than coming from the bit where she always imagined her own speech being created, down in her chest somewhere. She realised now what this strange quality was: lying.

'All right? You are sensible girl. You do as I ask, everything is OK. Nice and quiet and easy. No more like this, hmm?' He put his hand over his own mouth and mimed a brief struggle. 'Not necessary. Understand?' He waited and then went on as if she'd answered yes. 'Good girl. Not difficult like kids these days. And so pretty! OK? Now we're all friends. I am,' and he said something which sounded like Paul but with a slur in the middle. 'You?'

His smile had exactly the same thinness, the same hollowness, as his words.

'You miss mummy, yes? A little bit worried maybe?'

'How about a drink?' Jon said. 'Nice glass of water?'

'You have nasty cut. How you get cut like that? We look after you, OK? Mummy not have a bandage for you? We have upstairs. Jon? Up in bathroom. Go look.'

'You go look.'

The blond man shot a suddenly fierce glare back. 'Go upstairs. Please.'

The moment Jon had disappeared around the twist in the staircase the other man came close, too close, propping his arms on the sides of her stool. 'He's OK guy,' he said quietly and quickly, as though confiding a secret. 'But stupid. Says stupid things. Bad language. I don't like this. Don't worry, OK? I look after you, make sure you go home to mummy soon. You have little smile for me maybe?' One of his fingers touched her cheek, small and cold like the point of a nail: she could feel the hammer's weight and the bent arm poised behind it. From upstairs came clattering noises, things being tossed around. 'Smile hiding in there? Sorry I frighten you before. It's Jon, he makes me do these things. Always so stupid. It makes me crazy.' He swung around and shouted angrily up the stairs. 'What are you doing? Is one of boxes in the bathroom.'

'Fucking tip up here.' More banging. 'Why'd you pile all her shit in the bathroom?'

'This isn't your house,' Marina said. 'You don't live here.'

Surprised again, the man paused before arcing his thin eyebrows ruefully. 'You know Professor Lightfoot?' He said the name to rhyme with *hoot*. 'I come to help her. Months ago. When she first comes home. I try, but is impossible. Her legs, too badly hurt. And with snow, day after day . . .' He shook his head. 'Too difficult. Agency stops paying, you know? Before Christmas. Ever since then, no money. Hmm? But I come anyway. Even though they don't pay me I try. Professor is my friend now, I want to help. She's nice lady, I don't want her to be by herself with no one else. But you know, I come only from Truro but some days is impossible,

I don't get here till evening, Professor has nothing to eat all day, then I have to stay at night and try to get home next day but no bus, no train. Impossible.'

'Got them.'

He ignored Jon's shout. He leaned even closer, speaking rapidly. 'So Professor says to me one day, Pawel, this is crazy, I can't live here, I go to Falmouth with other old people, maybe go to friends in London. She tells me,' he tapped his own chest, 'to look after house. I trust you, she says. Many crazy people coming to village, someone has to look after house. All these beautiful things.' He waved at the shambles of dirty glasses and empty tins. 'Precious.' His eyes gleamed with sudden intensity, so close in front of hers she couldn't see anything else. As the bearded man came clumping back down the stairs he dropped his voice to a hungry whisper. 'Powerful things.'

'What the fuck are you doing?'

He leaned back and turned around, slowly. Marina realised she'd been holding her breath.

'Get out of her face, all right?'

'You stop swearing all the time in front of girl. Not surprise she won't talk to you. Give me that.'

'Nah.' Jon unrolled a length of white fabric from the reel he was holding. 'I'll do it.' Pawel made a brief grab at the bandage but Jon pushed his hand away. For a few moments they stared at each other; then the bearded man knelt by Marina's dangling feet. She saw Pawel shrug.

'Can't even see a cut.' His beard scratched her ankle. It felt like a horsehair brush. He fingered her foot all over.

'Shit. How can this be bleeding so much? Where's the . . .' He found the spot where the tiny man had stabbed her and began wrapping the bandage. 'There you go. Yeah? All better now.'

'Is enough.'

'Couple more turns. Nice and tight.' His fingers felt like fat cold caterpillars. He finished by making a loop and tying the torn end in a clumsy knot.

They were both looking at her, so she said, 'Can I go now?'

The silence went on too long before Pawel answered.

'In a little bit.'

The grimy roundels of Jon's spectacles no longer reflected the window, so Marina saw the way he looked. His eyes were as blank as Corbo's, as blank as the shallow eyes of the mask on the table.

'It's been ages,' he said, not to her, though his eyes didn't waver. 'Fucking months.'

'Shut up.'

'She's not all there anyway. Look at her. She won't even notice.'

Pawel kicked him, hard enough to tip him over and make him grunt in pain.

'Tell me,' he said, 'who is this man *Gah-van*?'

'Fuck that,' Jon muttered, rubbing his elbow and getting to his feet.

'You explain,' Pawel went on, ignoring the other man, 'then you go. Not before.'

'You mean Gawain,' Marina said, fixing on the idea of

leaving this heavy angry room. 'He's not a man, really. He's only a bit older than me.'

'Pav.'

'Shut up. Let her talk.'

Jon was breathing thickly. 'You can have your fucking chat after.'

Pawel leaned over the stool again and lowered his voice, talking as if the other man had left the room again. 'I want to know about Gawain who brought mask. He left it here, with message.' His eyes tracked intently over her face. 'Is that your friend? Who knows secret of these things? How to make them speak?'

'She doesn't know—' Pawel raised a hand sharply to silence the other man.

'You sit here until you tell me the truth,' he said.

I don't know, she'd been about to say, but the idea of echoing the bearded man's words disgusted her. She clenched her eyes shut, trying to remember. 'He said he was going to bring it back to her.' That miserable farewell. 'He said it belonged to her. He did know about it but he didn't tell me, just that the spirit isn't bad, it was the thing that was using it. He told me once about how it had come alive but I can't remember, I didn't understand.'

When Marina opened her eyes in the ensuing silence, everything seemed to be happening at half-speed, as though the threatening air had turned viscous. Pawel was turning to look at Jon, who lifted his hands to the top of his head, sweeping back his straggling fringe; his mouth had fallen open. The sound of a helicopter thudded in a distant crescendo, then faded. Some message passed between the two men without words; she could tell by the change in the way they looked at each other, then at her.

'So I can go now,' she said, and shuffled forward to hop off the stool.

Pawel stopped her. 'You say, "come alive"?' He sounded hoarse.

'Let's show it to her.'

Pawel ignored Jon. 'What did he say about this?'

'Just fucking show her. Hey. You. Come and see something.' He grabbed her arm and hurried her through into the other room. It was messier and even dimmer than the first one, so dim she couldn't distinguish most of the mess from mere shadow, but what she could see she liked better because it was things she recognised, books and coats and furniture. There were strange faces all around the walls, stranger even than the two men's, most of them hardly like people at all, but at least they were quiet and kept their distance. Most of the stuff in the room had been pushed to the edges, leaving a bit of clear space around a broad shin-high table. On the table was a circle of unlit candles arranged around something hidden under a cloth.

'Wait,' Pawel said, but the other man was already leaning over the table, still gripping Marina's arm with one hand while he reached for the cloth with the other.

'Here,' Jon said. 'Look.'

'Wait.'

He didn't wait. He whisked the cloth away. Underneath it was a thing she recognised completely even in the murk. She couldn't stop herself gasping in a little spasm of horror and hope.

'Idiot,' Pawel said.

'What?' Jon leered at her. 'Are you scared?' He sounded as if the idea of her fear excited him. 'Why?' He looked around impatiently. 'Where's that note? Where'd I put it?'

Marina's heart was alternating thrill and dread. It told her Gawain had come here, as they'd thought; they'd found his trail. The last time she'd seen the mask which was lying on the table, it had been in his hands. But then her heart contracted again with memories of a day she couldn't bear to think about at all, wrapped up in the blunt-muzzled face on the table, its pitilessly empty eyes staring up at her. She clutched at her chest.

'You know this?' Pawel's voice was at her ear, rapid and urgent. 'You see before? Come alive?'

Jon had let her go to rummage among a stack of books. He straightened with a sheet of paper in his hand. 'Here. This.' He held it out to her as if she'd asked for it.

'Girl already knows,' Pawel said, but the other man waved it at her face and then shoved it in her hands. 'What are you doing? Don't frighten her.'

'Can't see, can you?' Jon muttered, and began patting his pockets.

'It's the message,' Pawel said. 'From friend.'

Jon took out a box of matches. The first two he struck snapped in his hands.

'Careful!' But the third flamed and settled. He held it to the candles. They were anchored in congealed buttresses of their own wax. Yellow crescents danced around his glasses and in the sockets of the black dog's missing eyes. She looked away from them, and read handwriting.

Hester

Sorry I missed you. Owen Jeffrey said you've been in hospital but you've got someone helping you at home now. Hope you're OK. I don't know where to find you and I've got a long way to go so going to leave this for you.

I don't know what to say except thanks for looking after me when you did. You can probably guess now why I left while you were out. If you're here whenever I get back we can talk about it. Our friend won't come back, she's gone for good, but a lot of other things aren't gone any more.

I brought this. It's yours and I know you wanted it back. Remember you told me it was like a mouth? You were totally right, it opened and spoke. I see you're missing another one too, that was the same (had a voice in it). [In the margin here it said, *I don't know where it is by the way.*] *Three of the others do too, I won't say which ones, they're fine if you leave them alone. You've probably had enough voices.*

I wish there was something I could tell you about what's happening. Maybe when I get back. Though you probably won't be here. I hope you read this anyway and you're somewhere safe. Leaving a note doesn't feel right. I wish I'd seen you. Later on, I hope (but much later, I have a long way to go, the other side of the world

The paper fell from Marina's hands. Her heart beat in, in, in, contracting, sucking blood. Jon lunged before the note fell into the candles and batted it to the floor. He knelt to scrabble in the shadows by her feet.

'Is from your friend?' Pawel said, over her shoulder, his mouth almost on her ear.

The other side of the world. In her mind's eye Marina saw the tea-brown globe in her father's study, every line of which she'd memorised when she was small, from the little picture of *Timbouctoo* with its piled-up flat roofs to the puffy sea-monster that coiled in the ocean next to *Van Diemen's Land.* She felt as if she'd walked for ever since leaving Pendurra but she hadn't moved even the thickness of a dot on the globe, not even the width of one of her own hairs, and yet Gawain had gone . . .

She swayed, faint. The man at her back caught her. 'Is it him?' he hissed. 'What did he tell you? Tell me what he said.'

'She's still bleeding.' Jon knelt up, holding his hand out to the candlelight. It was smeared dark. 'Shit. Must be about to pass out.'

Pawel shook her. 'Open your mouth.' He was whispering but the whisper stung like a shout. 'I said open your mouth.'

'Fuck. She bled all over the floor. Through the fucking bandage.'

'I have enough of trying to be nice. Girl knows how to make this speak to us, hmm?' Another shake. Her neck was limp and the rattling hurt her. 'You go nowhere until I hear everything.'

'Yeah.' The other man pulled himself up in front of her until she was almost sandwiched between them. 'No mummy. You listening? No more mummy.'

'Hold it close. Show it to her face.'

'Oh yeah. Don't like it much, do you?' He made his grimace, exposing teeth stained as black as the mask. The grip on her arms tightened impossibly hard. She wriggled in hopeless resistance. The man behind her pulled her against his chest with a strange gasp. Jon reached to pick up the mask, his hands still streaked with her blood. She tried to push herself free but she was pinned completely, the mouse under the cat's paw, the minnow on the hook. She opened her mouth to scream.

A subterranean groan filled the room instead.

Jon yelped and stumbled away from the table. 'Fuck.' His voice was a squeak. 'It fucking moved.'

The candles wavered. Jagged shadows leaped from every corner. The blunt upthrusting jaws in the middle of the table appeared to twitch. There was an even darker blot at the muzzle's tip. The deep groan sounded again, undermining every other noise, the whole room vibrating as if the ground beneath it had stirred.

'What the fuck?' The little of Jon's face that showed had turned white. 'What's that?'

The candle flames suddenly stretched thin and tall, all together. Their glow began to redden. Jon dropped to his knees.

'Master,' he said, a cringing whine. 'I'm here.' As if answering, the sound came again, a straining towards speech, like a huge maw trying to open. The ringed flames went from russet to deep crimson, the whole room seen as if through a curtain of—

'Blood.'

Pawel's grip loosened as he said the word. She slumped. She remembered very little of the appalling day when Gwen had stopped being herself and her sheltered sanctuary had turned into a prison of horror, and the few fragments that refused to be forgotten hung separate from each other like stills from a nightmare, but the red light plunged her back among them. She would have fallen to the floor if the man hadn't hooked her waist to catch her again.

'Blood,' he said again. 'Is her blood.'

Jon stared until he understood, then knelt and pulled the bandage from her foot. When his fingers were dripping he turned to the mask again.

'Quick,' Pawel said.

'Master. Speak to us.'

'Do it! On the mouth.'

He wiped his shaking hands on the black snout. The flames roared up, blinding, and then vanished. All three people in the room cried out, but their cries were swallowed by a visceral rumble vibrating in the sudden darkness. It rose and rolled, taking on the shape of language, the silhouette of speech projected by an unseen fire. Pawel was shouting. Jon fumbled at Marina's feet. 'Pick her up!' he yelled. 'I can't see!' But none of them could hear the others. Marina felt hands clawing around her calves and kicked wildly. Her bloodied foot caught Jon in the face, sending his glasses flying. Pawel lost his grip and dropped her on top of him. Both men were swearing, as full of fury and empty of sense as the other language drowning them out. Its guttural cadence began to subside.

'Fuck. Master! Hold still, you little . . .'

'Cut her,' Pawel yelled.

'Where's your fucking . . . Ow!'

'Get knife. Hurry.' Pawel leaned down and pummelled the darkness until he got an arm across Marina's neck. She bucked and flailed her legs, connecting with the other man's face, the table, anything in reach. Her shift rolled up to her hips. Pawel slapped blindly at her. 'Hurry, idiot!' he shouted. 'I hold her!'

'Fuck you!'

'More blood. Knife, bowl, I cut her. Ah!' He'd left his hand too near Marina's face; she'd twisted her head up and bitten it. He shoved down on her neck again. His breath was a steaming roar in her face. 'For that I cut you deep.'

'Hold her arms,' growled the other voice. Marina could only tug at the weight on her windpipe. Other hands closed on her, down by her thighs. 'I'll make you fucking bleed.' The full brute darkness turned solid and crushed down on her. Its greasy hair and sour breath soiled her face. Her eyes opened wide, horribly wide, and saw the features of a man, and in the instant before it started she discovered something she hadn't known until then, which was that the human body far too close to her own was an alien species, no more akin to her than the hook to the fish.

There was a great deal of blood.

Thirty-One

T HE DOOR WAS open.

A wide crack, an arm's width. A little light came into
the room sidelong, as if it didn't want to look.

She was curled up on the low table. Her knees were tight
to her chest. An ugly lump of cold wax pushed against her
cheek.

One finger and thumb plucked at the skin of her calf,
pinching and twisting. From time to time a helicopter droned
somewhere beyond the roof.

'Ahem,' a small voice coughed, eventually.

Marina flinched and pushed her head away from the light.

'Ahem,' it said again. There was a momentary scrape and
jingle near her head. 'Ah. A somewhat awkward moment.'

She kept her eyes tight, tight shut.

'Though whether a more opportune occasion awaits at
any proximate hour is at the very best conjectural. Not to say
optimistic. Fantastical, even.'

With one hand she covered her ear. Her fingertips curled to scratch her skull.

'Summ mmghht rrggnn . . . Can yhrrmm?' The muffled voice strained squeakily to raise itself. 'Can you hear me?' More scraping and tinkling, and then it sounded closer. 'I said, can you hear me?' She pushed her hand down harder until her ear sang with hollow echoes. The little voice came floating in. 'You show little of your former courtesy.' It separated the words out one by one to make them heard. 'To be expected. Your state is grievously reduced.'

The scraping might have been small feet on the surface of the table next to her head.

'A common slattern, I fear. A soiled thing.'

Something touched her. It was as faint as the tickle of a blade of grass on the back of her hand, but she twitched away from it convulsively, a peep of fear escaping her tight-pressed mouth.

'Now now now. Mind your manners, saucebox. It's hard enough having to shout for a hearing. I'll be hoarse tomorrow, and lucky to say thirty words by the end of the week.'

Her hand tightened into a fist and kneaded her skull.

'Ah. There. Well, beggars can't be choosers. Which is to say, those sunk as low as you set no conditions, and would do better to listen when spoken to.'

She heard a minuscule sigh.

'That said . . . I confess an inability to shrug away the impression, however implausible, of bearing some share of responsibility.'

An expectant silence followed. She felt her fist trembling, close to the corner of her mouth.

'All right,' the voice continued. 'So be it. You choose not to notice my condescension. Granted, your former honour is dead and buried, but one might still have anticipated the very minimum of graciousness. The soles of its boots, you might say. The skin of its teeth. Still, if that little is too much to ask, I forgive the offence. I am, you see, magnanimous. The substance may be small but the soul is great.'

Thumb and forefinger plucked, twisted, released, plucked, twisted, released. There was a pinprick of pain each time.

'Mind you. Ahem. Whatever share of responsibility for your unhappy fall belongs to my part, the weightier balance lies with you. You had only to answer a simple question. Candour demands that we not forget the fact.'

Her eyes opened a little. Her hair was all over her face, smelling of man. She thought of water, to wash it out.

'The question in question – ha!' It interrupted itself with a satisfied chuckle, the shake of wooden dice in a closed hand. 'Excellent. As I was saying. The question in question being now moot. Mooter than moot. Never was enquiry so thoroughly redundant.'

Tap, tap, tap on the table near her head. She looked through the clotted screen of her hair. She had the impression of a small odd head with too much chin and nose, under a wide-brimmed hat.

'Let us be clear, from the start, that I owe you nothing at all. I am a free creature, and you a miserable wretch. Let that not be disputed. However. Your virgin blood made a fine draught.' A touch of faraway sweetness came into the voice. 'Exquisite. Matchless. And to think the vintage is forever spoiled. None but I will ever be qualified to sing songs in praise of that nectar. Glorious! Think of that.'

She thought of nothing.

'Can you really be ignorant of the virtue of your blood?'

The figure standing by her head appeared to shuffle from side to side, looking for a better view through her hair. 'Misery is the lot of your father's kind. A lesson this past hour has surely taught you more thoroughly than any disquisition of mine, I dare guess. But you're your mother's daughter also.'

No mummy. She quivered and mewled from the back of her throat. *No. No.*

'I see I'm wasting my breath. Very well. Cower and grovel and slink on all fours. Perhaps those undiscriminating vaga- bonds the weasels will applaud the performance and take you in. I might as well have showered my chivalry in their direction. Here, then, is the first and last and in between of what I came to tell you, rudely truncated, and delivered on this ensanguined platform in its raw state. Men could not but do to you, and now they cannot but be done to. And if the coarseness of my terms offends, your silence has earned it. Upbraid me if you dare. Trollop!'

She flinched weakly. The small person next to her head composed himself. He edged closer still, almost putting his nose in her hair.

'I'd trip those fools on a bramble and stab their eyes out myself, if I could,' he said, conspiratorially. 'Alas, I lack the puissance. We folk to our domain and they to theirs, is the way of it. But you, madam, were born to both. Your father went to his drowning like a sheep to slaughter. Your mother wielded the knife. Take a peck of counsel in return for that drop of your blood, and remember the one as well as the other. Now, good day to you. And should you see her again, don't neglect to tell her it wasn't my fault. Do you hear? Not. My. Fault.'

She thought she saw a tiny glittering eye, a snake's eye. Then with a tap and a skitter it was gone.

A little later she heard it start to rain.

Her shoes were stiff with dried blood. Bending over to clean them off hurt too much in the middle, and anyway her fingers wouldn't go straight. She prodded her toes into them. All down her legs were streaks like spilled brown paint.

On the floor near her shoes was a handwritten piece of paper with a name written at the bottom: *Gawain*. She sat on the edge of the table looking at it, while the array of masks looked at her.

Eventually she poked the paper with the toe of one shoe, pushing it around the right way so she could read. Every movement hurt. There was a big hard lump of pain in the middle of her. All of her was connected to it.

She couldn't read the whole paper. Some parts were obscure in the apologetic light. Others were defaced with dried bloody spots. She mouthed the words she could make out. It seemed like there ought to be some comfort in them, but she couldn't find it. She got to the point where she'd dropped the note. There was a bit more.

Later on, I hope (but much later, I have a long way to go, the other side of the world) I'll be back for sure. I promised someone important I would.

Gawain

Her eyes skimmed back and forth over the words a few times, barely touching them, like insects on water. After that she carefully manoeuvred her shoes to each side of the sheet of paper. Wiggling them towards each other, painstakingly, she crumpled up the note.

Water.

Nothing came between it and her. It fell pure, indifferent, unrestrained. Once it reached the ground it was fouled, picking up the world's wreckage, mixing with mud and rubbish. Where it touched her it rinsed off red.

She looked up the street and saw closed door after closed door. She turned the other way. She hadn't managed to get her shoes on properly so she walked in a stuttering limp, taking small steps. The pain wouldn't allow anything faster.

The rain had the most wonderful smell. It was coming down quite hard from a sky done in long brushstrokes of stone-grey and dove-grey. Very soon, before she'd passed the last house in the village, it had flushed the stench out of her hair and her tattered cotton shift.

There was a lot of debris around her feet. Old newspapers, so wet they'd printed themselves illegibly on the
tarmac. Cigarette butts, foil wrappers, plastic forks, crushed
cans, things, things, things, intended for vast oubliettes in the
ground but lying in plain sight instead, wind-blown and rain-
washed testimony to a catastrophic failure of the whole
science of forgetting.

Farther along the road she encountered a knot of people
carrying shopping bags and sticks, hurrying. More debris.
She aimed herself to the side of them but they stopped when
they saw her.

'God in heaven.'

'Are you all right?'

'Hello? Are you hurt?'

'What happened to you?' The wind blew them towards
her. 'She looks hurt.'

'Did they do this?'

'Where's your family?'

'Don't go crawling all over the poor thing. Give her some
room. All right, you? Who's with you?'

'That's blood. On her dress.'

'You must be half dead with cold. Are you all right, dear?
Do you have somewhere to go?'

'Jill?'

'You can tell us. It's all right. We won't hurt you.'

'Jill!'

'What?'

'Are you sure that's really a girl?'

Another invisible gust made some of the debris swirl away.

'They're coming!' someone shouted.

A car appeared down the road. The glare of its bright white eyes picked out cones of slashing raindrops. 'Here,' someone said, and tried to put arms around her shoulders. The arms sprang back at once.

'God! She's like ice!'

The car blared its horn. It was a big white car, with black letters written on it. The wreckage in the road was sucked under its black wheels, squashed and spat out to the side.

'They'll take you away,' a person near her said. 'This way, quick!'

'Leave it be, Jill.'

The person tried to touch her again. Marina raised her head and looked at her.

'Oh my . . .' The person's hand went to her mouth. She backed away and then began to run.

'What is it?'

'Let's go! Go!'

The car growled louder, closer, and then came to a sudden stop. Doors banged open on either side of it. Marina was going to walk past, but two people in lumpy black clothes got out, blocking the gaps. She came slowly towards them, stepping very carefully, putting her feet down softly each time.

'Hello,' said one of the people next to the car. 'Who's this, then?'

An angry shout came from behind. 'You leave her alone! Can't you see she's hurt?'

'Where's your mum?'

'Filth!' A stone came flying over her shoulder and banged

against the front of the car. The person unstrapped something from his bulky black clothes. The rain made it glisten darkly.

'Everyone calm down,' he said.

The writing on the car said POLICE, and the word was stitched on to the black clothes as well. Marina looked at the glistening thing.

'That's a gun,' she said, 'isn't it?' It was much shorter than the one Caleb used.

The person's eyes widened. He gave a short and uncomfortable laugh.

'Well, aren't we the clever one,' he said.

She looked over her shoulder at the people with the sticks and bags. Some of them had stopped hurrying and were watching from a distance, including the one who'd touched her. Marina turned back to the person with the gun.

'Can you shoot it at them?' she said, pointing.

It was much louder than Caleb's, too. It split the air like an axe. The people started screaming and running. The second of the two police people said something like *what the fucking*, though the screaming and the echoes of the shot obscured it. The one with the gun frowned mildly, looking sad, a little lost.

'Keep shooting,' she told him. He held his arm out and pulled the trigger repeatedly, his hand jerking each time. Five more deafening cracks cut through the screaming and swearing. Two of the running people stopped running and fell over. After that the gun only made a soft clicking sound. The person kept squeezing the trigger anyway, until finally he dropped the gun in the road. The other policeman was leaning against the car. His face had gone completely white and his mouth was opening and closing with a little noise like half a word. With trembling hands he undid a strap at his belt and took out another gun. The first man dropped to his knees in the road in front of Marina.

'What did you . . .' he began, but didn't finish the sentence because he put the back of his hand in his mouth and bit the skin. He and Marina both looked at the other one, the one unsteadily holding his weapon.

'Kill it,' the kneeling man said. 'Fucking shoot her.' The white-faced one grasped his gun in two hands and lifted it to point at Marina. His eyes were milky with shock.

'No,' she said. 'Him.'

He blinked. The gun wavered and fired again. The kneeling man stopped kneeling and became a limp flat thing, lying under the wheels of the car, waiting to be rolled over and crushed.

'No,' the policeman said, as if echoing her. For a moment he seemed puzzled. He stared at his own hands, then back at Marina.

'Does it work on yourself?' she said.

He frowned a little, then put the barrel in his mouth, pointing upwards and in.

'Oh,' she said. 'Of course.' She nodded at him.

Another vicious crack. More debris. Running water quickly nudged the scraps into the red pools guttering at the edge of the road. No one was in her way now, so she stepped past the car. The rain fell against it with a sound almost like the clatter of a storm on her bedroom windows.

She wasn't thinking about where she was going so she carried on downhill, like water. The tower of the church whose bells she used to hear ringing across the river overlooked her from a distance, through the upturned brooms of late-budding trees. She passed a field churned into mud and littered with abandoned tents like the coloured scraps of burst balloons. Turning a long corner in the lane, she gained a view out to part of the coast. To the north the greyscale sky was palled by a low drift of smoke. Eastwards was a slice of the sea. She stopped walking.

She put her hands over her ears and doubled up.

The pain in her middle was the centre of everything. It was a slashing tearing ache at the point where everything met, between front and back, top and bottom, inside and out, flesh and thought. Everything that had happened before was concentrated in it. It was like all the abandonment and loneliness and misery and not understanding rolled up into a tight wad and shoved inside her so she couldn't take a step without carrying them along.

She sat down on the tarmac.

After a while she heard someone half running, half stumbling along the lane ahead of her. The steps skidded to an abrupt stop.

'Marina?'

They started again, slipping and kicking through the rubbish. 'Marina? Marina?'

Someone was in front of her, kneeling down. For an instant her inside fluttered with a feeling other than pain as she recognised a face older than unhappiness, someone from the time before. Then she remembered it wasn't Gwen.

'What have they done to you? Marina? I heard shots, are you hurt? Marina, look at me.' It looked as if the woman was going to try and embrace her, but something must have held her back. 'Did someone hurt you?'

Marina didn't look at her. 'Yes,' she said.

The woman's face was running with rainwater. 'I told you not to go out of my sight. What happened? Can you stand up?'

'Yes,' she said, and stood up, ignoring the hands offered to help her.

'Oh God,' the woman said. 'You're bleeding. Marina? Were you shot? Oh God, oh God. She's only a girl!'

Marina raised her head to look at the woman.

'I'm not only a girl,' she said.

As well as the dribble of rain off her long wet hair, the woman's face was dripping tears. She was a picture of bedraggled misery.

'And you're not Gwen,' Marina continued. 'And you're not Gawain's mother, or my mother.'

The woman's arms opened again, tentatively. She might have been about to try hugging Marina again, but instead she hugged herself. Her shoulders shivered and rose and fell raggedly. She was out of breath.

'No more,' she said at last. 'That's it. I'm taking you home.' She reached out an arm. 'They can drown me or eat me, I don't care. I've had enough.' She took hold of Marina's hand, gasping slightly as their palms touched. 'Down to the river,' she said. 'Let's go.'

'Yes,' Marina said, looking across to the east, where the rain didn't blow in her face. 'Home.'

As they passed in front of the church the weather turned violent. The wind backed northwards and gathered strength as if to herd them into the valley. Remnants of the pilgrims' tent village blew past them and were impaled in the grave-yard hedge. Some were lifted higher and got caught in the Monterey pines beyond, flapping there like huge wounded birds. Marina's shift was soaked right through. It stuck to her skin, chafing. The hem flapped in the wind too. She stopped to take it off.

'What are you doing?'

It was too wet for the wind to play with. It sloughed on to the ground with all the other inert things.

'Marina, don't . . . Oh my God.' Iseult's hands went to her mouth in horror. 'Oh no. Oh no.'

Marina's shoes weren't interfering, so she left them on, the last two things from Pendurra to survive the journey. Rain scoured and bathed the rest of her.

'I'm so sorry.' Iseult shuffled close. Her voice had turned into a feeble croak. Marina could see she wanted to touch her but didn't quite dare. 'Oh, Marina. I . . . If I'd . . .' Iseult's fingers knotted helplessly through each other. 'I wouldn't have let it happen if I'd been there. Never, ever. I'm sorry. It's my fault.'

Marina looked at herself. The skin around where the pain was jammed was swollen and bruised black. Not all the blood had washed away there, either. But it would, she knew.

'Will you let me hold you for a bit? Please?'

'Don't.'

'Please, Marina.'

'No.'

The woman's eyes were very red. 'OK. I understand.'

The road ended at the church. A steep path descended through the pines to the river below, eroded by rain and the long thaw into little more than a scree of mud. Marina held on to branches to steady herself and went very slowly. When she looked down through the evergreen copse she saw white-caps dancing below, where the river met the sea.

Iseult, as thin and straggly as the branches, went slowly too, a little ahead, stopping often to look back.

'I wish you'd blame me,' she said. 'You should scream at me. At everyone. Just as long as you know that it's not your fault. Promise me you'll never think that?'

'I don't want you to say that word.'

'Which one?'

'*Promise.*'

The woman stayed quiet for a long time after that. They inched along and down, the last steps of two long journeys, one measured in miles, the other in years. The slope steadied at last and met the top of low cliffs above the river. Another choked and defaced track followed the line of the coast there. Upriver, to the west, it led out of the pines and down to the shore, dropping into a cove at the mouth of a brief tributary valley. The wind roared in the trees above, flexing the pines into a frenzy. Marina stopped again when she got to the overgrown clifftop and looked seaward. Everywhere water met land there was a turbulent fringe of spray. The noise was continuous inverted thunder, a pounding from below. In the wide mouth of the estuary a cargo ship lay three-quarters submerged, listing towards the open sea, waves racing over all but its feebly lifted bow and its bridge. It made all the other wrecks look like toy boats. Her gaze followed the line of the opposite shore, over dense woods, to where one corner of an old grey house jutted out from its deep cover.

'Is that it?' Iseult had followed her look.

Marina had never imagined seeing her house, her world, this way round. It occurred to her that the window she could just about see, far away, a dark blob as tiny as a fingernail, was the window in the narrow niche in the corner of the room above her father's study, the niche with the heart-shaped speckly stone she used to be able to sit on in a perfect fit until on the day of her ninth birthday her legs turned out to have grown too long, the room where one of the chairs had lion's faces carved on the ends of the arms, one of which was named Leo and the other Aslan, and she and Daddy used to make them argue with each other, Aslan always saying things like Aslan in the books and Leo being mischievous and silly and interrupting by saying he wanted to pop out for a wildebeest; if she sat in the niche, wiped a pane of glass and tucked her head close to it sideways (minding out for the sharp flake of iron in the frame of the window which used to miss her but got in the way now she was tall), she would be able to see the church tower and the stand of pines – so differently shaped from every other tree, their tops squashed flat like storm clouds – and, below them, the hump of cliff, which was where she was actually standing, now. *There* had become *here* and *here* was now *there*. Her home was away. Empty. Not her home; she was gone from it. One by one everyone had left it until no one at all remained.

The gulf between them and the southern shore heaved with rage. Tide against wind in the narrowing estuary mouth made the waves appear to be circling and surging, a mob waiting for the next victim to be thrown down.

'I didn't tell you this,' Iseult said, 'but when I met your mother before, she told me to go away and kill myself. She won't let me go across with you. But I don't mind. I couldn't look after you. I said I was going to and I couldn't. I couldn't look after Gavin either. Gawain. It doesn't matter about me. I just want to see you safe home. Are you ready? Shall we start down?' Iseult came and stood in front of her and bent to look in her face. It was odd how like Gwen she looked, especially when she was sad. Unhappiness pulled in her cheeks and softened the set of her mouth and so took away that grimness Gwen never had.

But then Gwen had turned into the worst thing in the world, or what she'd thought was the worst thing in the world until she'd gone over the gate and out into the world proper and discovered it was all like that.

Iseult's head dropped and she turned away.

'Never mind,' she said. 'I'm so tired of everything. I've had enough of being cold and wet, I really have. It'll be a relief. Come on.'

They edged and slipped their way along the coast path to the cove.

In the weeds at the back of the beach was a crude boat-house, its wooden door hacked and splintered. A rough circle of large flat stones had been assembled above the high-water line. There were bits of unlikely debris inside it, smeared with wet sand: metal tools, animal bones and scraps of shredded fur, books turned to soggy mush. The pilgrims had tried to propitiate the murderous river, perhaps, forgetting that the sea had plenty of sacrifices to choose from.

She came from the waves as soon as Marina and Iseult limped on to the sand. The wind shrieked in welcome and the rain hammered down as if it wanted to raise the river with her. She was as white as death. She stood upright where the breaking wave lifted her, at the foaming river's edge. This time she didn't reach out in supplication. Marina hobbled towards her anyway. Iseult came behind, her borrowed boots scraping pebbles and broken shells.

The sea-woman's voice had a terrifying heft. It was the seething exhalation of water chafing against rock.

'Curse them,' she said. 'Curse the men who did this to you. I curse them and I curse all men. All your father's race.'

Marina pulled herself closer, though the heavy pain tried to hold her back. She went on until the longest waves were tugging her shoes and breaking over her ankles: the dividing line.

It wasn't cold, or if it was she didn't feel it like that. It was *huge*, that was what she felt: huge enough to overwhelm the hurt in her middle. She waded farther out. Her mother folded gleaming white arms around her, and held her.

'My daughter.'

Marina had forgotten she still had her shoes on. She started trying to prise the heel of one shoe off with the toe of the other. She couldn't bend down, but she had her mother to hold her up while she worked at it.

'We were going to take her home,' Iseult said, from the beach, a few paces behind. She was difficult to hear. She was so much smaller than the wind and waves and the downpour. 'She'll be all right now, won't she?'

Her mother didn't answer, though Marina sensed her attention fall on the woman. The arms wrapped more tightly, one around her head, the other her back. She thought she could feel a thing like a heart beating beside her ear, but slow, hollow, effortless. Its pulse was the tranquil back-and-forth of sunken things.

'I brought your girl. I know an awful thing happened to her but I couldn't do anything, I wasn't there. At least you have her now. What about me? Can you bring me my boy? And don't say he's not mine, just . . . don't say that.'

One shoe came off. It floated up like a dead and bloated fish. A wave tipped it on to the sand. Marina's bare foot wasn't as good for pushing at the heel of the other one, but she tried anyway.

'You don't have anything to say at all, do you? Of course you don't. Marina? Can't you ask her? Please? Don't you care about Gawain any more?'

The soaked lining stuck to her skin, that was the problem. She tried to catch the heel in the wet sand and pull her foot free that way. There was a heavy scrunching noise, the noise (probably) of someone dropping on to the beach.

'I can't go any farther,' Iseult's voice said from back there, hoarse now. 'I'm sorry, Iggy. I just want to die.'

The shoe slipped. Marina kicked and squirmed and wriggled her foot, and at last it came free.

'Bye, Marina,' Iseult said.

'Peace.'

The sea-woman said the last word, yet the whole scene seemed to speak it with her. Its long final sibilance was the shuffle of pebbles under ebbing waves and the static crackle of rain. As soon as it was spoken the wind began to fade, as if abashed. She said it again – *Peace* – and again it was a kind of command. The storm curled up under it and turned into a shower. Without the gale driving it the rain turned gentle, falling straight. The river sloshed and broke without anger.

'Everything returns,' Swanny said. No one could have described her voice as kind, but a force had left it; it had calmed too. 'My daughter, today. My wedding band, to him to whom it was bequeathed. I myself, though it almost cost me my life. I've been patient for twelve years. Be patient.'

The second shoe bobbed up and grounded itself. Naked, Marina felt the terrible pain beginning to dissolve. Water was getting rid of it. When her mother's embrace began to draw her deeper into the river she felt a surge of happiness as irresistible as the sea itself.

'You found me my daughter.' She didn't care what her mother was saying, she only wanted to listen to her speak, to hear the liquid sound flow from the body she squeezed herself against. They went deeper. The water came up and over her shoulders. 'The river will bless you as the road has. You've gone far enough now. Cross in peace, and rest.'

Peace, Marina heard. She opened her lips and the river came in. *Rest. Ssss, sssss.* She opened her eyes too. They dipped down through a soft barrier, the world went away, and everything became infinitely hushed, infinitely the same.

Part VII

Thirty-Two

PACKING BOXES.

Whether it was the actual smell of cardboard or some more nebulous aura of transience, of dust and things unfinished, it was the packing boxes that gave it away.

She'd been trying to establish which of the various beds that counted as her own bed she'd woken up in. (Woken, she thought, by the distant shatter of breaking glass, or was it an accelerating engine, or a nocturnal shout?) It was, certainly, her own bed. Before she knew anything else she knew that. Instinct told her she was home. But . . . her bedroom next to Tess's, with the brass headboard where she hung medals from school and arranged hockey stickers from packs of gum? The basement apartment in Toronto, where condensation beaded on the paint above the bed because there wasn't an extractor fan in the shower? Or was it her place in Victoria? Which smelled of Chinese cooking from the restaurant backing on to the overgrown yard . . . In the absence of light or noise she thought about smells, and so caught the ambience of boxes and paper and stuff still not put away. Alice. Which meant the anglepoise lamp would be *there* (she stirred, reached out . . .)

Her arm moving in the dark: it was warm, dry. Or at least not cold, not wet. She held still, not feeling the metal bell of the shade (had she moved it? – when she, when she . . .)

Her consciousness drew its own outline and came back where it started. Whole, and home. She felt . . . fine. No pain, no hunger.

It was absolutely dark, a hundred per cent dark. Whatever fragment of noise had woken her had vanished, the pop of a bubble. She batted a cautious hand but still failed to find the lamp or its cord. No light. There ought to have been an infinitesimal electric shimmer from the kitchen, the LED on the stove, as well as a rectangular blur around the edge of the blind, but neither was where it should be, unless she'd forgotten which way around the room was.

She sat up. A soft presence sat up with her, attached; not sheets. She drew her own outline again and found she'd gone to sleep in her uniform shirt and pants. She never did that, no matter how tired she was when she got home, and anyway she couldn't have been that tired because the one thing she'd learned over the couple of weeks she'd been posted up here was that nothing ever happened. She should have finished unpacking days ago.

The clock she'd had since seventh grade (when she started having to wake herself up to go to school; she couldn't drive with Dad any more because Dad had moved out and her mother didn't like driving in the snow or before breakfast) had glow-in-the-dark hands. They weren't glowing. Unless she hadn't unpacked it yet, though she thought she had, on the second shelf of the unit by the bed. No light. The luminescent stuff needed something to reflect, of course. The power was out. She thought she remembered that. The power had been out since, since . . .

'Tell him to go home to his father,' someone said.

Goose looked around, or felt like she looked around, though the futility of the effort impressed itself on her straight away.

'Who's there?' she said. Not being able to see herself had the weird effect of disembodying her voice also.

'He can undo what was done to me. What I did. He can refuse it. He can go back and say no. Tell him that.'

The other voice was hard to place, close and far away at the same time. Was she listening to the neighbours talking, through the wall? She didn't remember a Brit woman living anywhere in the building, though. Not that she'd met everyone yet.

'And that I loved him. For the few days we were together. I carried him as far as I could. Remember.'

'Are you talking to me?' Goose tried to ask so quietly that only someone in the room would be able to hear. Hardly moving her lips, if at all.

'Tell Gawain.'

'What the hell are you doing in my apartment?'

'I can't stay any longer. Remember. Three things. Return. Refusal. Love.'

'How did you get in here?'

'Say them. Return, refusal, love.'

It must have been a neighbour after all, talking to someone else. Or perhaps a crazy person in the corridor. Goose put her feet down carefully. The problem with leaving packing boxes everywhere was that she couldn't remember where the clear space was in the room. She swept a half-circle with her toes and took a pace towards where she thought the door was. Repeat.

'You still there?'

A whisper of light. She was in the corridor outside, and over by the stairwell was something which wasn't entirely nothing. She must have left the apartment door open, another thing she never did. At least that accounted for hearing the voice.

'Who's out here?'

Or had she imagined it? Like she'd imagined, or dreamed, the other . . .

She certainly wasn't imagining the power outage. There was supposed to be one of those motion sensor lights in the corridor, and an exit sign, both over the stairwell. She remembered them working the day before, or whichever day it was, whenever she'd last come home. Anyway. Neither was working now, for sure. The something that wasn't nothing in the stairwell was a dim blur reflected from somewhere else, down at the bottom, by the door. She went that way. She did remember that things had started going wrong. Top to bottom. Her job was to know that sort of thing and be prepared.

She remembered fog.

She remembered it so vividly she knew it was true. She could feel the non-weight of it. The absence. She had a strong clear recollection of that absence, that hush, that shrouding invisibility, descending on the town and on the sea. And a ferry blasting through it. And a blind ferryman, and no passengers. Or one passenger, Goose herself, crossing dark water with the ferryman her guide.

Which couldn't be right, because here she was. *Here.* Corridor, stairwell. Alice. *Vous êtes ici.*

She went down towards the intimation of light.

The stairs didn't clank like usual. She must have been going extra carefully. It occurred to her that she hadn't put shoes on. The night seemed milder than recently. No wind, that made all the difference.

On the linoleum at the bottom of the stairwell was a blob of non-darkness. She went all the way down. The door there had a square window of frosted glass crossed by a lattice that looked like chicken wire. The square shimmered the eerie colour of a harvest moon.

Somewhere outside, glass popped and tinkled. Agitated voices rose for a moment, as distant as seabirds.

The power was gone, definitely, and communications were down. Everything had started to go wrong. She remembered the bank being out of money and having to suspend accounts because of the computer glitch: that was definite too, because she remembered it in lots of different ways (talking to her father, talking to Jonas, unspooling police tape outside the ATM, watching the news and seeing the pictures of people standing in long lines on the sidewalks in Toronto holding cups of takeaway coffee; they couldn't all be part of the same dream or nightmare). And the autumnal glimmer in the door was surely fire.

Was she on duty?

She thought she ought to get to the station anyway. She couldn't quite see where the door was. The crazy Brit woman must have come out ahead of her and left it open; by the glow of hidden firelight she found herself outside, on the uneven stones by the street. Sparks tumbled upwards into sight over the silhouette of the next-door building. The fire was towards town. Its light was all the light there was. The outage had blacked the whole place. A car screeched into hearing and then sight on the road below, going the other way, much too fast. She felt her way on to the street and down to the main road, where she noticed again that she'd forgotten shoes. The tarmac didn't seem wet and wasn't cold. Anyway, it was an emergency: best to hurry. She felt light, that slightly delirious convalescent feeling. Now she could look along the road and see the splintered outline of flames, strips of gossamer yellow tearing themselves off and vanishing into the dark. A house was burning. Another house.

Down by the inlet people were shouting.

As she jogged into town a set of headlights swung out from one of the side roads. They swept round and came head on, blinding her. She turned aside and got herself out of the way. As the vehicle accelerated past she waved from the side of the road to stop the driver. She leaned into the head-high brilliance of the headlights as far as she dared. Tyres squealed and skidded, the lights tipped away, there was a crack like a cannon. Goose cowered in shock. The truck had swerved into a pole and embedded the wood in its crumpled front. After the crunch of impact, silence: then something heavy thumped against the inside of the side window and stuck there, leaking darkness.

Goose uncurled herself, dumbstruck.

The headlights were still on, picking out long grass and the foot of the building on the corner. A window slid open somewhere above.

'Hello?' Goose called. She approached the side window where the unmoving silhouette was sprawled. 'Someone there?'

'You OK?' a voice shouted down.

'I think the driver's injured. Can you call an ambulance?'

'Anyone there?'

'I'm the police.' Shielding her eyes from the glare in front, she pushed her face to the glass. The silhouette became another face, looking back at her, pressed flat against the window, unmoving, cracked open at the temple. No need for an ambulance after all.

'*Tabarnac*.' She'd seen plenty of vehiculars but the impact of the empty-eyed faces never wore off. 'Fatal accident,' she called to whoever was leaning out of the building above.

'Hello?'

'I'm a police officer. Sir, I need you to—' She was about to say *call*: then she remembered (was it remembering? – it didn't feel quite like remembering, but there wasn't time to think about it) that the phone lines were down. She'd have to get help herself. Get the accident scene cordoned off, get back here with some light. If there was light. If she had time. She struggled to think of the proper procedure. The fire was more urgent, anyway; the accident was over. The blink of an eye, and another life snuffed out, another person's whole history of fears and desires and things done and undone all gone as quick as pressing the off switch, *wink* . . .

She backed away from the car.

'Anyone alive down there?'

'No survivors,' she called back. 'Please stay away from the incident scene, sir. We'll be back as soon as we can.' Insects flittered silently out of the dark to bathe in the beam of the lights. She stepped among them, looking up to where the man at the window seemed to be. 'I'm—' she began, and heard the window bang abruptly shut.

'Sir?'

A white-winged moth brushed by her face, too light for touch.

'I need your name, sir,' she called. 'For a statement later.' No one answered. 'That's an official police request.' Still no one answered. She glanced towards the fire again. She didn't have time for this. 'Small-town piece-of-crap losers,' she added. All she could see of the building above was the dim echo of firelight in panes of glass, as though the apartment block were thinking about smouldering too. She tried to get the truck's tag number but the glow behind was too dim, though when she looked down the road towards the fire it seemed taller now, its heart a deeper red. The station, she thought. She could get herself back on top of things once she was properly at work. She could get Jonas to bring her up to speed. She didn't like to leave the scene of an accident but there wasn't anything more she could do on her own and if there was a house burning in town she'd be needed there too, until the rescue squad came. She wondered how long it took them to get over from Hardy once they got the call—

No call. The phones were down.

She found herself jogging faster towards the firelight, imagining the volunteer firefighters in their beds in Hardy, on the other side of the island, thirty dark kilometres away. They couldn't hear or see the burning house and yet they were supposed to know and come racing. What happened when they didn't?

As she passed she glimpsed a few people standing on the doorsteps of houses back from the road. She yelled at them to stay clear. The inevitable bystanders, drawn to the fire like those insects in the headlights, would only be putting themselves in danger. She didn't wait to see whether they were listening. They probably couldn't see her in the dark anyway. The flames were rising from a property down near the water, where the road dipped closest to the inlet, not far from the dock. As she came closer the stillness of the night dissolved into the white noise of burning, a dry roar as constant as a waterfall. The heat was less fierce than she'd expected but the sound was overwhelming.

In the surrounding darkness the fire was the uncontested centre of the world. Trees and houses and trailers and the poles of dead street lamps and empty electrical wires came into being around it, made of red light and shadows, and the surrounding streets shone like expiring lava, cooling into black as they flowed away. She saw a few silhouettes scurrying back and forth around the house, some carrying pails. Two kids on a motorbike came roaring past. The one riding shotgun tossed a bottle into the conflagration, whooping. A family ferrying possessions out of a nearby property and into the back of a camper van stopped what they were doing long enough to shout tepid insults after the kids. A weak chain of maybe six or seven people stretched between the street and the inlet, ferrying pails of water. The man at the top of the chain edged as close to the burning lot as he dared before chucking his load on to the house. Goose could see at once that his efforts were hopeless. The rising glow turned the surface of the inlet into a sheet of submerged copper, punctured by dark holes where a handful of boats were moored. Someone was shouting about wetting the bushes around the yard. Other townspeople were just standing around, hands in the pockets of their nightgowns. No one looked her way. The air hissed and crackled and hummed.

'Has someone gone over to Hardy?' An older guy was standing by himself, leaning on a stick. Goose ran up next to him. 'Excuse me? Sir?' He didn't seem to hear her. She touched his arm. 'Sir?' He had the patiently bewildered expression common to most of the old guys. He turned it on her, or nearly on her; his eyes didn't focus. Half blind, perhaps, or half drunk. His mouth fell open but he didn't answer. She looked for someone who might have been in charge. The guy who'd been shouting about making a firebreak was trying to wrestle the pail away from someone else. Between the two of them they only managed to drop it. A tongue of spilled water licked across the road, reflecting the leaping brilliance as though the tarmac too had caught fire. She went over his way. 'Sir? Sir?' But the noise of the burning was deafening here, either that or he was ignoring her too: he ran back towards the inlet with the pail. Someone behind her screamed. A white spot rose on the road behind and rushed closer: the motorbike again, making a return pass, both of the kids now howling with anarchic joy. Goose turned to see where the scream had come from. Her gaze was caught by a ripple of shadow on a roofline at the edge of visibility. For an instant she thought something huge and dark had moved there, spreading massive wings; then it was gone, if it had been there at all.

'Get everyone out of these houses!' No one even stopped to listen. By the light of the flames their faces were all mask-like, flattened and filled with shadow. She imagined herself the same, another eerie phantom in the crowd. She needed the authority of her proper uniform, then maybe people would start recognising her and she could get something done. She turned her back to the burning house and started uphill towards the station, wondering where Jonas was. She'd gone the first block when it occurred to her that it was the middle of the night (wasn't it?) and she hadn't picked up her keys. She wasn't sure what she'd thought she was doing just running out of her apartment like that without even putting her shoes on, let alone grabbing anything else she might need; still, here she was. (Wasn't she?) She slowed down. Already, just a block and a half up the hill, the road was almost utterly dark, two rows of houses with their yards fed by Pacific rainfall between her and the blaze. In one picture window she saw candlelight, which, now that she thought about it, was probably how the fire had started in the other house. She considered knocking on the door, waking them up, ticking them off for leaving their candles lit, but she couldn't make herself do it. The little illumination would be all they had. Without it – *snuff*—

Up another block and then two more along the slope. She thought she'd made the right turns but it was hard to be sure. She heard screams again, floating up like the short-lived cinders. In consort with the fistful of fire surrounded by absolute darkness and the memory of the gruesome dead face in the truck, the shouts turned the scene below her momentarily hellish. The kids, she guessed, doing their best to terrify already fearful people. She promised herself she'd have the two of them in cells in the morning—

She halted, dizzy: or not exactly dizzy, because in the darkness she didn't feel stable on the earth anyway, but suddenly afflicted by a vertigo of uncertainty. She was remembering a girl in a cell one morning, a memory too concrete with consequences to be part of any nightmare. Jennifer Knox, The Girl Who Wouldn't Speak – except that Goose could recall the sound of her voice precisely.

It had just been the two of them, after all, with miles of nothing in every direction, the sea and the barren islands. She remembered Jennifer explained why it was OK to speak to Goose: *Talking with you's like talking with nobody*.

The cells were just here, if she was right. She tried to make some sense of the dark. Edging along the road, she saw a tall straight shadow suddenly come between her and the glow. The flagpole: she'd reached the station, then. But there wasn't a hint of light inside. The power had left it, the same as everywhere else. No one was there.

Jonas might be at home, though. She couldn't see whether or not the patrol car was out in front. It was hard to believe he wouldn't be out on duty somewhere on a night like this, but then if you'd have backed anyone to sleep through the apocalypse Jonas would be the guy. Anyway, her options were either getting lucky and finding him in or footing it back to the apartment for all the stuff she needed; she ought at least to give it a go while she was here. Unfortunately the half of the station where Jonas lived had its entrance at the back, where it was utterly dark. She remembered there were shrubs by the path but she couldn't see them at all, not even the suggestion of an outline. She went step by step, feeling for anything that might orient her. A few paces in off the road she thought she felt plants: something cool and living, at any rate. She prodded her way carefully past.

The ambience of the darkness changed: tighter, closer. The air smelled of inside things. She thought she must be right by the back fence, but when she put her hands out they met nothing.

'Goose?'

'Jonas?'

'Goose!'

She must have got all the way inside without knowing it.

So he'd left his door open too? Perhaps he'd been hoping for a trickle of light, though when she turned around there was nothing visible in that direction either.

'Hey, I didn't mean to just walk in. I can't see a thing. Where are you?'

'I'm right here, man.'

'Thanks, that helps. Don't you have a torch or something? What are you doing?'

'I'm sleeping.'

'You were asleep? Don't you know what's going on out there?'

'Lotta things been going on, Goose. What happened to you? Where did you go?'

'I—' She felt weightless again, as if her own history had fled from her, as invisible and intangible as the room she was (wasn't she?) standing in. 'I was—' *Was*, the past tense. *J'étais* . . . It felt like a grammatical trapdoor opening on to a bottomless drop. She edged away from it. 'Am I supposed to be on tonight? I guess I lost track. Sorry.'

'Aw, Goose. None of that works any more.'

'None of what?'

'Rotas and stuff. Normal service. Is that why you're here? Worrying about work even in my dreams?'

'You're not dreaming, Jonas. Where are you?' She reached around her ankles, feeling for the clutter she remembered in his room, the TV and the man-cave chair.

'Hey, you're right. If this was my dream you'd be naked.' He chuckled his gentle amusement, a soft slow belly laugh, at ease with itself. He sounded like he was over . . . *there*, but when she tried to connect the direction with wherever she was facing it didn't add up.

'You fell asleep in your chair?'

'I guess.'

'Couldn't even make it to the bedroom? Jeez.'

'Nah. I gave the kid the bed.'

'Kid?'

'You remember. You saw him first. The Chinese kid.'

Fog. She felt it vividly again – or rather *didn't* feel it; she felt or recalled or re-experienced the absence of anything to feel, the (non-)sensation of floating in the dense grey mist, not knowing up from down. She'd been with Jonas in his boat . . .

'I got him from the hospital.' Jonas sounded even dozier than usual. He hadn't even tried to get up from wherever he was. 'They couldn't deal with extra bodies. Doctor stopped me in the street and said they were gonna put him out on the sidewalk. When the power went they tried to send everybody home. Man, nobody knew where to go. Crazy couple o' days. I couldn't just leave him on his own. Some of the guys were running pretty wild in the streets.'

'The kid on the beach? The killer whale? He's here?'

'Yep. He's been OK. Freaks out sometimes but I think we're starting to get along. Said his name a couple of times. It's a start. Hey, you were right, maybe I was cut out to be a dad after all.'

Goose felt around, still trying to get her bearings in the room. She remembered the gigantic TV and was amazed she hadn't bumped into it yet. Her sweeping fingers tapped against something near knee level. 'Jonas? That you?' No, it was an object, not a body; in fact her hands identified it immediately, despite the darkness, as if its oval-eyed face had thrust out of the fog. The mask. Something about the rough solidity of the carved wood was unmistakable to the touch. 'Where the hell are you?' Now she noticed a smell so powerful she wondered how she could have missed it before. He must have been fishing and forgotten to put his catch in the freezer. No. The freezer wouldn't be working either, of course.

'You sound kinda troubled, Goose. You got something you need to tell me?'

'Can't you just get your ass in gear? There's a fire in town. Someone needs to get down there and keep some order.'

'Order?' She thought she heard him stirring, getting up, but it was only a whispery exhalation, the quietest version of his half-chuckle, half-sigh. 'Good luck with that. Order, heh. What, you want me to go wave my badge around, tell everyone to chill out, get back to work? Where've you been these last couple of days?'

Drifting. Nowhere. 'I—'

She couldn't answer that question. Not only because she didn't know: when she tried to know, when she thought about it, the terrible ungrounded vertigo made her spin. She glimpsed a reflection of her old childhood nightmare, the incommunicable horror of a solitary spot of consciousness moving in an infinite void.

'You not coming back, Goose? Here to say goodbye?'

'I'm trying to get to work. We're still mounties. Sworn to serve, remember?'

'Kalmykov left. Hoaglund too. Hoaglund was supposed to be watching the SavaMart. Know what he did? Filled the back of the car with ham and beer and bagels and took off. Dunno where they all think they're going. Last we heard things were getting pretty heavy down-island too. Before we stopped hearing anything. Me, I knew it was serious when they cancelled the play-offs.'

'Hoaglund's a prick. You're not, Jonas. Come on. Are you planning to sleep through it?'

'What are you, my guilty conscience? Cute. I should know myself better than that. I can't guilt myself out of bed in the middle of the night. Hey, I took that kid home, that oughtta be good enough for you. Me.'

If only she could find him she could kick him. 'How about you at least get up long enough to open the station? I don't have keys.'

'What's this about, Goose?'

She was trying to follow his voice but every time she took a hesitant step she seemed to have gone in the wrong direction. She thought she heard another sound, faintly, a suppressed rattle or rustle; perhaps he was getting dressed after all.

'Ah, never mind,' Jonas went on, peaceably. 'Whatever, it's good you came. Been missing you, you know? We had a good thing going.'

'Is that you moving?'

'Probably wake up after this, won't I? I hope I remember. This is kinda trippy.'

Someone or something was definitely moving. The reek

of fish was disorientingly strong. Could someone else have blundered in through the open door? She heard a kind of wheezing grumble from a direction that might have been outside.

'Jonas.' She tried one last time. As far as she knew he didn't touch weed or even drink, but she hadn't known him long and it wouldn't really have been a surprise if he had a secret habit. 'If you're drunk or stoned, whatever. Listen to me. You're not dreaming. We've got a problem in town. Up you get. We're partners. Right?'

Perhaps the scratchy sound was coming from the bushes outside. It had that quality, the massed bristling of stiff small twigs. A grunt went with it.

She went still, suddenly listening intently. The grunt hadn't sounded human.

Bear?

Distracted from her efforts to rouse Jonas, she was surprised when he spoke, very softly, very ruefully.

'I can't go with you, man. I'm not ready yet.'

The moving thing was big. Though she couldn't see a thing she could sense its weight, its presence: like the *chug-chug-chug* of the ferry in the fog, massive even in the absence of any shape or ratio. The reek seemed to bear down on her like an unseen vessel.

'Did you take my boat?' Jonas sounded farther away. 'I had a feeling that was you. When I heard you'd gone the same night. I'm right, aren't I? I guess that makes me partly responsible, something like that. You want me to tell someone the news, Goose? Kinda hard to imagine how, but sure, I'll do what I can. You want me to try and get word to your folks?'

His delirium passed her by, a mere mournful background hum compared to the gathering animal menace. 'Jeez, Jonas,' she muttered, though she was talking to herself, 'only you would take a kid home and then leave your freaking door wide open.' She took little sideways steps towards what she hoped was a corner of the room, looking to get solid walls at her back.

'You're not at peace,' he said, 'are you? Still fighting it. Still that kind of lady.'

Something rustled and crunched, very near by. 'Hey,' croaked a new voice, also close yet muffled, as if behind a thick curtain. 'White girl.'

'Wakin' up,' Jonas said, receding. 'Go easy, Goose. Don't fight it. I'll say some words for you, help you along.'

The other voice, husky and full of malice, chuckled. 'No help for you, white girl. Hear me? Get out here.'

Was Jonas finally rousing himself? She was so confused now about what was happening where that she couldn't place the creak of a body shifting, turning over in their sleep. The other person had the strong husky accent of the oldest First Nations people. Some old native bum stumbling by in the dark. Must have heard her voice and decided to pick a fight. 'Jonas?' she called again.

'No one in there listening to you no more. Lost your voice, white girl. Got no language. Just one message left to say and you're gonna forget it anyhow. Three words too many for you. Get out here. Gonna take you back to the water where you belong.'

They were all drunk, maybe. She could imagine how it had gone when order broke down; straight to the market, all of them, fighting for free booze. That was always the first thing to get stolen, before money even. Money would just be used to buy booze anyway; better to cut out the middleman. Curiously, she felt neither anger nor her usual thrill-coated anticipation. Normally she looked forward to these confrontations. Perhaps it was just that on a night like this dealing with an incoherently insulting native guy seemed tedious more than anything else, a waste of time. On the plus side it did sound as if Jonas had finally shrugged himself out of his weird stupor; she heard him – presumably him – making the furniture squeak and crack as he got himself upright.

'I'll go deal with this loser,' she said. 'See you round by the station, OK? Got that?' But no one answered.

'No more whispering and walking,' cackled the throaty voice. 'Time's up.'

She felt for the doorway, found something else under her hands – a damp and living something, life unburdened by thought: the bushes between the back of the house and the road – and, disoriented again, looked up. A tinge of fire-light marked the presence of the open sky. There was someone standing in the road, a very large shadow distinguished from the rest of the deep-shadowed world by the faintest glitter, as if its darkness were scaled where everything else was shrouded.

The bigger they came, she thought, the harder they fall. Especially the drunk ones.

'Sir,' she said, advancing, 'I'll be straight with you. You

freaking stink.' If the stench had been bad inside Jonas's house, it was twice as bad up close. The old guy must have stuck his head in a barrel of rancid fish oil.

'Don't you sir me,' rasped the big shadow, and Goose realised with brief surprise that it actually belonged to a woman, not a man; a gap-toothed-crone voice, a sixty-a-day throat-cancer voice. 'You got no house. Don't owe no one no respect.'

'OK, here's who you're messing with. I'm Constable Maculloch of the RCMP, Hardy detachment, on secondment to Alice. This here's my police station you're standing outside. Now. Do you have any alcohol on your person, ma'am?'

'Cuntsible Maculloch Arseyempee Hardy Alice. I'm eatin' your asshole white names and I'm spittin' them out and you know what's left?' With a many-voiced dry rattle the shadow suddenly loomed, the elusive glitter of its clothes coming alive with movement, as though a chain-mail sleeve had thrust itself at her. 'No name.'

A hand closed on her hand. Goose gasped airlessly: no breath escaped her but she felt a clutch of inward shock. The hand was immensely strong and bitterly cold. The foul smell enveloped her, and at the same moment she remembered it: it fell into a place in time, a beginning, before which everything had been unchanged and normal. It was the reek she'd smelled in the station (right next to her) when she'd come back from Traders with her coffee and found the cell open and the girl, impossibly, gone. In the wake of that inexplicable instant followed other things, the pursuit of Jennifer, the middle which came after the beginning, one thing after another until they came to an island in a cold sea, which was the—

'Down you go,' the coarse voice said, and Goose found herself being pulled along the road like a toddler. With every step the shadow beside her spoke in its other voice, the wordless chattering incantation of its clothes. As it dragged her away from the back of the station the myriad objects whose rustling and clicking made that murmur snagged more firelight from the sky. She saw that the huge old woman was draped in things, bone and horn and beaten metal and hollow wood, head to toe, and she had the sudden dreadful knowledge that she too was just another thing, a notch on a stick, a dry wordless voice among hundreds of thousands that had gone before, being carried along against her entirely useless will.

'Let me—' But trying to pull her hand away was like trying to uncuff herself, except the cuff was a shackle of stone. 'What are you—'

'Been walkin' out too late,' the woman growled. 'Don't know who let you go but they had their turn. I got you now for good. Gonna drag you under.'

'No,' she said. She thought she heard a door open behind them. 'Jonas!' she shouted. 'I'm here!' The woman pulled her around a corner and started down the dimly outlined street. Looking down its length, she saw the inlet below, a slash of darkness varnished in reflected fire. 'What's wrong with me?' She couldn't feel the road under her feet or the air on her face. All the sensation she'd ever had was compacted in the unspeakably icy grip around her hand. If Jonas had heard her he wasn't answering, if it was even Jonas at all. 'You can't do this to me. I'm . . .' She lost her breath as the woman made her stumble, or so she thought. 'I'm . . .' No stumble this time, and no breath: the incomplete sentence was simply that, a connection with only one end, a beginning that petered out. She couldn't have breathed anyway, not against the rank stench of rot filling the air. She groped for the next word, the one which went with *I*. It wasn't there. '*Je suis . . . Je m' . . . J' . . .*' Less than a word, less than a syllable: the only sound left to her matched the dumb rustle of the woman's coat. They were skirting the circle of things given visible substance by the fire, heading straight down the blocks below the station to the enveloping nothingness of the sea. One other person moved in the street, another mere shadow. The town she'd come to live in, a nice, backward, ordinary British Columbian town, a place of determined neighbourliness and pension-funded comfort, had turned into a solar system of chaotic darkness orbiting a raging blood-red sun. The oblivion of drowning loomed below. Goose gathered herself in desperate protest and tried one last time to remember herself, remember that she was still herself. 'I . . . am . . .'

The shadowed person ahead unfurled, standing tall, turning. Suspended in it were two unquenched sparks from the blaze.

'Séverine,' it said.

The old woman's fierce shamble abruptly stopped.

Goose seized on the word like a lifeline. 'I'm Séverine,' she said. 'Séverine Maculloch. I'm an officer. Let go of me. You have to let go.'

'Let her go,' the fire-eyed shadow repeated.

The cold chain dropped away from her hand.

'Freak thing,' the hulking woman spat. 'Monster.'

'Shut up,' said the shape ahead, stepping forward. The coals of its eyes lit patches of a death-pale face, hollows between pinched cheekbones and a narrow nose. Next to Goose the old woman in the cloak sewn with talismans shivered and bent, cloak and throat both making a gargle like a prolonged death rattle. 'You have no mouth. You lost it. Crawl away.' Goose knew it was all true, now, all the way from the beginning to the end. None of it was any kind of dream; the world really was dark and burning, and the demon that had ferried her to her desertion was walking its streets. The demon raised its hand, so pale that it resisted shadow and appeared as a glimmer of ember-tinged flesh: Goose saw a small ring blotting out a hoop of the finger that stretched out towards the cowering old creature. 'Go back to the sea. Séverine is mine.' The cloak chittered in violent alarm and rolled away out of sight. Its miasma went with it.

Along the road, towards the burning house, someone cried out. Glass smashed. There was a snatch of wild laughter.

The twin fires burned in Goose's vision, depthless and unblinking, close enough for her to touch.

She took a weightless pace backwards.

'I don't want any part of this,' she said.

'Séverine.' The voice was like fire too, all hissing and whispering and sharp pops and cracks. 'Séverine, Séverine.' It lingered over her name the way one might draw a silk scarf slowly over fingertips. 'Beautiful, strong Séverine. Have you not yet understood? Have you forgotten me? We shared a night, you and I. You were so brave. Other women would have been weak with terror, but not you. You and I, we sailed the dark hours together, and both of us found what we sought. None of it was a dream.' The eyes had drawn still closer. With a pulsing bittersweet shock Goose felt the withered hand touch her face, gently, lovingly. 'None of it. You can't go back.'

'Don't touch me.' But she didn't push the hand away. It was as caressing as the huge woman's grasp had been merciless. It was, she realised, the only thing she could feel at all. It stroked her brow and cheek and the corner of her mouth. She held still, knowing that if the stroking stopped she would be left with no sense of touch, no skin.

'You see, now, don't you?' The English vowels dripped sad sympathy. 'You understand your predicament. Don't you, Séverine?' The shadow was intimately close now. Goose sensed the clean salt-washed fabric of its ragged clothes, the cool drowned flesh beneath. 'Say it. Say the truth.'

'I'm not—' she began, but couldn't say the word. She couldn't be. If . . . *that* had happened to her, then none of this could be happening: nothing would be happening: there would be no *happening*, there would be no *her*. 'I didn't—' she tried again, and again fell short.

'You are,' the shadow whispered tenderly. 'You did.'

'No,' Goose said. 'No. I'm here. I still have a choice.'

'That's right.' Its substance touched her. Shredded and scoured leather pressed her front, draped around the weight of a dreadfully wasted body. She felt arms like brittle tentacles slide around her waist. 'I'm your choice, Séverine. Say yes.'

There was no recoil of horror. Not even the ghastly eyes bending over her close enough to kiss could rouse the symptoms of dread, the nausea, the prickling, the helplessly loosened guts. The only sensations allowed to her were in its touch.

'No,' she said.

'Listen to me, Séverine. I'll be your life and you'll be mine. We'll be together. Strong and beautiful and young, not like this ragged wreck I wear. We'll live for ever. You gave me back the secret of it yourself, my love. You took it from the foolish girl's neck and you threw it to me in the water. I want to share it with you. We'll go wherever we want and feel whatever we want and do everything we want. Say yes. Save yourself from the black water, as I did once. Say it.' Chill shrivelled fingers touched her lips. '*Oui*. Shape your lips for a kiss. *Oui*. Say it to me now.'

She couldn't feel horror, but she could know it. Knowledge meant thought, thought meant choice. 'No.'

The crepuscular face bent over her. The eyes burned but made no sound and gave out no heat; all they did was light up the finger's-width space between Goose and the demon, trapping the two of them together in their tiny refuge from the darkness.

'It's this,' the lifeless lips whispered, 'or nothing.'

'No.'

'It's cold below the sea, Séverine. Join me and you can

have everything, everything in the world. Without me you're alone in the dark. For ever.'

Tyres screeched, something banged. The background rage of the fire seemed to surge. If the sun ever rose, Goose thought, there'd be nothing for it to see but destruction.

'No,' she said again.

'Nothing can deny me for ever. I want your lips, Séverine. And your mouth. And I want your lungs and your voice and your shoulders, and your heart. Say yes. Only once. Without thinking. Once is enough. Watch my lips.' They puckered, bleached and cracked curves opening like the valves of a dried-up shell. '*Oui.*' They closed on Goose's mouth until all she could see was flame, swirling and dancing in silent rage. 'Say it. Kiss me.'

A sudden hollow cacophony swept above them, a beating of voiceless thunder. It was so loud and abrupt that it made Goose cringe, breaking out of the embrace. The demon sprang back with a hiss, looking up. A huge winged silhouette passed between them and the glow of the rising fire. Goose heard the thud of those wings descending, and then a scrape on the road.

'Here,' croaked a toneless voice, from the same nearby darkness where the scrape had come, a little way down towards the water. 'This way.'

The arms around Goose's waist tightened but the face had flinched away. 'Be quick,' the demon whispered. '*Sans moi, rien.*'

Goose thought of her mother drawing on her cigarette, making the tip glow with a rush of tainted oxygen, the impatient inhalation while she waited for her unglamorous tomboy daughter to confess to whatever she'd been accused of. She put her arms down by her sides and levered the skeletal embrace away.

'I should have said no to you from the start,' she said.

Another spot of fire appeared, coming up from the shore.

'End of the road,' said the croaking voice in the dark. The flame beyond it revealed itself to be a torch, smoking and sputtering. Under its umbrella of obscure light two people were walking close together. Only their faces and hands stood out from the night, but they were definitely human faces and human hands. The inhuman thing in front of Goose turned to watch them approach, folding its hands over its chest, where no heart beat.

Goose thought she heard it whisper something like a sigh: *I have and I hold.*

'Still not yours,' the grating voice said. The thing it belonged to, the thing that had winged overhead and come to rest on the road, was like a black hole: the approaching torchlight didn't seem to fall on it at all, leaving instead a boulder-sized seam of mere darkness. Both the people under the torch had the clear steady faces of children. One, Goose saw, was Jennifer Knox. The firelight had turned her skin copper, a ceremonial mask beaten perfectly smooth. The other was a boy of about the same age, almost as pale as the drowned white face with the burning eyes, and almost as thin as well.

'Not yet free, puka?' The demon had lost interest in Goose. Its mocking whisper was directed the other way. 'Is it that slavery suits you so well you choose it willingly? I can unbind you with a word, you know.'

'Up yours,' the impenetrably black lump replied. The two teenagers came up to stand beside it and halted. A sliding crackling boom echoed over the town, and the fan of fire over the rooftops spread wider, throwing off a sudden billow of fresh sparks. Another house must have gone up, or down. Goose saw a tree burning by the road, quivering black limbs torn upward in a relentless stream of flame: it looked like a soul in torment.

The fire-eyed thing raised its voice and its dead left hand together. The pendant ring Goose had thrown into the sea was fixed around its index finger. 'Too late,' it cried out, with hideously joyful emphasis. The boy, who was the one holding the bundle of glowing sticks, stepped forward on his own, passing the dark croaking shape, making something in its face glisten for a moment. 'You had better sail away again,' the triumphant voice went on. 'All of you. There'll be little here tomorrow but ruin and starvation.'

The look in the boy's face was strange. Goose didn't see a hint of fear there. It was more like teenage reluctance taken to a tragic extreme, as if the kid literally couldn't bear to look at the thing he was facing. Nevertheless, he kept coming, until the raised white hand pushed its palm out and spread its fingers.

'No farther,' the demon said. The boy stopped. By the tentative glow Goose saw he had no shoes on.

'There's nothing you can do now, once-boy,' the thing told him, a murmur almost sympathetic. 'Turn back. Go home. Or wander the world as the prophetess did. It makes no difference.'

The boy held out the hand that wasn't holding the torch.

'You'd better give it to me,' he said.

Goose somehow wasn't surprised that he had an English accent too. Alice, B.C. – of all places – had fallen under the spell of the changed England, ruled by madness and fire; invaded again, a tiny colony of the anarchic kingdom.

The demon folded its hands to its body again.

'Not this time,' it said. There was a twisted smile in its voice.

'She left it to me.'

'And you lost it. You let it go. It fled you. It was cast away. We took it fairly, once-boy. All that long journey of yours, and you came a day too late.'

'Cold,' muttered the black croaking thing with the shiny beak. 'Dark.'

'We think the puka would prefer it if you sailed southwards,' the demon said. 'Towards the summer. At least it won't go hungry. The world's ripe with carrion.'

'What do you want with the ring?' the boy said. He shook his head a little, as if genuinely puzzled. 'What's the point?'

The demon leaned towards him. It was just a shadow to Goose now, an outline of wild thick-tangled hair.

'To live,' it said softly. 'We want to live. It's nothing to you, is it? The stones under your feet, the smell of water. The music of that house alight. The dread of these people. To you it's all mere happenstance, isn't it? The weave of the world changes every instant and you barely notice, except perhaps to regret the change. Life is wasted on you. There's no magic more wonderful than this flesh.' It spread its hands, turning them over and back. 'This feeling. Pleasure and pain, constantly. We are legion, yet every moment we live there is sensation enough for each of us a hundred times over.'

'That flesh, as you call it.' The boy fought against the evident urge to avert his eyes. 'Was a person once. Someone I loved.'

'We feel your grief, too.' The withered hands rose in the air and held still. 'Small, rough, dry. Almost-forgotten. A nail sunk in wood.'

'Feel this,' the black thing croaked from behind the boy, and unfolded, and leaped forward, a cloak of feathered night thrown towards them. The torchlight showed talons wider than hands stretching towards the demon. It put the finger with the ring swiftly to its lips and spat three strange words: the cloak crumpled and dropped to the ground. 'Don't, Corbo,' the boy was saying, but by the time he'd said it the spasm of movement was over. They all stood as they had a moment before, except that the huge winged darkness was now sprawled near the boy's bare feet.

'Shall we let it free?' the demon asked, hand still near its lips. 'The puka's a long way from where we bound it. It would be lost here. Still. Shall we say the words?'

The boy crouched and touched some part of the black shape. 'Corbo.'

'Spirits are weak. How else would they have let themselves be forgotten for so long? The puka is still there, once-boy.

Don't trouble yourself. But it won't move that filthy body we gave it. Still. You have another companion for your homeward journey, we see.'

An unhealthy-sounding car came along the main road from the direction of the mill and passed just below them, pulled towards the rising fire. Goose wondered what the driver would have seen or thought if she'd looked up the street as she went by. Perhaps Jonas was right: once people lost their internet connection and saw their pay cheques dissolved into imaginary numbers confounded by an electronic plague, they'd gone as far into a nightmare as they needed to go; everything else was just scenery. Jennifer approached now, shuffling slightly. Her gaze had lost the disquieting intensity Goose remembered from the station cell. She too looked her age: awkwardly, nervously hostile. The demon surveyed the two of them.

'Well-suited companions,' it said. 'Both lost what you were given.'

Where the boy was quietly distressed, Jennifer was just angry. 'I know what you are,' she said, jutting her head forward beside the boy's shoulder. The night was so thick it swallowed the rest of her. She snarled a word in a language Goose didn't know. 'Ghost. Bad spirit. We got songs to put you down.'

'You,' the demon said, pointing the ringed finger at the girl, 'have no voice at all.' Jennifer's black eyes went wide. She clutched at her throat, staggering backwards. The boy winced. 'We banish the spirit from your mouth as easily as we bound the puka. We sent that spirit back to the sea.' Jennifer fell to her knees, gasping as if she couldn't breathe.

'Don't,' the boy said.

'And who are you to tell us what we may or may not do?' The triumph in the demonic voice was turning wild. Jennifer curled up, mouth wide open but soundless. Goose knew horror again and felt she ought to intervene. She remembered how she'd come *this* close to knocking the demon-woman overboard, out in Jonas's boat. Hitting hard and fast was all she knew how to do. She braced herself to accelerate: the demon raised a hand above its shoulder and she found herself unable to move at all, not paralysed or weighed down but as if she'd been turned to air, as if the idea of motion no longer applied in her case. 'You were created free,' it went on, with barely a pause. 'You were born into your own body. Do you grudge us who were insubstantial that same freedom? Do you not understand what it means, to will an act, and make it so?'

'She's choking,' the boy said. 'Stop it. She'll die.'

'Of course she will. All people die. Three have died tonight within earshot of where we stand. One was a child younger than this girl. The girl herself would have have died adrift in that boat if you and the puka hadn't sailed by and found her. Yesterday, today, another day, what does it matter when?'

'I'm not telling you.' He was tensely quiet, as if only just holding himself together. 'I'm asking you.'

'But her suffering!' The demon shivered, its whisper ecstatic. 'The pitch of fear! Can't you taste it? She knows herself on the very brink. Think how glittering life must be, in its final instants!'

'Then don't go any farther. That's enough.'

With a huge gasp Jennifer slumped to the road beside the winged beast. All Goose could see of her was a shoulder, twitching. Small strained noises escaped her.

The boy looked as if he wanted to help her somehow but had instead forced himself to stand where he was, facing up to his enemy. There was a long pause between them. Goose heard shouting around the burning houses. She could have sworn that one of the voices was Jonas's, only a few blocks away.

'Was it her,' the demon finally said, 'you came all this way to find?'

'That's right,' the boy said.

'Her?' It waved its left hand slowly. 'Or this?'

'Both. I knew she'd have it.'

'And you were wrong. A hard journey, to end in a mistake.'

'No.' The boy looked almost reluctant as he shook his head. 'I'm not wrong.'

'She had it. But she lost it, as you see.'

'I'm not wrong,' he said again, without stubbornness.

The demon sounded like it was smiling again. 'It's the price of your freedom. People are born with the gift of choice, and pay the cost of error. You follow your own will, knowing that it might lead you astray.'

'Remember what you called me?'

The demon didn't answer.

'*Once-boy*,' he went on. 'Once. Not any more. I left all that behind. I'm not a person at all.'

Still the demon said nothing, as if the boy's answer had defeated it.

'The journey really brought it home.' The torch was dwindling, not much more now than a few ashy embers with the occasional lick of soft yellow flame. He held it very steadily. 'I walked, do you know that? Sailed, then walked all the way. How could a boy do that? How could anyone still be a person after the distance I walked? The crossing took a long time too but sailing's different, after a while it's just waves and wind, waves and wind. But on land . . . The world's so big. I stayed a long way north. It was dark most of the time, everything was under snow. For weeks and weeks I didn't see a person. Not even a sign of people. Sometimes there'd be a line in the snow which must have been a kind of road, or pylons, but that's it. Day after day. Places no one's walked across ever, maybe. You start noticing how little the world has to do with yourself. It doesn't need freedom. It just . . .' He shrugged, struggling to say what he meant. 'Is. That's what you're not getting. You want to be alive, you want to feel everything, you want to do what you want. Like people do. That's not what she gave me, though. That's what I had to leave behind. All that walking stripped it out. I didn't have anything to do except,' he frowned and made a walking motion with his fingers, 'go through everything and see it for what it is. Like she did. That's why the ring belongs with me.' If this was meant to be an argument, it was utterly unpersuasive. The boy ended up almost mumbling, staring at his hands, his expression as confused as his speech. Nevertheless, he found nothing to add. There was another protracted silence between the two of them.

'So you think you've left behind a boy's desires,

once-boy?' The whisper had recovered its undertone of insidious glee. 'Shall we tell you what else you left behind?'

The boy looked up sharply, straight into the burning gaze: Goose saw the double fires reflected in his eyes.

'The half-girl has abandoned her sanctuary,' it said, taunting.

The boy's awkwardness vanished all at once. For the first time he looked afraid.

'She went out into the world. But why should you care? Let things be as they are.'

'She can't have.'

'You think we tell you an untruth, boy? You know better than that. Or is it that you hope we lie? Is that it? Is it desire you feel now? Longing, fear?'

'How can you know anything about her?' The boy's hands had clenched at his sides.

'Does it matter how? We know. You left her behind, and the pain of it was more than she could stand.'

'Give me the ring.' The boy thrust his arm out again.

'We will not.'

'You can't keep it. You can't use it. It's isn't for using. Give it to me.'

'You'll return empty handed, boy. And to an empty house. Do you love her? Is that the truth? We smell a strange doubleness in you. Pain and joy wound together. Is that love? Teach us.' The hand with the ring stretched forward towards the boy's face. 'We want to learn the secret of it.'

Something snapped in the boy. He jumped back as if the hand were a striking snake. The torch flared as he nearly dropped it. He clutched it with both hands but it still shook. Burnt ends dangled and dropped, dying before they hit the road. Jennifer whimpered and tried to struggle to her hands and knees.

'You can do nothing,' the demon hissed. 'None of you. The puka is a slave, the shaman has lost the spirit that gave her a voice, and you, once-boy, are as powerless as the prophetess.' Goose was forgotten. The affliction that had kept her motionless began to fade. She found herself retreating, pace by backward pace, up the hill, away from the light. None of what she'd seen made sense to her, except that she knew, somehow, that for a brief moment – a real moment, an instant in time, not any kind of dream – it had depended on her: the ring they were talking about had passed through her hands for a second, when she'd swept the necklace off Jennifer's neck and thrown it into the sea. She'd done the wrong thing, and now here she was, in fire and darkness, dumbly and helplessly watching some kind of consequence unfold, while the town burned and people crashed and died. There was nothing she could do, because she was . . .

She hadn't left the door of her apartment open. She never did that. Nor slept in her uniform. Jonas hadn't left his door open either. The night seemed mild and it didn't matter that she'd forgotten her shoes because she couldn't, she couldn't feel, she had no feeling . . .

Except.

Still fighting it. Still that kind of lady.

While she'd been in Jonas's place, feeling around in the dark, she'd touched something.

The boy was retreating down the hill towards the water, the demon striding after him, still talking, it seemed, though at a distance there was no difference between its voice and the whisper of the blaze. Goose had been backing unwillingly away, but now she set herself up the hill, looking again for any hint of the outline of the station. She remembered Jennifer staring mutely from the floor of the cell there, at the beginning. She remembered reading the file, thinking about the girl's refusal to speak. *The spirit that gave her a voice.* She thought of Jennifer up in the bedroom of her house on the night of 1 December, shouting 'crazy stuff'. Who wouldn't listen to her now? Forget about the lawyers and doctors and cops and her useless drunken mother, forget about the voices down phones and on Skype and broadcast by satellite from studios in Toronto or New York; hers was the language they needed.

She found the station, and the path between the hydrangea bushes, and the invisible back door. She went in and found the mask, the one thing her hands had clasped and recognised in the darkness.

'Mum?'

She held still, the carved wood in her arms.

'Is that you? I can't see.'

A younger child's voice, English accented (needless to say), with a spiky uncertainty to it.

'Hey,' Goose said. 'It's Horace, isn't it?'

'Who the hell's there?'

'I'm . . . no one. Doesn't matter.'

'Where's Mum? You better not be a burglar.'

'You're not at home, Horace. You've come a long way.'

'Can't you turn a flipping light on?'

'No,' she said. 'I'm afraid I can't.'

'Who is this? You're an American.'

'Actually I'm . . . not.'

'You the one who was calling, then?'

'Not me.'

'Someone was calling. I heard it. Where are we? Where's Mum?'

'I tried to call your mother. The phones stopped working, though. This is Canada.'

'Canada like in Canada? That top bit of America?'

'. . . Uh-huh.'

'What am I doing in Canada? That's ridiculous.'

'I couldn't tell you. I guess maybe it's like you said, someone called you.' She thought of the hospital report: Jennifer slipping out of bed when no one was looking and murmuring, swaying, dancing. 'You're OK. A friend of mine's been looking after you. He's—' *This is for you, Jonas*, she thought; a valedictory thought. 'He's good people.'

'Is that him with you?'

'Nah. He went out.'

'So who's that?' Something bumped. 'Ow. Where are you? Where's the lights?'

'There's no one else here. There's no lights either. Power's off.'

'There is, I heard him. I got sharp ears.' More bumping: something got knocked over. 'What's all' – he said it *wossall* – 'this stuff?'

Now Goose heard it too, and smelled and tasted it at the same time: it crept over every ambient sense like the first subsonic tremor of an earthquake. Her arms and hands vibrated with it.

'Maybe you should stay put a little bit,' she said. 'Jonas'll be back to help you.'

'Help me what? I don't need help.'

'I found you, you know.' Fog, and a slumped body alone on an island in the sea. 'Me and Jonas got you safe. I guess if it hadn't been for those guys when I was out in the kayak I might not have known. So that's one thing I did right, huh?'

The bumping had stopped.

'You're mental,' Horace said, warily.

'It's OK.' The other voice in the room rose to a deep, swift-slow hum, at rest yet full of immense power. It had a rough singing tone, but it went on rising, with no need to draw breath. 'I have to take this now.'

'Take what? Are you stealing stuff?'

'You take care, Horace. They thought you were lost, you know? Nothing's lost, I guess. Just went missing for a while.' The sound was swelling around her, too much for Jonas's cluttered front room to contain. She went out again, still holding the mask. It too had gone missing, she supposed, and perhaps was now back where it belonged. She had a memory as brief as a heartbeat: she'd gone to the museum in Victoria once and looked at a case full of masks, and she remembered thinking how odd their silence was. All those things with great mouths, beaks and jaws and muzzles – something about the way the old First Nations people carved them made them look as if they were all mouth – lined up there not saying a word, like they'd been in the middle of a sentence and simultaneously forgotten what they were saying. Forgotten for however many hundred years.

Not for ever, though.

The boy and the drowned thing were gone, or at least there was no torchlight and no other lights either. She found Jennifer by the soft gasping noises the girl made as she crouched in the street, though how she could hear anything over the yawning moan of the mask she didn't know. She smelled the sea again, foam and kelp and salt. It no longer revolted her. She put the mask in Jennifer's hands, or thought she did. It was too dark to know for sure.

Everything fell silent.

Then there was a single crack of thunder. Lightning splintered the dark, a white wound ripped from the zenith to the reflecting surface of the inlet. In its instant of shocking brilliance Goose saw a silhouette standing in front of her, upright: the girl with her head transformed. From the face of the mask came a cry as huge and fierce as the sky's.

It began to rain. Not the kind of storm rain the thunder had briefly promised, but Pacific rain, a sweetly irresistible drenching, the kind that feels as if it could go on for ever. Within moments it had made the town its instrument. Gutters dripped and spilled, skylights thrummed, every surface answered to the gentle percussion. The darkness had come alive. The blaze at its centre wilted visibly as Goose turned to look. Its noise was swamped. Instead of a hard-edged, blood-coloured divide between burning light and utter shadow, the town had become an equal sea of quiet music, streets and buildings and sidewalks and foliage and the handful of vehicles that hadn't yet been pressed into evacuation service all whispering their different presences by the different ways they testified to the unseen rainfall. There were voices everywhere. Everything had found its mouth.

Séverine, said one of them, close to her, deep, strong, calm. Goose saw the masked face turned in her direction. *Be on your way now.*

'I don't actually know where I go next,' she said.

Then follow me.

'Which one are you?' Though she knew, really. The voice was in front of her on the road. She recognised it, in a way. It was the thing that had been missing, the thing she'd been looking for. It was the voice that hadn't been in the cell in the station, and hadn't been in the reams and megabytes of Jennifer's file, the voice that was absent from those places: the voice which knew the answers to crazy things, which had nothing to say to all the wrong questions. Jennifer's other voice.

Song of the killer whale clan, it said, suddenly huge, surging. *Speaking for the house that won't be emptied. For the people who won't run away. Who's listening?* It became a bellow like the aftermath of thunder; it echoed between the houses. *Who's going to live here? Who's going to learn how to live in this house?* It moved away. Goose followed as if magnetised. She couldn't actually see where she was going at all but it didn't seem to matter. The voice was as good as a beacon. *There's roofs and hearths. Who hasn't forgotten? Who's not afraid?* A set of headlights appeared in the near distance, coming into town along the main road. They swept over the small rise by the WELCOME TO ALICE, B.C. sign and angled straight towards her, turning the rain white and opaque and lighting up the silhouette which marched in front. Goose saw the outline of Jennifer's sweatshirt and pants, and on top of them the great swelling ridges and fins of the mask, all now completely alive. It moved as if swimming through the air, ducking, turning, while the body it rode swayed and spun. The fire ahead was already almost gone. A ruined house and its half-ruined neighbour glowed dully at their outer edges, no more than that. The headlights picked out a few other people. Some ducked away and disappeared when they saw what was coming, others stayed where they were, frozen, Goose supposed, by sheer disbelief, or perhaps standing still to listen. Between English words the mask sang in its own almost-dead language. *Run away if you want to. Find somewhere else to go. Everything's looking for its own house.*

The song took over. If anything it was growing louder all the time. An angry note came into it. *Where's the ghost? Where's the bad spirit?* They were near what had been the heart of the blaze now. A motorcycle lay flat in the road, trapping a prone body by the legs; the body wasn't moving. Someone shouted something and ran uphill out of the light. The approaching car stopped with an audible screech. Its engine cut out, restarted with a frantic roar, and it began to reverse away. *Come out*, the voice roared. *Time to face the music, monster. You got no house here. You been turned away.* The transformed girl came to a halt by the smoking shell. Goose halted too. The mask turned to face the glow and leaned forward as if snatching prey. *Come out!*

The song stopped, and for a few moments the only sound was the polyphony of rain. The headlights swerved away in a jerky arc and turned back out of town. Someone else beating a retreat.

'Goose?'

He was near by but invisible. She looked towards where the hesitant voice had come from. In the diminishing firelight even the nearest corners and streets were entirely invisible. 'Jonas?'

'That really you? Ohh, man—'

The whispered exchange went no farther. Something moved among the embers and silenced them both.

The house had burned down to its timber frame, most of which was now piled in a charred and formless heap that sheltered the last of the fire. One of the upright black beams stirred and began to walk. Ash and sparks marked its passage. The pile settled, flaring, and the straight black thing became a body rather than a piece of the wreckage, going on stumbling black-booted feet. Two undimmed coals were housed in its head. It waded across the sputtering fire, and Goose saw how the scrawny white flesh had blistered, livid with burns and then blackened over with soot. Its waist-length hair smouldered with live sparks. Its clothes were frayed to shreds and its hands had curled into charred talons. The left one was hooked over the ring, whose soft gloss was undamaged and held the light.

Goose heard Jonas say, 'What the fuck,' and then the pop of a holster and the unmistakable click and slide of his pistol.

'Don't,' she said, in the same instant that Jonas fired. The demon staggered. Its right arm twitched and went slack below the elbow. Still it came forward. The pistol clicked again.

'Don't!' Goose repeated. 'Leave it to Jennifer.'

'That's Jennifer?'

'Watch.'

The demon shambled through a disintegrated doorway and on to the scorched ground of the yard. The soles of its boots had almost burned away. They flapped in the sodden ash like broken wings.

'So you found her after all,' Jonas said quietly, from wherever he was standing. 'Had a feeling you would.'

'Mountie always gets her man.'

'You did good, Goose.'

The walking corpse lifted what had once been its left hand. The firelight was fading visibly: the motion was little more than a stirring of different textures of black. Any semblance of air had gone out of its voice. When it spoke it sounded like dead leaves, or a stiff broom sweeping through ashes.

'Silence,' it hissed.

The mask swung its huge blunt prow upwards and bellowed.

'We.' The demon's mouth had roasted dry, and it could only make one word at a time. 'Banish. You.'

No. Jennifer began to dance again, just a clumsy-looking shuffle below the waist, and yet it gave the mask a restless energetic motion. *No you don't. Got no power to make me leave my own house.*

'This,' the demon croaked. The ring in its ruined fist gleamed. 'Is. Power.'

Open door, sang the mask. *Letting things come home. Magic don't belong to you. Only thing here out of its place is you, monster. This is where I live. I know the song to sing away bad spirits. You ready to hear it?*

There must have been another bystander – at least one other – hidden in the night near by, because an incongruously cheerful voice shouted, 'Yeah!'

You listening?

The same voice whooped, like someone in a hockey crowd watching the start of a fight.

Goose felt the mask turn her way and speak suddenly quietly, closely. *Song's gonna send you on your way too. Got any goodbyes to say?*

'Bye, Jonas,' she said.

'This is it?'

'Yup.'

'Man.' *Ma-aan.* 'I wish it wasn't.'

The mask had begun to chant. The girl's apologetic shuffle gained momentum. Her feet began to drum on the road with the rain.

'Too late for that. Look after Jennifer.'

'Check. Bye, Goose. Hey, what was your real name? I forgot.'

'Me too.'

'Goose, then. Fly north. Summer's coming.'

Jonas was somewhere at her back. She was starting to jog. She settled into the steady motion, relieved. She remembered how running obliterated everything else. Head steady, barely looking, just the pure feeling of going. The song gave her feet a wonderfully easy rhythm.

She glanced behind. The demon had fallen. Over its collapsed body a slender figure knelt: the boy, she saw, the barefoot boy, death's companion. She wondered whether he'd knelt over another fallen body once, out on a deserted island in the middle of the Inside Passage, and whispered words to help send her on her way. Something made his eyes sparkle in the light of the embers. He put his hand out to the burned claw and very gently eased the ring away. After he'd taken it he left his hand there, holding the scarred flesh in a surprisingly tender gesture. He stayed like that, kneeling, holding hands. She looked away again and faced up the dark road. For a few strides it felt as if there was something she might have said to him, but then it (and he, and everything) was gone.

Thirty-Three

RUNNING WITHOUT EFFORT, without pain, up through a wet deep invisible forest.

There was only one road. It went up away from light and habitation. The rain softened to a kind of mist, halfway between something and nothing. She rose with the road, running smoothly, lightly, as if she shared the mist's immunity to the pull of the earth.

At the top of the pass she came to a golden grove.

A light so beautiful it felt like you could drink it glowed among broad-leaved trees. She slowed. The trees were oaks and the light was like reflected sunrise, though it was long before dawn and there were no stands of oak among the birches and evergreens along the Hardy road. When she looked for the source which made this island of gold-green radiance in the otherwise infinite night, it seemed that the place was its own illumination, a glow-in-the-dark forest preserving the mellow warmth of an absent sun. The road led into it. She went under boughs sprouting with acorns. Everything was dry, though she heard the sound of running water ahead.

A golden man stood in the grove and watched her go by. Slung over his back was a quiver of arrows, which were plague, and in his hand was a bow. He smiled at her as beautifully as the light and opened his mouth, which was prophecy, though he said nothing. Walking now, she went on towards the water.

A wide shallow stream marked the edge of the grove. It ran dark. The road continued under the black waters and then emerged on the far side, where it went over the pass and was dark too.

On the distant shore stood a woman no longer young but not yet old, with a long, rather anxious face and an air of waiting not very optimistically for something no one was ever going to give her.

There was no particular margin where the road disappeared into the stream, just dry ground as far as the edge, and then the opposite. When she reached that edge she stopped, wondering whether she'd gone far enough now and should turn around and head back down the hill to town.

'Is someone there?' the other woman called. She peered across the stream. 'Has someone come?'

'Hey,' Goose said.

'Marina?' the woman called doubtfully. 'Is that you? Don't cross if that's you.'

Goose thought about a small voice speaking to her from somewhere very far away, too far to know. She turned to look back at the golden man as if for confirmation. He watched her, still smiling.

'Speak to me,' the other woman said, leaning across the stream as far as she dared. 'If you're there. Please.'

Goose heard inward echoes of a name. *Marina.* She remembered a child calling in tentative desperation. *Where's Gwen? Can I talk to her again?*

'You must be Gwen,' she said.

The other woman twitched in surprise. A look of confused hope appeared in her face. 'Yes,' she called. 'Yes! I must be.' She stepped hesitantly forward into the stream. 'Who's there? Did Marina send you?'

Goose hesitated for a moment. The golden man spoke behind her: 'Marie-Archange Séverine Gaucelin-Maculloch.' His voice was if anything more exquisite than his smile. It made her name a poem. While the poem lasted she remembered many things, so many that she thought they must in fact be all the things she had to remember, and all of them, even the embarrassing or frightening ones, now bathed in the marvellous light of the grove.

'I guess she tried to,' she called back. 'We got cut off.' The other woman splashed awkwardly in shallow water, the flow eddying around her boots. Goose had remembered the boots too, and the black skirt, and the black leather jacket with a silvery pattern sewn into it.

The poem finished. She saw the woman struggling to cross and stepped in.

They met somewhere near the middle. Gwen clasped her and held on for a long moment.

'Thank you,' she said.

'Ah. It's nothing.'

She looked towards the grove. 'I can see light there. Is that the road?'

'Yep. You just follow it all the way. Can't go wrong.'

'Bless you.'

'Not a problem,' the other woman said. The golden glow was fading behind her. She sped up again, carefully at first, with the water lapping around her, and then more steadily once she'd crossed. The road went over the pass and began its descent. Downhill was easy. Downhill was irresistible. She ran as easy as water, easy as air, weightless, senseless, running, running, on down into the dark.

In the best books, the ending often comes as a shock.
Not just because of that one last twist in the tale,
but because you have been so absorbed in their world,
that coming back to the harsh light of reality is a jolt.

If that describes you now, then perhaps you should track down
some new leads, and find new suspense in other worlds.

Join us at www.hodder.co.uk, or follow us on
Twitter @hodderbooks, and you can tap in to a
community of fellow thrill-seekers.

Whether you want to find out more about this book,
or a particular author, watch trailers and interviews, have
the chance to win early limited editions, or simply browse
our expert readers' selection of the very best books,
we think you'll find what you're looking for.

And if you don't, that's the place to tell us what's missing.

We love what we do, and we'd love you to be part of it.

www.hodder.co.uk

@hodderbooks

HodderBooks

HodderBooks